LP FIC Day

Day, S.
Captivated by you.

(3593/ke   )

CAPTIVATED BY YOU

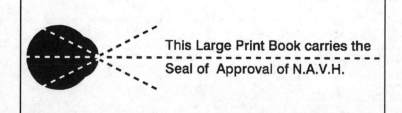

CROSSFIRE, BOOK 4

CAPTIVATED BY YOU

SYLVIA DAY

THORNDIKE PRESS

A part of Gale, Cengage Learning

GALE
CENGAGE Learning·

Farmington Hills, Mich • San Francisco • New York • Waterville, Maine
Meriden, Conn • Mason, Ohio • Chicago

GALE
CENGAGE Learning·

LIBRARY OF CONGRESS CATALOGING-IN-PUBLICATION DATA

Day, Sylvia.
    Captivated by you / by Sylvia Day. — Large print edition.
        pages cm. — (Crossfire ; #4) (Thorndike Press large print romance)
    ISBN 978-1-4104-7749-1 (hardcover) — ISBN 1-4104-7749-5 (hardcover)
    1. Large type books. I. Title.
    PS3604.A9875C37 2015
    813'.6—dc23   2014047547

Published in 2015 by arrangement with The Berkley Publishing Group, a member of Penguin Group (USA) LLC, a Penguin Random House Company

Printed in the United States of America
1 2 3 4 5 6 7 19 18 17 16 15

This one is for all the readers who waited patiently for this next chapter in Gideon and Eva's story.
I hope you love it as much as I do!

ACKNOWLEDGMENTS

There are innumerable people behind me who make it possible for me to write, keep up with my commitments, and stay sane.

Thanks to Hilary Sares, who keeps me on track by editing each book as I go. I rely on you more than you know.

Thanks to Kimberly Whalen, agent extraordinaire, for all that you do, but especially for all of your support. I'm grateful for you every day.

Thanks to Samara Day, for all the stress you take off my shoulders. I can't imagine how far behind I'd be without you.

Thanks to my children, who tolerate being without me for long stretches while I work (and all the inconveniences associated with that). I couldn't do what I do without your support. I love you.

Thanks to all the amazing teams at Penguin Random House: Cindy Hwang, Leslie Gelbman, Alex Clarke, Tom Weldon, Rick

Pascocello, Craig Burke, Erin Galloway, Francesca Russell, Kimberley Atkins . . . and that's just scratching the surface of the US and UK. There are teams hard at work in Australia, Ireland, Canada, New Zealand, India, and South Africa. I'm grateful to you all for the time and effort you put into publishing my books.

Thanks to Liz Pearsons and the team at Brilliance Audio for making audio editions readers rave about!

And thanks to all of my international publishers, who work tirelessly in their territories. I wish I could thank you all personally here. Please know that I feel blessed to work with you.

1

Icy needles of water bombarded my over-heated skin, the sting chasing away the clinging shadows of a nightmare I couldn't fully remember.

Closing my eyes, I stepped deeper into the spray, willing the lingering fear and nausea to circle the drain at my feet. A shiver racked me, and my thoughts shifted to my wife. My angel who slept peacefully in the apartment next door. I wanted her urgently, wanted to lose myself in her, and hated that I couldn't. Couldn't hold her close. Couldn't pull her lush body under mine and sink into it, letting her touch chase the memories away.

"Fuck." I placed my palms flat against the cool tile and absorbed the chill of the punishing deluge into my bones. I was a selfish asshole.

If I'd been a better man, I would've walked away from Eva Cross the moment I saw her.

Instead, I'd made her my wife. And I wanted the news of our marriage broadcast via every medium known to man, rather than hidden away as a secret between less than a handful of people. Worse, since I had no intention of letting her go, I would have to find a way to make up for the fact that I was such a fucking mess we couldn't even sleep in the same room together.

I lathered, quickly washing away the sticky sweat I'd woken up in. Within minutes I was heading out to the bedroom, where I pulled on a pair of sweats before heading to my home office. It was just barely seven in the morning.

I'd left the apartment Eva shared with her best friend, Cary Taylor, only a couple of hours earlier, wanting to give her time to catch a few hours of sleep before she headed into work. We had been at each other all night, both of us too needy and greedy. But there'd been something else, too. An urgency on Eva's part that gnawed at me and left me uneasy.

Something was bothering my wife.

My gaze drifted to the window and its view of Manhattan beyond it, then settled on the empty wall where photos of her and us hung in the same space in my penthouse office in our home on Fifth Avenue. I could imagine the collage clearly, having spent countless hours studying it over the last few months. Looking out at the city had once been the way I encapsulated my world. Now, I accomplished that by looking at Eva.

I sat at my desk and woke my computer with a shake of the mouse, taking a deep slow breath as my wife's face filled my monitor. She wore no makeup in the photo that was my desktop wallpaper, and a smattering of light freckles on her nose made her appear younger than her twenty-four years. My gaze slid over her features — the curve of her brows, the brightness of her gray eyes, the fullness of her lips. In the moments when I let myself think of it, I could almost feel those lips against my skin. Her kisses were benedictions, promises from my angel that made my life worth living.

With a determined exhalation, I picked up the phone and speed-dialed Raúl Huerta. Despite the earliness of the hour, he answered swiftly and alertly.

"Mrs. Cross and Cary Taylor are heading to San Diego today," I said, my hand curling into a fist at the thought. I didn't have to say more.

"Got it."

"I want a recent photo of Anne Lucas and

a detailed rundown of where she was last night on my desk by noon."

"At the latest," he affirmed.

I hung up and stared at Eva's captivatingly beautiful face. I'd caught her in a happy, unguarded moment, a state of being I was determined to keep her in for the rest of her life. But last night she'd been distressed by a possible run-in with a woman I'd once used. It had been a while since I'd crossed paths with Anne, but if she was responsible for aggravating my wife, she'd be seeing me again. Soon.

Opening my inbox, I started sifting through my e-mails, drafting quick answers when required and working my way toward the subject line that had caught my eye the moment my e-mail opened.

I felt Eva before I saw her.

I lifted my head and my keystrokes slowed. A sudden rush of desire soothed the agitation I felt whenever I wasn't with her.

I leaned back to better appreciate the view. "You're up early, angel."

Eva stood in the doorway with her keys in hand, her blond hair in a sexy tangle around her shoulders, her cheeks and lips flushed from sleep, her curvy body clad in a tank top and shorts. She was braless, her lush tits swelling softly beneath the ribbed cotton. Petite and built to take a man to his knees, she often pointed out how different she was from the women I'd been photographed with before her.

"I woke up missing you," she replied, with the throaty voice that never failed to make me hard. "How long have you been up?"

"Not long." I pushed the keyboard drawer in to make room for her on my desk.

She padded over on bare feet, effortlessly seducing me. The moment I first saw her I'd known she would wreck me. The promise was there in her eyes and the way she moved. Everywhere she went, men stared at her. Coveted her. Just like I did.

I caught her by the waist when she came close enough, choosing to pull her onto my lap instead. Bending my head, I caught her nipple in my mouth, drawing on her with long, deep sucks. I heard her gasp, felt her body jolt at the sensation, and smiled inwardly. I could do whatever I wanted to her. She'd given me that right. It was the greatest gift I had ever been given.

"Gideon." Her hands went to my hair, sifting through it.

I felt infinitely better already.

Lifting my head, I kissed her, tasting the cinnamon of her toothpaste and the underlying flavor that was uniquely her. "Hmm?"

She touched my face, her gaze searching. "Did you have another nightmare?"

I exhaled in a rush. She'd always been able to see right through me. I wasn't sure I would ever get used to it.

I stroked the pad of my thumb over the damp cotton clinging to her nipple. "I'd rather talk about the wet dreams you're inspiring right now."

"What was it about?"

My lips thinned at her persistence. "I don't remember."

"Gideon —"

"Drop it, angel."

Eva stiffened. "I just want to help you."

"You know how to do that."

She snorted. "Sex fiend."

I cuddled her closer. I couldn't find the words to tell her how she felt in my arms, so I nuzzled her neck, breathing in the well-loved scent of her skin.

"Ace."

Something in the tone of her voice set me on edge. I pulled back slowly, my gaze gliding over her face. "Talk to me."

"About San Diego . . ." Her eyes dropped and she caught her lower lip between her teeth.

I stilled, waiting to see where the conversation would go.

"Six-Ninths is going to be there," she said finally.

She hadn't tried to hide what I'd already known, which was a relief. But a different kind of tension flooded me instead.

"You're telling me that's a problem." My voice remained steady, but I was anything but calm.

"No, it's not a problem," she said softly. But her fingers were tangling restlessly in my hair.

"Don't lie to me."

"I'm not." She took a deep breath and then held my gaze. "Something's not right. I'm confused."

"About what, exactly?"

"Don't be like that," she said quietly. "Don't get all icy and freeze me out."

"You'll have to forgive me. Listening to *my wife* tell me she's confused over another man doesn't put me in a good mood."

She squirmed out of my lap and I let her, so I could watch her — gauge her — with some distance between us. "I don't know how to explain it."

I deliberately ignored the cold knot in my gut. "Try."

"It's just —" Looking down, she chewed on her lower lip. "There's something . . . not finished."

My chest grew tight and hot. "Does he turn you on, Eva?"

She stiffened. "It's not like that."

"Is it the voice? The tattoos? His magic dick?"

"Stop it. It's not easy talking about this. Don't make it harder."

"It's damned hard for me, too," I snapped, pushing to my feet.

I raked her from head to toe, wanting to fuck her and punish her at the same time. I wanted to tie her up, lock her up, safe from anyone who could threaten my grip on her. "He treated you like shit, Eva. Did seeing the 'Golden' video make you forget that? Is there something you need that I'm not giving you?"

"Don't be an ass." Her arms crossed, a defensive pose that angered me further.

I needed her open and soft. I needed her completely. And there were times when I was maddened by how much she meant to me. She was the one thing I couldn't imagine losing. And she was saying the one thing I couldn't bear hearing.

"Please don't be ugly about this," she whispered.

"I'm being remarkably civilized, considering how violent I feel at the moment."

"Gideon." Guilt darkened her gray eyes,

16

and then tears glistened.

I looked away. "Don't!"

But she saw into me the way she always did.

"I didn't mean to hurt you." The diamond on her ring finger — my claim to her — caught the light and shot sparks of multi-hued fire against the wall. "I hate that you're upset and pissed off at me. It hurts me, too, Gideon. I don't want him. I swear I don't."

Restless, I went to the window, trying to find the calm I needed to deal with the danger Brett Kline presented. I'd done everything I could. I had said the vows, slid the ring on her finger. Bound her to me in every way. Yet it still wasn't enough.

The city spread out before me, the view obstructed by taller buildings. From the penthouse, I could see for miles. But from the Upper West Side apartment I'd taken next door to Eva's, the vista was limited. I couldn't see the endless ribbons of streets clogged with yellow taxis or sunlight glinting off the many skyscraper windows.

I could give Eva New York. I could give her the world. I couldn't love her more than I did; it consumed me. And still, an asshole from her past was making strides on edging me out.

I remembered her in Kline's arms, kissing

17

him with a desperation she should feel only for me. The possibility that lust for him might still affect her made me want to tear something apart.

My knuckles popped as my hands fisted. "Do we need to take a break already? Take some time for Kline to clear up your confusion? Maybe I should do the same and help Corinne deal with hers."

She sucked in a shaky breath at the mention of my former fiancée. "Are you *serious*?"

There was a terrible stretch of silence.

Then, "Congratulations, dickhead. You just hurt me worse than he ever did."

I turned in time to see her stalking out of the room, her back rigid and tense. The keys she'd used to let herself in were left on my desk, and the sight of them abandoned triggered something desperate. *"Stop."*

I caught her and she struggled, the dynamic between us so familiar — Eva running, me chasing.

"Let me go!"

My eyes closed and I pressed my face against her. "I won't let him have you."

"I'm so mad at you right now, I could hit you."

I wanted her to. Wanted the pain. "Do it."

She clawed at my forearms. "Put me

down, Gideon."

I turned her around and pinned her to the hallway wall. "What am I supposed to do when you tell me you're *confused* about Brett Kline? I feel like I'm hanging on the edge of a cliff and my grip is slipping."

"So you're going to tear at me to hold on? Why don't you get that I'm not going anywhere?"

I stared down at her, scrambling for something to say that would make things right between us. Her lower lip began to quiver and I . . . I unraveled.

"Tell me how to handle this," I said hoarsely, circling her wrists and exerting gentle pressure. "Tell me what to do."

"Handle *me,* you mean?" Her shoulders went back. "Because I'm what's wrong here. I knew Brett during a time in my life when I hated myself but wanted other people to love me. And now he's acting the way I wanted him to back then and it's giving me a head trip."

"Christ, Eva." I pressed harder, flattening my body against her. "How am I not supposed to feel threatened by that?"

"You're supposed to trust me. I told you because I didn't want you to get weird vibes and jump to conclusions. I wanted to be honest about it so you *wouldn't* feel threatened. I know I've got some stuff to work out in my head. I'm going to see Dr. Travis this weekend and —"

"Shrinks aren't a cure-all!"

"Don't yell at me."

I fought the urge to slam my fist into the plaster behind her. My wife's blind faith in the healing properties of therapy frustrated the hell out of me. "We're not running to a damned doctor every time we've got a problem. It's you and me in this marriage. Not the goddamned psychiatric community!"

Her chin lifted, her jaw taking on the determined slant that drove me crazy. She never gave me an inch unless my cock was inside her. Then she gave me everything.

"You may think you don't need help, ace, but I know I do."

"What I need is you." I cupped her head in my heads. "I need my wife. And I need her thinking about me and not some other guy!"

"You're making me wish I hadn't said anything."

My lip curled in a sneer. "I knew how you felt. I've seen it."

"God. You jealous, crazy . . ." She moaned softly. "Why don't you understand how much I love you? Brett's got nothing on you. *Nothing.* But honestly, I don't want to be around you right now."

I felt her resistance, the pushback of her trying to get away. I clutched her like a lifeline. "Can't you see what you're doing to me?"

Eva softened in my arms. "I don't get you, Gideon. How can you just flip a switch and turn your feelings off? Knowing how I feel about Corinne, how could you throw her in my face like that?"

"You're the reason I breathe, I can't turn it off." I slid my mouth across her cheek. "I think of nothing but you. All day. Every day. Everything I do, I do with you in mind. There's no room for anyone else. It kills me that you have room for him."

"You're not listening."

"Just stay the hell away from him."

"That's avoidance, not a solution." Her fingers dug into my waist. "I'm broken, Gideon, you know that. I'm piecing myself back together."

I loved her just the way she was. Why wasn't that enough?

"Thanks to you I'm stronger than I've ever been," she went on, "but there are still cracks, and when I find them, I have to figure out what made them and how to seal them up. Permanently."

21

"What the fuck does that mean?" My hands pushed beneath her top, seeking her bare skin.

She stiffened and pushed at me, rejecting me. "Gideon, no . . ."

I sealed my mouth over hers. Lifting her off her feet, I took her to the floor. She struggled and I growled, "Don't fight me."

"You can't just screw our problems away."

"I just want to screw you." My thumbs hooked into the waistband of her shorts and shoved them down. I was frantic to be in her, possessing her, feeling her surrender. Anything to drown out the voice in my head telling me I'd fucked up. *Again.* And this time, I wouldn't be forgiven.

"Let me go." She rolled onto her stomach.

My arms banded around her hips when she tried to crawl away. She could throw me off as she'd been trained to and she could cut me off with a word. Her safe word . . .

"Crossfire."

Eva froze at the sound of my voice and the one word meant to convey the riot of emotions she shattered me with.

It was in that eye of the storm that something snapped. A fierce and familiar quiet exploded within me, silencing the panic shaking my confidence. I stilled, absorbing the sudden absence of turmoil. It had been

22

a long time since I'd last felt the dizzying switch between chaos and control. Only Eva could rock me so deeply, sending me hurtling back to a time when I'd been at the mercy of everything and everyone.

"You're going to stop fighting me," I told her calmly. "And I'm going to apologize."

She went lax in my arms. Her submission was total and swift. I had the upper hand again.

I pulled her up and back, so that she was sitting on my thighs. Eva needed me in control. When I was reeling, she scattered, which only shook me more. It was a vicious cycle and I had to get a better grip on it.

"I'm sorry." Sorry for hurting her. Sorry for losing my command of the situation. I'd been edgy after the nightmare — something she'd intuited — and getting hit with Kline immediately after hadn't given me time to get my shit together.

I would deal with him. I'd keep a tight grasp on her. Period. There were no other options.

"I need your support, Gideon."

"I need you to tell him you're married."

She leaned her temple against my cheek. "I'm going to."

I shifted her to sit across my lap and leaned back against the wall, cradling her

23

close. Her arms wrapped around my neck and my world righted itself again.

Her hand slid down my chest. "Ace . . ."

The coaxing note in her voice was one I knew well. I was hard in an instant, my blood hot and thick. Submitting to me turned Eva on, and that reaction from her fired me up like nothing else.

I pushed my hand into her hair and fisted the soft gold strands, watching the way her eyes grew heavy-lidded at the feel of the gentle tug. She was restrained and at my mercy, and she loved it. Needed it, just as much as I did.

I took her mouth.

Then I took her.

While Angus drove Eva and me to work, I scrolled through my appointment calendar and thought of my wife's eight-thirty flight.

I glanced at her. "You'll take one of the jets to California."

She had been looking out the window of the Bentley, city-scoping with her usual eager interest. She turned her gaze to me.

I was born in New York. I'd grown up in and near the city and eventually began to make it my own. At some point, I'd stopped noticing it. But Eva's fascination and delight with my hometown had reintroduced it to me. I didn't study the city with the intensity she did, but I saw it with fresh eyes all the same.

"Will I?" she challenged, her eyes betraying her countering attraction to me.

Her fuck-me look kept me redlined constantly.

"Yes." I closed my tablet case. "It's faster, more comfortable, and safer."

Her mouth curved. "All right."

That hint of teasing amusement captivated me, made me want to do everything wicked and raw to her until only complete surrender remained.

"You get to tell Cary," she went on, switching the cross of her legs and revealing the lacy edge of her stockings and a peek of her garter.

She was wearing a red sleeveless shirt and a white skirt with strappy heels. A perfectly acceptable businesslike outfit that was elevated by the body inside it to understated sexiness. Electricity arced between us, the instinctive recognition that we had been made to fit together perfectly.

"Ask me to come with you," I said, hating the thought of her being away from me for an entire weekend.

Her smile faded. "I can't. If I'm going to start telling people we're married, I have to start with Cary, and I can't do that with you around. I don't want him to feel like he's on the outside of a life I'm creating with you."

"I don't want to be on the outside, either."

She linked her fingers with mine. "Spending private time with friends doesn't make us any less of a couple."

"I prefer to spend time with you. You're the most interesting person I know."

Her eyes widened and she stared at me. Then she exploded into movement, hitching up her skirt and straddling me before I realized what she was doing. Cupping my face in her hands, she pressed her gloss-slick lips to mine and kissed me senseless.

"Umm," I moaned, as she pulled away breathlessly. My fingers flexed into the generous curve of her gorgeous ass. "Do that again."

"I'm so hot for you right now," she breathed, rubbing my lips clean with her thumb.

"I'm good with that."

Her husky laugh slid all around me. "I feel so awesome right now."

"Better than you did in the hallway?" Her joy was infectious. If I could've stopped time, I would have at that moment.

"That's a different kind of awesome." Her

fingertips tap-danced on my shoulders. She was . . . *radiant* when she was happy, and her pleasure brightened everything around her. Even me. "That was the best compliment, ace. Especially coming from *the* Gideon Cross. You meet fascinating people every day."

"And wish they'd go away so I can get back to you."

Her eyes glistened. "God, I love you so much it hurts."

My hands shook and I dug them into the backs of her thighs to hide it from her. My gaze wandered, trying to latch on to something that would anchor me.

If she only knew what she did to me with those three little words.

She hugged me. "I want you to do something for me," she murmured.

"Anything. Everything."

"Let's have a party."

Seizing the opportunity to move on to other topics . . . "Great. I'll set up the swing."

Pulling back, Eva shoved at my shoulder. "Not *that* kind of party, fiend."

I sighed. "Bummer."

She gave me a wicked smile. "How about I promise the swing in return for the party?"

"Ah, now we're talking." I settled back,

enjoying her immensely. "Tell me what you have in mind."

"Booze and friends, yours and mine."

"All right." I considered the possibilities. "I'll see you your booze and friends, and raise you a quickie in a dark corner somewhere during."

Her throat worked on a quick swallow and I smiled inwardly. I knew my angel well. Indulging her closet exhibitionism was a complete 360 turnaround for me, and though it still amazed me when I thought about it, I didn't mind in the least. There was nothing I wouldn't do for those moments when the only thing that mattered to her was being filled with my cock.

"You drive a hard bargain," she said.

"Exactly my intention."

"Okay, then." She licked her lips. "I'll see you your quickie and raise you a hand job under the table."

My brows rose. "Clothed," I countered.

Something that sounded like a purr rumbled in the air between us. "I think you need to revisit and revise, Mr. Cross."

"I think you'll need to work harder to convince me, Mrs. Cross."

She was, as always, the most invigorating negotiation of my day.

■ ■ ■ ■

We separated on the twentieth floor, where she exited the elevator into the Waters Field & Leaman foyer. I was determined to get her on my team and working for me. It was an objective I strategized every day.

When I reached my office, my assistant was already at his desk.

"Good morning," Scott greeted me, standing as I approached. "PR called a few minutes ago. They're fielding an unusual amount of inquiries about a rumored engagement between you and Miss Tramell. They'd like to know how to respond."

"They should confirm." I passed him and went to the coatrack in the corner behind my desk.

He followed. "Congratulations."

"Thank you." I shrugged out of my jacket and slung it on a hook. When I glanced at him again, he was grinning.

Scott Reid handled myriad tasks for me with quiet care, which led others to often underestimate him and allow him to go unnoticed. On more than one occasion, his detailed observations of individuals had proven extremely insightful, and so I overpaid him for his position to keep him from going anywhere else.

"Miss Tramell and I will marry before the end of the year," I told him. "All interview and photo requests for either of us should be routed through Cross Industries. And tell security downstairs the same. No one should get to her without going through me first."

"I'll let them know. Also, Mr. Madani wanted to be notified when you got in. He'd like a few minutes with you before the meeting this morning."

"I'm ready when he is."

"Great," Arash Madani said, walking in. "There used to be days when you were here before seven. You're slacking off, Cross."

I shot the lawyer a warning look that carried no heat. Arash lived to work and was damned good at it, which is why I hired him away from his former employer. He'd been the toughest counsel I had ever run across, and in the years since, that hadn't changed.

Gesturing at one of the two chairs in front of my desk, I took my seat and watched him take his. His dark blue suit was simple but bespoke, his wavy black hair tamed by a precision cut. Sharp intelligence marked his dark brown eyes, extending to a smile that was more warning than greeting. He was a friend as well as an employee, and I valued his lack of bullshit.

"We've received a respectable bid on the property on Thirty-sixth," he said.

"Oh?" A tangle of emotions held my reply for a moment. The hotel Eva hated remained a problem as long as I owned it. "That's good."

"That's curious," he shot back, setting one ankle on the opposite knee, "considering how slowly the market's recovering. I had to dig through several layers, but the bidder is a subsidiary of LanCorp."

"Interesting."

"Cocky. Landon knows the next highest bid is a ways off — about ten million ways. I recommend we pull the property off the market and revisit in a year or two."

"No." Sitting back, I waved away the suggestion. "Let him have it."

Arash blinked. "Are you shitting me? Why are you in such a hurry to get rid of that hotel?"

Because I can't keep it in my holdings without hurting my wife. "I have my reasons."

"That's what you said when I advised you to sell it a few years ago and you chose to sink millions in renovations into it instead. An expense that you're just finally breaking even on, and *now* you want to offload it in

31

a still-shaky market to a guy who wants your head?"

"It's never a bad time to sell real estate in Manhattan." And certainly, never a bad time to dump something Eva called my "fuck pad."

"There are better times, and you know it. Landon knows it. You sell to him, you'll only be encouraging him."

"Good. Maybe he'll up his game."

Ryan Landon had an ax to grind; I didn't hold it against him. My father had decimated the Landon fortune and Ryan wanted a Cross to pay for that. He wasn't the first or last businessman to come after me because of my father, but he was the most tenacious. And he was young enough to have plenty of time to dedicate to the task.

I looked at the photo of Eva on my desk. All other considerations were secondary.

"Hey," Arash said, lifting his hands in mock surrender, "it's your business. I just need to know if the rules have changed."

"Nothing's changed."

"If you believe that, Cross, you're further out of the game than I thought. While Landon's plotting your ruin, you're off at the beach."

"Stop kicking my ass for taking a weekend off, Arash." I'd do it again in an instant.

Those days I'd spent with Eva in the Outer Banks had been every fucking dream I'd never allowed myself to have.

I stood and walked to the window. LanCorp's offices were in the high-rise two blocks over, and Ryan Landon's office had a prime view of the Crossfire Building. I suspected he spent more than a few moments every day staring at my office and planning his next move. Occasionally, I stared back and dared him to bring it harder.

My father was a criminal who'd destroyed countless lives. He was also the man who'd taught me how to ride a bike and to sign my name with pride. I couldn't save Geoffrey Cross's reputation, but I could damn sure protect what I'd built out of his ashes.

Arash joined me at the window. "I'm not going to say I wouldn't hole up with a babe like Eva Tramell if I could. But I'd have my goddamn cell phone with me. Especially in the middle of a high-stakes negotiation."

Remembering how melted chocolate tasted on Eva's skin, I thought a hurricane could've been ripping shingles off the roof and I wouldn't have given it a second's attention. "You're making me pity you."

"LanCorp's acquisition of that software set you back years in research and development. And it's made him cocky."

That was what really got Arash's blood up, Landon's pleasure in his own success. "That software's next to worthless without PosIT's hardware."

He glanced at me. "So?"

"Agenda item number three."

He faced me. "It said *To Be Determined* on my copy."

"Well, it says *PosIT* on my mine. That game enough for you?"

"Damn."

My desk phone beeped, followed by Scott's voice projecting from the speaker. "A couple things, Mr. Cross. Miss Tramell is on line one."

"Thank you, Scott." I headed for the receiver with the thrill of the hunt coursing through my blood. If we acquired PosIT, Landon would be back to square one. "When I'm clear, I need Victor Reyes on the line."

"Will do. Also, Mrs. Vidal is at reception," he went on, stopping me in my tracks. "Would you like me to postpone the morning meeting?"

I looked out the glass partition that divided my office from the rest of the floor, even though I couldn't see my mother from that distance. My hands clenched at my

34

sides. According to the clock on my phone, I had ten minutes to spare and my wife on the line. The urge was there to make my mother wait until I could fit her in my schedule, not hers, but I shoved it down.

"Buy me twenty minutes," I told him. "I'll take the calls with Miss Tramell and Reyes, then you can bring Mrs. Vidal back."

"Got it."

I waited a beat. Then I picked up the phone and hit the rapidly blinking button.

2

"Angel."

The impact of Gideon's voice on my senses was as hard-hitting as it had been the first time I'd heard it. Cultured yet smoky with sensuality, it knocked me for a loop both in the darkness of my bedroom and over the phone, where I couldn't be distracted by that incomparably gorgeous face of his.

"Hi." I slid my swivel chair a little closer to my desk. "Is it a bad time?"

"If you need me, I'm here."

Something in his voice didn't hit me right. "I can call back later."

"Eva." The authoritative bite when he said my name had my toes flexing in my nude sling-back Louboutins. "Say what you need."

You, I almost said, which was more than a little insane considering he'd just fucked my brains out only a couple hours before. After he'd fucked my brains out damn near all night long.

Instead, I told him, "I need a favor."

"I'll enjoy the payback."

Some of the tension left my shoulders. He'd hurt me by mentioning Corinne the way he had, and the argument that followed was still fresh in my mind. But I had to push it aside, let it go. "Does security have the home addresses of everyone who works in the Crossfire?"

"They have copies of IDs. Tell me why you're asking."

"The receptionist here at work is a friend of mine and she's been out sick all week. I'm worried about her."

"If you're hoping to head over to her place and check up on her, you should get the address from her."

"I would if she'd return my calls." I ran my fingertip around the lip of my coffee mug and stared at the collage of pictures of Gideon and me that decorated my desk.

"Are you not on speaking terms at the moment?"

"No, we're not fighting or anything. It's just not like her to not get in touch with me, especially when she's calling in sick to work every day. She's a chatty girl, you know?"

"No," he drawled. "I have no idea."

If it had been any other guy who'd said that, I would think he was being sarcastic. But not Gideon. I didn't think he'd ever really talked with women in any meaningful way. He was too often clueless when interacting with me, as if his social development hadn't quite been well rounded when it came to dealing with the opposite sex.

"Then you'll have to take my word for it, ace. I just . . . I want to make sure she's all right."

"My lawyer's standing right here, but I don't have to ask him about the legality of giving you the information you're asking for via the means you've suggested. Call Raúl. He'll find her."

"Really?" An image of the dark-haired, dark-eyed security specialist ran through my mind. "Is he going to be okay with that?"

"Angel, he's paid to be okay with everything."

"Oh." I fiddled with my pen. I knew I shouldn't feel uncomfortable using Gideon's resources, but it made me feel as if our relationship were unbalanced in his favor. While I didn't believe he would ever hold that over me, I didn't think he'd see me as equal to him, either, and that was really important to me.

He had already taken care of issues on his own that I should've been a part of. Like Sam Yimara's horrid sex tape of Brett and me. And Nathan.

Still, I asked, "How do I reach him?"

"I'll text you his number."

"Okay. Thanks."

"I want either myself, Angus, or Raúl with you when you go see her."

"And that wouldn't be awkward at all." I glanced at Mark's office to make sure my boss didn't need me for anything. I tried not to make personal calls at work, but Megumi had been out for four days straight without a single returned call or text the whole time.

"Don't throw me that 'chicks before dicks' line, Eva. You need to give me something here."

I got the subtext. He was worried about me going to San Diego and was letting that issue slide. I had to bend a little somewhere else in return. "Okay, okay. If she's not back in the office on Monday, we'll figure out how to handle it."

"Good. Anything else?"

"No. That's it." My gaze returned to a photo of him and my heart hurt just a little, the way it always did when I looked at him. "Thank you. I hope you have an amazing day. I love you madly, you know. And no, I don't expect you to say it back while your lawyer's hanging around."

"Eva." There was an aching note in his voice that moved me more than words ever could. "Come see me when you get off work."

"Sure. Don't forget to call Cary about taking your jet."

"Consider it done."

I hung up and sat back in my chair.

"Good morning, Eva."

I swiveled to face Christine Field, the executive chairman. "Good morning."

"I wanted to congratulate you again on your engagement." Her gaze went past my shoulder to the framed photos behind me. "I'm sorry, I hadn't realized you and Gideon Cross were dating."

"That's okay. I try not to talk about my personal life at work."

I made the statement casually, because I didn't want to antagonize one of the partners. Still, I hoped she got the hint. Gideon was the center of my life, but I needed some parts of it to belong only to me.

She laughed. "That's good! But just goes to show that I'm not keeping my ear close enough to the ground."

40

"I doubt you're missing anything important."

"Are you the reason Cross approached us with the Kingsman campaign?"

I winced inwardly. Of course she'd think I would recommend my employer to my boyfriend, because she'd assume Gideon and I had been dating at least long enough to make an engagement plausible. Telling her I had been with Waters Field & Leaman longer than I'd been with Gideon, when I had been employed there only a couple of months, would open up speculation I didn't want floating around.

Worse, I was pretty certain Gideon *had* used the vodka campaign as an excuse to draw me into his world on his terms. That didn't mean Mark hadn't done a phenomenal job on the request for proposal. I didn't want my relationship with Gideon to shift any of the focus away from my boss and his accomplishments.

"Mr. Cross approached the agency on his own," I replied, sticking to the truth. "Which was a great decision. Mark rocked that RFP."

Christine nodded. "He did. All right. I'll let you get back to work. Mark's been singing your praises, too, by the way. We're glad to have you on our team."

I managed a smile, but my day was off to a rocky start. First, Gideon knocked me sideways with his Corinne bullshit. Then, finding Megumi still out sick. Now, I'd rolled into being treated differently at work because my name was connected to Gideon's in a significant way.

Opening my inbox, I started going through the morning's e-mail. I understood that Gideon wanted to make me feel what he was feeling, so he'd leveraged Corinne against me. I'd known talking about Brett was going to be a problem, which was why I'd put it off, but I hadn't had an ulterior motive in bringing it up or when I'd kissed Brett, either. I had hurt Gideon, yes, but could sincerely say I hadn't consciously intended to do so.

On the flip side, Gideon had deliberately set out to hurt me. I hadn't realized he was capable of that or willing to do it. Something important had shifted between us that morning. I felt as if a core column of trust had been shaken.

Did he know that? Did he understand how big a problem that was?

My desk phone rang and I answered with my usual greeting.

"How long were you going to wait to tell me about your engagement?"

42

A sigh escaped me before I could hold it back. My Friday really was shaping up to be a trial. "Hi, Mom. I was going to call you during my lunch."

"You knew last night!" she accused. "Did he ask you on the way to dinner? Because you didn't say anything about a proposal when we talked about him asking your father and Richard for permission. I saw the ring at Cipriani's and was pretty sure, but when you didn't say anything, I didn't push because you've been so touchy lately. And —"

"And you've been violating the law lately," I shot back.

"— Gideon was wearing a ring, too, so I thought maybe it was some kind of promise thing or something —"

"It is."

"— and then I read about your engagement online! I mean, really, Eva. No mother should find out on the Internet that her daughter is getting married!"

I stared at my monitor blankly, my heart rate kicking up. "What? Where on the Internet?"

"Take your pick! Page Six, Huff Post . . . And let me tell you again, there is *no way* I can pull together a proper wedding before the end of the year!"

My daily Google alert hadn't hit my inbox yet, so I did a quick search, typing so quickly I spelled my own name wrong. It didn't matter.

Socialite Eva Tramell has nabbed the brass ring. Not literally, of course. Multibillionaire entrepreneur Gideon Cross, whose name is synonymous with excess and luxury, wouldn't slide anything less than platinum onto the finger of the woman who'll bear his name. (see photo at left) A source at Cross Industries confirmed the significance of the giant rock on Tramell's left hand. No comment was made regarding the ring Cross has been seen wearing. (see photo at right) A wedding is planned before year's end. We have to wonder what the rush is. Operation Gideva Baby Bump Watch has commenced.

"Oh my God," I breathed, horrified. "I have to go. I have to call Dad."

"Eva! You need to come over after work. We have to talk about the wedding."

Thankfully my dad was on the West Coast, which bought me at least three hours, depending on his work schedule. "I can't. I'm going to San Diego this weekend with Cary."

"I think you need to put off any travel for a while. You need to —"

"Start without me, Mom," I said desperately, glancing at the clock. "I don't have anything specific in mind."

"You can't be seri—"

"Gotta go. Have to work." I hung up, then pulled open the desk drawer that held my smartphone.

"Hey." Mark Garrity leaned over the top of my cubicle and offered me one of his charming crooked smiles. "Ready to roll?"

"Uh . . ." My finger hovered over the home button on my phone. I was torn between doing what I was paid to do — work — and making sure my dad heard about the engagement from me. Usually, it wouldn't be a dilemma at all to choose. I loved my job too much to risk it by slacking off. But my dad had been in a funk since he'd messed around with my mom and I was worried about him. He wasn't the kind of guy to take sleeping with a married woman lightly, even one he was in love with.

I put the phone back in the drawer. "Absolutely," I replied, pushing back from my desk and grabbing my tablet.

When I settled into my usual seat in front of Mark's desk, I sent my dad a quick text from my tablet saying I had something important to share with him and that I'd call at noon.

It was the best I could do. I could only hope it was enough.

3

"Man, you are smooth."

I looked up at Arash after setting the receiver back in its cradle. "Are you still here?"

The attorney laughed and settled back in his seat on my office sofa. The view wasn't nearly as pleasant as the one my wife had given me not too long ago.

"Schmoozing the father-in-law," he said. "I'm impressed. I expect Eva will be impressed, too. Bet you're counting on that heading into the weekend."

Damn right. I would need all the points I could earn when I met up with Eva in San Diego. "She's about to go out of town. And you have to head into the conference room before they get too restless in there. I'll join you as soon as I can."

He stood. "Yes, I heard. Your mother's here. Let the wedding insanity begin. Since you're free this weekend, how about we round up some of the usual suspects at my place tonight? It's been a while, and your bachelor days are numbered. Well, technically they're over, but no one else knows that."

And he was bound by attorney-client privilege.

It took me a beat to decide. "All right. What time?"

"Eight-ish."

I nodded, then caught Scott's eye. He got the message and rounded his desk to head up to reception.

"Great." Arash grinned. "See you at the meeting."

During the two minutes I had alone, I texted Angus about getting to California. I still had unfinished business there, and taking care of it while Eva was visiting her dad gave me a legitimate excuse to be where she was. Not that I absolutely needed one.

"Gideon."

As my mother entered, my fingers curled into my palms.

Scott followed and asked, "Are you sure I can't get you something, Mrs. Vidal? Coffee, maybe? Or water?"

She shook her head. "No, thank you. I'm fine."

"All right." He smiled and left, pulling the

door closed behind him.

I hit the remote on my desk that controlled the opacity of the glass wall, blocking the view from everyone on the main floor. My mother approached, looking slim and elegant in dark blue slacks and white blouse. She'd pulled her hair back into a sleek ebony bun, showing off the flawless face that my father had adored. Once, I'd adored it, too. Now, I had trouble looking at her.

And since we looked so much alike, I sometimes had trouble looking at myself.

"Hello, Mother. What brings you into the city?"

She set her purse on the edge of my desk. "Why is Eva wearing my ring?"

The small pleasure I'd felt at seeing her dissipated instantly. "It's *my* ring. And the answer to your question is obvious: She's wearing the ring because I gave it to her when I proposed."

"Gideon." She pulled her shoulders back. "You don't know what you're getting into with her."

I forced myself to remain facing her. I hated when she looked at me with hurt in her eyes. Blue eyes that were so like mine. "I don't have time for this. I've put an important meeting on hold to see you."

"I wouldn't have to come to your office if

you'd answer my calls or come home once in a while!" Her pretty pink mouth tightened with disapproval.

"That is *not* my home."

"She's using you, Gideon."

I retrieved my coat. "We've had this discussion."

She folded her arms across her chest like a shield. I knew my mother; she was just getting started. "She's involved with that singer, Brett Kline. Did you know that? And she's got an ugly side you've never seen. She was downright vicious to me last night."

"I'll speak with her." Straightening my coat with a brisk tug on the lapels, I headed toward the door. "She shouldn't be wasting her time."

My mother's breath caught. "I'm trying to help you."

"It's a little too late for that, don't you think?"

She took a shaky step back from the look I gave her. "I know Geoffrey's death was hard on you. It was a difficult time for all of us. I tried to give you —"

"I'm not doing this here!" I snapped, furious that she would bring up something as personal as my father's suicide while I was working. That she would bring it up at all. "You've hijacked my morning and pissed

50

me off. Let me make it clear to you. There is no scenario pitting you against Eva where you come out on top."

"You're not listening to me!"

"There's nothing you could say that would affect anything. If she wanted my money, I'd give her every cent. If she wanted another man, I'd make her forget him."

She lifted an unsteady hand to her hair, smoothing it although not a single glossy strand was out of place. "I only want the best for you, and she's stirring up crap that has been put away a long time. It can't be a healthy relationship for you. She's creating a rift with your family that —"

"We've been estranged, Mother. Eva has nothing to do with that."

"I don't want it to be like this!" Stepping closer, she held out her hand. A strand of black pearls peeked out from between the lapels of her blouse, and a sapphire-faced Patek Philippe adorned her wrist. She hadn't rebooted her life after my father's death; she'd done a complete wipe and restart. And never looked back. "I miss you. I love you."

"Not enough."

"That's not fair, Gideon. You won't give me a chance."

"If you need a ride, Angus is at your

51

service." I caught the handle of the door and paused. "Don't come here again, Mother. I don't like arguing with you. It would be best for both of us if you just stay away."

I left the door open behind me and headed toward the conference room.

"You took this shot today?"

I looked up at Raúl, who stood in front of my desk. Dressed in a plain black suit, he had the steady, watchful gaze of a man who made his living by seeing and hearing everything.

"Yes," he answered. "Not more than an hour ago."

I returned my attention to the photo in front of me. It was difficult looking at Anne Lucas. The sight of her foxlike face, with its sharp chin and sharper eyes, brought back memories I wished I could erase from my mind. Not just of her, but of her brother, who'd been similar in ways that made my skin crawl.

"Eva said the woman had long hair," I murmured, noting that Anne still had cropped hair. I remembered the plastic feel of it, the sharp-gelled spikes scratching my thighs as she deep-throated my cock, working desperately to get me hard enough to fuck her.

I handed the tablet back to Raúl. "Find out who it was."

"Will do."

"Did Eva call you?"

He frowned. "No." But he pulled out his smartphone and checked it. "No," he said again.

"She may wait until you fly out to San Diego. She wants you to find a friend of hers."

"No problem. I'll take care of it."

"Take care of *her*," I said, holding his gaze.

"Doesn't need to be said."

"I know. Thank you."

As he left my office, I sat back in my chair. There were a number of women in my past who might cause problems for me with my wife. The women I'd slept with were aggressive by nature, ones who put me in the position of needing to take the upper hand. Eva was the only woman who'd ever grabbed the lead and made me want more.

It was getting harder to let her be away from me, not easier.

"The team from Envoy is here," Scott said through the speaker.

"Send them in."

I powered through my day, wrapping up the

week's agenda and laying the groundwork for more to come. There was a lot I needed to get off my plate before I could take time off with Eva. Our daylong honeymoon had been perfect, but far too short. I wanted at least two weeks away with her, preferably a month. Someplace far away from work and other commitments, where I could have her all to myself with no interruptions.

My smartphone vibrated on my desktop and I looked at it, surprised to see my sister's face on the screen. I'd texted Ireland earlier to let her know about the engagement. Her reply had been a short and simple, Yay! Stoked. Congrats, bro!

I'd barely answered the call with a quick hello when she cut me off.

"I'm so fucking excited!" she yelled, forcing me to pull the phone away from my ear.

"Watch the mouth."

"Are you kidding? I'm seventeen, not seven. This is so awesome. I've wanted a sister forever, but figured I'd be old and gray before you and Christopher stopped bouncing around and settled down."

I sat back in my chair. "I live to serve."

"Ha. Yeah, right. You done good, you know. Eva's a keeper."

"Yes, I know."

"Thanks to her, I get to harass you now.

Always a highlight of my day."

My chest tightened, forcing me to take a minute before I could reply in an easy tone of voice. "Oddly enough, it's a highlight of mine as well."

"Well, yeah. It should be." Her voice lowered. "I heard Mom losing her shit over it earlier. She told Dad she went to your work and you guys got in a fight or something. I think she's kinda jealous. She'll get over it."

"Don't worry about it. Everything's fine."

"I know. It just sucks that she couldn't keep it together today of all days. Anyway, I'm thrilled and wanted you to know that."

"Thank you."

"But I'm not going to be the flower girl. I'm too old for that. I'm up for being a bridesmaid, though. Even a groomswoman or whatever. Just sayin'."

"All right." My mouth curved. "I'll pass that along to Eva."

I'd just hung up when Scott buzzed through my office line.

"Miss Tramell is here," he announced, making me realize how late in the day it was. "And, as a reminder, your videoconference with the development team in California is in five minutes."

Pushing back from the desk, I saw Eva

55

round the corner and come into view. I could watch her walk for hours. She had a sway to her hips that made me ache to fuck her and a determined tilt to her chin that challenged every dominant instinct I had.

I wanted to fist her ponytail in my hand, take her mouth, and grind against her. Just the way I'd wanted to the first time I saw her. And every time since.

"Send along the proposal deck to the team," I told Scott. "Tell them to review and I'll join in shortly."

"Yes, sir."

Eva swept through the door.

"Eva." I stood. "How was your day?"

She rounded the desk, then grabbed me by the tie.

I was instantly hard and totally focused on her.

"I fucking love you," she said, before yanking my mouth down to meet hers.

I hooked one arm around her waist and felt around for the opacity controls with my other hand, all the while letting her kiss me as if she owned me. Which she did. Absolutely.

The feel of her lips against mine and the unmistakable possessiveness of her actions were exactly what I needed after the day I'd had. Holding her close, I turned and half-sat on the edge of the desk, pulling her in between my thighs. I could say it was a more secure way to hold her, but honestly, my knees were weak.

Her kisses did that to me. Did what three hours of sparring with my trainer couldn't do.

Inhaling through the rising lust, I breathed her in, allowing the delicate fragrance of her perfume and the provocative scent that was hers alone to intoxicate me. Her lips were soft and damp against mine, demanding in the subtlest of ways. Her tongue licked delicately, savoring, teasing and arousing me effortlessly.

Eva kissed me as if I were the most delicious thing she'd ever tasted, a flavor she craved and was helplessly addicted to. The feeling was heady and had become necessary. I lived for her kisses.

When she kissed me, I knew I belonged right where I was.

Tilting her head, she moaned into my mouth, a soft sound of pleasure and surrender. Her fingers were in my hair, sliding through it, tugging it. That sensation of being caught — *claimed* — challenged me on the deepest level. I drew her closer, until the firmness of her belly pressed against the hardness of my erection.

My dick was throbbing, aching.

"You'll make me come," I murmured. All the effort I'd once had to expend to become aroused enough to orgasm was unnecessary with my wife. The fact that she existed stirred my blood. The strength of her desire was enough to set me off.

She leaned back slightly, breathless like me. "I don't mind."

"I wouldn't, either, if I didn't have a meeting waiting."

"I don't want to hold you up. I just want to thank you for what you said to my dad."

Smiling, I gave her ass a two-handed squeeze. "My lawyer said I'd score major points for that."

"Work was so busy, and I didn't have a chance to call him until lunch. I was so worried he'd hear about our engagement before I could tell him." She shoved at my shoulder. "You could've given me a heads-up that you were announcing it to the world!"

I shrugged. "It wasn't planned, but I wasn't going to deny it when asked."

Her lips twisted wryly. "Of course not. Did you see that ridiculous post about a baby bump?"

"A frightening thought at this point," I said, trying to keep my tone light despite the sudden rush of alarm I felt. "I'm planning on keeping you all to myself for a while."

"I know, right?" She shook her head. "I was freaked out that my dad would think I was engaged *and* pregnant, and just couldn't be bothered to let him know. It was such a relief to call him and find out you'd explained everything and smoothed the way."

"My pleasure." I would set the world on fire to clear a path for her, if that's what it took.

Her hands went to work unbuttoning my vest. My brows arched in silent query, but I wasn't going to stop her.

"I haven't even left yet, and I'm missing you already," she said quietly, straightening my tie.

"Don't go."

"If I were just going to hole up with Cary for a bit, I'd do it here at home and not in San Diego." She lifted her gaze to my face. "But he's a head case over Tatiana being pregnant. Plus, I need to spend time with my dad. Especially now."

"Is there something you should be telling me?"

"No. He sounded good when I talked to him, but I think he was hoping we'd have more time together before I got married. To him, it seems like you and I just met."

I knew I should keep my mouth shut, but I couldn't. "And we can't forget Kline."

Her jaw hardened. She dropped her attention back to where her fingers were buttoning my vest. "I'm leaving soon. I don't want to fight again."

I caught her hands. "Eva. Look at me."

Staring into her stormy eyes, I felt the tug in my chest: a slow wrenching that could turn me upside down. She hadn't stopped being angry with me, and I couldn't stand it. "You still don't understand what you do to me. How crazy you make me."

"Don't give me that. You shouldn't have brought up Corinne the way you did."

"Maybe not. But be honest, you brought up Kline this morning because you're worried about seeing him."

"I'm not worried!"

"Angel." I gave her a patient look. "You're worried. I don't think you'd sleep with him, but I do think you're anxious about crossing a line you shouldn't. You needed a strong reaction from me, so you were blunt and you got it. You needed to see what it would do to me. How just the thought of you with him makes me insane."

"Gideon." She gripped my biceps. "*Nothing* is going to happen."

"I'm not making excuses." I brushed my

fingertips across her cheek. "I hurt you and I'm sorry."

"I'm sorry, too. I wanted to avoid causing any problems and they happened anyway."

I knew she regretted our fight. I could see it in her eyes. "We're learning as we go. We'll fuck up now and again. You just have to trust me, angel."

"I have, Gideon. It's why we've gotten so far. But the fact that you'd hurt me at all — *on purpose . . .* " She shook her head and I could see how what I'd said was eating at her. "You were always supposed to be the one I could count on to never hurt me deliberately."

Hearing her doubt her trust in me was a hard blow. I took the hit, then explained myself the way I'd only ever done with her. I would explain anything, talk for hours, write the promise in blood . . . if that was what it took to make her believe in me.

"There's a difference between deliberation and malicious intent, wouldn't you agree?" I cupped her face in my hands. "I promise I'll never cause you pain just to hurt you. Don't you see that I'm just as vulnerable? You have the same power to hurt me."

Her face softened, became even more stunning. "I wouldn't."

"But I did. You'll have to forgive me."

She stepped back. "I hate when you use that tone of voice."

Inclined toward self-preservation, I didn't allow the smile I felt to show. "But it makes you wet."

Tossing a glare at me over her shoulder, Eva moved to the window and stood in the same spot I'd occupied that morning. Her ponytail showed off her beauty — and left her no way to conceal her emotions. Hot color rose in her cheeks.

Did she know how often I thought about tying her up when she was riled like this? Not to cage her or leash her, but to hold that vibrant energy of hers, that lust for life I'd never learned to have. She gave that to me, surrendered it fully.

"Don't try to control me with sex, Gideon," she said with her back to me.

"I don't want to control you at all."

"You manipulate me. You do things . . . say things . . . just to get a particular response out of me."

My arms crossed as I remembered her kissing Kline. "As do you, which we just discussed."

She faced me. "I'm allowed to, I'm a woman."

"Ah." I smiled then. "I knew that."

"You're such an enigma to me." She sighed and I could see her letting the lingering resentment go. "But you've got me pegged. You know all my buttons and just how to push them."

"If you think I don't spend a good percentage of every day trying to figure you out, you're not paying attention. Think about that while I handle this meeting, and then we'll say good-bye properly."

As I sat in my chair, her gaze followed me. I adjusted the fit of my headset and paused when I realized she was staring. She liked looking at me. And hers was the only avid hunger that had ever made me feel good about myself. I'd never had the knee-jerk defensive reaction to her sexual interest that others provoked. She made me feel loved and wanted in a way that wasn't the least threatening.

"Watching you get into business mode makes me hot," she explained, her voice just husky enough to prevent me from fully focusing on work. "Sexy as hell."

My lips twisted wryly. "Angel, behave for fifteen minutes."

"What would be the fun in that? Besides, you like me bad."

Damn straight.

"Fifteen minutes," I reiterated. Considering I'd planned for the meeting to take close to an hour, that was a major concession.

"Do what you have to do." Eva stopped by my chair and bent over like a pinup girl to breathe in my ear. "I'll find something to occupy myself with while you're on the phone playing with your millions."

My cock was abruptly, painfully hard. She had said something similar to me when we'd first started dating, and I had dreamed of it in the weeks since.

I would have told her to wait, but I knew she wouldn't. She had a determined look in her eye and a taunting swing to her hips as she circled my desk. I'd fucked up and she wanted to get a piece of her own back. Some couples punished each other with pain or deprivation. Eva and I, we punished each other with pleasure.

The moment she stepped out of view, I logged into the meeting without activating my camera and I muted my microphone. All half-dozen participants were actively discussing the materials Scott had provided. I gave them a moment to register that I'd logged in . . .

. . . and used the time to stand and open my fly.

Eva kicked off her heels. "Good. It'll go easier on you if you cooperate."

"You don't actually believe having your mouth wrapped around my dick while I'm on a videoconference is going to be easy at any level." Even then, the team in California was chiming in with greetings through my headset. I ignored them for the moment, thinking only of what was about to happen right there in my office.

Only weeks ago the possibility that I'd play while working would've been nonexistent. If Eva had been wired any differently, I would've made her wait until I had the time and attention to devote fully to her.

But my angel was a dangerous lover, one who got off on the thrill of being *this close* to discovery. I would never have known I enjoyed that edge if not for her. There were times I wanted to fuck her for the entire world to see, so it would be known definitively how completely I possessed her.

Her grin was pure wickedness. "If you liked things easy, you wouldn't have married me."

And I was going to marry her again, as soon as possible. It wouldn't be the last time. We'd be renewing our vows often, reminding each other that we made a promise to be together forever, no matter what life threw at us.

Lowering gracefully to her knees on the

far side of my desk, Eva set her hands on the floor and prowled toward me like a lioness on the hunt. Through the smoked-glass surface of my desktop, I watched her move into place, her tongue darting out to wet her lips.

Anticipation coursed through me, the rush of the challenge and erotic expectation. Everything about my wife gave me pleasure, but her mouth was in a class by itself. She sucked me off as if she were starved for my cum, as if the taste were something she was hooked on. Eva gave me head because she loved it. Watching me unravel while she did it was just a bonus.

I adjusted the spread of my fly and pushed down the waistband of my boxer briefs, studying her face as I revealed how she'd affected me. Her lips parted as her breath quickened, her body shifting back until she was sitting on her heels like a supplicant.

Settling into my chair, I absorbed the unaccustomed feeling of restraint around my thighs and the pull of elastic beneath my balls. My reaction was swift and unpleasant, the sensation of being bound dredging up memories I kept ruthlessly buried.

Reconsidering, I started to roll back in my desk chair, my heart rate rising . . .

Eva swallowed me.

"Fuck," I hissed, my fingers digging into the armrests as her fingers dug into my hips.

The rush of wet heat over the sensitive crown of my cock was shockingly intense. Hard suction tightened around me and a satin-soft tongue massaged the perfect spot. Through the pounding of my heart, I heard the team questioning whether my webcam and headset were working properly . . .

Straightening my spine, I slid forward and activated my feeds. "Excuse the delay," I said briskly as Eva took more of me. "Now that you've had the chance to review the deck, let's discuss the steps you'll be taking to implement the recommended adjustments."

Eva hummed her approval and the vibration reverberated through me. I was hard enough to drive nails and her slender fingers were teasing me, stroking with just enough pressure to make me want more.

Tim Henderson, the project manager and team leader, spoke first. I could barely focus, seeing him more from memory than the monitor in front of me. A tall, painfully thin man with pale skin and a wild mane of dark curls, he liked to talk, which was a blessing considering how dry my mouth had become.

"I'd like more time to review this," he

began, "but off the cuff, I'm thinking this is a seriously accelerated schedule. Some of this is great and I'm excited about seeing what we can do with it, but phasing into consumer beta testing is at least a year away, not six months."

"That's what you told me six months ago," I reminded him, my fist clenching as Eva took my cock to the back of her throat. Sweat bloomed on the back of my neck when she pulled off, her mouth a hot velvet suction.

"We lost our top designer to LanCorp —"

"And I offered a replacement, which you declined."

Henderson's jaw tightened. He was a coding genius with a brilliant creative mind, but he didn't play well with others and was resistant to outside intervention. That would be his prerogative . . . if he weren't eating my time and money.

"A creative team is a delicate balance," he argued. "You can't just plug a random person into the void. We've got the right man on the job now —"

"Thank you," Jeff Simmons interjected, his angular face breaking into a grin at the praise.

"— and we're making progress," Tim went on. "We —"

"— keep blowing through your self-imposed deadlines." My tone was gruffer than I intended due to my wife's wickedly agile tongue. Soft, playful licks from root to tip were driving me half out of my mind. My thighs ached with strain, the muscles hardened by the force it took to keep me in my chair. She was following the line of every sensitive vein, stroking over the throbbing ridges with the flat of her tongue.

"While creating an exceptional and groundbreaking user experience," he shot back. "We're getting the job done and we're doing it right."

I wanted to bend Eva over my desk and fuck her. Hard.

To do that, I needed to get through the damn meeting.

"Excellent. Now, you just need to do it faster. I'm sending out a team to help you achieve the objectives on time. They'll —"

"Now, wait a minute, Cross," Henderson snapped, leaning closer to the webcam. "You send some corporate bean counters over to breathe down our necks and you're only going to slow us down! You need to leave the development to us. If we need your help, we'll ask for it."

"If you thought I'd give you my money and be a silent partner, you didn't do your homework."

"Uh-oh," Eva murmured, her eyes bright with laughter beneath the glass.

I reached beneath the desk and cupped her nape, squeezing. "The app space is highly competitive. That's why you approached me. You presented me with a unique and intriguing gaming concept, and a one-year development-to-rollout timeline, which was judged by my team to be reasonable and achievable."

I paused on a breath, tormented by the feel of warm lips gliding up and down my raging dick. Eva was working with purpose now, driving me on with hard pumps of her fist. There was no more buildup, no teasing. She wanted me to come. Now.

"You're looking at this from the wrong perspective, Mr. Cross," Ken Harada said, running his hand over a blue goatee. "Technical timelines don't make allowances for an organic creative process. You don't understand how —"

"Don't make me the villain here." The urge to thrust, to fuck, was clawing. Aggression built in me like a tidal wave, forcing me to fight for any semblance of civility. "You guaranteed on-time delivery of all elements on a schedule you created and you're not holding up your end. I'm now forced to help you keep the promises you made."

The artist slumped back in his seat, muttering under his breath.

Tightening my grip on Eva's neck, I tried to slow her down. Then I gave up and started moving her, urging her roughly to suck faster. Harder. To drain me. "This is how this is going to play out. You'll work with the team I'm sending. If you miss another deadline, I'm pulling Tim off oversight."

"Bullshit!" he shouted. "This is my fucking app! You can't take it from me."

I needed finesse but had none, my brain hazed with the animal need to mate. "You should've read the contract more carefully. Do that tonight and we'll revisit tomorrow after the team arrives."

After I come . . .

Tingles raced along my spine. My balls drew up. I was a minute away, and Eva knew it. Her cheeks were hollowing with the force of her suction, her tongue fluttering over the sensitive underside of my cockhead. My heart was pounding, my palms damp with perspiration.

Staring into a half-dozen angry faces with a riot of protests exploding from my earpiece, I felt the orgasm hit me like a freight train. I fumbled for the mute button and let the groan tear from my throat as I spurted powerfully into Eva's greedily working mouth. She moaned and milked my dick with both hands, pulling and squeezing as I kept coming in a flood I couldn't stop.

I felt the heat race up into my face. Staring stonily into my monitor, I fought the urge to close my eyes and throw my head back, to free myself to absorb the singular pleasure of coming for my wife. Coming *because* of her.

As the pressure eased, I released her hair and touched her cheek with my fingertips.

I unmuted my microphone.

"My admin will call you in a few minutes," I cut in, my voice hoarse, "to arrange tomorrow's meeting. I hope we can come to an amicable agreement. Until then."

I shut down my browser and yanked off my headset. "Come here, angel."

My chair was shoved back and I'd hauled her out before she had the chance to come out on her own.

"You're a machine!" she gasped, her voice as rough as mine, her lips red and swollen. "I can't believe you didn't even twitch! How can you — Oh!"

The tiny scrap of lace she wore as underwear dropped to the floor in pieces.

"I liked those panties," she said breath-lessly.

Lifting her, I set her bare ass on the cool glass, aligning her perfectly to take my cock. "You'll like this more."

"Angel."

Like a sleepy kitten, Eva blinked at me as I stepped out of my office washroom. "Hmm?"

I grinned at finding her still slumped in my desk chair. "I assume you're okay."

"Never better." She reached up and ran a hand over her hair. "Missing the brain you just fucked out of me, but otherwise, I'm feeling excellent, thank you very much."

"You're welcome." I headed toward her with a warm damp washcloth.

"Are you trying to set a new record for most orgasms in a single day?"

"An intriguing proposition. I'm willing to give it a shot."

She held out her hand as if to ward me off. "No more, maniac. You screw me again and I'll be a drooling, babbling idiot."

"Let me know if you change your mind." I kneeled in front of her and urged her legs open. Waxed smooth and pretty pink, her cunt was lovely. Perfect.

She watched me as I cleaned her, her

73

fingers reaching out to comb through my hair. "Don't work too hard this weekend, okay?"

"As if there's something else worth doing without you around," I murmured.

"Sleep in. Read a book. Plan a party."

My mouth quirked. "I haven't forgotten. I'm asking the guys tonight."

"Oh?" The laziness left her eyes. I pulled back before her legs closed. "What guys?"

"The ones you want to meet."

"You're calling them?

I stood. "We're getting together."

"To do what?"

"Drink. Hang out." Returning to the bathroom, I tossed the washcloth in the hamper and washed my hands.

Eva followed me. "At a club?"

"Maybe. Probably not."

She lounged against the doorjamb and crossed her arms. "Are any of them married?"

"Yes." I slung the hand towel back on the rack. "Me."

"That's it? Is Arnoldo going to be there?"

"Maybe. Likely."

"What's up with the short answers?"

"What's up with the interrogation?" I asked the question, but I knew. My wife was a jealous, possessive woman. Lucky for both

74

of us, I liked it. A lot.

She shrugged, but it was a defensive gesture. "I just want to know what you're doing, that's all."

"I'll stay home if you will."

"I'm not asking you to do that."

There was a smudge of dark makeup beneath her eyes. I loved mussing her up and giving her that just-fucked look. No woman wore it better. "Get to the point, then."

She made a frustrated noise. "Why won't you tell me what you guys have planned?"

"I don't know, Eva. Usually we meet at one of our places and drink. Play cards. Sometimes we go out."

"Trolling. A group of hot guys who've got a buzz and want a good time."

"That's not a crime. And who said they're attractive?"

She shot me a look. "They're trolling with you. That means they're either hot enough not to completely pale in your shadow or too confident to worry about it."

I held up my left hand. The bloodred rubies in my wedding band caught the light. I never took the ring off and never would. "Remember this?"

"I'm not worried about you," she muttered, her arms dropping to her sides. "If

75

I'm not fucking you enough, you need help."

"Says the wife who couldn't wait fifteen minutes."

She stuck her tongue out at me.

"That's what got you fucked right there."

"Arnoldo doesn't trust me, Gideon. He doesn't really want you with me."

"It's not his decision to make. And some of your friends aren't going to like me, either. I know Cary's on the fence."

"What if Arnoldo tells the others how he feels about me?"

"Angel." I went to her and caught her by the hips. "Talking about feelings is predominantly female territory."

"Don't be sexist."

"You know I'm right. Besides, Arnoldo knows how it is. He's been in love before."

She looked up at me with those uniquely beautiful eyes. "Are you in love, Mr. Cross?"

"Irrevocably."

Manuel Alcoa slapped me on the back as he rounded me. "You just cost me a thousand dollars, Cross."

I leaned against the kitchen island and shoved my hand into the pocket of my jeans, wrapping it around my smartphone. Eva was mid-flight and I was alert for any word from her or Raúl. I'd never feared flying,

76

never worried over someone's safety while traveling. Until now.

"How so?" I asked, before taking a swig of my beer.

"You are the last man I figured would tie the knot and you turn out to be the first." Manuel shook his head. "Kills me."

I lowered the bottle. "You bet against me?"

"Yeah. Although I suspect someone had the inside scoop." The portfolio manager narrowed his eyes across the island at Arnoldo Ricci, who lifted one shoulder in a shrug.

"If it's any consolation," I said, "I'd have bet against me, too."

Manuel grinned. "Latinas rule, my friend. Sexy, curvy. More than a handful in bed and out. Hot tempered. Passionate." He hummed. "Good choice."

"Manuel!" Arash yelled from the living room. "Bring those limes over here."

I watched Manuel leave the kitchen with the bowl of lime slices. Arash's condo was modern and spacious with a panoramic view of the East River. There was a notable lack of walls except for those hiding the bathrooms.

Circling the granite-topped island, I approached Arnoldo. "How are you?"

"Good." His gaze dropped to the amber

liquid he swirled in a tumbler. "I'd ask you the same, but you look well. I'm glad."

I didn't waste time with small talk. "Eva worries that you've got a problem with her."

He glanced at me. "I've never been disrespectful to your woman."

"She never said you were."

Arnoldo drank, taking a moment to savor the fine liquor before swallowing it. "I understand that you are — what's the word? — held captive by this woman."

"Captivated," I provided, wondering why he didn't just speak in Italian.

"Ah, yes." He gave me a slight smile. "I have been there, my friend, as you know. I don't judge you."

I knew Arnoldo understood. I'd found him in Florence, recovering from the loss of a woman by drowning in liquor and cooking like a madman, producing so much five-star cuisine he was giving it away. I had been fascinated by the totality of his despair and unable to relate.

I'd been so certain I would never know anything like it. Like the opacity and soundproofing of the glass wall in my office, my view of life had been dulled. I knew I'd never be able to explain to Eva how she'd appeared to me the first time I saw her, so vibrant and warm. A colorful explosion in a

78

black-and-white landscape.

"Voglio che sia felice." It was a simple statement, but the crux of the issue. *I want her to be happy.*

"If her happiness depends on what I think," he answered in Italian, "you ask too much. I will never say anything against her. I'll always treat her with the respect I feel for you as long as you are together. But what I believe is my choice and my right, Gideon."

I looked over at Arash, who was lining up shot glasses on the bar in the living room. As my lead attorney, he knew about both my marriage and Eva's sex tape, and he didn't have a problem with either one.

"Our relationship is . . . complex," I explained quietly. "I've hurt her as much as she's ever hurt me — likely more."

"I'm not surprised to hear that, but I am sorry." Arnoldo studied me. "You couldn't choose one of the other women who've loved you and would give you no trouble? A comfortable ornament who would settle into your life without a ripple?"

"As Eva says, what would be the fun in that?" My smile faded. "She challenges me, Arnoldo. Makes me see things . . . think about things, in ways I didn't before. And she loves me. Not like the others." I reached

79

for my phone again.

"You didn't allow the others to love you."

"I couldn't. I was waiting for her." A thoughtful expression crossed his face and I said, "I can't imagine your Bianca was hassle-free."

He laughed. "No. But my life is simple. I can use complications."

"My life was ordered. Now, it's an adventure."

Arnoldo sobered, his dark eyes growing serious. "But that wildness in her that you love is what worries me most."

"Stop worrying."

"I will mention this only once, then never again. You may be angry with me for what I say, but understand that my heart is in the right place."

My jaw tightened. "Get it off your chest."

"I sat with Eva and Brett Kline at dinner. I observed them together. There is chemistry there, not unlike what I saw between Bianca and the man she left me for. I wish I believed Eva would ignore it, but she's already proven that she can't."

I held his gaze. "She had her reasons. Reasons I gave her."

Arnoldo took another drink. "Then I'll pray that you don't give her more reasons."

"Hey," Arash shouted. "Cut it out with

80

the Italian and get your asses in here."

Arnoldo touched his glass to my bottle before passing me.

I finished my beer alone, taking a moment to consider what Arnoldo had said.

Then I joined the party.

4

"What's got you frowning, baby girl?" Cary asked, his voice low and sleepy from the Dramamine he'd downed at takeoff.

Staring at the choices in the dropdown menu my cursor hovered over, I debated which to pick. *Engaged* or *It's complicated*? Since *Married* also applied, I thought *All of the above* should've been an option.

Wouldn't that be fun to explain?

Glancing across the luxurious cabin of Gideon's private jet, I found my best friend sprawled along the white leather sofa with his hands tucked behind his head. Long and lean, he was a pretty picture with his shirt riding high and his cargo pants riding low, exposing the amazing abs that were helping Grey Isles to sell jeans, underwear, and other men's clothing.

Cary had no problem whatsoever accustoming himself to the luxurious conveniences of Gideon's immense wealth. He'd settled immediately and comfortably into the elegant appointments of the ultra-modern cabin. And somehow, even casually dressed, he looked perfectly at home amid the brushed steel and gray oak.

"I'm trying to set up some social media accounts," I answered.

"Whoa." He sat up with effortless grace, his posture surprisingly and instantly alert. "Big step."

"Yeah." Nathan had kept me hiding, afraid to put myself out there and risk making it easy for him to find me. "But it's time. I feel like . . . Never mind. It's just time."

"All right." He set his elbows on his knees and tapped his fingertips together. "Then why is your face all scrunched up like that?"

"Well, there's a lot to consider. I mean, how much do I share out there? I don't have to worry about Nathan anymore, but Gideon is under constant scrutiny."

With my thoughts on Gideon, I ran a search for his profile. It popped up with the little blue check mark that told me it was verified as belonging to him. The sight of his picture, a shot of him in a black three-piece suit and the blue tie I loved, sent a pang of longing through me. He'd been photographed on a rooftop with the skyline of Manhattan fuzzily out of focus behind him, while he was sharply and vividly captured by the camera's lens.

He was even sharper and more vibrant in reality. I stared into Gideon's eyes, getting lost in that impossible blue. His black hair framed that perfect fallen-angel face in strands of glossy, inky silk.

Poetic? Yes. But then his looks could inspire sonnets. To say nothing of spur-of-the-moment marriage.

When had the photo been taken? Before we'd met? He had the implacable, remote look that made him seem like such an impossible dream.

"I'm married," I blurted out, tearing my gaze away from the most gorgeous man I'd ever seen. "To Gideon, of course. Who else would I be married to?"

Cary froze while I rambled. "Come again?"

I rubbed my palms on my yoga pants. It was a cop-out telling him the news while motion sickness drugs lulled his brain, but I'd take any advantage I could get. "When we went away last weekend. We eloped."

He was quiet for a long, weighted minute. Then he exploded to his feet. "Are you shitting me?"

Raúl's head turned in our direction. The movement was casual and unhurried, but his gaze was vigilant and watchful. He sat in the far corner, being eerily unobtrusive for such a hard-to-miss guy.

"What's the damned rush?" Cary snapped.

"It just . . . happened." I couldn't explain it. I'd thought it was too soon. Still did. But Gideon was the only man I would ever love so completely. When I considered that, I knew Gideon had been right; we'd only be postponing the inevitable. And Gideon needed my promise that I was his forever. My amazing husband who found it so hard to believe he could be loved. "I'm not sorry."

"Not yet." Cary shoved both hands into his hair. "Jesus, Eva. You don't up and marry the first guy you have a serious relationship with."

"It's not like that," I protested, awkwardly avoiding looking at Raúl. "You know how we feel about each other."

"Sure. You two are whack jobs separately. Together, you're a goddamn nut house."

I flipped him the bird. "We'll work on it. Wearing a ring doesn't mean we stop figuring things out."

He dropped into the chair across from me. "What incentive has he got to fix anything? He's bagged and tagged the prize. You're stuck with his psychotic dreams and Grand

Canyon–sized mood swings."

"Wait a minute," I said tightly, feeling the sting of truth in his words. "You didn't get upset when I told you we were engaged."

"Because I figured it'd be a year, at the very least, before Monica got the wedding worked out. Maybe a year and a half. At least some time for you two to try living together."

I let him rant. Better that he did it at thirty thousand feet than in some public venue where the whole world could hear.

He leaned closer, his green eyes fierce. "I'm having a baby and I'm not getting married. You know why? Because I'm too fucked up and I know it. I've got no business hitching a passenger on this wild ride. If he loved you, he'd be thinking about *you* and what's best for *you*."

"I'm so glad you're happy for me, Cary. That means a lot."

The words dripped with sarcasm, but they were honest in their own way. There were girlfriends I could call who would tell me what an amazingly lucky bitch I was. Cary was my closest friend because he always gave it to me straight, even when I desperately wanted sugarcoating.

But Cary was thinking only about the darkness. He didn't understand the light

Gideon brought into my life. The acceptance and the love. The safety. Gideon had given me my freedom back, a life without terror. Giving him vows in return was too simple a repayment for that.

I turned my attention back to Gideon's profile, scrolling down to see that the most recent post was a link to an article about our engagement. I doubted he'd posted it himself; he was too busy to bother with something like that. But I figured he'd approved it. If not, he had somehow already made it clear that I was important enough to become the one bit of personal news that was okay to be shared on an otherwise business-focused profile.

Gideon was proud of me. Proud to be marrying me, a hot mess with a history of bad choices. Whatever anyone else thought, I knew *I* was the one who'd bagged and tagged the prize.

"Fuck." Cary slouched into the chair. "Make me feel like an ass."

"If the shoe fits . . ." I muttered, clicking on the link to view other photos of Gideon.

It was a mistake.

All the pictures posted by his social media admin were business-related, but the unofficial pictures he'd been tagged in weren't. There, in living color, were images of him

87

with beautiful women. And they hit me hard. Jealousy clawed and twisted my stomach.

God, he looked amazing in a tuxedo. Dark and dangerous. His face savagely beautiful, his cheekbones and mouth chiseled perfection, his posture confident and more than a little arrogant. An alpha male in his prime.

I knew the photos weren't recent. I knew the women in them didn't have firsthand knowledge of his insanely mad skills in bed; he had a rule about that. Neither of which stopped the images from making me twitchy.

"Am I the last to know?" Cary asked.

"You're the only one." I glanced at Raúl. "At least on my side. Gideon wants to tell the world, but we're going to keep it under wraps."

He studied me. "For how long?"

"Forever. The next wedding we have will be our first as far as anyone else is concerned."

"You having second thoughts?"

It killed me that Cary didn't care that we had an audience. I was hyperaware that every move I made, every word I said was being witnessed.

Not that Raúl's presence had any effect on my answer. "No. I'm glad we're married.

I love him, Cary."

I was glad Gideon was mine. And I missed him. Worse after seeing those pictures.

"I know you do," Cary said with a sigh.

Unable to help myself, I opened the messaging app on my laptop and sent Gideon a text. I miss you.

He texted back almost instantly. Turn the plane around.

That made me smile. It was so like him. And so unlike me. Wasting the pilots' time, the fuel . . . it seemed so frivolous to me. More than that, though, would be the proof of how dependent on Gideon I'd become. That would be the kiss of death in our relationship. He could have anything, any woman, at any time. If I ever became too easy for him, we'd both lose respect for me. Losing his love wouldn't be far behind.

I returned to my new profile and uploaded a selfie I'd taken with Gideon that I synced from my smartphone. I made it the masthead image. Then I tagged him and gave it a description: *The love of my life.*

After all, if his photos were going to include him with women, I wanted at least one of them to be me. And the one I'd chosen was undeniably intimate. We lay on our backs, our temples touching, my face bare of makeup and his relaxed with a smile in his eyes. I dared anyone to look at it and not see that I had a private bond with him the world would never know.

I suddenly wanted to call him. So badly that I could almost hear that amazingly sexy voice, as intoxicating as top-shelf liquor, smooth with just a hint of bite. I wanted to be with him, my hand in his, my lips against his throat where the smell of his skin called to something hungry and primitive inside me.

It scared me sometimes, how much I needed him. To the exclusion of everything else. There was no one I wanted to be with more, including my best friend, who was at that moment needing me almost as fiercely.

"It's all good, Cary," I assured him. "Don't worry."

"I'd be more worried if I thought you actually believed that." He shoved the bangs off his forehead with an impatient hand. "It's too soon, Eva."

I nodded. "But it'll work out."

It had to. I couldn't imagine my life without Gideon in it.

Cary's head dropped back and his eyes closed. I might have thought he was succumbing to the motion sickness pills, except his knuckles were white from gripping the armrests too tightly. He was taking the news hard. I didn't know what I could say to re-assure him.

You're still heading in the wrong direction, Gideon texted.

I almost asked him how he knew that, but caught myself. Are you having a good time with the guys?

I'd have more fun with you.

I grinned. I would hope so. My fingers paused, then: I told Cary.

The answer wasn't instantaneous. Still friends?

He hasn't disowned me yet.

He didn't say anything to that, and I told myself not to read too much into his silence. He was out with his guys. It had been asking a lot to even hear from him at all.

Still, I was super happy to get a text from him ten minutes later.

Don't stop missing me.

I looked over at Cary and found him watching me. Was Gideon facing similar disapproval from his friends?

Don't stop loving me, I texted back.

His answer was simple and very much Gideon. Deal.

"SoCal, baby, I missed you." Cary de-scended the steps from the plane to the tar-mac, tilting his head back to look up at the night sky. "God, it's good to leave that East Coast humidity behind."

I scrambled down after him, eager to get to the tall, dark figure waiting by a shiny black Suburban. Victor Reyes was the kind of male who commanded attention. Part of that was due to his being a cop. The rest was all him.

"Dad!" I ran full bore toward him and he unfolded from where he'd been leaning against the SUV and opened his arms to me.

He absorbed the crash of my body into his and lifted me off my feet, squeezing me so tightly I couldn't breathe. "It's good to see you, baby," he said gruffly.

Cary sauntered up to us. My dad put me down.

"Cary." My dad clasped Cary's hand, then pulled him in for a quick hug and a hearty slap on the back. "Looking good, kid."

"I try."

"Got everything?" my dad asked. He eyed Raúl, who'd exited the plane first and now stood silently near a black Benz that had been parked and waiting close by.

Gideon had told me to forget that Raúl was there. That wasn't easy for me to do.

"Yep," Cary answered, adjusting the weight of his duffel strap on his shoulder.

He carried my bag, which was lighter than his, in his hand. Even with all my makeup and three pairs of shoes, Cary had packed more than me.

I loved that about him.

"You two hungry?" My dad opened the passenger door for me.

It was just past nine in California, but after midnight in New York. Too late for me to eat usually, but we hadn't grabbed dinner.

Cary answered before climbing into the backseat. "Starved."

I laughed. "You're always hungry."

"So are you, sweet cheeks," he shot back, sliding into the center seat so he could lean forward and be in the mix. "I've just got no guilt about it."

We pulled away from the jet and I watched it grow smaller as we cruised down the tarmac toward the exit. I glanced at my dad's profile, looking for any hint of his thoughts about the lifestyle I'd be living as Gideon's wife. The private jets. The full-time bodyguards. I knew how he felt about Stanton's wealth, but that was my stepdad. I was hoping a husband would be cut some slack.

Still, I knew the change in routine was glaring. Previously, we would've flown into San Diego's harbor. We would have headed to the Gaslamp and grabbed a table at Dick's Last Resort, spending an hour or more laughing at the silliness and enjoying a beer with dinner.

There was tension now that hadn't been there before. Nathan. Gideon. My mom. They were all hovering between us.

It sucked. Massively.

"What about that place in Oceanside with the slushy beer and peanut shells on the floor?" Cary suggested.

"Yeah." I twisted in my seat to give him a grateful smile. "That'd be fun."

Laid-back and familiar. Perfect.

I could tell my dad thought so, too, when I looked at him and his mouth quirked. "You got it."

We left the airport behind. I dug out my phone and turned it on, wanting to sync it to the Suburban's sound system so we could listen to music that would take us back to less complicated times.

Texts popped up so fast, they filled my screen then scrolled off.

The most recent one was from Brett. Call me when you get into town.

And right on cue, "Golden" started playing on the radio.

I was climbing the steps of my dad's tiny

porch the next day when my phone started vibrating. I pulled it out of my shorts pocket and felt a tingle of happiness at the sight of Gideon's picture on the screen.

"Good morning," I answered, settling into one of the two cushioned wrought-iron chairs near the front door. "Did you sleep well?"

"Well enough." The beloved soft rasp of his voice slid sweetly through me. "Raúl says Victor's coffee could wake a hibernating bear."

I glanced at the Benz parked across the narrow street. The tinted windows were so dark I couldn't see the man inside. It was a bit freaky that Raúl had somehow managed to talk to Gideon about the coffee I'd just barely taken over to him before I even made it back to the house. "Are you trying to intimidate me with how closely you're watching me?"

"If intimidation were my goal, I wouldn't be subtle about it."

I picked up the mug I'd dropped off on the small patio table prior to making my java delivery to Raúl. "You do know that tone of voice makes me want to irritate you back, don't you?"

"Because you like the way I rise to the challenge," he purred, sending little goose bumps across my skin despite the warmth of the summer day.

My mouth curved. "So, what exactly did you guys end up doing last night?"

"The usual. Drink. Give each other a hard time."

"Did you go out?"

"For a couple of hours."

My grip tightened on the phone as I pictured a pack of hot guys out on the prowl. "I hope you had fun."

"It wasn't bad. Tell me your plans for the day."

I picked up the same note of tightness in his words that I'd just had. Unfortunately, marriage wasn't a cure for jealousy. "When Cary wakes up and rolls his ass off the couch, we'll grab a quick lunch with my dad. Then we're going down to San Diego to see Dr. Travis."

"And tonight?"

I took a sip of my coffee, steeling myself for an argument. I knew he was thinking about Brett. "The band's manager sent me an e-mail about where to claim VIP tickets, but I've decided not to see the show. I figure Cary can take a friend, if he wants. What I have to say won't take very long, so either I'll see Brett tomorrow before I leave or we can chat on the phone."

He exhaled softly. "I expect you have an idea of what you're going to tell him."

"I'm gonna keep it simple. With 'Golden' and my engagement, I don't think it's appropriate for us to see each other socially. I hope we'll be friends and keep in touch, but e-mail and texts are better, unless you're with me."

He was silent long enough that I thought maybe the call had dropped. "Gideon?"

"I need to know if you're afraid to see him."

Uneasy, I took another drink. The coffee had cooled, but I barely tasted it anyway. "I don't want to fight about Brett."

"So your solution is to avoid him."

"You and I have enough shit to fight about without throwing him into the mix. He's not worth it."

Gideon was quiet again. This time, I waited him out.

When his voice came again, it was confident and decisive. "I can live with that, Eva."

My shoulders relaxed and something inside me eased. And then, paradoxically, my chest tightened. I remembered what he'd said to me once, that he'd live with me loving another man just so long as he had me.

He loved me so much more than he loved

himself. It broke my heart that he'd sell himself short like that. It made it impossible to hold myself back.

"You're everything to me," I breathed. "I think about you all the time."

"It's no different for me."

"Really?" I lowered my voice further, trying to keep it down. "Because I have it so bad for you. I get — well, hot. Like I'm overcome with this desperate *need* to be touching you. My brain scatters and I have to take a minute to ride it out, but it's so hard to deal. So many times I've almost dropped whatever I'm doing to get to you."

"Eva —"

"I have fantasies about barging into one of your meetings and just running right into you. Have I told you that? When the craving is really bad, I can almost *feel* you pulling at me."

I rushed on when I heard him growl softly. "I lose my breath every time I see you. If I close my eyes, I can hear your voice. I woke up this morning and I panicked a little because you're so far away. I would've given *anything* to be able to get to you. I wanted to cry because I couldn't."

"Christ. Eva, please —"

"If you're going to worry about anything, Gideon, it should be *me*. Because I can't be rational when it comes to you. I'm crazy about you. Literally. I can't think about a future without you — it freaks me out."

"Goddamn it. You'll *never* be without me. We're going to grow old together. Die together. I'm not going to live a single day without you."

A tear slid from the corner of my eye. I scrubbed it away. "I need you to understand that you'll never have to settle for pieces of me. You shouldn't be settling at all. You deserve so much better. You could have anyone —"

"That's enough!"

I jumped at the lash of his voice.

"You will not ever say anything like that to me again," he snapped. "Or I swear to God, angel, I will punish you."

Shocked silence filled the space between us. The words I'd spoken circled restlessly in my mind, taunting me with how pathetic I could be. I never wanted to be dependent on him, but I already was.

"I have to go," I said hoarsely.

"Don't hang up. For God's sake, Eva, we're *married*. We're in love. There's no shame in that. So what if it's crazy? It's *us*. It's who we are. You need to come to grips with that."

The screen door squeaked as my dad

stepped onto the porch. I looked at him and said, "My dad's here, Gideon. I'll have to talk to you later."

"You make me happy," he said, in the deep firm tone he used when making an unswayable decision. "I'd forgotten what that feels like. Don't devalue what you mean to me."

God.

"I love you, too." I ended the call and set the phone down on the table with a shaky hand.

My dad settled into the other chair with his coffee. He wore long shorts and a dark olive T-shirt, but his feet were bare. He'd shaved and his hair was still damp, the ends curling slightly as they dried.

He was my father, but that didn't stop me from appreciating the fact that he was ridiculously attractive. He kept himself in great shape and had a naturally confident bearing. I could see why my mother hadn't been able to resist him when they'd met. And apparently still couldn't.

"I heard you talking," he said without looking at me.

"Oh." My stomach dropped. It was bad enough spilling my guts to Gideon. Knowing that my dad had heard me do it only made it worse.

"I was going to talk to you about whether you knew what you were doing, getting engaged so soon and so young."

I pulled my legs up and crossed them under me. "I figured you would."

"But now I think I understand what you're feeling." He looked at me, his gray eyes soft and searching. "You express it far better than I ever could, back in the day. The most I could ever get out was 'I love you,' and it's just not enough."

I could see he was thinking about my mom. I knew it must be hard not to when I looked so much like her. "Gideon doesn't think those words are enough, either."

I looked down at my rings. The one Gideon had given me to express his need to hold on to me, and the other both a symbol of his commitment and a tribute to a time in his past when he'd last felt loved. "He shows me, though. All the time."

"I've talked to him a few times now." My dad paused. "I have to remind myself that he's in his twenties."

That made me smile. "He's very self-possessed."

"He's also very hard to read."

My smile widened. "He's a poker player. But he means what he says."

I believed Gideon implicitly. He always

told me the truth. The problem was, there was a lot he didn't tell me.

"And he wants to marry my daughter."

I shot him a look. "You gave him your blessing."

"He said he would always take care of you. He promised to keep you safe and make you happy." He stared across the street at the Benz. "I still don't know why I believe him, even with him staking out my place for you. Doesn't help that he lied about waiting to ask you."

"He couldn't wait, Dad. Don't hold it against him. He loves me too much."

He looked at me again. "You didn't sound happy when you were just talking to him."

"No. I sounded desperate and insecure." I sighed. "I love him like mad, but I hate when I get needy with it. We should be balanced in our relationship. Equals."

"Good goal. Don't lose sight of it. Does he want that, too?"

"He wants us to be together. In everything. But he's built a reputation and an empire, and I want to build my own. Not necessarily the empire, but the reputation for sure."

"Have you talked to him about this?"

"Oh yeah." My mouth quirked. "But he believes Mrs. Cross should naturally play on Team Cross. And I can see his point."

"It's good to hear that you've been thinking this through."

I heard the pause. "But?"

"But that could be a serious issue, couldn't it?"

I loved the way my dad urged me to explore without trying to sway me or judge. He'd always been that way. "Yes. I don't think it would become a deal breaker for us, but it could cause problems. He isn't used to not getting what he wants."

"Then you're good for him."

"He thinks so." I shrugged. "Gideon isn't the problem. It's me. He's been through a lot in his life and he's had to deal with it on his own. I don't want him to feel like he's got to handle everything himself anymore. I want him to feel like we're a unit and that I'm here to support him. That's a hard message to send when I want my own independence, too."

"You're a lot like me," he said with a soft smile, looking so handsome that my heart swelled with pride.

"I know you'll get along with him. He's a good man, with a beautiful heart. He'd do anything for me, Dad." *Even kill for me.*

The thought made me queasy. The possibility that Gideon would have to answer for Nathan's death in some way was all too real. I couldn't let anything happen to him.

"Would he let me pay for the wedding?" My dad snorted out a laugh. "I guess I should ask how much of a fight you think your mother would give me."

"Dad . . ." My chest tightened again. After the discussions we'd had about paying for my college tuition, I knew better than to say he didn't have to stretch his finances to the breaking point for me. It was a point of pride and my father was a very proud man. "I don't know what to say except thank you."

He gave me a relieved smile and I realized that he'd been expecting me to be resistant, too. "I've got about fifty large. I know it's not much —"

I reached for his hand. "It's perfect."

I could already hear my mom's freakout in my head. I'd cope with that when the time came.

It would be worth it for the look on my father's face at that moment.

"It hasn't changed." Cary paused on the sidewalk outside the former recreation center and pulled the sunglasses off his face. His gaze slid over the gym's entrance. "I've missed this place."

I reached for his hand and linked our fingers. "Me, too."

We headed up the walk and nodded at the couple standing by the door smoking. Then we went inside and were greeted by the sights and sounds of a hoops match in progress. Two teams of three played a half-court game, taunting each other and laughing. I knew from experience that sometimes Dr. Travis's unusual offices were the only place one felt free and safe enough to laugh.

We waved at the players, who paused just long enough to register us, and then we made a beeline for the door that still had *Coach* emblazoned on the glass inset. It was ajar and a beloved figure lounged in a worn desk chair with his feet propped on the desk. He tossed a tennis ball against the wall and caught it deftly, over and over, while a fellow patient I knew from before vaped on an electronic cigarette and talked.

"Oh my God." Kyle stood in a rush, her pretty red mouth falling open and a cloud of vapor billowing out. "I didn't know you two were back!"

She launched herself at Cary, barely giving me time to let his hand go.

Dr. Travis folded his legs and then stood, his kind face splitting with a welcoming grin. He was dressed in his usual khakis and dress shirt, with the leather sandals on his feet and the earrings in his ears giving him away as a tad unconventional. His sandy brown hair was shaggy and messy, and his wire-rimmed glasses were slightly skewed on the bridge of his nose.

"I wasn't expecting you two until sometime after three," he said.

"It's after three in New York," Cary rejoined, disentangling himself from Kyle.

I had my suspicions that Cary had slept with the pretty blonde at some point, and that she hadn't brushed it off as easily as he had.

Dr. Travis caught me up in a quick hug, then did the same to Cary. I watched my best friend's eyes close and his cheek rest for a moment on Dr. Travis's shoulder. My eyes stung as they always did whenever I saw Cary happy. Dr. Travis was the closest thing to a father that he had and I knew how much Cary loved him.

"You two still watching each other's backs in the Big Apple?"

"Of course," I replied.

Cary jerked his thumb at me. "She's getting married. I'm having a baby."

Kyle gasped.

I elbowed Cary in the ribs.

"Oww," he complained, rubbing his side.

Dr. Travis blinked. "Congratulations. Quick work, both of you."

"I'll say," Kyle muttered. "What's it been? A month?"

"Kyle." Dr. Travis tucked his chair into his desk. "Would you give us a minute?"

She snorted and sauntered toward the door. "You're good, Doc, but I think you're going to need more time than that."

"Engaged, huh?" Kyle took another drag off her e-cigarette, her eyes on Cary as he leaped above Dr. Travis's head and made a slam dunk. We sat on the worn bleachers about three rows from the top, enough distance away that we couldn't overhear the therapy session taking place on the court.

Cary got restless when he opened up. Dr. Travis had quickly learned to keep Cary physically active if he wanted to keep him talking.

Kyle looked at me. "I always kinda figured you and Cary would end up together."

I laughed and shook my head. "It's not like that with us. Never has been."

She shrugged. Her eyes were the color of the San Diego sky and heavily rimmed with electric blue liner. "You known this guy you're marrying long?"

"Long enough."

Dr. Travis nailed a bank shot and then ruffled Cary's hair affectionately. I saw him glance at me and knew it was my turn.

I stood and stretched. "Catch you later," I said to Kyle.

"Good luck."

My mouth twisted wryly and I made my way down the stairs until I reached Dr. Travis.

He was about Gideon's height, so I stopped before I hit the bottom stair so that we were briefly at eye level. "You ever consider moving to New York, Doc?"

He smiled his crooked smile. "As if California taxes aren't bad enough."

I sighed dramatically. "I had to try."

His arm slung around my shoulders when I joined him courtside. "So did Cary. I'm flattered."

We went to his office. I shut the door while he nabbed a dinged metal chair and spun it around to sit facing backward with his arms draped along the backrest. It was one of his quirks. He sat in the desk chair when he was just hanging out; he straddled the relic when he got down to business.

"Tell me about your fiancé," he said, when I took my usual spot on the green vinyl sofa that was held together with duct tape and decorated with signatures of former and existing patients.

"Come on," I chided. "We both know Cary filled you in."

Cary always started his sessions with talk about my life and me. That eventually dovetailed into talk about him.

"And I know who Gideon Cross is." Dr. Travis tapped his feet in that way he had that somehow never seemed restless or impatient. "But I want to hear about the man you're going to marry."

I thought for a minute and he sat quietly while I did, not waiting, just observing. "Gideon is . . . God, he's so many things. He's complicated. We have some issues to work out, but we'll get there. My more immediate problem is the feelings I'm having for this singer I used to . . . see."

"Brett Kline?"

"You remember his name."

"Cary reminded me, but I remember our discussions about him."

"Yeah, well." I looked at my stunning wedding ring, twisting it around my finger. "I'm so in love with Gideon. He's changed my life in so many ways. He makes me feel beautiful and precious. I know it seems too fast, but he's the one for me."

Dr. Travis smiled. "It was love at first sight for me and my wife. We were in high school when we met, but I knew she was the girl I was going to marry."

My gaze drifted to the pictures of his wife on his desk. There was one when she was younger, and another more recent. The office itself was a mess of papers, sports equipment, books, and ancient posters of bygone sports personalities, but the frames and glass protecting the photos were spotless.

"I don't understand why Brett has any effect on me at all. It's not that I want him. I can't imagine being with anyone else but Gideon. Sexually or otherwise. But I'm not indifferent to Brett."

"Why should you be?" he asked simply. "He was a part of your life at a pivotal time, and the end of your relationship caused a bit of an epiphany for you."

"My . . . interest — that's not the right word — doesn't feel like nostalgia."

"No, I'm sure it doesn't. I would guess you're feeling some regret. Thinking about what-ifs. It was a highly sexual relationship for you, so there may be some lingering attraction, even if you know you'd never go there again."

I was almost sure he was right about that.

His fingertips drummed on the back of the chair. "You said your fiancé is a complicated man and you're working on some issues. Brett was very simple. You knew what you were getting with him. In the last few months, you've had a big move, you're closer to your mother, and you're engaged. You may, occasionally, wish things were simpler."

I stared at him as that sank in. "How do you make sense like that?"

"Practice."

Fear made me say, "I don't want to screw things up with Gideon."

"Do you have someone you're talking with in New York?"

"We're in couples therapy."

He nodded. "Practical. That's good. He wants it to work, too. Does he know?"

About Nathan? "Yes."

"I'm proud of you, kiddo."

"I'm going to avoid Brett, but I wonder if that means I'm not dealing with the root of the problem. Like an alcoholic who doesn't drink is still an alcoholic. The problem is still there, they're just staying away from it."

"Not quite true, but interesting that you'd use an addiction analogy. You're prone to self-destructive behavior with men. A lot of individuals with your history are, so it's not unexpected and we've addressed that before."

"I know." That was why I was so afraid of getting lost in Gideon.

"There are a few things you have to consider," he continued. "You're engaged to a man who, on the surface, is very much the sort of man your mother would want for you. Considering how you feel about your mother's dependence on men, there might be some resistance you're feeling."

My nose wrinkled.

He wagged his finger at me. "Ah, a possibility? The other is that you might not feel you deserve what you've found with him."

A rock settled in my gut. "And I deserve Brett?"

"Eva." He gave me a kind smile. "The fact you're even asking that question . . . that's your problem right there."

5

"I didn't even recognize you without the suit and tie," Sam Yimara said, as I settled into the seat across from him. He was a compact man, well shy of six feet in height but muscled. His head was shaved and tattooed, his earlobes pierced so that I could see right through them.

Pete's 69th Street Bar wasn't located on Sixty-ninth Street, so I had no idea where the name originated. I did understand that Six-Ninths had derived their name from it, after playing on its stage for a number of years. I also understood that the restrooms in the back had provided a place for Brett Kline to screw my wife.

I wanted to lay my fists into him for that. She deserved palaces and private islands, not seedy bar bathroom stalls.

Pete's wasn't quite a dive, but it was classless. A beach bar that looked best under cover of darkness and known mostly as a place for SDSU students to hook up and drink 'til they couldn't remember what they did or whom they fucked.

After I tore the place to the ground, they wouldn't remember the bar, either.

The choice in venue was deliberate and quite brilliant on Yimara's part. It put me on edge and drove home what was at stake. If my decision to show up alone and dressed in jeans and T-shirt threw him off in return, I'd consider the challenge well met.

I leaned back in my seat, watching him carefully. The bar had a few patrons, most of whom were seated on the patio. Only a handful of us occupied the beach-themed interior. "Have you decided to accept my offer?"

"I've considered it." He crossed his legs and angled so that he could lay his arm along his seat back. Overconfident and not smart enough to exercise caution. "But hey, considering what you're valued at, I'm surprised Eva's privacy isn't worth more than a million dollars to you."

I smiled inwardly. "Eva's peace of mind is priceless to me. But if you think I'll up my offer, you aren't thinking clearly. The injunction against you *will* go through. And then there's the pesky little detail regarding the legality of filming Eva without her consent, a very different scenario from a mutually agreed-upon private sex tape gone public."

His jaw tightened. "I thought you wanted to keep this quiet, not make it part of public record. Eva would be on her own with any lawsuit, you know. I've already talked to Brett and we've worked things out."

Tension tightened my shoulders. "He's seen the footage?"

"He has it." Sam reached into his pocket and pulled out a flash drive. "Here's a copy for Eva. I figured you should see what you're paying for."

The thought of Kline viewing sexual images of Eva sent rage surging through me. His memories were bad enough. A recording was unacceptable.

My hand fisted around the flash drive. "It's going to come out that the footage exists; I can't stop it. You contacted too many reporters with your offer to sell it. What I can do is destroy you. Personally, that would be my preference. I want to watch you burn, you piece of shit."

Sam shifted in his seat.

I leaned forward. "You got more than Eva and Kline with your cameras. There are dozens of other victims who didn't sign releases. I own this bar. Hell, I own the band. It didn't take much effort to find the regulars and Six-Ninths followers who were here when you were illegally filming in the bathrooms."

The last bit of avarice in his gaze dimmed, then blinked out completely.

"If you were smarter," I went on, "you would've leveraged for long-term gain instead of an immediate payout. Instead, you're going to sign the contract I'm about to put in front of you and walk away with a check for a quarter million."

He straightened. "Fuck that! You said one million. That was the deal."

"Which you didn't accept." I stood. "It's no longer on the table. And if you take any longer to decide, the new offer won't be, either. I'll just run you into the ground and straight into a jail cell. It's enough that I can tell Eva I tried."

As I walked away, I shoved the flash drive into my pocket, where it promptly burned a hole I couldn't ignore. My gaze met Arash's as I passed where he sat at the bar waiting for his cue to step in.

He hopped off his bar stool. "Always a pleasure watching you scare the hell out of someone," he said, before heading toward the seat I'd just vacated, the necessary contract and check in hand.

I stepped outside the dim bar into the

bright San Diego sunshine. Eva didn't want me to view the footage; she'd made me promise I wouldn't.

But she was feeling something for Kline. He remained a very real threat. Seeing them together, intimately, might give me the information I needed to fight him off.

Had she been as sexually raw with him as she was with me? Had she been as desperate and greedy for him? Could he make her come like I could?

I squeezed my eyes shut against the images in my head, but they wouldn't go away.

Remembering my promise, I crossed the parking lot to my rental car.

Is it silly that I'm nearly as excited to be your "friend" as I am to be your wife?

I laughed inwardly as I read Eva's text and replied. I'm as excited to be your lover as I am to be your husband.

OMG . . . fiend.

That had me laughing aloud.

"What was that sound?" Arash looked at me over the edge of his tablet, having made himself at home on the couch in my hotel suite. "Was that a laugh, Cross? Were you seriously just laughing? Or were you having a stroke?"

I flipped him off.

"Seriously?" he shot back. "The finger?"

"Eva says it's a classic."

"Eva's hot enough to get away with it. You're not."

I opened a new window on my laptop and logged into my social media profile, linking it to Eva's with the *Engaged to* designation now that we were "friends." As I waited for her to accept the relationship link, I clicked on her profile and smiled again at the cover image she'd selected. She was exposing herself to the world for the first time, and she was doing so as the woman who was mine.

I texted her back when she approved our joined status. Now you're both.

☺ I'm keeping my half of our deal.

My gaze moved from the message window to the photo of us on her profile. I brushed over her face with my fingertips, resisting the urge to go to her. It was too soon. She needed what space I could bear to give her.

So am I, angel mine.

The theater in the casino wasn't a huge venue, but it wasn't small, either, and it was easier to fill. It was better for Six-Ninths to boast sold-out concerts than to risk embarrassingly empty seats, even in their hometown. Christopher would've thought of that.

My brother was good at what he did. I'd learned not to tell him so, though. It only made him more of an asshole.

As the rows of seats slowly emptied, I made my way toward backstage. Not my turf, despite the all-access pass I carried as primary shareholder of Vidal Records. Kline definitely had the advantage.

But I hadn't been able to stay away until morning, even though I knew it was the wiser move. Then, he'd be exhausted. Possibly hungover. *I* would have the upper hand then.

I couldn't wait that long. He had the footage. He would've watched it at least once. Maybe more than that. I couldn't stomach the thought of him watching it again. Getting it away from him was the most important thing on my agenda.

And I wanted him to know I was close by before he met with Eva. I was marking my territory, so to speak, and I chose to do so in the jeans and T-shirt I'd worn when I met Yimara. Anything to do with Eva was a personal matter, not business, and I wanted that to be clear the moment Kline saw me.

I entered stage left and walked straight into chaos. Scantily clad women fucked up on their drug or booze of choice lined the scuffed, narrow corridor. Dozens of tattooed and pierced men broke down and packed up equipment with efficient, practiced skill and speed. Hard-grinding music piped out of hidden speakers, clashing with the tunes spilling out of individual rooms. I weaved through the pandemonium, searching for a distinctive head of frosted spikes.

An achingly familiar blonde stumbled out of an open doorway several feet away, her hair falling around her shoulders and drawing attention to the lush curves of a great ass.

My footsteps slowed. My heartbeat quickened. Kline followed her out, a beer in one hand and the other reaching for her. She caught it and pulled him out into the wing.

I knew how that delicate hand felt, how smooth the skin was. How firm the grip. I knew how those nails felt digging into my back. How those fingers tugged at my hair as she came against my mouth. The electric sizzle of her touch. The primal awareness.

I stood frozen, my gut knotting. She stood close, too close, to Kline. Her shoulder leaned against the wall. Her hip was cocked provocatively, her fingertips brushing suggestively over Kline's stomach. He gave her a cocky, flirtatious smile, his hand rubbing her upper arm in a far too intimate way.

No one who saw them together could

mistake that they were lovers.

Rage fired my blood. A sick darkness radiated through me.

Pain. Searing and soul deep. It took my breath and every ounce of control.

A woman's arm draped over my shoulder. Her hand slid beneath the neck of my T-shirt to touch my chest, while her other wrapped around my hip to stroke my dick. Cloying perfume assaulted my nose, spurring me to shrug her off violently even as a model-thin brunette with heavily made-up blue eyes tried to sandwich me from the front.

"Back off!" I growled, glaring at both in a way that had them stumbling back and calling me an asshole.

In another time, I would've fucked them both, turning the feel of being hunted into one of complete control.

I'd learned how to handle sexual predators after Hugh. How to put them in their place.

I surged forward, pushing through the crowd, remembering the feel of Kline's jaw against my fist. The unforgiving hardness of his torso. The grunt of air leaving his body when I hit him with everything I had.

I wanted him laid out and battered. Bloody. Broken.

Kline bent over her, speaking close to her ear. My hands clenched. She threw her head back and laughed, and I stumbled to a halt. Startled and confused. Despite the volume of noise, the sound struck me as wrong.

It wasn't Eva's laugh.

It was too high. My wife's laugh was low and throaty. Sexy. As unique as the woman it belonged to.

The blonde turned her head and I saw her in profile. She wasn't Eva. The body and hair were similar. Not the face.

What the fuck?

My mind caught up with reality. The girl was the one from the "Golden" music video. The Eva stand-in.

Roadies and groupies filtered around me, but I remained fixed in place as Kline caressed and seduced a pale imitation of my incomparable wife.

My phone vibrated in my pocket, startling me. I cursed and pulled it out, reading the text from Raúl: She just arrived at the casino.

So, she'd changed her mind about seeing Kline. Working the situation to my benefit, I typed back: Get her to the left wing now.

Got it.

I backed up against the wall, sidestepping into an alcove half hidden by steel equipment cases stacked on hand trucks. The minutes ticked by slowly.

I sensed her before I saw her, felt the frisson of recognition. Turning my head, I found her easily. Unlike her imitator, who wore a small tight dress, Eva was dressed in jeans that hugged every curve and a simple gray tank top. She wore heeled sandals and hoop earrings, casual and relaxed.

Hunger hit me with brutal force. She was the most beautiful woman I'd ever seen and easily the sexiest woman alive. Other women turned their heads to follow her when she walked by, envying her effortless beauty and sexuality. Men eyed her with heated interest, but she didn't seem to notice, her attention on Kline.

Her gaze narrowed as she took in the same scene I had moments earlier. I watched her assess the situation and knew when she reached the same conclusion I had. A myriad of emotions crossed her face. It had to be odd for her, seeing a former lover so desperate to recapture what he'd once had with her.

It was inconceivable to me. If I couldn't have Eva, I would have no one.

Her shoulders went back. Her chin lifted. Then a smile curved her mouth. I could see the acceptance settle over her, a new kind of peace. Whatever she'd needed, she had found it.

Eva passed by without spotting me, but Raúl joined me.

"Awkward," he said, his attention on Kline as the singer looked up and spotted my wife, his body visibly stiffening.

"Perfect," I replied, as my wife greeted Kline by extending her left hand to him. My ring on her finger sparkled brilliantly, impossible to miss. "Keep me posted."

I left.

As my muscles burned through my eightieth push-up, my gaze was on the flash drive lying on the carpet in front of me. The way I'd dealt with Yimara and Kline had been effective but unsatisfying. I was still tense and aggravated, spoiling for a fight.

My eyes stung as rivulets of sweat ran down my forehead. My chest heaved with exertion. Knowing Eva was out clubbing with Cary and some of their SoCal friends only sharpened the edge I hovered on. I knew how primed she got when out drinking and dancing. I loved nailing her when her body was damp and steamy with perspiration, her cunt slick and greedy.

Jesus. My dick throbbed and hardened further. My arms trembled as I neared the point of muscle fatigue. Veins stood out in harsh relief along my forearms and hands. I needed a cold shower, but I wouldn't get myself off. I always saved it for Eva. Every thick, creamy drop.

The message app on my laptop pinged and I slowed the vicious pace, hitting one hundred before I pushed to my feet. I grabbed the flash drive and dropped it on the desk, then retrieved the towel I'd hung over the back of the chair. Wiping my face before opening the window on my laptop, I expected to read the latest update on Eva's evening. What I saw was a text from her.

What room are you in?

I stared at the screen for a moment, processing the question. Another ping announced a text from Raúl: She's heading toward your hotel.

Anticipation shifted my focus from working out to my delectable, clever wife. I typed a reply to her: 4269.

I reached for the phone on the desk and called room service. "A bottle of Cristal," I ordered. "Two flutes, strawberries, and whipped cream. Have it here in ten. Thanks."

Returning the receiver to its base, I slung the towel around the back of my neck. A quick glance at the clock told me it was half past two in the morning.

By the time the doorbell chimed, I'd turned on all the lights in both the living room and bedroom and opened the curtains that had been blocking the view of the moonlit ocean.

I went to the door and opened it, finding both Eva and room service waiting. Dressed as I'd seen her earlier, Eva looked like a bad girl, renewing my hard-on in an instant. Her hair was limp and her face shiny, her mascara running slightly. She smelled like clean sweat and alcohol.

If the server hadn't been standing behind her, I would've had her on her back on the foyer tile before she knew what hit her.

"Holy fuck," she breathed, eyeing me from head to toe.

I glanced down. I was still overheated, my skin shiny with sweat. The waistband of my sweats was wet with it, drawing attention to the erection I didn't even try to will away. "Sorry, you caught me mid-workout."

"What are you doing in San Diego?" she demanded from the hallway.

Stepping back, I gestured for her to come in.

She didn't move. "I'm not getting sucked into your sex-god vortex until you answer me."

"I'm here on business."

"Bullshit." Her arms crossed.

Reaching out, I caught her by the elbow and tugged her in. "I can prove it."

Room service rolled the cart in after her.

"You're way too optimistic," she muttered, looking at the order as I signed the receipt.

I handed the bill and stylus back, waited for the server to leave, then walked over to the phone by the sofa. I dialed Arash's room.

"Are you serious?" he answered, sounding groggy. "Some of us sleep, Cross."

"My wife wants to talk to you."

"What?" Sheets rustled. "Where are you?"

"In my room." I held the receiver out to Eva. "My attorney."

"Are you nuts?" she asked. "It's five in the morning in New York! On a Sunday!"

"He's in the room next door. Take it. Ask him if I've been working today."

She marched over and snatched the phone out of my hand. "You should get a new job," she told him. "Your boss is insane."

He replied and she sighed. "Before." She glanced at me. "Thank God he's hot. Still, I might get my head checked. Sorry he woke you up. Go back to sleep."

Eva held the phone out to me.

I took it and put it to my ear. "As she said, go back to sleep."

"I like her. She gives you shit."

My gaze slid over her. "I like her, too. Good night."

I hung up and reached for her.

She backed up, avoiding my grasp. "Why didn't you tell me you were here?"

"Didn't want to cramp your style."

"Don't you trust me?"

My brows rose. "Asks the wife who tracked my phone to my hotel."

"I was just curious if you were staying in the penthouse or not!"

She pouted when I only continued to eye her. "And . . . I missed you."

"I'm right here, angel." I opened my arms to her. "Come and get me."

Her nose wrinkled. "I have to shower. I stink."

"We're both sweaty." I went to her. This time, she didn't pull away. "And I love the way you smell. You know that."

I put my hands on her waist, sliding them up until I hugged her delicate rib cage just beneath the full swell of her tits. I cupped them through her top, gently hefting their weight, squeezing softly.

I'd never had a fetish for particular parts of the female body, until Eva. I worshipped every inch of her, cherished all of her generous curves.

The pads of my thumbs circled her nipples, feeling them harden. "I love the way you feel."

Lowering my head, I found the crook of her neck and nuzzled her, rubbing my damp hair against her.

She moaned. "No fair. You're all ripped and shiny and mostly naked, and I have no willpower."

"You don't need any." I pushed my hands beneath her tank and freed the clasp of her bra. "Let me have you, Eva."

I sucked in a slow, deep breath as she reached under the elastic of my waistband and gripped my cock.

"Yum," she whispered. "Look what I found."

"Angel." I cupped her ass. "Tell me you want it exactly the way I want to give it to you."

She looked up at me with heavy-lidded eyes. "And how would that be?"

"Here. On the floor. Your jeans caught around one ankle, your shirt pushed up, your underwear shoved to the side. I want my cock inside you, my cum filling you." I slid my tongue along the racing pulse in her neck. "I'll take care of you once I get you to bed, but right now . . . I just want to use you."

She trembled. "Gideon."

Banding one arm behind her thighs, I pulled her feet out from under her and lowered her carefully to the carpet. My mouth found hers soft and hot and wet, her tongue licking mine. Her arms wrapped around my neck, trying to hold me. I let her, my knees straddling her hips, my fingers opening her jeans.

Her belly was flat and silky smooth, concaving with a giggle when my knuckles brushed her sides. Her ticklishness made me smile into our kiss, joy filling my chest until it felt too small to contain it.

"You'll stay with me," I told her. "Wake up with me."

"Yes." Her hips lifted to help me yank her pants down.

I freed one leg and left the other trapped, my hands pushing her thighs open so I could see her. Her panties were skewed from pulling off her jeans, giving her just the look I wanted.

She was my wife. My most valuable possession; I treasured her. But I loved her slutty and dirty, too. A sexual object for my pleasure. The one woman who could silence the memories in my head and set me free.

"Angel." I slid down, lying prone, my mouth watering for the taste of her.

"No," she protested, her hands covering herself.

I pinned her wrists at her sides and glared. "I want you like this."

"Gideon —"

I licked her through the silk and she arched with a whimper, her heels digging into the carpet and lifting her cunt to my mouth. I pulled her panties aside with my teeth and uncovered the impossibly soft skin. A rough sound left me, my dick hardening to the point of pain.

Wrapping my lips around her clit, I sucked her, licked her. Felt her tense up. I released her hands, knowing she was mine now, helpless to fight me.

"Oh God," she breathed, writhing. "Your mouth . . ."

Spreading her wide with my shoulders, I tongued her, driving her to come. Her fingers pulled at my hair, tugging painfully at the roots, spurring me on until she climaxed with a startled cry. I licked inside her, fucking her, feeling her quiver around my tongue. She grew slicker, hotter.

I rubbed against her clit and slid two fingers inside her, grinding my hips into the floor at the feel of her tight plushness. My cock ached to sink into that snug heat, knowing how amazing it felt, craving the constriction.

"Please," Eva begged, grinding into the thrust of my fingers, needing the slide of my dick to fill her.

I wanted to fuck. To come. Not because I needed sex, but because I needed *her.*

Her body twisted and tensed with another orgasm, her neck arching as she cried out.

Wiping my wet mouth on her inner thigh, I rose to my knees and shoved my sweats down. I placed one hand on the floor and used the other to aim my cock, levering over her and notching the throbbing head against her. I thrust hard, putting the weight of my body behind it, surging through the tight clasp with a groan.

"Gideon."

"Christ." I rubbed my sweat-slick forehead against her cheek, wanting her to smell like me. Her nails were in my back, digging in. I wanted them to mark me, scar me.

Cupping her ass, I lifted her, angled her, digging my feet into the carpet for the leverage I needed to push all the way in. Eva gasped and churned her hips, working to fit me.

"Take me," I hissed through clenched teeth, fighting the need to come before she took all of my cock. "Let me in."

Her cunt rippled, sucking at me. I pinned

her shoulder to hold her still and thrust harder. She gave, letting me have her.

The feel of her clutching the entire length of my dick was all I needed. Wrapping myself around her, I held her against me, kissing her roughly, coming with a violence that left me trembling in her arms.

Steam curled around us as I cradled Eva in the suite's massive sunken tub. Her wet hair clung to my chest, her arms draped over mine where they hugged her waist.

"Ace."

"Hmm?" I pressed my lips to her temple.

"If we couldn't be together — not that it would ever happen, just hypothetically — would you sleep with someone who looked like me? I mean, I know I'm not your usual type, but would you want to pretend with someone who reminded you of me?"

"I'm not going to speculate on situations that will never occur."

"Gideon." She leaned to the side, tilting her head back to look at me. "I get it. I tried to think if I would find any comfort in being with someone similar to you. Like maybe if it was dark and his hair was your length —"

My hold tightened. "Eva. Don't tell me about fantasies of other men."

"God. As usual, you're not listening."

"What the fuck is this about?" I knew, of course. But there were no avenues in the topic I wanted to explore.

"Brett's sleeping with that girl from the 'Golden' video. The one who looks like me."

"No one looks like you."

She rolled her eyes.

"She may have your curves," I conceded, "but she doesn't sound like you. She doesn't have your sense of humor, your wit. She doesn't have your heart."

"Oh, Gideon."

I brushed wet fingertips over her brow. "Turning off the lights wouldn't help me at all. A random, stacked blonde wouldn't smell like you. She wouldn't move the way you do. She wouldn't touch me the same way, need me the same way."

Her face softened and she pressed her cheek against my shoulder. "That's what I thought, too. I couldn't do it. And the moment I saw Brett with that girl, I knew that you wouldn't do it, either."

"Not with anyone. Ever." I kissed the tip of her nose. "You've changed what sex means to me, Eva. I couldn't go back. I wouldn't even try."

She shifted around to straddle me, sending water sloshing up and over the rim of the tub. I looked at her, taking in the slicked-back hair the color of wheat, the smudges left by her makeup, the sheen of water on her golden skin.

Her fingers massaged the nape of my neck. "My dad wants to pay for the wedding."

"Does he now?"

She nodded. "I need you to be okay with that."

I was okay with anything when I had my naked, wet, and frisky wife wrapped around me. "I've had the wedding I wanted. You can do whatever you like this time around."

Her brilliant smile and enthusiastic kiss were all the reward I needed. "I love you."

I pulled her closer.

She bit her lower lip, then said, "My mom is going to have a fit. She can blow through fifty thousand dollars in just flowers and invitations."

"So tell your parents your dad is paying for the wedding and your mom can pitch in for the reception. Problem solved."

"Ooh. I like that. You're handy to have around, Mr. Cross."

I lifted her and licked across her nipple. "Let me prove it."

The bedroom was lightening with the coming dawn when Eva's breathing settled into the deep, even rhythm of sleep. I extricated myself from both her arms and the sheets as carefully as possible, standing beside the bed to watch her. Her hair was tumbled around her shoulders, her lips and cheeks flushed from sex. I rubbed my chest, pained by how tight it had become.

Leaving her like this was always hard and became more difficult by the day. My skin hurt from being parted from hers.

I closed the curtains in the bedroom, then moved into the living room and did the same there, plunging the room into darkness.

Then I settled on the sofa and fell asleep.

A sudden flash of light woke me. Blinking, I scrubbed at my gritty eyes and saw that the curtains had been parted to send sunlight shafting across my face. Eva walked toward me, the light haloing around her naked body.

"Hey," she whispered, sinking to her knees beside me. "You said I'd wake up with you."

"What time is it?" I looked at my watch, saw I'd only been asleep an hour and a half. "You were supposed to sleep longer."

She pressed her lips to my abs. "I don't sleep well without you."

Regret pierced me. My wife needed things I couldn't give her. She woke me with light instead of a touch because she feared my reaction. She was right to be cautious. In the grip of a nightmare, the stroke of a hand might have me waking up with fists flying.

I brushed her hair back from her face. "I'm sorry." *For everything. For all you're giving up to be with me.*

"Shh." She lifted the elastic waistband of my sweats and pushed it down past my cock. I was hard for her. How could I help it when she came to me naked and sleepy-eyed?

Her mouth wrapped around the head of my dick.

I squeezed my eyes shut and groaned, surrendering.

Knocking at the door woke me the next time. Eva stirred in my arms, cuddled against me on the narrow stretch of the sofa.

"Goddamn it," I muttered, pulling her tighter against me.

"Ignore it."

The knocking continued.

I leaned my head back and yelled, "Go away."

"I come bearing coffee and croissants," Arash shouted back. "Open up, Cross, it's

137

after noon and I want to meet your lady."

"Christ."

Eva blinked up at me. "Your lawyer?"

"He was." I sat up and shoved my hands through my hair. "We're going away, you and me. Soon. Far away."

She kissed the small of my back. "Sounds good."

I shoved my feet into the legs of my sweats, then stood to pull them up. Eva took the opportunity to smack me on the bare ass.

"I heard that!" Arash yelled. "Cut it out and open up."

"You're fired," I told him, striding toward the door. I glanced back to tell Eva to cover herself, but she was already running into the bedroom.

I found Arash waiting outside my suite with a room service cart. "What the fuck is the matter with you?"

I had to back out of the way before he rolled right through me.

"Quit your bitching." He grinned, pushing the cart off to the side and raking me with a glance. "Save the marathon sex for your honeymoon."

"Don't listen to him!" Eva shouted through the bedroom door.

"I won't." I turned away from him. "He

138

doesn't work for me anymore."

"You can't hold it against me," Arash said, following me into the living room. "Wow. Your back looks like you got into a brawl with a mountain lion. No wonder you're tired."

"Shut up." I snatched my shirt off the floor.

"You didn't tell me Eva was in San Diego, too."

"It was none of your business."

He held up both hands in surrender. "Truce."

"Don't say a word about Yimara," I told him quietly. "I won't have her worrying about that."

Arash sobered. "It's done. I won't mention it again."

"Good." I went to the cart and poured two cups of coffee, preparing Eva's the way she liked it.

"I'll take a cup," he said.

"Serve yourself."

His lips curved wryly as he joined me. "Is she coming out?"

I shrugged.

"She's not mad, is she?"

"I doubt it." I took both mugs to the coffee table, then went to the wall where the controls for the drapes were. "It takes some

139

work to piss her off."

"You're good at it." He smiled and settled into one of the armchairs. "I recall that viral video of you two scrapping in Bryant Park."

I shot him a look as sunlight began pouring into the room. "You must really hate your job."

"Tell me you wouldn't be curious if I eloped with a chick I knew only a couple of months."

"I'd send her my condolences."

He laughed.

The bedroom door opened and Eva stepped out dressed in her clothes from the night before. Her face was freshly washed, but the dark circles under her eyes and her swollen mouth made her look both well fucked and extremely fuckable. With her bare feet and barely tamed hair, she was stunning.

Pride swelled my chest. Uncovered by the lack of makeup, the dusting of freckles on her nose made her adorable. Her body told you she was a dream to fuck, the confidence in her posture told you she'd take no shit from anyone, and the mischievous amusement in her eyes told you there would never be a dull moment.

She was every promise, every hope, every

fantasy a man could have. And she was mine.

I stared. Arash stared, too.

Eva shifted her stance and smiled shyly. "Hi."

The sound of her voice snapped him out of it. He pushed to his feet so quickly he spilled his coffee. "Shit. Sorry. Hi."

He set his mug down and brushed the stray droplets off his pants. He went to her and held out his hand. "I'm Arash."

She shook it. "Nice to meet you, Arash. I'm Eva."

I joined them, pushing Arash back with my forearm. "Stop drooling."

He glanced at me. "Funny, Cross, you ass."

Eva laughed and leaned into me when I slid my arm around her shoulders.

"It's good to see he works with people who aren't afraid of him," she said.

Arash winked, blatantly flirting. "I know how he operates."

"Really? I'd love to hear all about it."

"I think not," I drawled.

"Don't be a spoilsport, ace."

"Yeah, ace," Arash taunted. "What have you got to hide?"

I smiled. "Your corpse."

He looked at my wife and sighed. "See what I have to deal with?"

6

A late-afternoon outdoor lunch, in beautiful San Diego, with the three most important men in my life definitely ranked at the top of my best-moments-ever list. I sat between Gideon and my dad, while Cary lounged in the seat directly across the table from me.

If you had asked me a few months ago, I would have said I was apathetic about palm trees. I had a new appreciation for them now that I hadn't seen one in a while. I watched them sway gently in the warm ocean breeze and felt the kind of peace I chased but rarely caught. Seagulls competed with pigeons for the scraps under tables, while the not-too-distant crash of waves against the beach underpinned the bustle of the packed restaurant.

My best friend's mirrored shades hid his eyes, but his smile came often and easy. My dad wore shorts and a T-shirt and had started out the meal unusually quiet. He'd loosened up after a beer and now looked as comfortable as Cary. My husband wore tan cargo pants and a white T-shirt, the first time I'd ever seen him in light-colored clothing. He looked cool and relaxed in aviators, his fingers linked with mine on the arm of my chair.

"An early-evening wedding," I thought aloud. "Around sunset. Just family and close friends." I looked at Cary. "You'll be the man of honor, of course."

His mouth curled up on one side in a lazy smile. "I better be."

I glanced at Gideon. "Do you know who you'll ask to stand with you?"

The tightening of his lips was nearly imperceptible, but I caught it. "I haven't decided yet."

My happy mood dimmed a little. Was he debating whether Arnoldo would be suitable, considering the chef's feelings toward me? It made me sad to think I might strain that relationship.

Gideon was such a private person. Although I didn't know for sure, I suspected he was tight with his friends but that there weren't many of them.

I squeezed his hand. "I'm going to ask Ireland to be a bridesmaid."

"She'll like that."

"What do we do about Christopher?"

"Nothing. With luck, he won't come."

My dad frowned. "Who are we talking about?"

"Gideon's brother and sister," I answered.

"You don't get along with your brother, Gideon?"

I explained, not wanting my dad to hold anything against my husband. "Christopher's not a nice guy."

Gideon's head turned toward me. He didn't say it aloud, but I got the message: He didn't want me speaking for him.

"He's a total douche, you mean," Cary interjected. "No offense, Gideon."

"None taken." He shrugged and then elaborated for my father. "Christopher views me as a competitor. I'd have it differently, but it's not my choice."

My dad nodded slowly. "That's too bad."

"While we're discussing the wedding," Gideon segued smoothly, "it would be my pleasure to provide transportation. It would give me a chance to contribute, which I'd appreciate."

I took a deep breath, understanding — as I knew my father would — that my husband's directness and tact made him hard to refuse.

"That's very generous of you, Gideon."

"It's a standing offer. With an hour's notice, we can have you in the air and on your way. It'll make it easier for you and Eva to work around your schedules and maximize your time together."

My dad didn't answer right away. "Thank you. It might take me a while to get used to the idea. It's a bit extravagant, and I don't want to be a burden."

Gideon pulled his shades off, baring his eyes. "That's what money's for. All I want is to make your daughter happy. Make that easy on me, Mr. Reyes. We all want to see Eva smiling as much as possible."

It sank in then why my dad was so opposed to Stanton paying for anything. My stepdad didn't do it for me; he did it for my mom. Gideon would only ever consider *me* when making decisions. I knew my dad could live with that.

I caught Gideon's gaze and mouthed, *I love you.*

His grip on my hand tightened until it hurt. I didn't mind.

My dad smiled. "Making Eva happy. How can I argue with that?"

The smell of freshly brewed coffee brought my well-trained senses to life the following morning. I blinked up at the bedroom ceiling of my Upper West Side apartment and gave a sleepy smile when I discovered Gideon standing beside my bed, stripping out of his shirt. The sight of his leanly muscular torso and washboard abs almost made up for the fact that I'd obviously spent the night alone after falling asleep in his arms.

"Good morning," I murmured, rolling onto my side as he pushed his pajama bottoms down and kicked them off.

Whoever said Mondays sucked had obviously never woken up to a naked Gideon Cross.

"It will be," he said, lifting the covers and sliding between the sheets with me.

I shivered as his cool skin touched mine. "Yikes!"

His arms slipped around me, and his lips touched my neck. "Warm me up, angel."

By the time I was done with him he was sweating and the coffee he'd brought me was cold.

I didn't mind in the least.

I was in an excellent mood when I got to work. Morning sex contributed to that, of course. Also the sight of Gideon getting dressed for the day, watching him transform from the private man I knew and loved into the dark and dangerous global magnate. The day only got better when I exited on the twentieth floor and saw Megumi sitting at her desk.

I waved at her through the glass security doors, but my smile faded the moment I got a good look at her. She was pale and had dark circles under her eyes. Her usually sassy asymmetrical haircut looked limp and overlong, and she was wearing a long-sleeved blouse and dark slacks that were out of place with the August mugginess.

"Hey," I greeted her when she buzzed me through. "How are you? I've been worried about you."

She gave me a weak smile. "I'm sorry I didn't call you back."

"Don't worry about it. I'm totally antisocial when I get sick. I just want to curl up in bed and be left alone."

Her lower lip quivered and her eyes grew shiny with tears.

"Are you okay?" I glanced around, worried about her privacy as other employees passed through the reception area. "Did you see a doctor?"

She started crying.

Horrified, I stood frozen for a minute. "Megumi. What's *wrong*?"

She pulled off her headset and stood, tears spilling down her face. She shook her head violently. "I can't talk about it now."

"When is your break?"

But she was already hurrying to the bathroom, leaving me staring after her.

I headed to my cubicle and dropped off my bag, then went down the hall to Will Granger's desk. He wasn't there, but I found him in the break room when I stopped to grab some coffee.

"Hey, you." His eyes behind his square-framed glasses looked as worried as I felt. "Did you see Megumi?"

"Yeah. She looks wiped out. And she started crying when I asked how she's doing."

He slid the carton of half-and-half over to me. "Not good, whatever it is."

"I'm bad with not knowing. My imagination runs wild. I'm bouncing between cancer, pregnancy, and everything in between."

Will shrugged helplessly. With his neatly trimmed sideburns and subtly quirky-patterned shirts, he was the sort of affable and easy-natured guy who was hard to dislike.

"Eva." Mark stuck his head in the door. "I've got news."

My boss's bright eyes told me he was

excited about something. "I'm all ears. Coffee?"

"Sure. Thanks. See you in my office." He ducked back out again.

Will grabbed his mug off the counter. "Have a good one."

He left. I hurried to get the coffee ready, then went to Mark's office. He'd taken his jacket off and was studying something on his monitor. He looked up, smiling when he saw me.

"We've got a new RFP request." His smile widened. "And they asked for me specifically."

I tensed. Setting his coffee down, I asked warily, "Is it another Cross Industries product?"

As much as I loved Gideon and admired all that he'd accomplished, I didn't want to be totally overshadowed by his world. Part of who we were as a couple was two people who had separate working lives. I enjoyed riding to work with my husband, but I needed to say good-bye to him, too. I needed those few hours when he didn't consume me.

"No, it's bigger."

My brows rose. I couldn't think of anything or anyone bigger than Cross Industries.

Mark slid a picture of a silver-and-red box across the desk to me. "It's the new PhazeOne gaming system from LanCorp."

I settled into the seat in front of his desk with an inner sigh of relief. "Sweet. Sounds fun."

It was a little after eleven when Megumi called to see if I was free for lunch.

"Of course," I told her.

"Someplace quiet."

I considered our options. "I've got an idea. Leave it to me."

"Great. Thanks."

I sat at my desk. "How's your morning been?"

"Busy. I have to get caught up."

"Let me know if I can help with anything."

"Thank you, Eva." She took a deep, shaky breath, her composure slipping. "I appreciate you."

We hung up. I called Gideon's office, and his secretary answered.

"Hey, Scott. It's Eva. How are you?"

"I'm good." I could hear the smile in his voice. "What can I do for you?"

My feet tapped restlessly. I couldn't help but be worried about my friend. "Could you ask Gideon to give me a call when he has a free minute?"

"I'll put you through now."

"Oh. Okay, great. Thanks."

"Hang on."

A moment later I heard the voice I loved. "What do you need, Eva?"

I was startled for a minute by his brusqueness. "Are you busy?"

"I'm in a meeting."

Fuck. "My bad. Bye."

"Eva —"

I hung up, and then called Scott again to discuss how we should handle calls in the future so I didn't come out looking like an ass. Before he answered, the secondary line flashed with an incoming call. I switched over. "Mark Garrity's office —"

"Don't ever hang up on me," Gideon snapped.

I bristled at his tone. "Are you in a meeting or not?"

"I was. Now I'm dealing with you."

Hell if anyone was going to "deal" with me. I could be as pissy as him any day of the week. "You know, I asked Scott to give you a message when you had time for it and he patched me through. He shouldn't have done that, if you were busy with —"

"He has standing orders to always connect your calls. If you want to leave me a message, send a text or an e-mail."

"Well, excuse me for not knowing the etiquette for getting in touch with you!"

"Never mind that now. Say what you need."

"Nothing. Forget it."

He exhaled roughly. "Don't play games with me, angel."

I was reminded of the last time I'd called him at work and how off he'd sounded then, too. If something was bugging him, he sure wasn't sharing it.

I hunched over my desk and lowered my voice. "Gideon, your attitude pisses me off. I don't want to *deal with you* when you're aggravated. If you're too busy to talk to me, you shouldn't have standing orders that interrupt you."

"I'm never going to be unreachable."

"Really? 'Cause you seem that way right now."

"For fuck's sake."

Hearing his exasperation gave me a surge of satisfaction. "I didn't text you because I didn't want to bother you in a meeting. I didn't send an e-mail, because it's a time-sensitive favor and I don't know how often you get to your inbox. I figured a message with Scott would get the job done best."

"And now you have my complete attention. Tell me what you want."

"I want to get off the phone, and I want you to get back to your meeting."

"What you're going to get," he said, with dangerous evenness, "is me at your desk if you don't cut the shit and explain why you called."

I glared at his photo. "You make me want to find a job in New Jersey."

"You make me crazy." He growled softly. "I can't function when we're fighting, you know that. Just say what you need, Eva, and forgive me for now. We can argue and have makeup sex later."

The tension left me. How could I stay mad at him after he admitted how vulnerable I could make him?

"Damn you," I muttered. "I hate when you get reasonable after irritating me."

He made a low sound of reluctant amusement. I instantly felt better.

"Angel mine." His voice took on the sexy, raspy warmth I needed to hear. "Definitely not a quiet, comfortable ornament."

"What are you talking about?"

"Don't worry about it. You're perfect. Tell me why you called."

I knew that tone. I'd turned him on somehow. "You're a maniac. Seriously."

Lucky me.

"Anyway, ace, I wanted to see if I could

154

borrow one of your conference rooms for lunch with Megumi. She's back, but she's a mess and I think she wants to talk about it but there's really not a good place to go nearby that's private and quiet."

"Use my office. I'll have something ordered in and you'll have the space to yourself while I'm out."

"For real?"

"Of course. However, I have to remind you that when you work for Cross Industries you'll have your own office to lunch in."

My head fell back. "Shut up."

The research involved in prepping for the PhazeOne RFP kept me hopping, but I was antsy for information from Megumi, so the hour seemed to drag anyway.

I met up with her at the reception desk at noon. "If it's not too weird," I said, as she pulled her purse out of a drawer, "we're going to use Gideon's office for lunch. He's out and it's private."

"Oh man." She shot me an apologetic look. "I'm sorry, Eva. I should've congratulated you. Will told me about your engagement, but I spaced."

"It's totally okay. Don't worry about it."

She reached out and squeezed my hand. "I'm really happy for you."

"Thank you."

My concern deepened. Megumi always followed the latest gossip. The friend I knew would've heard about the engagement almost before I did.

We took an elevator to the top floor. The Cross Industries vestibule was as striking as Gideon himself. It was much bigger than others in the building and decorated with lilies and ferns in hanging baskets. CROSS INDUSTRIES was etched into the smoked-glass security doors in a masculine but elegant font.

"Impressive," Megumi murmured, as we waited for the receptionist to buzz us through.

The redhead I was used to seeing at the reception desk must have been out to lunch, because a guy with dark hair let us in.

He stood when we approached. "Good afternoon, Miss Tramell. Scott said you should just go right in."

"Has Mr. Cross left?"

"I'm not sure. I just took over here."

"All right. Thank you." I led Megumi back. We rounded the corner to reach Gideon's office just in time to see him stepping out.

Fierce pride and possession moved me. Pleasure, too, when his stride faltered just a bit when he saw me. We met each other halfway.

"Hi," I greeted him.

He gave me a nod in return and held his hand out to Megumi. "I don't think we've been officially introduced. Gideon Cross."

"Megumi Kaba." She gave him a firm shake. "Congratulations to you and Eva."

A ghost of a smile touched his sexy mouth. "I'm a lucky man. Make yourselves comfortable. If you need anything, just call up to reception and Ron will see to it."

"We'll be fine," I told him. "You won't even know we had a raging party in there while you're gone."

He smiled outright. "Good. I have a meeting later. Shot glasses and streamers would be interesting to explain."

I expected him to head out. Instead, he cupped my face, tilted my head to the angle he wanted, and pressed his lips to mine in an unhurried, chaste kiss that left me with little stars in my eyes.

Then he whispered in my ear, "Looking forward to making up later."

My toes curled.

Pulling back, he slid easily into the reserved persona he showed the rest of the world. "Enjoy your lunch, ladies."

He walked away with the confident, innately sexual stride that turned heads.

"And you're still standing upright," Megumi murmured, shaking her head. "Kills me."

I couldn't explain how weak Gideon made me. How shaken and needy I could so easily become. "Come on," I said breathlessly. "Let's eat."

She followed me into Gideon's office. "I don't think I can."

While she took in the sprawling space with its panoramic views and monochromatic color scheme, I went to the bar, where lunch awaited us. I remembered how I'd felt the first time I walked into the room. Despite the multiple seating areas that might have invited guests to sit and stay awhile, the progressively contemporary, cutting-edge design kept visitors from getting too comfortable.

There were so many sides to the man I'd married. His office reflected only one. The classically European style of his penthouse reflected another.

"Have you ever experimented with BDSM?" Megumi asked, seizing my attention.

Surprise made me drop the napkin-rolled utensils I'd been holding. I spun to face her and found her staring out the window at the city. "That acronym covers a lot of ground."

She rubbed her wrist. "Being tied up and gagged. Helpless."

"I've been helpless, yes."

Her head turned. Her eyes were twin shadows in her pale face. "Did you like it? Did it turn you on?"

"No." I walked over to the nearest couch and sat. "But I wasn't with the right person."

"Were you scared?"

"Terrified."

"Did he know that?"

The formerly appetizing smell of lunch started to turn my stomach. "Why are you asking me these questions, Megumi?"

She answered by rolling up her sleeve, exposing a wrist so bruised it was nearly black.

7

It was after eight when I let myself into Eva's apartment and found her sitting with Cary on the living room's white sectional sofa, holding a glass of red wine in both hands.

My wife gravitated toward modern traditional furnishings, but I could see touches of her mother and roommate in the décor. I didn't resent those pieces of Monica and Cary, but I looked forward to the day when I shared a home with Eva that reflected *us,* undiluted.

Still, the apartment would always be a special place to me. I would never forget the way Eva had looked the first time I'd come over. Naked beneath a thigh-length silk robe, her face made up for the night ahead, a diamond anklet winking at me. Teasing me.

I had lost all rational thought. I'd put my mouth on her, my hands all over her, and my fingers and tongue inside her. I hadn't even thought about getting her to the "fuck pad." I wouldn't have been able to wait, even if I had. She wasn't like any woman who'd come before her. Not just because of who she was, but also because of who *I* was when I was with her.

It was unlikely I would ever allow the property management to lease the space out again. It held too many memories, both good and bad.

I tipped my chin at Cary in greeting and sat beside Eva. My wife's best friend was dressed to go out, while Eva wore a Cross Industries T-shirt and had her hair twisted up in a clip. They both glanced at me, and I knew something was wrong.

There were things to discuss, but whatever was troubling Eva was the pressing priority.

Cary stood. "I'm heading out. Call me if you need me."

She nodded. "Have fun."

"My middle name, baby girl."

The front door shut behind him as Eva's head fell gently against my shoulder. Sliding my arm around her, I settled deeper into the sofa and tucked her closer. "Talk to me, angel."

"It's Megumi." She sighed. "There's this guy she was into and things weren't work-

161

ing out — he was hot-and-cold and couldn't commit — so she broke it off. But afterward, he stepped it up and she let him come over. They started messing around with a little bondage, but things got out of hand in a bad way."

The mention of bondage put me on alert. I ran my hand down her back and tucked her tighter against me. I was nothing if not patient in aligning my desires with her fears. Setbacks were expected and accommodated, but I didn't want someone else's misadventures to create new hurdles for Eva and me to face.

"Sounds like bad judgment all around," I said. "One of them should've known what they were doing."

"That's the thing." She pulled away and faced me. "I went over it with Megumi. She said no — *a lot* — until he gagged her. He got off on her pain, Gideon. And now he's terrorizing her with texts and photos he took of her that night. She's asked him to stop, but he won't. He's sick. Something's wrong with him."

I weighed how best to respond. I went with blunt. "Eva. She broke it off, and then took him back. He might not realize she's serious this time."

She recoiled, then slid off the couch in a

rush of curvy, golden legs. "Don't make excuses for him! She's bruised everywhere. It's been a week and the bruises are still dark. She couldn't sit down for days!"

"I'm not excusing him." I stood with her. "I would never justify an abuser — you know that. I don't have the whole story, but I know *your* story. Her situation isn't like yours. Nathan was an aberration."

"I'm not projecting here, Gideon. I saw the pictures. I saw her wrists, her neck. I saw his texts. He's crossed a line. He's dangerous."

"Even more reason for you to stay out of it."

Her hands went to her hips. "Oh my God. You did not just say that! She's my friend."

"And you're my wife. I know that look on your face. There are some battles that aren't yours to fight. You will not confront this man the way you did my mother and Corinne. You will not put yourself in the middle of this."

"Did I say I was going to do that? No, I didn't. I'm not an idiot. I asked Clancy to find him and talk to him."

I went still inside. Benjamin Clancy was her stepfather's man, not mine. Totally outside my control. "You shouldn't have done that."

"What was I supposed to do instead? Nothing?"

"Preferably. At most, you should've asked Raúl."

She threw up her hands. "Why would I do that? I don't know Raúl enough to ask him for a personal favor."

I checked my exasperation. "We discussed this. He works for you. You don't have to ask him for favors, you just need to tell him what you need done."

"Raúl works for *you.* Besides, I'm not some godfather sending out hired thugs to teach people lessons. I asked someone I trust, as a friend, to help another friend of mine."

"However you rationalize it, the result is the same. You forget, Ben Clancy is employed to protect your stepfather's interests. He looks after you only because it gives him more control in securing Stanton's safety and reputation."

She bristled. "How would you know what his motives are?"

"Angel, let's simplify. Focus on the fact that your mother and Stanton have been invading your privacy for some time. You're keeping that door open by using their resources."

"Oh." Eva caught her lower lip in her

teeth. "I hadn't thought of it that way."

"You sent a trained professional to 'talk' to this guy. But you didn't fully assess the possibility of blowback. If you'd tapped Raúl to help you, he would've known to be extra vigilant." My jaw clenched. "Damn it, Eva. Don't make it hard for me to keep you safe!"

"Hey." She reached for me. "Don't worry, okay? I told you what was happening as soon as you walked in the door. And Clancy was with me until an hour ago, when he dropped me off after my Krav Maga class. Nothing's happened yet that would put me in danger."

I pulled her into me and held on, wishing I could be certain she was right. "I want Raúl to escort you wherever you go," I said gruffly. "To your classes, the gym, shopping . . . whatever. You need to let me look after you."

"You do, baby," she said soothingly, her temper cooled. "But you can be obsessive about it."

I would always be obsessive when it came to her. I'd come to accept that. Eventually, she would, too. "There are things I can't give you. Don't fight me on the things I can."

"Gideon." Her face softened. "You give

165

me everything I need."

I brushed my fingers across her jaw. She was so soft. Delicate. I had never anticipated my sanity hinging on something so fragile. "You come home to another guy. You make your living by working for someone else. I'm not as necessary to you as I'd like to be."

Her eyes brightened with humor. "While I'm about as dependent on you as I can stand to be."

"It's mutual." Running my hands down her arms, I caught her by the wrists and squeezed with just enough pressure to capture her focus. I watched her pupils dilate and her lips part, her body instinctively responding to the restraint. "Promise you'll come to me first from now on."

"Okay," she breathed.

The undercurrents of arousal and surrender in her voice sent my blood humming. She swayed into me, her body softening. "I'd like to come now, actually."

"I am, as always, at your service."

Gideon.
The shock of hearing panic in Eva's voice reverberated through me. My body jolted, jerking me out of the deepest sleep. Rolling to my side with a low moan, I struggled

awake, shoving my hair out of my face to find her kneeling on the edge of the bed.

A heavy, inescapable sense of dread had my heart racing and cold sweat coating my skin.

I pushed up onto one elbow. "What's wrong?"

Moonlight slanted through the room and haloed her. She'd come to me in our bedroom in the apartment next door to hers. Something had woken her, and I was afraid. Fear chilled me to the bone.

"Gideon." She slid into me in a rush of silken skin and shining hair. Curled against me, she reached up and touched my face. "What were you dreaming about?"

The stroke of her fingertips left a trail of wet across my skin. Startled, horrified, I scrubbed at my eyes and smeared more tears across my cheek. In a corner of my mind, I sensed the lingering shadow of a dream.

The brush of memory had me shivering, spiraling further downward.

I rolled into her and pulled her tight against me, hearing her gasp as I squeezed too hard. Her skin was cool to the touch, but her flesh was warm beneath and I absorbed her heat, breathed in her scent, felt the terrible lingering grief inside me ease with her nearness.

I couldn't grasp the dream I'd had, but it refused to let go of me.

"Shh," she crooned, her fingers pushing through the sweat-damp roots of my hair, her hand stroking up and down my back. "It's okay. I'm here."

I couldn't breathe. I fought for air and a horrible sound ripped from my burning lungs.

A sob. Christ. Then another. I couldn't stop the violent contractions.

"Baby." She hugged me harder, her legs tangling with mine. She rocked us gently, whispering words I couldn't hear over the pounding of my heartbeat and the outcry of my phantom pain.

I wrapped myself around her, holding on to the love that could save me.

"Gideon!"

Eva's back arched as I thrust hard, my knees spreading her thighs wide, my cock tunneling deep. Her wrists were pinned by my hands, her head thrashing as I fucked her hard.

Some days I woke her with tenderness. Today wasn't one of those mornings.

I'd woken to a throbbing erection, the head of my dick wet with pre-cum against the curve of Eva's ass. I aroused her hungrily, impatiently, sucking her nipples to hard points, slickening her cunt with the demanding drive of my fingers. She'd ignited to my touch, gave herself over to me, gave herself *to* me.

God. I loved her so much.

The need to come was like a vise around my balls, the pressure exquisite. She was tight, so amazingly snug, and so wet. I couldn't get enough. Couldn't get deep enough, even when I felt the end of her clasping at the head of my cock.

She thrashed beneath my pounding drives, her heels sliding across the sheets, her tits rocking with the force of my thrusts. She was so small, so soft, and I was fucking her lush body with everything I had in me.

Take me. Take all of me. The good and the bad. Everything. Take it all.

The headboard banged into the shared wall between our two apartments in a hard-driving rhythm that screamed *crazed sex* to anyone listening. As did the growls spilling from my throat, the animalistic sounds of my pleasure I didn't try to hold back. I loved fucking my wife. Craved it. Needed it. And I didn't care who knew what she did to me.

Eva arched up, sinking her teeth into my

biceps, her bite sliding over my sweat-slick skin. The mark of possession drove me wild, had me thrusting so hard I shoved her up the bed.

She cried out. I hissed as she tightened around me like a greedy fist.

"Come," I bit out, my jaw clenched against the urge to do the same, to let go and pump every drop I had into her.

Rolling my hips, I ground against her clit, pleasure sizzling up my spine when she moaned my name and climaxed around me in pulsing ripples.

I kissed her roughly, drinking in her taste, spilling into her with a shuddering groan.

Eva stumbled a little as I helped her out of the back of the Bentley in front of the Crossfire.

A hot flush spread across her face and she shot me a look. "You suck."

My brows rose questioningly.

"I'm shaky and you're not, sex machine."

I smiled innocently. "I'm sorry."

"No, you're not." Her wry smile faded as she glanced down the street. "Paparazzi," she said grimly.

I followed her gaze and spotted the photographer aiming a camera out of the open passenger window of his car. Gripping her by the elbow, I led her into the building.

"If I have to start actually styling my hair every day," she muttered, "you're dealing with morning wood on your own."

"Angel," I tugged her into my side and whispered, "I'd hire a fulltime hairdresser for you before I gave up your cunt every morning."

She elbowed me in the ribs. "God, you're crude, you know that? Some women take offense to that word."

She went ahead of me through the security turnstiles and joined the mass of bodies waiting for the next elevator car.

I stood close behind her. "You're not one of them. However, I might be willing to revise. I recall *orifice* being a favorite of yours."

"Oh God. Shut up," she said, laughing.

We separated when she exited on the twentieth floor and I went up to Cross Industries without her. I wouldn't be doing so for long. Someday, Eva would be working with me, helping to build our future as a team.

I was debating the myriad avenues to achieving that goal when I rounded the corner on approach to my office. My stride slowed when I saw the willowy brunette waiting by Scott's desk.

171

I steeled myself to deal with my mother again.

Then her head turned and I saw it was Corinne.

"Gideon." She rose gracefully to her feet, her eyes brightening with a look I'd come to recognize, having seen it on Eva's face.

It gave me no pleasure to see that warmth in Corinne's eyes. Unease slid down my spine, stiffening my back. The last time I had seen her had been shortly after she'd tried to kill herself.

"Good morning, Corinne. How are you feeling?"

"Better." She came toward me and I took a step back, causing her to slow and her smile to waver. "Do you have a moment?"

I gestured to my office.

With a deep breath, she turned and preceded me. I glanced at Scott. "Give us ten."

He nodded, his gaze sympathetic.

Corinne walked to my desk and I joined her, hitting the button that closed the door behind us. I kept the glass clear and didn't remove my jacket, sending her every signal that she shouldn't settle in for long.

"I'm sorry for your loss, Corinne." Saying the words wasn't enough, but they were all I could give her. The memories of that night in the hospital would be with me for a while.

172

Her lips whitened. "I still can't believe it. All these years of trying . . . I thought I couldn't get pregnant." She picked up the photo of Eva on my desk. "Jean-François told me you called a couple times asking about me. I wish you'd called me. Or returned my calls."

"I don't think that's appropriate, under the circumstances."

She looked at me. Her eyes weren't the same shade of blue as my mother's, but they were close, and their sense of style was similar. Corinne's elegant blouse and trousers were notably like something I'd once seen my mother wear.

"You're getting married," Corinne said.

It wasn't a question, but I answered anyway. "Yes."

Her eyes closed. "I'd hoped Eva was lying."

"I'm very protective when it comes to her. Tread lightly."

Opening her eyes, she set the picture down hard. "Do you love her?"

"That's none of your business."

"That's not an answer."

"I don't owe you one, but if you need to hear it, she's everything to me."

The tightness of her mouth softened with a quiver. "Would it make a difference if I told you I'm getting divorced?"

"No." I exhaled roughly. "You and I will never be together again, Corinne. I don't know how many times or in how many ways I can say it. I could never be what you want me to be. You dodged a bullet when you broke our engagement."

She flinched, her hair sliding over her shoulder to flow down to her waist. "Is that what's keeping us apart? You can't forgive me for that?"

"Forgive you? I'm thankful." My voice softened when tears filled her eyes. "I don't mean to be cruel. I can guess how painful this might be. But I didn't want you to have hope when there isn't any."

"What would you do if Eva said these things to you?" she challenged. "Would you just give up and walk away?"

"It's not the same." I raked a hand through my hair, struggling to find the words. "You don't understand what I have with Eva. She needs me as much as I need her. For both our sakes, I wouldn't ever give up trying."

"*I* need you, Gideon."

Frustration made me curt. "You don't know me. I played a role for you. I let you see only what I wanted you to see, what I thought you could accept." And in return, I saw only what I wanted to see in her, the girl she'd once been. I had stopped paying real attention long ago, and so I'd failed to see how she had changed. She'd been a blind spot for me, but no longer.

She stared at me in shocked silence for a moment. "Elizabeth warned me that Eva was rewriting your past. I didn't believe her. I've never known you to be swayed by anyone, but I guess there's a first time for everything."

"My mother believes what she wants and you're welcome to join her." They were similar in that way, too. Good at believing what they wanted and ignoring any proof to the contrary.

It was a revelation to realize I had been comfortable with Corinne because I'd known she wouldn't pry. I'd been able to fake normalcy with her and she never dug deeper. Eva had changed that for me. I wasn't normal and I didn't need to be. Eva accepted me the way I was.

I wasn't going to reveal my past to everyone, but my days of playing along with the lies were over.

Corinne reached a hand out to me. "I love you, Gideon. You used to love me, too."

"I was grateful to you," I corrected. "And I will always be. I was attracted to you, had fun with you, for a time I even needed you, but it would never have worked out between us."

She dropped her hand back to her side.

"I would have found Eva eventually. And I would've wanted her, given up everything to have her. I would have left you to be with her. The end was inevitable."

Corinne turned away. "Well . . . at least we'll always be friends."

It was an effort to strip any apology out of my tone. I wouldn't encourage her. "That won't be possible. This is the last time you and I will speak to each other."

Her shoulders shook with a ragged indrawn breath, and I turned my head, fighting with discomfort and regret. She'd been important to me once. I would miss her, but not in the way she wanted me to.

"What do I have to live for if I don't have you?"

I turned at her question and barely caught her when she ran into me, holding her at bay with a grip on her upper arms.

The devastation on her beautiful face got to me before I could process what she'd said. Then it registered. Horrified, I shoved her away. She stumbled back as her heels caught in the carpet.

"Don't put that on me," I warned, my voice low and hard. "I'm not responsible for your happiness. I'm not responsible for you at all."

"What's *wrong* with you?" she cried. "This isn't you."

"You wouldn't know." I went to the door and yanked it open. "Go home to your husband, Corinne. Take care of yourself."

"Fuck you," she hissed. "You're going to regret this, and I might be too hurt to forgive you."

"Good-bye, Corinne."

She stared at me for a long minute and then stormed out of my office.

"Damn it." I pivoted, not knowing where to go or what to do, but I had to do *something.* Anything. I paced.

I'd pulled out my smartphone and called Eva before I consciously made the decision to do so.

"Mark Garrity's office," she began.

"Angel." The one word betrayed my relief at hearing her voice. She was what I needed. Something in me had known that.

"Gideon." She read me immediately, as she so often did. "Is everything all right?"

I glanced out at my staff in the distant cubicles getting into the groove of the day. I hit the controls to frost the glass, carving out a moment alone with my wife.

I lightened my tone, not wanting to cause

177

her stress. "I miss you already."

She waited a beat before replying, adjusting to my mood. "Liar," she shot back. "You're too busy."

"Never. Now, tell me how much you're missing me."

She laughed. "You're terrible. What am I going to do with you?"

"Everything."

"Damn straight. So what's up? It's going to be a busy day and I have to get going."

I went to my desk and studied her photo. My shoulders relaxed. "Just wanted you to know I'm thinking about you."

"Good. Don't stop. And FYI, it's nice to hear you not grumpy at work."

It was nice to hear her, period. I'd given up trying to figure out why she affected me the way she did. I just appreciated that she could reset my day. "Tell me you love me."

"Madly. You rock my world, Mr. Cross."

I stared into her laughing eyes, my fingertip brushing lightly over the glass. "You're the center of mine."

The rest of the morning passed swiftly and uneventfully. I was wrapping up a meeting regarding a possible investment in a proposed resort chain when yet another personal interruption showed up. So much for workflow.

"You've got to fuck up everything, don't you?" my brother accused, barging into my office with Scott on his heels.

With a look, I gave Scott the okay to back out. He shut the door behind him.

"Good afternoon to you, too, Christopher."

We shared blood but could not have been less alike. Like his father's, his hair was wavy and fell somewhere between brown and red. His eyes were a gray mixed with green, while I was most definitely our mother's son.

"Did you forget that Vidal Records is Ireland's legacy, too?" he snapped, his eyes hard.

"I never forget that."

"Then you just don't give a shit. Your vendetta against Brett Kline is costing us money, damn you. You're hurting all of us, not just him."

Moving to my desk, I leaned against it and crossed my arms. I should've seen it coming, considering how irate Christopher had become at the Times Square launch of the "Golden" video. He wanted Kline and Eva together. More than that, he wanted Eva and me apart.

It was the sad truth that I brought out the

worst in my brother. The only times he ever acted cruelly or rashly was when he was trying to hurt me. I'd seen him give brilliant speeches, charm people with his natural charisma, and impress board members with his industry savvy, but he never displayed those traits toward me.

Frustrated by his unprovoked animosity, I baited him. "I'm assuming you're going to get to the point soon."

"Don't play innocent, Gideon. You knew exactly what you were doing when you systematically destroyed every media opportunity Vidal secured for Six-Ninths."

"If those opportunities were centered on Eva, they had no business being pursued to begin with."

"That's not your decision to make." His mouth twisted in a scornful smile. "Do you even comprehend the damage you've done? *Behind the Music* has delayed their special because Sam Yimara no longer owns the rights to the footage he compiled of the band's early years. *Diners, Drive-Ins and Dives* can't include Pete's 69th Street Bar in their San Diego episode, because it's being demolished before they can film their segment. And *Rolling Stone* isn't interested in pursuing their proposed piece on 'Golden' since your engagement was announced. The song loses its interest without the happy ending."

"I can get you the footage VH1 wants. Put them in touch with Arash and he'll take care of it."

"After you remove all traces of Eva? What's the point?"

My brows lifted. "The point is supposed to be Six-Ninths, not my wife."

"She's not your wife yet," he shot back, "and that's your problem. You're afraid she's going to go back to Brett. You're not really her type and we all know it. You can eat her pussy at parties, but what she really likes is blowing rock stars in public —"

I was on him before he blinked. My fist hit his jaw; his head jerked back. I caught him with a follow-up left and he stumbled, crashing into the glass wall.

Through it, I glimpsed Scott shoving to his feet, and then I braced for the impact of Christopher's body hurtling into mine. We went down. I rolled, punching his ribs until he groaned. He slammed his head into my temple.

The room spun.

Dazed, I rolled away and clambered to my feet.

Christopher pulled himself up by the coffee table, blood running from the side of his

181

lips and onto the carpet. His jaw was swelling and he gasped for air, dragging in harsh breaths. My fists ached and I flexed my hands, tensing with the need to hit him again. If he'd been anyone else, I would have.

"Do it," he taunted, wiping his mouth on his sleeve. "You've wanted me dead since the day I was born. Why stop now?"

"You're insane."

Two security guards rounded the corner at a run, but I held up a hand to stop them.

"I'm fucking onto you, asshole," my brother growled, pushing heavily to his feet. "I've talked to members of the board. Explained what you're doing. You want to take me down, I'm fighting you all the way."

"You've lost it, you fucking idiot. Take your crazy somewhere else. And leave Eva alone. You want to make an enemy out of me, screwing around with her is the way to do it."

He stared at me for a long minute, then laughed harshly. "Does she know what you're doing to Brett?"

I winced through a deep breath, a dull ache in my side from a forming bruise. "I'm not doing anything to Kline. I'm protecting Eva."

"And the band is just collateral damage?"

"Better him than her."

"Fuck that," he snarled.

"Fuck you."

Christopher stalked toward the door.

I should've let him go but found myself speaking instead. "For Christ's sake, Christopher, they're talented. They don't need a gimmick to be successful. If you weren't so damned eager to make me pay for something you've imagined I've done, you'd be concentrating on better angles than making them into a one-hit wonder."

He rounded on me with clenched fists. "Don't tell me how to do my job. And don't get in my way or I'll shove you out."

I watched him leave, escorted by security. Then I went to my desk and checked my message log. Scott had noted that two of Vidal Records' board members had called over the course of the day.

I opened the line between Scott and me. "Get me Arash Madani."

If Christopher wanted a war, I'd give him one.

I arrived at Dr. Lyle Petersen's office on time at six o'clock. The psychologist greeted me with a welcoming smile, his dark blue eyes warm and friendly.

After the day I'd had, spending an hour

183

with a shrink was the last thing I wanted to do. Spending an hour alone with Eva was what I needed more.

Our session began as they always did, with Dr. Petersen asking how my week had been and me answering as succinctly as possible. Then he said, "Let's talk about the night-mares."

I leaned back, laying my arm on the sofa's armrest. I'd been up front about my sleep problems from the beginning in order to get the prescription medication that made me marginally safer for Eva to be near at night, but dissecting the dreams had never been one of the topics on discussion.

That meant someone else had brought them up. "You talked to Eva."

It wasn't a question, since the answer was evident.

"She sent me an e-mail earlier," he confirmed, folding his hands atop his tablet screen.

My fingers drummed silently.

His gaze followed the movement. "Does it bother you that she contacted me?"

I weighed my response before giving it. "She worries. If talking to you alleviates that, I won't complain. You're also *her* therapist, so she has a right to discuss it with you."

"But you don't like it. You'd prefer to choose which issues you share with me."

"I'd prefer Eva to feel safe."

Dr. Petersen nodded. "That's why you're here. For her."

"Of course."

"What does she hope the outcome of our sessions will be?"

"Don't you know?"

He smiled. "I'd like to hear your answer to that question."

After a moment, I gave it to him. "Eva previously made bad decisions. She learned to rely on the advice of therapists. It worked well for her and it's what she knows."

"How do you feel about that?"

"Do I have to feel anything?" I countered. "She asked me to try it out and I agreed. Relationships are about compromise, aren't they?"

"Yes." Picking up his stylus, he tapped at the screen of his tablet. "Tell me about your previous experience with therapy."

I took a breath. Let it out. "I was a child. I don't remember."

He glanced at me over the rim of his glasses. "How did you feel about seeing someone? Angry, frightened, sad?"

Glancing down at my wedding ring, I replied, "A little of all that."

"I imagine you felt similarly about your father's suicide."

I stilled. Studying him, my gaze narrowed. "Your point?"

"We're just talking, Gideon." He leaned back. "I often feel like you're wondering what the angle is. I don't have an angle. I just want to help you."

I forced my posture to relax.

I wanted the nightmares to stop. I wanted to share the same bed as my wife. I needed Dr. Petersen to help me do that.

However, I didn't want to talk about things that couldn't be changed to get there.

186

8

"Hey, girl. What are your thoughts on karaoke?" Shawna Ellison asked the second I answered the phone.

I dropped my pencil onto the notepad I'd been scribbling in, then sat back on the couch and curled my legs onto the cushion. It was rolling past nine o'clock and I hadn't heard from Gideon yet. I didn't know if that was a good or bad sign, considering he'd had an appointment with Dr. Petersen earlier.

The sun had set nearly an hour before, and I'd been trying not to think of my husband every five seconds since. Chatting with Shawna was a welcome distraction.

"Well," I hedged, "since I'm tone deaf, my thoughts on singing in public are pretty much nonexistent. Why?"

In my head, I pictured the vibrant redhead who was quickly becoming a friend. In a lot of ways, she was like her brother Steven, who happened to be engaged to my boss. They were both fun and easygoing, quick to tease and yet rock solid, too. I liked the Ellison siblings a lot.

"Because I was thinking we could go to this new karaoke bar I heard about today at work," she explained. "Instead of those cheesy background tracks, this place has a live band. You don't have to sing if you don't want to. A lot people go just to watch."

I reached for the tablet lying on the coffee table. "What's the name of this place?"

"The Starlight Lounge. I thought it might be fun for Friday."

My brows went up. Friday was our bringing-the-crew-together night. I tried to imagine Arnoldo or Arash singing karaoke and just the thought made me smile. Why the hell not? At the very least, it'd break the ice.

"I'll mention it to Gideon." I ran a search for the bar and pulled up its website. "Looks nice."

The name had conjured thoughts of old-school crooner hangouts, but the images on the site were of a contemporary club decorated in shades of blue with chrome accents. It looked upscale and swank.

"Right? I thought so, too. And it'll be entertaining."

188

"Yeah. Wait 'til you see Cary with a mic. He's shameless."

She laughed and I grinned at the sound, which was as bubbly as champagne. "So is Steven. Let me know what you decide. Can't wait to see you."

We hung up, and I tossed my phone onto the cushion beside me. I was leaning forward to get back to my project when I heard the ping of a text message.

It was from Brett. We need to talk. Call me.

I stared at his picture on the screen for a long minute. He'd been calling all day but hanging up when he got my voice mail. I would be lying if I said I wasn't conflicted about him still reaching out, but it was a dead end. Maybe we'd be friends someday, but not now. I wasn't up for it or the stress it caused Gideon.

I used to think facing issues that made me uncomfortable showed strength and responsibility. Now, I realized that sometimes resolution wasn't the purpose. Sometimes, you just had to take the opportunity to examine yourself better.

I'll give you a ring when I can, I typed back. Then I set the phone aside again. I'd call him when Gideon was with me. No secrets and nothing to hide.

"Hey." Cary strolled into the living room from the hallway dressed in pajama bottoms and a threadbare T-shirt. His dark brown hair was still damp from the shower he must have taken after Tatiana left an hour earlier.

I was glad she hadn't spent the night. I wanted to like the woman who said she was carrying my best friend's baby, but the leggy model didn't make it easy for me. I felt like she deliberately baited me whenever she could. I got the strong impression that she would like nothing more than to keep Cary all to herself and I was viewed as a big roadblock to that end.

My best friend sprawled facedown on the other section of the sofa, his head near my thigh and his long legs stretched out. "Whatcha working on?"

"Making lists. I want to get started on something for abuse survivors."

"Yeah? What are you thinking?"

One of my shoulders lifted in a helpless shrug. "I don't really know. I keep thinking about Megumi and how she didn't tell anyone. I didn't tell anyone, either. Neither did you, until way later."

"Because who's going to give a shit?" he said gruffly, propping his chin on his hands.

"And it's scary to talk about it. There are a lot of hotlines and shelters for victims. I want to find something else that makes a difference, but I don't have any ground-breaking ideas."

"So talk to idea people."

My mouth curved. "You make it sound so easy."

"Hell, why reinvent the wheel? Find someone who's doing it right and help 'em out." He rolled onto his back and scrubbed at his face with both hands.

I knew that gesture and what it signified. Something was eating at him.

"Tell me about your day," I said. I'd ended up spending more one-on-one time with Gideon in San Diego than I had with Cary, and I felt bad about that. Cary said he'd had a good time hanging with his old crowd, but that hadn't been the purpose of our trip. I felt like I'd let him down, even though he didn't accuse me of doing so.

He dropped his hands to his sides. "I had a shoot this morning, and then I saw Trey for a late lunch."

"Did you say anything to him about the baby?"

He shook his head. "I thought about it, but I couldn't do it. I'm such a dick."

"Don't be hard on yourself. It's a rough spot you're in."

Cary's eyes closed, shuttering the vivid

green of his irises. "I was thinking the other day how much easier it'd be if Trey swung both ways. Then we could both be banging Tat and each other, and I could have it all. Then I realized I didn't want to share Trey with Tat. Don't mind sharing her. But not him. Tell me that doesn't make me a total douche."

Reaching out, I ruffled my fingers through his dark hair. "It makes you human."

I'd been in a similar situation with Gideon, thinking I could work out a way to be friends with Brett, even while I was aggravated that Gideon was friends with Corinne. "In a perfect world, none of us would be selfish, but that's not the way it goes. We just do our best."

"You're always making excuses for me," he muttered.

I thought about that for a second. "No," I corrected gently, bending over to press a kiss to his forehead. "I just forgive you. Someone has to, since you won't forgive yourself."

Wednesday morning came and went in a flurry. Lunch was on me before I knew it.

"We were celebrating our engagement two weeks ago," Steven Ellison said, as I settled into the chair he held out for me. "Now we get to celebrate yours."

I smiled; I couldn't help it. There was something infectiously joyful about my boss's fiancé, which you couldn't help but pick up on. "Must be something in the water."

"Must be." He glanced at his partner, then back at me. "Mark's not losing you, is he?"

"Steven," Mark admonished, shaking his head. "Don't."

"I'm not going anywhere," I answered, which earned me a surprised and pleased grin from my boss. His goatee-framed smile was as contagious as Steven's gregariousness. Really, our scheduled lunches were worth the price of admission.

"Well, I'm happy to hear that," Mark said.

"Me, too." Steven opened his menu with a decisive snap, as if something important had been decided. "We want you to stick around, kid."

"I'm sticking," I assured them.

The server set a basket of olive oil–drizzled garlic bread on the table between us, then rattled off the day's specials. The restaurant the guys had selected had two menus: Italian and Greek.

Like most Manhattan eateries, the location was small and the tables packed tightly together, close enough that one party flowed into the next and you had to watch your elbows. The scents flowing out of the kitchen and wafting from the trays of passing servers had my stomach growling audibly. Thankfully the noise from the lunch crowd frenzy was loud enough to cover me.

Steven ran a hand through the bright red hair many women would kill for. "I'm having the moussaka."

"Me, too." I closed my menu.

"Pepperoni pizza for me," Mark said.

Steven and I teased him about being adventurous.

"Hell," he shot back, "marrying Steven is adventure enough."

Grinning, Steven set his elbow on the table and his chin on his fist. "So, Eva . . . how'd Cross propose? I'm guessing he didn't blurt it out in the middle of the street."

Mark, who was sitting on the bench seat next to his partner, gave him an exasperated look.

"No," I agreed. "He broke the news to me on a private beach. I can't say he asked, because he pretty much just told me that we're getting married."

Mark's mouth twisted in thought, but Steven was blunt as always. "Romance, Gideon Cross style."

I laughed. "Absolutely. He'll be the first to tell you he's not romantic, but he's wrong about that."

"Let me see the ring."

I held my hand out to Steven and the Asscher cut diamond shot sparks of multihued fire. It was a beautiful ring, which held beautiful memories for Gideon. Elizabeth Vidal's thoughts on the subject couldn't touch that.

"Whoa. Mark, darlin', you have got to get me one of those."

The picture in my head of the flame-haired, burly contractor wearing a ring like mine was comical.

Mark shot him a look. "So you can shatter it on a job site? Let me get right on that."

"Diamonds are tough little beauties, but I'll take good care of it."

"You'll have to wait until I run an agency of my own," my boss retorted with a snort.

"I can do that." Steven winked at me. "You register anywhere yet?"

I shook my head. "You?"

"Hell, yeah." He twisted to open the messenger bag next to him and pulled out his wedding binder. "Tell me what you think about these patterns."

Mark raised his gaze heavenward with a long-suffering sigh. I grabbed a piece of garlic bread and leaned forward with a happy hum.

I worked on the LanCorp RFP the remainder of the afternoon.

When my day ended, I headed to my Krav Maga class with Raúl. On the way, I reread Clancy's reply to my text saying I wouldn't need a ride from him. He had typed back that it was no problem, but I felt the need to explain further.

Gideon wants to have his ppl with me moving forward, so you're free from now on. ☺ TY for all your help.

It didn't take him long to answer. Anytime. Holler when you need me. BTW, your friend shouldn't have any more trouble.

The "thank you" I sent back didn't seem like enough. I made a note to send him something that would better express my gratitude.

Raúl parked outside the brick-faced converted warehouse that was Parker Smith's Krav Maga studio and then escorted me inside, taking a seat on the bleachers. His presence threw me off a little bit. Clancy had always waited outside. Having Raúl watching made me a little self-conscious.

The massive open space still managed to look crowded, thanks to all the clients on the mats and in one-on-ones with instructors. The noise was nearly deafening, a cacophony of bodies hitting padding, flesh colliding with flesh, and the various shouts as participants psyched themselves up while psyching each other out. Giant metal delivery-bay doors added to both the industrial feel of the studio and the heat, which even the air-conditioning and multiple standing fans couldn't quite alleviate.

I was stretching in preparation for the grueling drills ahead when a pair of lanky legs came into my line of sight. I straightened and faced NYPD detective Shelley Graves.

She wore her curly brown hair in a bun as severe as her face, and her blue eyes assessed me with sharp impassiveness. I was afraid of her and what she could do to Gideon, but I admired her a lot, too. She was fierce and confident in a way I could only aspire to.

"Eva," she greeted me.

"Detective Graves." She was dressed for work in dark slacks and a red jersey top. She wore a black blazer that didn't hide either her badge or her firearm. Her boots were scuffed and no-nonsense, much like her attitude.

"Spotted you on my way out. Heard about

your engagement. Congratulations."

My stomach flipped a little. Part of Gideon's alibi — if one could call it that — was that we'd been broken up when Nathan was killed. Why would a powerful, upstanding public figure kill a guy over an ex he'd left behind without looking back?

Getting engaged so quickly had to look suspicious. Graves had told me she and her partner had moved on to other cases, but I understood what kind of cop she was. Shelley Graves believed in justice. She believed Nathan had gotten his, but I knew something inside her questioned whether Gideon had something to pay for, too.

"Thank you," I replied, pulling my shoulders back. In this, Gideon and I were a team. "I'm a lucky girl."

She glanced at the bleachers. At Raúl. "Where's Ben Clancy?"

I frowned. "I don't know. Why?"

"Just curious. You know, one of the feds I talked to about Yedemsky also has the last name Clancy." Her gaze bored into me. "You think they're any relation?"

The blood drained out of my head at the mention of the Russian mobster whose corpse had been sporting Nathan's bracelet. I swayed a little with a sudden rush of dizziness. "What?"

She nodded, as if she'd expected as much. "Probably not. Anyway, I'll see you later."

I watched her walk away, her attention on Raúl. Then, she paused and faced me again. "You inviting me to the wedding?"

I fought through the buzzing in my head to say, "The reception. We're keeping the wedding small, just family."

"Really? Didn't expect that." Something like a smile transformed her thin face. "He's full of surprises, isn't he?"

I couldn't even begin to decipher what that meant. I was too busy trying to process everything else she'd said. I didn't even realize I'd chased after her until I had her elbow in my hand.

She stopped, her body taut in a way that told me to let go. Which I did. Immediately.

I stared at her for a beat, trying to pull my thoughts together. Clancy. Gideon. Nathan. What the hell did it mean? Where was she going with it?

Most of all, why did I feel as if she were helping me? Looking out for me. For Gideon.

What I ended up saying startled me. "I'm looking to support an organization that does good work for abuse survivors."

Her brows rose. "Why are you telling me?"

"I don't know where to start."

She shot me a look. "Try Crossroads," she said dryly. "I've heard good things about that one."

I was sitting cross-legged on the floor of my bedroom's sitting room when Gideon came home. He walked in wearing loose-legged jeans and a V-neck white T-shirt, the keys to my place spinning around his finger.

I stared. I couldn't help it. Would he always stop my heart? I hoped so.

The room was small and girly, decorated by my mother with antiques, such as the silly escritoire I was supposed to use as a desk. Gideon infused a drugging dose of testosterone into the space, making me feel soft and feminine and eager to be ravished.

"Hi, ace." The love and longing he inspired were exposed in those two words.

The keys were caught in his hand abruptly and he came to a stop, looking down at me much as he had that first day in the Crossfire lobby. His eyes took on the brooding fierceness I found wildly exciting.

For some reason I would probably never understand, he felt the same about me.

"Angel mine." He dropped gracefully into a crouch, his hair sliding briefly along his cheekbones in a loving caress. "What are you working on?"

His fingers rifled through the papers scattered on the floor around me. Before my research into his Crossroads Foundation distracted him, I caught his hand and squeezed it.

I blurted out what I knew, as abruptly as the info had been sprung on me. "It was Clancy, Gideon. Clancy and his brother in the FBI planted Nathan's bracelet on that mobster."

He nodded. "I figured."

"You did? How?" I smacked him on the shoulder. "Why didn't you say something? I've been worried sick."

Gideon settled on the floor in front of me, crossing his long legs in a pose mirroring mine. "I don't have all the answers yet. Angus and I have been narrowing it down. Whoever was responsible was either watching Nathan or me and following our movements, so we started there."

"Or watching both of you."

"Precisely. Who would do that? Who had a stake in it? In you?"

"Jesus." I searched his face. "Detective Graves knows. The FBI. Clancy —"

"Graves?"

"She brought it up at Parker's studio tonight. Tossed it at me in passing just to see how I'd take the news."

His gaze narrowed. "Either she's fucking with you or she wants you to stop worrying. My bet is on the latter."

I almost asked why, but then I realized I'd come to the same conclusion. The detective was tough as nails, but she had a heart. I had caught glimpses of it during the few times we'd interacted with one another. And she was good at her job, obviously.

"We have to trust her, then?" I asked, crawling over the brochures and paperwork to curl into his lap.

He pulled me into him, fitting me into the hard planes of his body as if I were meant to be there always. I felt that way when he held me. Safe. Treasured. Adored.

His lips touched my forehead. "I'm going to talk to Clancy just to be sure, but he's no fool. He wouldn't leave anything to chance."

My hand tightened around a fistful of his T-shirt, hanging on to him with everything I had. "Don't keep things like this from me, Gideon. Stop trying to protect me."

"I can't." His grip on me tightened, too. "Maybe I should have said something, but we have only a few hours alone every day and I want them to be perfect."

"Gideon. You've got to let me in."

His chest expanded beneath my cheek, his heart beating strong and sure. "I'm working on it, Eva."

That was all I could ask for.

The next morning I padded into the kitchen on bare feet to find Gideon pouring coffee. I could say the smell of java is what added a spring to my step, but it was the sight of my husband, freshly shaved and dressed with his vest hanging open, that did it. I loved seeing him a little undone.

He looked me over as I went to him, my heels rapping on the marble, his face impassive and his eyes warm. Did he get the same kick when he caught sight of me ready to tackle my day? I doubted it. I was convinced men just saw hot . . . or not.

Wrapping my fingers around his wrist, I led his hand around me and up the back of my skirt to cup the undercurve of my buttock.

A smile teased the corners of his lips. "Hello to you, too, Mrs. Cross."

He snapped the back of my garter against my thigh. I jumped at the sting and gasped as warmth spread outward from the spot.

"Hmm . . . you like that." He smirked.

My lower lip stuck out in a pout. "It hurt."

Gideon shifted to lean back against the counter and pulled me between his spread legs, both of his hands lightly gripping the back of my thighs. He nuzzled his nose against my temple and massaged the place that burned. "I'm sorry, angel."

Then he snapped my garter on the other side.

I arched in surprise, my body aligning with his. He was hard. Again. A low moan escaped me. "Stop it."

"It's turning you on," he murmured in my ear.

"It hurts!" I complained, even as I rubbed against him. He'd woken me with soft kisses and provocative hands. I had thanked him in the shower with my mouth. Still, he could go again. I could, too. We were addicted to each other.

"Want me to kiss it and make it better?" His fingers slid between my thighs and found me warm and ready. He groaned. "Christ. What you do to me, Eva. I've got so much to do . . ."

God, he felt good. Smelled even better. My arms wrapped around his neck. "We have to go to work."

He yanked me up to my toes, grinding me against his erection. "We're playing with these garters later."

I kissed him. I put my open mouth over his and devoured him, my tongue touching his. Stroking it greedily. Sucking.

Gideon's hand fisted in my ponytail, holding me in place as he took over the kiss, fucking my mouth, drinking me in. In an instant, I was hot, my skin humid with perspiration.

His lips were firm yet soft against my own, his grip angling me just the way he wanted, his teeth scraping gently across my lower lip. The taste of him, flavored delectably with a hint of rich black coffee, intoxicated me. Drunk on him, I clutched his hair in my hands, holding on, my toes flexing to push me closer. Always closer. But never close enough.

"Whoa." Cary's voice broke me out of the sensual spell Gideon had cast. "Don't forget we eat in here."

I started to pull away from my husband, but he held me tight, allowing me only to break the kiss. My gaze met his. His eyes were sharply alert beneath heavy lids, his lips softened and damp.

"Good morning, Cary," he said, his attention shifting to my best friend as Cary joined us by the coffeemaker.

"For you two, maybe." Cary opened the cupboard that held the mugs and pulled one out. "Sadly, I'm too tired to get turned on by the show. Not making me feel too optimistic about the rest of the day."

He was dressed in skinny jeans and a navy T-shirt, his hair skillfully arranged in a trendy pompadour. I pitied the single Manhattanites who'd see him out and about that day. He was such a striking man, both physically and in the false confidence he exuded.

"Do you have a shoot today?" I asked.

"No. Tat does, and she wants me there. She's got morning sickness and shit, so I'm going to be around to help her out if she's not feeling well."

I reached out and rubbed his biceps in sympathy. "That's awesome, Cary. You're the best."

His lips twisted wryly as he lifted his steaming cup to his mouth. "What else can I do? I can't get sick for her, and she's got to work as long as she can."

"You'll let me know if there's anything I can do?"

He shrugged. "Sure."

Gideon's hand stroked up and down my back, offering wordless support. "If you've got the time, Cary, I'd like you to be there for the appointment with the designer who's renovating our place on Fifth Avenue."

"Yeah, I've been thinking about that." Cary cocked his hip into the counter. "I haven't totally worked things out with Tat, but I figure we'll be shacking up together at some point. You guys aren't going to want a screaming baby next door. When you're ready for that, you'll have your own, not put up with mine."

"Cary . . ." My best friend rarely looked beyond the next fifteen minutes of his life. To hear him stepping up to the plate so solidly made me love him all the more.

"Both sections of the penthouse are fully soundproofed," Gideon said, his voice holding the firm note of command that reassured everyone who heard it. "We can make anything work, Cary. You just tell me what concerns you have and we'll address them."

Cary looked into his mug, his beautiful face suddenly looking worn and tired. "Thanks. I'll talk to Tat about it. It's hard, you know? She doesn't want to think about what's next and I can't stop thinking about it. There's going to be this person who's totally dependent on us, and we need to be prepared for that. Somehow."

I stepped back and Gideon let me go. It was hard to watch Cary struggling. It was scary, too. He didn't handle challenges well and I was so afraid he'd slip back into familiar, self-destructive coping mechanisms. It was a threat we both faced on a daily basis. I had a group of people who kept me anchored. Cary had only me.

"That's what families are for, Cary." I offered a smile. "To drive each other crazy and straight into therapy."

He snorted, then hid his face behind his mug. The lack of a glib reply made me even more anxious. A heavy silence descended.

Gideon and I both gave him a minute, taking the time to grab our own cups of java and caffeinate ourselves. We didn't speak or even look at each other, not wanting to create a unit that left Cary out, but I felt how in sync we were. It meant so much to me. I'd never had someone in my life who was a true partner, a lover who was there for more than just a good time.

Gideon was a miracle in so many ways.

It struck me then that I had to make some adjustments, compromise a little more on the issue of working with Gideon. I had to stop thinking of Team Cross as being his alone. I had to own it, too, so I could share in it with him.

"I've got time next week," Cary said finally, looking at me, then Gideon.

Gideon nodded. "Let's plan on Wednesday, then. Give us some room to recover from the weekend."

Cary's mouth twitched. "So it's that kind of party."

I smiled back. "Is there any other kind?"

"How are you?" I asked Megumi when we sat down for lunch on Thursday afternoon.

She looked better than she had on Monday, but she was still overdressed for the heat of the summer. Because of that, I'd ordered salads for delivery and we settled in the break room instead of braving the steamy day outside.

She managed a wan smile. "Better."

"Does Lacey know what happened?" I wasn't sure how close Megumi was to her roommate, but I hadn't forgotten that Lacey had dated Michael first.

"Not all of it." Megumi pushed at her salad with a plastic fork. "I feel so stupid."

"We're always quick to blame ourselves, but no means no. It's not your fault."

"I know that, but still . . ."

I knew just how she felt. "Have you thought about talking to someone?"

She glanced at me, tucking her hair behind her ear. "Like a counselor or something?"

"Yes."

"Not really. How do you even start looking for someone like that?"

"We've got mental health benefits. Call the number on the back of your insurance card. They'll give you a list of providers to choose from."

"And I just . . . pick one?"

"I'll help you." And if I got my act together, I'd find a way to help more women like her and me. Something good had to come of our experiences. I had the motivation and the means. I just had to find the way.

Her eyes glistened. "You're a good friend, Eva. Thanks for being here."

I leaned over and hugged her.

"He hasn't texted me lately," she said when I pulled back. "I keep dreading that he's going to, but every hour that goes by that he doesn't, I feel better."

Settling back in my seat, I sent a silent thank-you to Clancy. "Good."

At five o'clock, I left work and took the elevator up to Cross Industries, hoping to catch some time with Gideon before our appointment with Dr. Petersen.

I'd been thinking about him all day, about the future I wanted *us* to have together. I wanted him to respect my individuality and my personal boundaries, but I also wanted him to open up some of his own. I wanted more moments like this morning with Cary, when Gideon and I stood together, facing a situation as one. I couldn't really push for that if I wasn't willing to make the same effort.

The redheaded receptionist at Cross Industries buzzed me in. She greeted me with a hard smile that didn't reach her eyes. "Can I help you?"

"No, I'm good, thanks," I replied, breezing past her. It would be nice if all of Gideon's employees could be as easy-natured as Scott, but the receptionist had an issue with me and I'd just come to accept it.

I headed back to Gideon's office and found Scott's desk empty. Through the glass, I saw my husband at work, presiding over a meeting with casual authority. He stood in front of his desk, leaning back against it with one ankle crossed over the other. He wore his jacket and faced an audience composed of two suit-clad gentlemen and one woman wearing a great pair of Louboutins. Scott sat off to the side, taking notes on a tablet.

Settling into one of the chairs by Scott's desk, I watched Gideon as raptly as the others in the room with him. It never ceased to amaze me how self-assured he was for a man who was only twenty-eight. The men he was meeting with looked to be twice his age, and yet their body language and focused attention told me they respected my husband and what he was saying.

Yes, money talked — loudly — and Gideon had tons of it. But he conveyed command and control with subtle actions. I recognized that after living with Nathan's father, my mom's first husband, who'd wielded power like a blunt instrument.

Gideon knew how to own a room without thumping his chest. I doubted the setting made any difference; he would be a formidable presence in anyone's office.

His head turned and his gaze met mine. There was no surprise in those brilliantly blue eyes of his. He'd known I was there, had sensed me just as I often sensed his approach without looking. We were connected somehow, on a level I couldn't explain. There were times when he wasn't with me and I just wished he was, but I still felt him nearby.

I smiled, then dug in my bag for my phone. I didn't want Gideon to feel like I was just sitting around waiting, not that doing so would pressure him at all.

There were dozens of e-mail messages from my mother with photo attachments of dresses and flowers and wedding venues, reminding me that I needed to talk with her about Dad paying for the ceremony. I'd been putting off that conversation all week, trying to steel myself for her reaction. There was also another text from Brett, telling me that we needed to talk . . . urgently.

Standing, I looked around for a quiet corner where I could make that call. What I saw was Christopher Vidal Sr. rounding the corner.

Gideon's stepfather was dressed in the khakis and loafers I'd come to expect, with a pale blue dress shirt open at the collar and rolled up at the sleeves. The dark copper waves he'd passed on to Christopher Jr. were neatly cut around his neck and ears, and his slate green eyes were capped with a frown behind old-school brass-framed glasses.

"Eva." Chris slowed as he neared me. "How are you?"

"Good. You?"

He nodded, looking over my shoulder at Gideon's office. "Can't complain. Do you have a minute? I'd like to talk to you about something."

"Sure." The door opened behind me and I turned to see Scott stepping out.

"Mr. Vidal," he said, coming toward us. "Miss Tramell. Mr. Cross will be another fifteen minutes or so. Can I get either of you something to drink while you wait?"

Chris shook his head. "Nothing for me,

thank you. But if you have a private room we could use, that would be great."

"Of course." Scott looked at me.

"I'm good, thanks," I answered.

Leaving his tablet on his desk, Scott led us to a conference room with a sweeping view of the city. A long, polished wood table gleamed beneath the recessed lighting, with a matching cabinet covering one wall and a large monitor lining the other.

"If you need anything," he began, "just dial one and we'll take care of it. There's coffee in the cabinet there, and water."

Chris nodded. "Thank you, Scott. Appreciate it."

Scott left. Chris gestured for me to sit, then took the chair to the right of mine, spinning it to face me.

"First, let me congratulate you on your engagement." He smiled. "Ireland speaks very highly of you, and I know you've been instrumental in bringing her and Gideon closer together. I can't thank you enough for that."

"I didn't do much, but I appreciate the thought."

He reached for my left hand, which was resting on the table. His thumb rubbed gently over my engagement ring and his mouth curved ruefully.

Was he thinking about the fact that Geoffrey Cross had selected the ring for Elizabeth?

"It's a beautiful ring," he said finally. "I'm sure it meant a great deal to Gideon to give it to you."

I didn't know what to say to that. It meant a lot to my husband because it was a symbol of the love between his parents.

Chris released my hand. "Elizabeth is taking this very hard. I'm sure there are a lot of complicated emotions a mother must feel when her first child decides to get married, especially with a son. My mother used to say that a son is a son until he gets married — then he's a husband — but a daughter is a daughter for life."

The conciliatory explanation rubbed me the wrong way. He was trying to be kind, but I was tired of all the excuses, especially when it came to Elizabeth Vidal. The pretending had to end or Gideon would never stop hurting.

I needed the pain to stop. Every time he woke up crying, it shattered me a little more. I could only imagine the damage it was doing to him.

Still, I debated letting it go for now. I could argue and push forever, but Gideon needed to be the one to demand the answers and hear them given.

Put it away. When the time is right, it'll happen.

But I found myself leaning forward instead, unable to hold the silence Gideon had kept for too long.

"Let's be honest," I insisted quietly. "Your wife didn't have this reaction when Gideon became engaged to Corinne." I didn't know that for sure, but having seen Elizabeth with Corinne's parents at the hospital, it seemed likely.

His sheepish smile proved me right. "I think that was different because Gideon had been with Corinne awhile and we knew her. You and Gideon haven't been together long, so there's still some adjusting to do. I don't want you to take it personally, Eva."

The smile chafed, but it was the words that were too much for me. Resentment welled and flowed over the wall I tried to contain it behind.

Chris wasn't blameless, either. Taking a grieving, troubled boy into his home had to have been hard — especially when he'd been building his own family with Christopher Jr. and Ireland on the way. But he'd accepted the role of stepfather when he married Elizabeth. He shared responsibility for pursuing justice for a wounded and exploited child. Hell, a *stranger* would have an obligation to report the crime.

Leaning forward, I let him see how angry I was. "It's *very* personal, Mr. Vidal. Elizabeth is feeling threatened because I'm not going to put up with this bullshit anymore. You both owe Gideon an apology and she needs to admit to the abuse. I'm going to keep pressuring her to make things right. You can count on that."

His posture stiffened visibly. "What are you talking about?"

I snorted with disgust. "Seriously?"

"Elizabeth would never abuse her children," he said tightly when I didn't reply. "She's a wonderful, devoted mother."

I blinked, then stared at him. Was he as delusional as Elizabeth? How could they both act like they didn't know?

"I think you'd better explain yourself, Eva. Fast."

I sagged back into the chair, stunned. If he was acting, he deserved a goddamned Academy Award.

He surged forward without getting up, bristling and aggressive. "Start talking. *Now.*"

My voice came quiet. Small. "He was raped. By the therapist he was seeing."

Chris froze. For a long minute, he didn't

even breathe.

"He told Elizabeth, but she didn't believe him. She knows he was telling the truth, but she's denied it for whatever screwed-up reason she's come up with."

He straightened, shaking his head vehemently. "No."

The one-word rebuff pushed me to my feet. "Are you going to deny it, too? Who would lie about something like that? Do you have any idea how hard it was for him to admit to what was happening? How confused he must have been that a man he trusted would do those things to him?"

Chris looked up at me. "Elizabeth would never ignore . . . something like that. There's a misunderstanding. You're confused."

I took in his dilated pupils and white-rimmed lips but refused to feel bad for him. "She went through the motions. That's all. When push came to shove, she chose to side with everyone but her own child."

"You don't know what you're saying."

I grabbed the handle of my bag and slung it over my shoulder. I bent into him, meeting him at eye level. "Gideon was raped. One of these days, you and your wife are going to look him in the eye like I'm looking at you and you're going to admit it. And you're going to apologize for all the years he's lived with that alone."

"Eva."

Gideon's voice cracked through the air, making me jump. Straightening in a rush, I stumbled as I faced him.

He stood in the open doorway, his hand gripping the handle with such force it should've broken off. His face was hard, his body stiff, his gaze searing me with a different kind of heat.

Fury. I'd never seen him so angry.

Chris pushed heavily to his feet. "Gideon. What's going on? What is she saying?"

Gideon's arm shot out and grabbed me. He yanked me into the hallway with such force I yelped in alarm. I felt the bite of his fingers even after he released me.

With his hand at the small of my back, he propelled me forward, his stride so long and quick I had to scramble to keep pace.

"Gideon, wait," I said breathlessly, my heart pounding. "We —"

"Not a fucking word," he snapped, pushing me roughly through the etched glass security doors into the elevator vestibule.

I heard Chris calling Gideon's name. I caught sight of him rushing toward us just before the elevator doors shut him out.

9

As I led Eva out of the Crossfire, Angus took one look at my face and his smile disappeared. He opened the rear door to the Bentley and stepped aside, watching me urge my wife into the backseat.

Our gazes met over her head as she slid into the back. I read the message in his faded blue eyes. *Be gentle with her.*

He didn't know how hard it was for me to show as much restraint as I was managing. I could feel the vein pulsating in my temple, echoing the driving pulse beat that had my cock throbbing.

I'd nearly stopped the elevator halfway down to fuck Eva against the wall like an animal. The only things that deterred me were the security cameras and watchful guard eyes monitoring the feed.

I wanted to leash her. Sink my teeth into her shoulder as I nailed her. Dominate her. She was a tigress, clawing and hissing at everyone she felt had done me wrong, and I needed to pin her down. Make her submit.

"Goddamn it," I bit out, rounding the back of the car to get in on the other side. Eva was a wild card. I couldn't control her.

I folded into the seat and slammed the door shut, staring out the window because I was afraid of what I'd do if I looked at her. She was the air I breathed and at the moment, I couldn't catch my breath.

She set her hand on my thigh. "Gideon . . ."

Grabbing that slender hand wearing my ring, I shoved it between my legs and thrust my aching dick into her palm. "Open your mouth again and that's what I'm putting in it."

She gasped.

Angus slid behind the wheel and started the car. I felt Eva's gaze on the side of my face. Her hand pulled away and I nearly groaned at the loss of her touch. Then she shifted, curling into my side. Her other hand slid back between my legs, cupping my cock possessively. Her lips pressed a kiss against my jaw.

My arm went around her back. I took a deep breath, inhaling her scent.

The Bentley pulled away from the curb and we melded into midtown traffic.

■ ■ ■ ■

It wasn't until we pulled over in front of the office building where Dr. Petersen kept his office that I remembered our appointment. I'd been counting the minutes until we got home and I could take Eva the way I needed to . . . fast . . . hard . . . furious.

She started sitting up when Angus got out of the car. I tightened my arm around her. "Not today," I said tightly.

"Okay," she whispered, kissing my jaw again.

Angus opened the door. She pulled away, then got out of the car anyway. She spun through the revolving doors and left me staring after her.

"Jesus."

Ducking down, Angus peered in at me. "Couples therapy means the both of you."

I glared at him. "Stop enjoying this."

The smile in his eyes curved his lips into a broad grin. "She loves you, lad, whether you like it or naw."

"Of course I like it," I muttered, glancing over my shoulder to check the traffic before opening my door and stepping out. I rounded the trunk. "That doesn't mean she's not a loose cannon."

Angus shut the door. A rare summer breeze ruffled the graying red hair that peeked out from beneath his chauffeur's hat. "Sometimes you'll lead, sometimes you'll follow. Expect you'll grumble about the following part for a while yet."

I growled, exasperated. "She talked to Chris."

His brows rose with surprise even as he nodded. "I saw him go in."

"Why won't she leave it the hell alone?" I stepped onto the sidewalk, tugging my vest into place and wishing I could straighten my thoughts as easily. "She can't change the past."

"It's not the past she's thinking of." He set his hand briefly on my shoulder. "It's the future."

I found Eva pacing in Dr. Petersen's office, her hands waving as she spoke. The good doctor sat in his customary chair, his attention on his tablet as he took notes.

"The whole situation makes me so mad," she seethed. Then she caught sight of me standing in the doorway and paused mid-stride.

"Gideon." A brilliant smile lit up her beautiful face.

There wasn't anything I wouldn't do to

put that happy look on her. The fact that she smiled like that just because she saw me . . .

"Eva. Doctor." I took a seat on the sofa. How much had she told him?

Dr. Petersen followed me with his gaze. "Hello, Gideon. I'm glad you could join us after all."

I patted the cushion next to me and waited for Eva to sit.

"We're making plans to move back into the penthouse on Fifth with Cary," I said smoothly once she'd settled beside me, deflecting the conversation into territory I was more comfortable addressing. "I expect it will be a rocky transition for all of us."

Eva gaped.

Dr. Petersen set his stylus down. "Eva was just telling me about a visit with your stepfather. I would like to hear more about that before we move on."

I linked my fingers with Eva's. "It's not open for discussion."

She stared at me. I turned my head to meet her gaze and my breath left me in a pained rush.

The new look on her face made me ache for a different reason altogether.

The session had barely started and already it couldn't end soon enough for me.

■ ■ ■ ■

I told Angus to take us home — to the penthouse.

It was obvious Eva was lost in her own thoughts by the surprise she displayed when the valet opened the door for her. We were in the subterranean garage beneath the building.

She glanced at me.

"I'll explain," I told her, as I took her elbow and led her to the elevator.

We rode up in silence. When the car doors opened into our private foyer, I felt her tense beneath my hand. We hadn't been to the penthouse together in nearly a month. The last time we'd been in the foyer had been the night she confronted me about Nathan's death.

I'd been afraid then, too. Terrified I had done something she couldn't forgive me for.

We'd had many explosive moments here. The penthouse hadn't seen as much joy and love between us as the secret apartment on the Upper West Side. But we would change that. One day, we would look back and this place would remind us of all the steps in our journey together, good and bad. I refused to envision anything else.

I opened the door, gesturing her in before me. She dropped her purse into an armchair and kicked off her shoes. I shrugged out of my jacket, hung it on the back of one of the bar stools in the kitchen, and then pulled a shiraz off the wine rack.

"You're disappointed in me," I called out, uncorking the wine.

Eva padded to the open archway and leaned against the tumbled stone. "No, not in you."

Retrieving a decanter and two glasses, I considered my reply. It was difficult bargaining with my wife. In every other deal, I went in with the knowledge that I could take it or leave it. There was no agreement anywhere I couldn't walk away from.

Except those that endangered my hold on Eva.

As I poured the wine from its bottle into the decanter, she joined me at the island.

Her hand came to rest on my shoulder. "We haven't been together long, Gideon, and you've come so far already. I'm not going to push you to go farther so soon. These things take time."

I let the decanted wine sit and turned to face her, pulling her close. She'd felt so far away the last hour or so and the distance had been killing me.

"Kiss me," I murmured.

Tilting her head back, Eva lifted her mouth to me. I pressed my lips to hers but otherwise did nothing else, wanting her to be the one to reach out. Needing her to be.

The stroke of her tongue over the seam of my lips made me groan. The feel of her fingers sliding into the hair at my nape soothed me. There was an apology in the softness of her lips gliding across mine and love in her quiet moan of surrender.

I caught her up, lifting her feet from the floor, so relieved she still wanted me that I felt dizzy with it. "Eva . . . I'm sorry."

"Shh, baby, it's okay." She pulled back and touched my face, cupping it in both hands. "You don't have to apologize to me."

The back of my throat burned. I lifted her onto the counter, stepping between her spread legs. Her skirt rose up, baring the ends of her garters. I wanted her. In every way.

My forehead touched hers. "You're upset that I didn't want to talk about Chris."

"I wasn't expecting you to avoid it so completely, that's all." She kissed my brow, her fingers brushing the hair from my face. "I should've considered the possibility, considering how angry you were when we left the Crossfire."

"Not with you."

"At Chris?"

"At the situation." I exhaled roughly. "You're expecting people to change and that doesn't happen. In the meantime, you're stirring up trouble at a time when we've got enough on our plates. I just want to have some peace with you, Eva. Days when we're alone and happy and free of any bullshit."

"And nights where you go to sleep in another bed? In another room?"

My eyes squeezed shut. "Is that what this is all about?"

"Not completely, but some of it, yeah. Gideon, I want to be with you. Waking and sleeping."

"I understand, but —"

"That peace you're looking for? You're pretending you have it during the day and suffering without it at night. It's tearing you up from the inside, and it's shredding me watching it happen to you. I don't want you to live like this forever. I don't want *us* to live forever like this."

I looked at her, my soul bared to those amazing steel-colored eyes that didn't let me hide anything. There was so much love in the look she gave me. Love and worry, disappointment and hope. The pendant lamps over the island backlit her blond hair, reminding me of how precious she was. A gift I'd never expected.

"Eva . . . I am talking to Dr. Petersen about the nightmares."

"But not about what's causing them."

"You're assuming Hugh is the problem," I said evenly, feeling the burn of hatred and humiliation in my gut. "We've been talking about my father instead."

She pulled back. "Ace . . . I don't know exactly what's in your dreams, but I've seen you wake up in two different ways: ready to beat up someone or crying like your heart is breaking. When you come out swinging, the things you say make me damn near certain you're fighting off Hugh."

I sucked in a quick, deep breath. It infuriated me that my former therapist — and molester — could reach out from the grave and touch Eva through me.

"Listen." She wrapped her legs around my hips. "I said I wasn't going to push you and I meant it. If we were two years into our relationship, I'd put up a fuss, maybe. But it's only been a few months, Gideon. The fact that you're seeing someone and talking about your dad is enough for now."

"Is it?"

"Yes. But there are things we can never discuss that are haunting you, too. Dr.

Petersen is already working with a handicap because of that. The more you keep from him, the less he can help."

Nathan. She didn't have to say the name.

"I'm making an effort, Eva."

"I know." Her hands smoothed over my shoulders, then reached for the buttons of my vest. "Just tell me that you're not hoping to avoid talking about it forever. Tell me you're just working up to it."

My heart rate sped up. I reached for her wrists, holding them firmly, anchoring myself to her. I felt cornered, trapped between her needs and my own, which seemed terribly divergent at that moment.

Her lips parted at the pressure of my grip, her breasts lifting with a quickened breath. A restraining touch, a heated look, the tone of my voice . . . Eva reacted to my unspoken demands as if she'd been trained to.

"I'm doing my best," I told her.

"That's not an answer."

"It's all I've got right now, Eva."

She swallowed, her thoughts scattering as her body stirred. "You're playing with me," she said quietly. "You're manipulating me."

"I'm not. I'm giving you the truth, even though it's not what you want to hear. You told me you wouldn't push. Did you mean it?"

Wetting her lower lip with a brush of her tongue, she stared up at me. Then nodded. "Yes."

"Good. Let's have some wine and dinner. Afterward, if you'd really like to play, let me know."

"Play? How?"

"I have some silk cord I bought for you."

Her eyes widened. "Silk cord?"

"Crimson, of course." I released her and stepped back, giving her some space to think while I reached for the decanter to pour her a glass. "I'd like to tie you down when you're ready for that. If not tonight, then someday. I won't push you, either."

We were both steering each other in directions that were uncomfortable. She chose to believe an educated observer was part of the answer we were looking for. I believed we could find a lot of the answers on our own, just the two of us connecting in the most intimate ways possible.

Sexual healing. What could be more perfect for two people who had the history Eva and I shared?

Eva accepted the wine I handed her. "When did you buy that?"

"A week ago. Maybe two. I had no expectation of using it soon, but you made me want to today." I took a sip, letting the shiraz roll around my tongue. "That said, I'm perfectly happy with just fucking you hard."

The wine sloshed a little in her glass as she lifted it to her mouth. She gulped it down, leaving a few drops in the bottom. "Because you're mad at me for talking to Chris."

"I told you I wasn't."

"You were furious when we left."

"Furiously turned on." I smiled wryly. "I can't explain why, because I don't understand it myself."

"Try."

I reached up and brushed the pad of my thumb over her lips. "I see you angry, passionate, ready to fight, and I want all that violence trapped beneath me. You make me want to hold you down, clawing and screaming, your cunt milking my cock as I pound it into you. Mine. All mine."

"Gideon." She set her glass aside and grabbed me, claiming my mouth with a wild hunger I hoped would never abate.

"How come you never told Chris about what happened with Hugh?"

That unwelcome question came out of the fucking blue. I paused midchew, suddenly finding the bite of pizza in my mouth unappetizing. Dropping what was left of my slice onto the plate in front of me, I grabbed a napkin and wiped my mouth. "Why are we discussing this again?"

Eva frowned at me from where she sat beside me on the floor in between the coffee table and the couch in the living room. "We didn't talk about it."

"Didn't we? In any case, it doesn't matter. My mother told him."

Her frown deepened. She reached for the TV remote and lowered the volume, muting the voices of the NYPD detectives on the screen. "I don't think so."

I pushed to my feet and grabbed my plate. "She did, Eva."

"Do you know that for sure?" She followed me into the kitchen.

"Yes."

"How?"

"They discussed it at the dinner table one night, something I don't want to do."

"He acted like he didn't know." She braced her hands against the counter as I dropped my leftovers into the trash. "He seemed genuinely confused and horrified."

"Then he's as conveniently obtuse as my mother. You shouldn't be surprised."

"What if he didn't know?"

"So what?" I set the plate in the sink, the lingering smell of food making my stomach roil. "What the fuck does it matter now? It's done, Eva. Done and over with. Let it go."

"Why are you so mad?"

"Because I was settled in for the night with my wife. Dinner, wine, a little TV, a couple hours making love . . . after a long, rough day." I left the kitchen. "Forget it. I'll see you in the morning."

"Gideon, wait." She grabbed my arm. "Don't go to bed pissed. Please. I'm sorry."

I paused and removed her hand from my arm. "So am I."

"Start out slow," he whispers, his lips near my ear.

I can feel him becoming excited. He reaches around my hip to where I'm stroking my penis. His hand covers mine. His breath is quick and shallow. His erection brushes against my buttocks.

My stomach feels sick. I'm sweating. I can't stay hard, even as my oiled fist slides up and down, guided by his.

"You're thinking too much," he tells me. "Concentrate on how good it feels. Look at that woman in front of you. She wants you to fuck her. Imagine how it'd feel to push your cock into her. Soft. Hot. Wet. And tight." His grip closes harder over mine. "So tight."

I look at the centerfold spread over the top

of my toilet's water tank. She's got dark hair and blue eyes, and her legs are long. They always look like that, the women in the pictures Hugh brings.

He pants in my ear, and the sickness is back. Wrong. There's something wrong with me. *This* feels wrong. His eagerness makes me feel dirty. Bad. I'm a bad boy, even Mom says so. She yells it at me when she's crying, when she's angry with me about Dad.

A low moan cuts through the sound of his heavy breaths. It's me making that noise. It feels good, even though I don't want it to.

It's hard to breathe, to think, to fight . . .

"That's it," he coaxes. His other hand pushes between my buttocks.

I try to pull away, but he's got me trapped. He's bigger than me, stronger. No matter how I struggle, I can't push him off.

"Don't," I tell him, squirming.

"You like it," he grunts. His hand pumps me harder. "You shoot off like a geyser every time. It's okay. It's supposed to feel good. You'll be better once you've come. You won't fight with your mother so much . . . ."

"No. Don't! Oh, God . . ."

He pushes two slick fingers inside me. I cry out, writhing away, but he won't quit. He's rubbing and thrusting into me, hitting the spot that makes me want to come more than anything. The pleasure grows despite the tears burning my eyes.

My head falls forward. My chin touches my heaving chest. It's coming. I can't stop it . . .

Abruptly, I look down from a higher vantage. My hand is suddenly bigger, my forearm thicker and coursing with veins. Dark hair dusts my arms and chest, my abdomen ripples with muscle as I fight the orgasm I don't want.

I am not a child anymore. He can't hurt me anymore.

There's a knife atop the centerfold, gleaming in the light from the vanity beside me. I grab it and jerk free of the fingers fucking me. I turn and the blade sinks into his chest.

"Don't touch me!" I roar, grabbing his shoulder and yanking him into the knife, all the way to the hilt.

Hugh's eyes widen with horror. His mouth falls open in a silent scream.

His face morphs into Nathan's. My childhood bathroom shimmers and transforms. We're in an eerily familiar hotel room.

My heart pounds harder. I can't be here. They can't find me here. Can't find any trace of me. I have to leave.

I stumble back. The knife withdraws in a smooth, blood-soaked glide. Nathan's eyes turn milky with death. They're gray. Gray eyes. Beautiful, beloved dove gray irises. Eva's eyes. Clouding over . . .

Eva is bleeding in front of me. *Dying* in front of me. I've killed her. My God . . .

Angel!

Can't move. Can't reach her. She crumples and pools onto the floor, those stormy eyes dull and sightless —

I jerked awake with a gasp, sitting up in a rush that sent an air-conditioned breeze across my sweat-soaked skin. I couldn't breathe through the panic and fear choking me. Shoving off the sheet tangled around my legs, I stumbled out of bed, blind with terror. My stomach heaved in protest and I lurched into the bathroom, barely reaching the toilet before I vomited.

I showered, washing away the sticky sweat covering me.

The grief and despair weren't so easy to get away from. As I scrubbed a dry towel over my skin, they weighed heavily, suffocating me. The memory of Eva's pale face etched with betrayal and death haunted me. I couldn't get it out of my head.

I stripped the bed with rough, jerky movements, then yanked a clean fitted sheet over the mattress.

"Gideon."

I straightened and turned at the sound of

Eva's voice. She stood in the doorway to my bedroom, her hands twisting in the hem of the T-shirt she wore. Regret hit me hard. She'd gone to sleep alone in the room I'd had redesigned to look like her bedroom on the Upper West Side.

"Hey," she said softly, tentatively, shifting on her feet in a way that told me how uncomfortable she felt. How wary. "Are you okay?"

The light from the bathroom lit her face, revealing dark circles and reddened eyes. She'd fallen asleep crying.

I'd done this to her. I had made her feel unwelcome, unwanted, her thoughts and feelings less of a concern to me than my own. I'd let my past drive a wedge between us.

No, that wasn't true. I had let my fear push her away.

"No, angel, I'm not."

She took a single step closer, then stopped herself.

Opening my arms, I said hoarsely, "I'm sorry, Eva."

She came to me in a rush, her body lush and warm. I held her too tightly, but she didn't complain. Pressing my cheek to the top of her head, I breathed in her scent. I could face anything — I *would* face anything

— as long as she stayed with me.

"I'm afraid." My voice was scarcely a whisper, but she heard it.

Her fingers dug into the muscles of my back as she pulled me closer. "Don't be. I'm here."

"I'll try harder," I promised. "Don't give up on me."

"Gideon." She sighed, her breath soft against my chest. "I love you so much. I just want you to be happy. I'm sorry for pushing you after I said I wouldn't."

"It's my fault. I fucked up. I'm sorry, Eva. So sorry."

"Shh. You don't have to apologize."

I picked her up and carried her to the bed, laying her down carefully. I crawled into her arms, wrapping myself around her and resting my face against her belly. She ran her fingers through my hair, massaging my scalp, then my nape, then my back. Accepting me, despite all my flaws.

The cotton of her T-shirt grew wet with my tears and I curled in tighter, ashamed.

"I love you," she murmured. "I'll never stop."

Gideon.

I stirred at the sound of Eva's voice, then at the feel of her hand sliding down my chest. Opening my tired, burning eyes, I saw her leaning over me, the room softly lit by the coming dawn, her hair aglow in the meager light.

"Angel?"

She shifted, sliding a leg over me. Rising, she straddled me. "Let's make today our best ever."

I swallowed hard. "I'm on board with that plan."

Her smile rocked my world. She reached for something she'd left on her pillow and a moment later, haunting strains of music piped softly out of the speakers in the ceiling.

It took me a moment to recognize it. "Ave Maria."

She touched my face, her fingertips gliding over my brow. "Okay?"

I wanted to answer her, but my throat was too tight. I could only nod. How could I tell her it felt like a dream, a breathtaking heaven I didn't deserve?

She reached behind her to push the sheet below my hips and out of the way. Her arms crossed her torso to pull her shirt up and over her head. She threw it aside.

Awed, I struggled for my voice. "God, you're beautiful," I said hoarsely.

My hands lifted, gliding over the plush

curves and valleys of her voluptuous body. I sat up and dug my heels into the bed, pushing us backward until I was leaning against the headboard. My hands went into her hair and down her throat. I could touch her for days and not get my fill.

"I love you," she said, tilting her head to take my mouth in a hot, demanding kiss.

I let her have me, opening to her. Eva licked deep, stroking me with her tongue, her lips soft and wet against mine.

"Tell me what you need," I murmured, lost to the gently muted music. Lost to her.

"You. Just you."

"Take me, then," I told her. "I'm yours."

"I hate to be the one to break it to you, Cross," Arash said, his fingers drumming on the armrest of the chair in front of my desk, "but you've lost your killer instinct. Eva's tamed you."

I glanced up from my monitor. After spending two hours of my morning making love with my wife, I could concede that I wasn't feeling particularly aggressive. Slaked and relaxed was more apt. Still . . . "Just because I don't think LanCorp's PhazeOne gaming system is a threat to the GenTen doesn't mean I'm not paying attention."

"You're aware," he corrected, "which isn't

the same as paying attention, and I guarantee Ryan Landon has noticed. You used to do something every week or two to poke at him, which — for better or worse — gave him something to do."

"Wasn't it just last week that we closed the PosIT deal?"

"That's reactive, Cross. You need to make a move he didn't prompt."

My office phone started ringing on the line synced to my smartphone. Ireland's name popped up on the screen and I reached for the receiver. "I have to take this."

"Of course you do," he muttered.

I narrowed my eyes at him as I answered. "Ireland, how are you?"

It wasn't like my sister to call. We usually texted back and forth, a form of communication we were both comfortable with. No awkward silences, no need to fake cheeriness or ease.

"Hey, sorry to call you in the middle of the day." Her voice was off.

I frowned, concerned. "What's wrong?"

Ireland paused. "Maybe now's not a good time."

I cursed inwardly. Eva had similar reactions when I was too brusque. The women in my life needed to cut me some slack. I had a big learning curve when it came to social interactions. "You sound upset."

"So do you," she shot back.

"You can call Eva and complain about it to her. She'll sympathize. Now, tell me what's wrong."

She sighed. "Mom and Dad were fighting all night. I don't know what about, but Dad was yelling. He never yells, you know that. He's the most laid-back guy ever. Nothing gets to him. And Mom hates fighting. She's a conflict avoider."

Her astuteness both startled and impressed me. "I'm sorry you had to hear that."

"Dad took off early this morning and Mom's been crying ever since. Do you know what's going on? Is it about Eva and you getting married?"

A strange but recognizable quiet settled over me. I didn't know what to say to her, and I refused to jump to conclusions. "That probably has something to do with it."

The only thing I knew for certain was that I didn't want Ireland listening to her parents fighting. I remembered what it had felt like when my parents fought in the days after my dad's financial fraud had been exposed. I could still feel echoes of the panic and fear. "Is there a friend you can stay with over the weekend?"

"You."

The suggestion was unnerving. "You want to stay with me?"

"Why not? I've never seen your place."

I stared at Arash, who was watching me. He leaned forward, setting his elbows on his knees.

I didn't know how to refuse, but I couldn't agree. The only person who'd ever spent the night with me was Eva, and obviously, that hadn't turned out well.

"Never mind," she said. "Forget it."

"No, wait." Damn it. "Eva and I have plans with friends tonight, that's all. I'll need some time to change them."

"Oh, gotcha." Her voice softened. "I don't want to fuck up your plans. I've got some friends I can call. Don't worry about it."

"I'm worried about *you.* Eva and I can make some adjustments; it's not a problem."

"I'm not a kid, Gideon," she said, clearly exasperated. "I don't want to hang around your place knowing you and Eva were supposed to be out having fun. That would totally suck, so no thanks. I'd rather chill with my own friends."

Relief relaxed my spine. "How about dinner on Saturday instead?"

"Yeah? I'm down. Can I stay the night then?"

I had no idea how I was going to manage it. I had to trust that Eva would know what to do. "That can be arranged. Will you be okay until then?"

"Jeez, listen to you." She laughed. "You sound like a big brother. I'll be fine. It was just weird, you know, hearing them going at it. It freaked me out. Most people are probably used to their parents fighting, but I'm not."

"They'll be fine. All couples fight eventually." I said the words, but I was both uneasy and curious.

Eva couldn't have been right about Chris not knowing. I found that impossible to believe.

I'd just finished rolling up the sleeves of my black dress shirt when Eva stepped into the reflection of the mirror. I froze, my gaze raking over her.

She had chosen short shorts, a sheer sleeveless blouse, and high-heeled sandals. She'd pulled her hair up in its usual pony-tail, but she had done something to it to make it look wild and bedhead messy. Her eye makeup was dark, her lips pale. Big gold hoops hung from her ears, and bangles decorated her wrists.

I'd woken up to an angel. I would be going to bed with a different woman entirely.

I whistled in appreciation, turning my back to the mirror to take in the real deal. "You look like a bad, bad girl."

She wiggled her ass and gave a cocky toss of her head. "I am."

"Come here."

She eyed me. "I don't think so. You've got the fuck-me look and we have to go."

"We can be a little late. What would it take to talk you into wearing those shorts just for me?"

I wanted others to want her and know she was mine. I also wanted to keep her all to myself.

Her eyes took on a calculating gleam. "We could renegotiate the hand job."

Remembering the deal we'd struck — a quickie for a clothed hand job — I realized the shorts were going to make the former a bit more difficult than it could be. As for the latter, I could work something out.

Tilting my head in agreement, I told her, "Put on a skirt, angel, and let's get this party started."

"Was this your idea?" Arash asked, when we met him outside the ground-floor entrance to the Starlight Lounge.

Through the lobby glass, I watched a bouncer oversee the number of patrons entering the elevator that would take them to the rooftop. Two more bouncers stood guard at the exterior door, holding back the surging crowd hoping to get in based on their looks, their clothes, and/or their charm.

"It's as much of a surprise to me as it is to you."

"I meant to tell you." Eva was literally hopping with excitement. "Shawna's heard good things about this place and I thought it'd be fun."

"Great reviews online," Shawna said, "and some of my regulars were raving about it."

Manuel checked out the eager crowd behind the ropes, while Megumi Kaba stood cautiously between Cary and Eva. Mark Garrity, Steven Ellison, and Arnoldo all stood back, keeping the way clear for those whose names were on the VIP List.

Cary slung his arm around Megumi. "Stick with me, kid." He gave her a wide smile. "We'll show 'em how it's done."

Eva grabbed my arm. "Your surprise is here."

I followed her gaze, spotting a couple approaching us. My brows rose when I recognized Magdalene Perez. Her hand was linked with that of the man next to her and her dark eyes were brighter than I'd seen in a long time.

"Maggie," I greeted her, clasping her extended hand and leaning down to kiss her cheek. "I'm glad you came."

Gladder still that Eva had asked her. The two women had gotten off to a rocky start, which was entirely Maggie's fault. The rift between them had strained my relationship with Maggie in the weeks since, and I'd been prepared to accept that as an indefinite state of affairs. It was nice, however, that I didn't have to.

Maggie grinned. "Gideon. Eva. This is my boyfriend, Gage Flynn."

I took the man's hand after he shook Eva's, noting the strength of his grip and the steady way he met my perusal. He gave me a once-over, too, but mine would be more thorough. Before the week was out, I would know everything worth knowing about the man. Maggie had been through enough with Christopher. I didn't want to see her hurt again.

"And here's Will and Natalie," Eva said, as the last of our group arrived.

Will Granger had a retro beatnik look that worked for him. His arm was snug around the small blue-haired woman next to him, who dressed in the same fifties style and sported twin sleeves of tattoos.

While Eva made the introductions, I nodded at the bouncer to signal the arrival of the final members of our party. He held the line and cleared the doorway for us.

My wife shot me a suspicious glance. "Don't tell me you own this place."

"Okay, I won't."

"You mean you do?"

My hand slid down her back and rested lightly on the curve of her hip. She'd ditched the shorts in favor of a fitted skirt with a split up the back. I almost wished she hadn't changed. The shorts had shown off her legs; the skirt showed off her amazing ass.

"You need to decide if you want me to answer the question or not," I said, as we made our way into the club. The music was loud, the amateur singer on the stage louder. Strategic lighting illuminated walkways and tables while still allowing the Manhattan nightscape to dazzle patrons. Air-conditioning pumped out of the walls and floors, cooling the open air to a comfortable temperature.

"Is there anything you *don't* own in New York?"

Arash laughed. "He doesn't own the D'Argos Regal on Thirty-sixth anymore."

Eva stopped walking, causing Arash to bump into her from behind and send her stumbling. I shot him a glare.

Grabbing my arm, Eva yelled over the volume of the crowded club. "You got rid of the hotel?"

I looked down at her. The wonder and hope on her face more than made up for the financial hit I'd taken. I nodded.

She threw herself at me, her arms twining around my neck. She peppered my jaw with quick, fierce kisses and I smiled, my gaze meeting Arash's.

"And suddenly," he said, "it all makes sense."

10

"God, those two are so sweet," Shawna said, watching Will and Natalie sing "I Got You, Babe" on the stage.

"They're giving me diabetes." Manuel stood with his drink. "Excuse me, everyone. I see something interesting."

Gideon's voice near my ear was laced with amusement. "Say good-bye, angel. We won't be seeing him again."

I followed his line of sight and saw a pretty brunette giving Manuel a blatant once-over.

"Bye, Manuel!" I yelled after him, waving. Then I leaned into Gideon, who was semi-sprawled on the expensive leather uphol-stery. "How come all the guys you work with are hot?"

"Are they?" he drawled, nuzzling my neck and along the curve of my ear. "Maybe they won't be working with me much longer."

"Oh God." I looked up at the starry sky. "Whatever, caveman."

His arm tightened around my hips, tugging me closer so that I was pressed fully against him from knee to shoulder. Joy spread through me. After all the crap we'd been through the day before, it was so awesome to just enjoy each other.

Megumi leaned over the low coffee table that filled the center of the rectangular seating area we occupied. Bordered by two sectionals, the VIP section held our entire party comfortably. "When are *you* getting up there to make fools of yourselves?" she asked.

"Um . . . never."

It had taken a few drinks and Cary's undivided attention to make Megumi comfortable enough to enjoy herself. My best friend had kicked things off with a rousing rendition of "Only the Good Die Young," and then he'd dragged Megumi up there to sing "(I've Had) The Time of My Life." She'd come back to the table glowing.

I owed Cary big-time for taking care of her. Even better, he seemed to have no intention of ditching us to cruise the place for conquests like Manuel had. I was really proud of him.

"Come on, Eva," Steven coaxed. "You picked this place. You have to sing."

"Your sister picked this place," I shot

back, looking to her. Shawna just shrugged innocently.

"She's sung twice!" he countered.

I deflected. "Mark hasn't sung anything."

My boss shook his head. "I'm doing you all a favor, trust me."

"You're telling me. Squealing tires sound more lyrical than I do!"

Arnoldo pushed the tablet with the song choices my way. It was the first time all night he'd made any overture toward me, aside from saying hello at the entrance. He'd spent most of the evening focused on Magdalene and Gage, which I tried not to take as a personal snub.

"No fair," I complained. "You're all ganging up on me! Gideon hasn't sung yet, either."

I glanced at my husband. He shrugged. "I'll go up if you will."

Astonishment widened my eyes. I'd never heard Gideon sing, had never even imagined it. Singers exposed and expressed emotion with their voices. Gideon's still waters ran very deep.

"Hell, you gotta do it now," Cary said, reaching over to tap the menu open at a random page.

My stomach twisted a little. I looked helplessly at the songs in front of me. One jumped out and I stared at it.

Taking a deep breath, I stood. "Okay. Just remember, you all asked for this. I don't want to hear any shit about how bad I suck."

Gideon, who'd risen to his feet when I had, pulled me close and murmured in my ear, "I think you suck excellently, angel."

I elbowed him in the ribs. His low laughter followed me as I made my way to the stage. I loved hearing that sound, loved spending time with him when we forgot our troubles and had fun with people who loved us. We were married, but we still had so much dating to catch up on, so many nights with friends yet to experience. Tonight was just the first of many, I hoped.

I regretted threatening the fragile peace with my song choice. But not enough to change my mind.

I high-fived Will as he and Natalie passed me on the way back to our group. I could have input my song choice into the tablet at the table, the same way we placed our food and drink orders, but I didn't want Gideon seeing the title.

Plus, I'd noticed that every other party in the place had to wait for their turn in the queue, but our selections were fast-tracked. I was hoping that adding my name to the list in person would buy me some time to build up the courage I needed.

I should've known better. When I gave the hostess my selection, she typed it into the system and said, "Okay, stay right here. You're next."

"You're kidding." I glanced back at our table. Gideon winked at me.

Ooh, he was going to pay for that later.

The chick on the stage singing "Diamonds" wrapped it up, and the place exploded into applause. She'd been decent, but really, the live band made up for a lot of faults. They were really good. I had my fingers crossed that they'd be good enough for me, too.

I was shaking when I climbed the short steps to the stage. When the loud whistles and cheers erupted from our table, I couldn't help but laugh despite my nervousness. I gripped the mic in its stand and the beat kicked in immediately. The familiar song, one I loved, gave me the boost I needed to start.

Looking at Gideon, I warbled my way through the opening lyrics, telling him he was amazing. Even over the music, I could hear the laughter at my horrible voice. My own table erupted with it, but I had expected that.

I'd chosen "Brave." I had to be it to sing

it — that, or crazy.

I stayed focused on my husband, who wasn't laughing or smiling. He just stared intently at my face as I told him via Sara Bareilles's lyrics that I wanted to see him speak up and be brave.

The catchy composition plus the skill of the band backing me began to win over the crowd, who started singing along, more or less. My heart strengthened my voice, giving power to the message meant only for Gideon.

He needed to stop holding his silence. He needed to tell his family the truth. Not for me or for them, but for him.

When the song ended, my friends surged to their feet in applause and I grinned, energized. I gave a lavish bow and laughed when the strangers at the tables in front of the stage joined in the unearned praise. I knew my strengths. My singing voice certainly wasn't one of them.

"That was fuckin' awesome!" Shawna shouted when I got back to the table, grabbing me in a fierce hug. "You owned that, girl."

"Remind me to pay you later," I said dryly, feeling my face heat as the rest of our party kicked in with praise. "You guys are full of it."

"Ah, baby girl," Cary drawled, his green eyes bright with laughter, "you can't be good at everything. It's a relief to know you're flawed like the rest of us."

I stuck my tongue out at him and picked up the fresh vodka cranberry sitting in front of my spot.

"Your turn, lover boy," Arash goaded, grinning at Gideon.

My husband nodded, then looked at me. His face held no hint to his thoughts, and I began to worry. There was no softness on his lips or in his eyes, nothing to give me a clue.

And then some idiot started singing "Golden."

Gideon stiffened, his jaw visibly tightening. Reaching for his hand, I gave it a squeeze and felt a bit of relief when he squeezed back.

He kissed my cheek and headed to the stage, cutting through the crowd with easy command. I watched him go, seeing other women's heads turn to follow him. I was biased, of course, but knew for a certainty that he was the most striking man in the room.

Seriously, it should be criminal for a man to be that sexy.

I looked at Arash and Arnoldo. "Have

either of you heard him sing?"

Arnoldo shook his head.

Arash laughed. "Hell, no. With any luck, he'll sound like you. Like Cary says, he can't be good at everything or we'd all have to hate him."

The guy onstage wrapped it up. A moment later, Gideon walked on. For some reason, my heart started pounding as badly as it had when I was up there. My palms grew clammy and I wiped them on my skirt.

I was afraid of what it would be like to watch Gideon up there. Much as I hated to think it, Brett was a hard act to follow and hearing "Golden," even sung by someone who shouldn't ever have access to a microphone, brought those two worlds too close together.

Gideon grabbed the mic and pulled it off the stand as if he'd done the move a thousand times before. The women in the audience went crazy, yelling about how hot he was and making suggestive remarks I chose to ignore. The man was delicious physically, but his commanding, confident presence was the real kicker.

He looked like a man who knew how to fuck a woman senseless. And God, did he ever.

"This one," he said, "is for my wife."

With a pointed glance, Gideon signaled the band to start. An instantly recognizable bass beat ratcheted up my pulse.

"Lifehouse!" Shawna crowed, clapping her hands. "I love them!"

"He's calling you his wife already!" Megumi yelled, leaning toward me. "How freakin' lucky are you?"

I didn't glance at her. I couldn't. My attention was riveted on Gideon as he looked directly at me and sang, telling me in a lusciously raspy voice that he was desperate for change and starving for truth.

He was answering my song.

My eyes burned even as my heart began to beat with a different rhythm. Had I thought he'd be unemotional? My God, he was killing me, baring his soul in the rough timbre of his voice.

"Holy fuck," Cary said, his eyes on the stage. "The man can sing."

I was hanging by a moment, too, hanging on to every word, hearing his message about chasing after me and falling more in love. I shifted in my seat, turned on beyond bearing.

Gideon dominated the attention of everyone in the bar. Of all the voices we'd heard that night, his was truly professional grade. He stood in the single spotlight, feet set a foot apart, dressed elegantly while singing a rock song, and he made it work so well I couldn't imagine it sung any other way. There was no comparison to Brett, not in Gideon's delivery or my reaction to it.

I was on my feet before I knew it, making my way through the crowd to get to him. Gideon finished the song and the bar went ballistic, cutting off my route to him. I became lost in the crush, too short to see beyond the shoulders around me.

He found me, pushing his way through to catch me up in his arms. His mouth claimed mine, kissing me roughly, inciting a new round of catcalls and cheers. In the periphery, I heard the band begin a new song. I practically climbed up Gideon, panting in his ear, "Now!"

I didn't have to explain. Setting me down, he grabbed my hand and led me across the bar and back through the kitchen to the service elevator. I plastered myself against him before the doors closed behind us, but he was pulling out his phone and lifting it to his ear, tilting his head back as my mouth slid feverishly over his throat.

"Bring the limo around," he ordered gruffly, and then the phone was back in his pocket and he was kissing me back with all the passion he'd once kept locked inside.

Ravenous, I devoured him, catching his lower lip between my teeth and tasting it with swift lashes of my tongue. He groaned when I pushed him against the elevator's padded wall, my hands running down his chest to cup the heft of his erection in my palms.

"Eva . . . Christ."

We stopped descending and he exploded into movement, grabbing me by the elbow and pushing me ahead of him out the doors with brisk, impatient strides. We exited from a service hallway into the lobby, once again maneuvering through a crowd until we stepped out into the summer night heat. The limo idled in the street.

Angus jumped out, quickly pulling the rear door open.

I scrambled in with Gideon crowding in behind me.

"Don't go far," he told Angus.

We settled onto the bench seat with a foot of distance between us, both of us looking anywhere but at each other as the privacy partition slowly rose and the limo began to move.

The moment the divider locked into place, I fell back against the seat and yanked my skirt up, brazenly tearing off my own clothes in my eagerness to be fucked.

As Gideon dropped to his knees on the floorboard, his hands went to his waistband, opening his slacks.

I shimmied out of my underwear, kicking them off along with my sandals.

"Angel." His growl had me moaning with anticipation.

"I'm wet. I'm wet," I chanted, not wanting him to play with me or wait.

Still, he tested me, cupping my sex in his hand. His fingers parted me, stroking over my clit, pushing inside me.

"Jesus, Eva. You're soaked."

"Let me ride you," I begged, pushing away from the seat back. I wanted to set the pace, the depth, the rhythm . . .

Gideon pushed his pants and boxer briefs down to his knees, then sat on the bench, yanking his shirttails out of the way. His cock rose up thick and long between his thighs, as savagely beautiful as the rest of him.

I slid down to kneel between his legs, stroking his penis with my hands. He was hot and silky soft. My mouth was on him before I formulated the thought. His breath hissed out between his teeth, one hand grasping my ponytail as his head fell back.

His eyes squeezed shut. *"Yes."*

I swirled my tongue around the broad

head, tasting him, feeling the thick veins throbbing against my palms. Tightening my lips, I pulled off, then sucked him back in.

He groaned and arched upward, pushing into my mouth. "Take it deep."

I squirmed as I obeyed him, ragingly turned on by his pleasure. Gideon's eyes opened, his chin lowering so he could take in the sight of me.

"Come here." The low command sent a shiver of desire through me.

I crawled up his magnificent body, straddling his hips and draping my arms over his shoulders. "You are so fucking hot."

"Me? You're burning up, angel."

I moved my hips to position him. "Wait 'til you feel me from the inside."

He reached around me and gripped his cock, holding himself steady as I began to sink down. My legs shook as the thick crest of his penis pushed inside me, stretching me.

"Gideon." The feeling of being taken, possessed, was one I never got over.

Gripping my hips, he supported me. I took him deeper, my eyes on his as they grew heavy. A rumbling sound filled the space between us and I grew slicker, hotter.

It didn't matter how many times I had him, I always wanted more. More of the way he responded to me, as if nothing had ever felt the same, as if I gave him something he could get nowhere else.

I clung to the back of the seat and rolled my hips, taking a little more. I could feel him pressing against the deepest part of me, but I couldn't fit all of him. I wanted to. I wanted everything he had.

"Our first time," he said hoarsely, watching me. "You rode me right here, drove me out of my mind. You blew the top of my fucking head off."

"It was so good," I breathed, dangerously close to coming. He was so thick, so hard. "Ah, God. It's better now."

His fingers dug into my hips. "I want you more now."

Gasping, I pressed my temple to his. "Help me."

"Hold on." Yanking my hips down, he thrust upward, shoving into me. "Take it, Eva. Take it all."

I cried out and ground into him, moving on instinct, taking the last of him.

"Yes . . . yes . . ." I gasped, slamming my hips into his, pumping my sex up and down the rigid length of his erection.

Gideon's face was harsh with lust, brutally etched with his need. "I'm going to come so hard for you," he promised darkly. "You'll feel me in you all night."

The sound of his voice . . . the way he'd looked onstage . . . I'd never been so excited. He wasn't the only one who'd be coming hard.

His head fell back against the seat, his chest heaving, harsh sounds of pleasure scraping from his throat. His hands released me, clenching into fists against the seat. He let me fuck him the way I needed to, let me use him.

Arching back, I climaxed with a cry, my entire body shaking, my sex grasping, rippling along his cock. My rhythm faltered, my vision blackened. An endless moan poured out of me, the relief dizzying.

The world shifted and I was on my back, Gideon rising over me, his arm hooking beneath my left leg to lift it to his shoulder. He dug his feet into the floorboard, thrusting again and again, sinking deep. So deep.

I writhed, the feel of him so good it hurt.

He kept me pinned, opened and defenseless, using me as I'd used him, his control shattered by the need to orgasm. The power of his body as he pounded into me, the force with which he drove his cock into my tender sex, had me quivering on the verge again.

"I love you," I moaned, my hands stroking down his flexing thighs.

He growled my name and started coming, his teeth clenching, his hips pressed tight to my own, screwing deep. It set me off, the feel of him coming inside me.

"So good," he groaned, rocking into the spasms of my sex.

We strained together, grasping at each other.

He buried his face in my throat. "Love you."

Tears stung my eyes. He said the words so rarely.

"Tell me again," I begged, holding on to him.

His mouth found mine. "I love you . . ."

"More," I demanded, licking my lips.

Gideon glanced over his shoulder at me. Bacon sizzled in the pan in front of him and my mouth watered for another slice. "And here I'd thought two packs of bacon would last us all weekend."

"Grease is a must after a night of drinking," I told him, wiping some off my plate with my fingertip and lifting it to my mouth. "When you're not hung over, that is."

"Which I am," Cary muttered, walking into the kitchen in just his jeans, which he hadn't bothered buttoning all the way. "Got any beer?"

Gideon pointed at the fridge with his tongs. "Bottom drawer."

I shook my head at my best friend. "Hair of the dog this morning?"

"Hell, yeah. My head feels like it's splitting in two." Cary pulled a beer out and joined me at the island. He popped the cap off and tipped the bottle back, gulping down half the contents at once.

"How'd you sleep?" I asked, mentally crossing my fingers.

He'd stayed the night in the attached single-bedroom apartment, and I hoped he loved it. It had all the beautiful prewar details of Gideon's penthouse and was furnished similarly. I knew Cary's style was more contemporary, but he couldn't fault the view of Central Park. All the rest could be changed, if he just said the word.

He lowered the bottle from his mouth. "Like the dead."

"Do you like the apartment?"

"Of course. Who wouldn't?"

"Do you want to live there?" I persisted.

Cary gave me a lopsided smile. "Yeah, baby girl. It's a dream. Thank you for the pity fuck, Gideon."

My husband turned away from the stove with a plate of bacon in his hand. "There is neither pity nor fucking included in the offer," he said dryly. "Otherwise, you're welcome."

I clapped my hands. "Yay! I'm stoked."

Gideon snagged a piece of bacon and stuck it in his mouth. Leaning forward, I parted my lips. He bent toward me, letting me bite off the end.

"Come on," Cary groaned. "I'm fighting nausea as it is."

I shoved him gently. "Shut up."

He grinned and finished his beer. "Gotta give you guys a hard time. Who else is going to stop you two from singing 'I Got You, Babe' in a few years?"

Thinking of Will and Natalie made me smile. I'd discovered even more to like about Will and found that I got along well with his girl, too. "Aren't they adorable? They've been together since high school."

"Exactly my point," he drawled. "Spend enough years with someone and either you start bickering or you fall down the lovey-dovey hole, never to be seen again."

"Mark and Steven have been together for years, too," I argued. "They don't fight or moon at each other."

He shot me a look. "They're gay, Eva. No estrogen in the mix to cause drama."

"Oh my God. You sexist pig! You did not just say that."

Cary glanced at Gideon. "You know I'm right."

"And with that," Gideon declared, grabbing three strips of bacon, "I'm out."

"Hey!" I complained after him, as he exited to the living room.

My best friend laughed. "Don't worry. He hitched himself to your brand of female."

I glared at him as I munched another piece of bacon. "I'm giving you a pass, because I owe you for last night."

"It was fun. Megumi's good people." His humor fled, his face darkening. "I'm sorry she's going through what she is."

"Yeah, me, too."

"You make any decisions about how you're going to help others like her?"

I set my elbows on the island. "I'm going to talk to Gideon about working with his Crossroads Foundation."

"Hell. Why didn't you think of that before?"

"Because . . . I'm stubborn, I guess." I glanced over my shoulder at the living room, then lowered my voice. "One of the things Gideon likes about me is that I don't always do everything he wants just because he wants it. He's not like Stanton."

"And you don't want to be like your mom.

Does this mean you're keeping your maiden name?"

"No way. It means a lot to Gideon for me to become Eva Cross. Besides, it sounds kick-ass."

"It does." He tapped the end of my nose with his finger. "I'm here for you when you need me."

Sliding off the stool, I hugged him. "Same goes."

"I'm taking you up on that, obviously." His chest heaved with a deep sigh. "Big changes happening, baby girl. You ever get scared?"

I looked up at him, feeling the affinity that had gotten us both through some hard times. "More than I let myself think about."

"I have to run to the office," Gideon interjected, stepping back into the kitchen wearing a Yankees ball cap. He'd kept the same gray T-shirt on but had swapped out his pajama bottoms for sweats. A ring of keys twirled around his finger. "I won't be long."

"Is everything all right?" I asked, backing away from Cary. My husband was wearing his game face, the one that told me his mind was already on whatever he was going to deal with.

"Everything's fine." He came to me and

gave me a quick kiss. "I'll be back in a couple of hours. Ireland won't be here 'til six."

He left. I stared after him.

What was important enough to drag him away from me on a weekend? Gideon was possessive about a lot of things when it came to me, but our time together topped the list. And the key-twirling thing was kind of weird. Gideon wasn't a man given to wasted movement. The only times I'd seen him fidget were when he was completely relaxed or the opposite — ready to throw down.

I couldn't shake the feeling that he was hiding something from me. As usual.

"I'm gonna take a shower," Cary said, grabbing a bottled water out of the fridge. "You want to watch a movie when I get out?"

"Sure," I said absently. "Sounds like a plan."

I waited until he'd gone back into the attached apartment, then went to find my phone.

11

"Where's Eva?"

I rounded the front of the Benz and stepped onto the curb in front of Brett Kline. My fingers twitched, the habit of extending my hand in greeting ruthlessly suppressed. The singer's hands had touched my wife intimately in the past . . . and recently. I didn't want to shake them. I wanted to break them.

"At our home," I answered, gesturing at the entrance to the Crossfire Building. "Let's go up to my office."

Kline smiled coldly. "You can't keep me from her."

"You did that all by yourself." I noted the worn Pete's T-shirt he was wearing with black jeans and leather boots. Without a doubt, his choice of attire wasn't a coincidence. He wanted to remind Eva of their history together. Maybe even remind me, too. Had Yimara given him the idea? I wouldn't be surprised.

It was the wrong move for both men to have made.

He walked through the revolving doors ahead of me. Security took his information and printed out a temporary ID, then we headed through the turnstiles to the elevators.

"You can't intimidate me with your money," he said tightly.

I entered the car and hit the button for the top floor. "There are eyes and ears all over the city. At least in my office, I know we won't be putting on a show."

His lip curled in disgust. "Is that all you care about? Public perception?"

"An ironic question, considering who you are and what you want."

"Don't act like you know me," he growled. "You know shit."

In the confined space of the elevator car, Kline's aggression and frustration permeated the space between us. His hands gripped the handrail behind him, his stance hostile and expectant. From the platinum tips of his spiked hair to the black-and-gray tattoos covering his arms, the front man of Six-Ninths couldn't be more different from me in appearance. I used to feel threatened by that and his history with Eva, but no longer.

Not after San Diego. And certainly not after last night.

I could still feel the marks of Eva's nails in my back and ass. She'd pushed me to my limits all night and into the early hours of the morning. The insatiable hunger she felt for me left no room for anyone else. And the catch in her voice when she told me she loved me, the sheen of tears in her eyes when I yielded to what she did to me . . .

I leaned back against the opposite wall and tucked my hands into the pockets of my sweats, knowing my nonchalance would goad him.

"Does she know we're meeting like this?" he asked harshly.

"I figured I'd leave it up to you to decide whether to mention it."

"Oh, I'm mentioning it all right."

"I hope you do."

We exited into the Cross Industries foyer and I led him through the security doors and back to my office. There were a few people at their desks and I took note of them. Those who worked on their days off weren't always better employees than those who didn't, but I respected ambition and rewarded it.

When we got to my office, I shut the doors behind us and frosted the glass. A folder sat on my desk, as I'd instructed before leaving the penthouse. I set my hand atop it and gestured for Kline to take a seat.

He remained standing. "What the fuck is this about? I come into town to see Eva and your goon brings me here instead."

The "goon" was security provided by Vidal Records, but he wasn't wrong in thinking the man worked for me. "I'm prepared to offer you a great deal of money — along with other incentives — for the exclusive rights to the Yimara footage of you and Eva."

He gave me a hard smile. "Sam told me you were going to try this. That tape is none of your business. It's between me and Eva."

"And the entire world if it leaks, and that would destroy her. Does that matter to you at all, how she feels about it?"

"It's not going to leak, and of course I give a shit about how she feels. It's one of the reasons we need to talk."

I nodded. "You want to ask her what you can use. You think you can talk her into letting you exploit some of it."

He rocked back on his feet, a restless move that signaled a direct hit.

"You're not going to get the answer you

hope for," I told him. "The very existence of that tape horrifies her. You're an idiot if you think otherwise."

"It's not all sex. There's some good stuff of us hanging out. Her and I, we had something. She wasn't just a lay to me."

Piece of shit. I had to control the impulse to deck him.

He smirked. "Not that you'd understand. You had no problem banging away at that brunette until I came back into the picture, then you changed up your game. Eva's a toy you got bored with. Until someone else wanted her."

His mention of Corinne hit a harsh chord. The charade of dating my ex had nearly cost me Eva, a close call that still haunted me.

That didn't prevent me from noticing how good he was at shifting the blame. "Eva knows what she means to me."

He stepped closer to my desk. "She's too blinded by your billions to realize there's something really wrong with you hiding that bogus wedding in a foreign country. Is it even legal?"

It was a question I'd anticipated. "Absolutely legal."

Opening the folder, I pulled out the photo inside. It was taken on the day of my wedding, at the very moment I first kissed Eva

276

as her husband. The beach and the pastor who had officiated at the ceremony were behind us. I cupped her face, our lips touching softly. Her hands held my wrists, my ring sparkling on her finger.

I turned the picture around so that it faced him. I slid a copy of the marriage license into place beside it. I used my left hand, proudly displaying my ruby-encrusted wedding band.

I wasn't sharing such personal things to prove a point. I intended to provoke Kline, which I'd been deliberately doing from the moment he arrived in New York. When he reached out to my wife again, I wanted him off-balance and at a disadvantage.

"So you and Eva are done," I said evenly. "If you doubted it, now you know it for sure. In any case, I don't think you want my wife as much as you want the memory of her for the band's use."

Kline laughed. "Yeah, paint me as the sleaze. You can't handle the thought of her seeing that tape. You've never made her get that wild and you never will."

My forearms twitched with the need to pound the smugness out of his face. "Believe what you like. Here are your options: You can take the two million I'm offering, give me the footage, and walk away —"

"I don't want your damn money!" Setting his hands on the edge of my desk, he leaned toward me. "You don't get to own my memories. You may have her — for now — but I have those. Fuck if I'm selling them to you."

The thought of Kline watching the footage . . . watching himself fuck my wife . . . set my blood on a slow boil. The thought of him suggesting that Eva sit through a viewing of it, knowing how that would shatter her, pushed me to the raw edge of violence.

Keeping my tone even was a struggle. "You can reject the money and keep the existence of the footage to yourself until you die. Make it a secret gift to Eva she never has to know about."

"What the fuck are you talking about?"

"Or you can be a selfish asshole," I continued, "and hit her up with it, shocking her with the goal of destroying her marriage and making yourself more famous."

I stared him down. Kline stood his ground, but his gaze dropped for a fraction of a second. A small victory, for what it was worth.

With a swipe of my hand, I withdrew the contract Arash had drawn up. "If you care about her at all, you'll make a different decision than the one that brought you to New York."

He grabbed the documents off my desk and ripped them in half, throwing the pieces back onto the glass. "I'm not leaving until I see her."

Kline strode out of my office, bristling with anger.

I watched him go. Then I placed a call via a secure line. "Did I give you enough time?"

"Yes. We took care of the laptop and tablet in his luggage as soon as you took him upstairs. We're handling his e-mail and backup provider servers as we speak, and the backups to those servers. We searched his residence over the weekend, but he hasn't been there in weeks. We cleaned everything on both Yimara and Kline's equipment, as well as the accounts and equipment of those who received teasers of the full-length footage. One of the execs at Vidal had a full copy on his hard drive, but we wiped it. We found no evidence that he forwarded it anywhere."

Ice slid through my veins. "Which executive?"

"Your brother."

Fuck. I gripped the edge of my desk so hard my knuckles cracked with the strain. I remembered the video of Christopher with

Magdalene, knew how perverse his hatred toward me was. Thinking about him seeing Eva so intimately . . . so vulnerable . . . took me to a place I hadn't been since I'd first heard about Nathan.

I had to believe that the private military security firm I'd hired had dealt with the situation thoroughly. Their tech teams were trained to handle far more sensitive information.

I shoved the mess on my desk into the folder. "I need that footage to cease to exist anywhere."

"Understood. We're on it. Still, it's possible there's a hard copy floating around, although we've searched Kline and Yimara's transaction records for security deposit boxes and the like. We'll continue to monitor the situation until you say otherwise."

I never would. I'd search for a lifetime, if that was what it took, for any hint that the footage survived somewhere outside of my control. "Thank you."

Hanging up, I left my office and headed home to Eva.

"You're really good with those," Ireland said, eyeing Eva as she lifted a chopstickful of kung pao chicken from its white box to her mouth. "I never got the hang of 'em."

"Here, try holding them like this."

I watched my wife adjust my sister's grip on the slender sticks, her blond head a bright contrast against Ireland's black hair. Sitting on the floor at my feet, they both wore shorts and tank tops, their tanned legs stretched out beneath the coffee table, one long and lean, the other petite and voluptuous.

I was more of an observer than a participant, sitting on the couch behind them and envying their easy rapport even while I was grateful for it.

It was all so surreal. I hadn't ever imagined a night like that, a quiet evening at home with . . . family. I didn't know how to contribute or even if I could. What could I say? How should I feel?

Besides awed. And thankful. So very thankful for my amazing wife, who brought so much to my life.

Not long ago, on a similar Saturday night, I would have been at a highly publicized social function or event, focusing on business unless or until a woman's keen interest spurred a need to fuck. Whether I returned to the penthouse by myself or ended up at the hotel with a one-night stand, I'd be alone. And since I hardly remembered what it felt like to belong anywhere, to anyone, I didn't know what I was missing.

"Ha! Look at that," Ireland crowed, holding up a tiny bit of orange chicken, which she promptly ate. "Made it to my mouth."

I swallowed the wine in my glass in a single gulp, wanting to say *something.* My mind raced with options, all of which sounded insincere and contrived. In the end what came out was, "The chopsticks have a large target. Ups your chances."

Ireland turned her head toward me, revealing the same blue eyes I saw in the mirror every day. They were much less guarded, far more innocent, and bright with laughter and adoration. "Did you just call me a big mouth?"

Unable to resist, I ran my hand over the crown of her head, touching the silky soft strands of her hair. Those, too, were like mine and yet not. "Not my words," I said.

"Not *in so many* words," she corrected, leaning briefly into my touch before turning back to Eva.

Eva glanced up at me, offering an encouraging smile. She knew I drew strength from her, and she gave it unconditionally.

My throat tight, I rose from the couch and grabbed Eva's empty wineglass. Ireland's glass of soda was still half full, so I left it and headed to the kitchen, trying to regain enough equanimity to make it through the rest of the evening.

"Channing Tatum is so hot," Ireland said, her voice traveling from the living room. "Don't you think?"

I frowned. My baby sister's idle question triggered uncomfortable thoughts of her dating. She had to have started a few years ago — she was seventeen. I knew it was unrealistic to want her to stay away from boys. I knew it was my fault that I'd missed so much of her childhood. But the thought of her having to deal with younger versions of men like me and Manuel and Cary roused an unfamiliar defensive reaction.

"He's very good-looking," Eva agreed.

Possessiveness rose to join the mix. My gaze narrowed on the two glasses in front of me as I refilled them.

"He's this year's Sexiest Man Alive," Ireland said. "Look at those biceps."

"Ah, now on that, I have to totally disagree. Gideon is way sexier."

My mouth curved.

"You're such a goner," my sister teased. "Your pupils turn into little hearts when you think about Gideon. It's so cute."

"Shut up."

Ireland's musical laugh floated through the air. "Don't worry. He's goofy over you, too. And he's been on every Sexiest Man Alive list for ages. I never hear the end of it from my friends."

"Gah. Don't tell me stuff like that. I'm jealous by nature."

Laughing inwardly, I dropped the empty bottle into the recycling bin.

"So is Gideon. He's going to flip out when you start hitting the Hottest Women Alive lists. No way to avoid it now that everyone's heard of you."

"Whatever," Eva scoffed. "They'd have to Photoshop fifteen pounds off my ass and thighs to sell that."

"Um, have you seen Kim Kardashian? Or Jennifer Lopez?"

I paused on the threshold of the living room, taking in the picture Ireland and Eva made over the rim of my glass. An ache bloomed in my chest. I wanted to freeze the moment, protect it, keep it safe forever.

Ireland looked up and spotted me, then rolled her eyes. "What did I tell you?" she said. "Goofy."

Sitting back in my chair, I sipped coffee and studied the spreadsheet on my monitor. I rolled my shoulders back, trying to loosen the kink in my neck.

"Dude. What the hell? It's three in the

morning."

I looked up to find Ireland standing in the doorway to my home office. "Your point?"

"Why are you working so late?"

"Why are you Skyping so late?" I countered, having heard her laughter and occasionally raised voice over the last hour or so since I'd left Eva sleeping.

"Whatev," she muttered, coming in and dropping into one of the chairs in front of my desk. She slouched, her shoulders even with the chair back and her legs sprawled out in front of her. "Can't sleep?"

"No." She didn't know how literally true that was. With Ireland sleeping in Eva's bed and Eva sleeping in mine, I couldn't risk going to sleep myself. There was only so much I could expect Eva to take, only so many times I could frighten her before it destroyed the love she felt for me.

"Christopher texted me a bit ago," she said. "Guess Dad's staying at a hotel."

My brows rose.

She nodded, her face forlorn. "It's bad, Gideon. They haven't spent a night apart ever. At least that I can remember."

I didn't know what to say. Our mother had been calling me all day, leaving messages on my voice mail and ringing the penthouse so often I'd been forced to disconnect the main receiver so that none of the phones would ring. I hated that my mother was struggling, but I had to protect my time with Ireland and Eva.

It felt heartless to focus on myself, but I'd already lost my family twice before — once when my father died and again after Hugh. I couldn't afford to lose any more. I didn't think I could survive it a third time, not with Eva in my life.

"I just wish I knew what caused the fight," she said. "I mean as long as they didn't cheat on each other, they should be able to get through it, right?"

Exhaling roughly, I straightened. "I'm not the person to ask about relationships. I have no idea how they work. I'm just stumbling my way through, praying not to fuck things up, and grateful that Eva is so forgiving."

"You really love her."

I followed her gaze to the collage of photos on the wall. It hurt sometimes, looking at those pictures of my wife. I wanted to recapture and relive every moment. I wanted to hoard every second I'd ever had with her. I hated that time slipped away so quickly and I couldn't bank it for the uncertain future.

"Yes," I murmured. I'd forgive Eva any-thing. There was nothing she could do or say that would break us apart, because I couldn't live without her.

"I'm happy for you, Gideon." Ireland smiled when I looked at her.

"Thank you." The worry in her eyes lingered and sparked restlessness. I wanted to fix the problems troubling her, but I didn't know how.

"Could you talk to Mom?" she suggested. "Not now, of course. But tomorrow? Maybe you can find out what's going on?"

I hesitated a moment, knowing a conversation with our mother was certain to be unproductive. "I'll try."

Ireland studied her nails. "You don't like Mom very much, do you?"

Weighing my answer carefully, I said, "We have a fundamental difference of opinion."

"Yeah. I get it. It's like she's got this weird form of OCD that applies to her family. Everyone has to be a particular way or at least pretend to be. She's so worried about what people think. I saw an old movie the other day that reminded me of her. *Ordinary People*. Ever seen it?"

"No, can't say I have."

"You should watch it. It has Kiefer Sutherland's dad in it and some other people. It's sad, but it's a good story."

"I'll look it up." Feeling the need to

explain our mother, I tried my best. "What she dealt with after my father died . . . It was brutal. She's insulated herself since then, I think."

"My friend's mother says Mom used to be different before. You know, when she was married to your dad."

I set my cooled coffee aside. "I do remember her differently."

"Better?"

"That's subjective. She was more . . . spontaneous. Carefree."

Ireland rubbed at her mouth with her fingertips. "Do you think it broke her? Losing your dad?"

My chest tightened. "It changed her," I said quietly. "I'm not sure how much."

"Ugh." She sat up, visibly shaking off her melancholy. "You going to be awake awhile?"

"Probably all night."

"Wanna watch that movie with me?"

The suggestion surprised me. And pleased me. "Depends. You can't tell me what happens. No spoilers."

She shot me a look. "I already told you it's sad. If you want happily ever after, she's sleeping down the hall."

That made me smile. Standing, I rounded

my desk. "You find the movie, I'll grab the soda."

"A beer would be good."

"Not on my watch."

She pushed to her feet with a grin. "Okay, fine. Wine, then."

"Ask me again in a few years."

"You'll have kids by then. It won't be as fun."

I paused, hit by anxiety sharp enough to mist my skin with sweat. The thought of having a baby with Eva both thrilled and terrified me. It wasn't safe for my wife to live with me. How could it ever be safe for a child?

Ireland laughed. "Holy fuck, you should see your face! A classic case of playboy panic. Didn't they tell you? First comes love, then comes marriage, then comes the baby in the baby carriage."

"If you don't shut up, I'm sending you to bed."

She laughed harder and linked her arm with mine. "You're a riot. Seriously. I'm just messing with you. Don't flip out on me. I've got enough family members doing that."

I willed my heart to stop pounding so damn hard.

"Maybe *you* should have a drink," she suggested.

"I think I will," I muttered.

"I'm going to give major props to Eva for getting a ring out of you. Did you have a panic attack when you proposed, too?"

"Stop talking, Ireland."

Leaning her head against my shoulder, she giggled and led me out of my office.

The sun had been up for over two hours by the time I returned to bed. I stripped silently, my gaze roaming over the delectable bump under the covers that was my wife.

Eva was curled in a ball, mostly hidden except for the bright strands of hair splayed over the pillow. My mind filled in the blanks, knowing she was naked between the sheets.

Mine. All mine.

It killed me to sleep away from her. I knew it hurt her, too.

Lifting the edge of the blankets, I slid in beside her. She gave a soft little moan and rolled toward me, her lush warm body wriggling into place against me.

I was instantly hard. Desire simmered in my blood; awareness tingled along my skin. It was combustible sexual chemistry but also something more. Something deeper. A strange, wonderful, frightening recognition.

She filled an emptiness in me I hadn't

known was there.

Eva buried her face in my throat and hummed softly, her legs tangling with mine, her hands gliding over my back. "Hard and yummy all over," she purred.

"All over," I agreed, cupping her ass and pulling her tighter against my hard-on.

Her shoulders shook with a silent laugh. "We have to be quiet."

"I'll cover your mouth."

"Me?" She nipped at my throat. "You're the noisy one."

She wasn't wrong. As rough and impatient as I could get when aroused, I'd never been loud . . . until her. It was a struggle to be discreet when situations called for it. She felt too good, made me feel too much.

"So we'll take it slow," I murmured, my hands roaming greedily over her silky skin. "Ireland will be sleeping for hours; there's no rush."

"Hours, huh?" Laughing, she pulled back and rolled away from me, reaching for the nightstand drawer. "Overachiever."

Tension stretched across my shoulders as she dug out the breath mints she kept handy. I was reminded of similar situations, when women had reached into the night-stand drawer for condoms.

Eva and I had used condoms only twice.

Before her, I'd never fucked a woman without one. Avoiding pregnancy was something I'd religiously adhered to.

Yet since those first two times with Eva, we'd gone bare, relying on her birth control to prevent conception.

It was a risk. I knew that. And considering how often I had her — at least two, sometimes three or four times a day — the risk was not inconsiderable.

I thought of it sometimes. I questioned my control, my selfishness in putting my own pleasure above the consequences. But the reason for my recklessness wasn't as simple as pleasure. If it were, I could deal. Be responsible.

No, it was much more complicated.

The need to come inside her was primitive. It was a conquest and surrender in one.

I had wanted to fuck her raw before I'd even had her the first time, before I knew definitively how explosive it would be between us. I'd gone so far as to warn her prior to our first date that I needed it, needed her to give me that, something I'd never wanted with anyone else.

"Don't move," I said roughly, sliding over her while she was still stretched out on her stomach. My hand pushed between her hip and the bed, reaching between her legs to cup her cunt in my palm. She was moist and warm. My stroking fingers made her slick and hot.

She muffled a moan.

"I want you just like this," I told her, brushing my lips across her cheek.

Reaching for my pillow with my free hand, I yanked it over and then shoved it under her, lifting her hips to an angle that would let me sink balls-deep.

"Gideon . . ." The way she said my name was a plea, as if I wouldn't get down on my knees and beg for the privilege of having her.

I shifted, urging her legs apart and pinning her wrists beside her head. Holding her down, I thrust into her. She was ready for me, plush and tight and wet. My teeth gritted together to restrain the growl that surged from my throat, a tremor racking my body from head to toe. My chest heaved against her back, my violent exhalations ruffling her hair lying across the pillow.

Just like that, just by taking me, she had me right on the edge.

"God." My hips churned without volition, screwing my cock into her, pushing me deeper until I was in her to the hilt. I could feel her all around me, from root to tip, clenching in ripples that milked me like a greedy little mouth. "Angel —"

The pressure at the base of my dick was insistent, but I was capable of staving it off. It wasn't a question of control, but of will.

I *wanted* to come inside her. Wanted it enough to consider the risk — as terrifying as it was — acceptable.

Closing my eyes, I dropped my forehead to her cheek. I inhaled the scent of her and let go, coming hard, my ass flexing as I filled her up in thick, hot spurts.

Eva whimpered, writhing under me. Her cunt tightened, then trembled around my cock. She climaxed with a soft, sweet moan.

I growled her name, searingly aroused by her orgasm. She came because I did, because my pleasure turned her on as much as my touch. I would reward her for that, show her the depth of my gratitude. She would get hers, over and over again, as many times as she could take it.

"Eva." I rubbed my damp cheek against hers. "Crossfire."

Her fingers tightened their grip on mine. Her head turned, her lips seeking.

"Ace," she breathed into the kiss. "I love you, too."

It was shortly after five in the evening when I drove the Bentley through the gates of the

Vidal estate in Dutchess County and into the circular drive out front.

"Aw, you drove too fast," Ireland complained from the backseat. "We're here already."

I put the SUV in park and left it idling. One look at the house, and a knot tightened in my gut. Eva reached over, taking my hand and giving it a squeeze. I focused on her steely gray eyes instead of the Tudor-style mansion at her back.

She didn't say a word, but she didn't have to. I felt her love and support and saw the glimmer of anger in her eyes. Just knowing she understood gave me strength. She knew every dark and dirty secret I had, and yet she believed and loved me anyway.

"I want to stay over again sometime," Ireland said, poking her head between the two front seats. "It was fun, right?"

I looked at her. "We'll do it again."

"Soon?"

"All right."

Her smile more than made the promise worth what it would cost me in sleep and anxiety. I'd stayed away from her for many reasons, but the main one was that I didn't know what I could offer her of any value. I'd channeled everything into keeping Vidal Records afloat for her well into the future, taking care of her the only way I knew I wouldn't screw up.

"You'll have to help me out," I told her honestly. "I don't know how to be a brother. You will probably have to forgive me. Frequently."

The smile left Ireland's face, transforming her from a teenager to a young woman. "Well, it's like being a friend," she said somberly. "Except you *have* to remember birthdays and holidays, you have to forgive me for everything, and you should introduce me to all your hot, rich guy friends."

My brow lifted. "Where's the part about me picking on you and giving you a hard time?"

"You missed those years," she shot back. "No do-overs."

She meant to tease, but the words struck home. I *had* missed years and I couldn't get them back.

"You get to pick on her boyfriends instead," Eva said, "and give *them* a hard time."

Our eyes met and I knew she understood exactly what I was thinking. My thumb stroked over her knuckles.

Behind her, the front door opened and my mother stepped out. She stood on the wide top step dressed in a white tunic and matching pants. Her long, dark hair hung loosely around her shoulders. From a distance, she looked so much like Ireland, more of a sister than a parent.

My grip on Eva's hand tightened.

Ireland sighed and opened her door. "I wish you guys didn't have to work tomorrow. I mean, what's the point of being a gazillionaire if you can't play hooky when you want?"

"If Eva worked with me," I said, looking at my wife, "we could."

She stuck her tongue out. "Don't start."

I lifted her hand to my mouth and kissed the back. "I haven't stopped."

Opening my door, I stepped out of the car and hit the hatch release. I rounded the back of the car to retrieve Ireland's bag and found my arms full of her instead. She hugged me tightly, her slender arms wrapped around my waist. It took me a moment to unfreeze from my surprise, and then I hugged her back, my cheek coming to rest on the crown of her head.

"I love you," she mumbled into my chest. "Thanks for having me over."

My throat closed tight, preventing me from saying anything. She was gone as quickly as she'd come at me, her duffel in hand as she met Eva on the passenger side and hugged her, too.

Feeling as winded as if I'd been punched, I closed the hatch and watched as my mother met Ireland halfway across the blue-gray gravel drive. I was about to return to the wheel and leave, when she signaled at me to wait.

I glanced at Eva. "Get in the car, angel."

She looked as if she might argue, and then she nodded and slid back into the front passenger seat and closed the door.

I waited until my mother came to me.

"Gideon." She caught me by the biceps and lifted onto her tiptoes to press a kiss to my mouth. "Won't you and Eva come in? You drove all this way."

I took a step backward, breaking her hold. "And we have to drive back."

Her gaze reflected her disappointment. "Just for a few minutes. Please. I'd like to apologize to both of you. I haven't handled the news of your engagement well and I'm sorry about that. This should be a happy time for our family, and I'm afraid I've been too worried about losing my son to appreciate it."

"Mom." I caught her arm when she moved toward the passenger side. "Not now."

"I didn't mean all those things I said about Eva the other day. It was just a shock,

298

seeing the ring your father gave me on another woman's hand. You didn't give the ring to Corinne, so I was surprised. You can understand that, can't you?"

"You antagonized Eva."

"Is that what she told you?" She paused. "I never meant to, but — Never mind. Your father was very protective, too. You're so like him."

I looked away, gazing absently at the trees beyond the drive. I never knew how to take comparisons to Geoffrey Cross. Were they meant as praise or a backhanded compliment? There was no telling with my mother.

"Gideon . . . please, I'm trying. I said some things to Eva I shouldn't have, and she responded as any woman would under the circumstances. I just want to smooth things over." She set her hand over my heart. "I'm happy for you, Gideon. And I'm so glad to see you and Ireland spending time together. I know it means so much to her."

I pulled her hand away gently. "It means a lot to me, too. And Eva made it possible in ways I won't explain. Which is just one of the reasons I won't have her upset. Not now. She has to work in the morning."

"Let's make plans for lunch this week, then. Or dinner."

"Will Chris be there?" Eva asked through the window before pushing the door open again and stepping out. She stood there, so small and bright against the dark hulking SUV, formidable in the way her shoulders were set.

My wife would fight the world for me. It was miraculous to know that. When no one else had fought for me, I'd somehow found the one soul who would.

My mother's lips curved. "Of course. Chris and I are a team."

I noted the brittleness of her smile and doubted her, as I so often did. Still, I conceded. "We'll make plans. Call Scott tomorrow and we'll work something out."

My mother's face brightened. "I'm so glad. Thank you."

She hugged me and I braced myself, my body stiff with the need to push her away. When she approached Eva with her arms outstretched, Eva thrust out her hand between them to shake instead. The interaction was awkward, with both women so obviously on the defensive.

My mother didn't want to mend fences; she wanted an agreement to pretend the fences were sound.

We said good-bye, and then I slid into the driver's seat. Eva and I took off, leaving the estate behind us. We hadn't gone far when she said, "When did your mother talk to you?"

Damn it. I knew what that bite in her tone signified.

Reaching over, I set my hand on her knee. "I don't want you worrying about my mother."

"You don't want me worrying about anything! That's not the way this is gonna work. You don't get to deal with all the crap alone."

"What my mother says or does isn't important, Eva. I don't give a shit and neither should you."

She twisted in the seat to face me. "You need to start sharing stuff. Especially things that have to do with me, like your mother saying things behind my back!"

"I won't have you getting pissed off over an irrelevant opinion." The road curved. I accelerated out of the turn.

"That would be better than me getting pissed off at *you*!" she snapped. "Pull over."

"What?" I glanced at her.

"Pull the damn car over!"

Cursing inwardly, I removed my hand from her leg and gripped the wheel. "Tell me why."

"Because I'm mad at you, and you're sitting there looking all hot and sexy driving and you need to stop."

Amusement warred with exasperation. "Stop what? Looking hot and sexy? Or driving?"

"Gideon . . . don't push me right now."

Resigned, I eased off the gas and pulled to a stop on the narrow shoulder. "Better?"

She got out of the car and went around the hood. I stepped out, giving her a questioning glance.

"*I'm* driving," she announced when she was standing in front of me. "At least until we get to the city."

"If that's what you want."

I knew next to nothing about relationships, but it was a no-brainer to make concessions when your woman was mad at you. Especially when you entertained hopes of getting laid in a few hours, which I most definitely was. After spending the weekend with friends and Ireland, I was feeling a renewed need to show my wife just how much I appreciated her.

"Don't look at me like that," she muttered.

"Like what?" I raked her with a glance, admiring how pretty she looked in a strappy white sundress. The evening was hot and muggy, but she looked airy and fresh. I wanted to strip off my clothes and press up against her, cool off a little before heating things up.

"Like I'm a ticking time bomb ready to go off!" Her arms crossed. "I am *not* being irrational."

"Angel, that's not the look I'm giving you."

"And don't try to distract me with sex," she bit out, her jaw clenched. "Or you won't get any for a week!"

My arms crossed, too. "We've already talked about issuing ultimatums like that. You can bitch at me all you like, Eva, but I'll have you when I want you. Period."

"Never mind whether I want you?"

"Asks the wife who gets wet watching me drive a damn car," I drawled.

Her gaze narrowed. "I may just leave you here on the side of the road."

Clearly, I wasn't navigating the situation well. So I switched tactics, taking the offensive position.

"You don't tell me everything," I countered. "What about Kline? Has he completely stopped communicating with you since San Diego?"

I'd been holding back the question all weekend, wondering how Kline was going to handle Eva.

I was torn about how I wanted him to proceed. If he approached her about the tape he no longer possessed, it would hurt her but also drive her closer to me. If he walked away for her sake, it would betray deeper feelings for her than I was comfortable with. I hated that he wanted her, but I feared he might actually love her.

She gasped. "Oh my God. Have you been looking at my phone again?"

"No." My reply was swift and decisive. "I know how you feel about that."

I followed her every move, knew where she was and who she was with at every moment of the day, but she'd set a hard limit with her cell phone and I honored it, even though it drove me crazy.

Eva studied me a minute but must have seen the truth on my face. "Yes, Brett has sent me a few texts. I was going to talk to you about it, so don't even try to say it's the same thing. I totally intended to tell you. You had absolutely no intention of telling me."

A car rushed by on the road, turning my concern toward her safety. "Get in and drive. We'll talk in the car."

I waited until she climbed into the seat, and then I shut the door behind her. By the time I settled in the passenger side, she'd adjusted the mirrors and seat to suit her and put the car in gear.

The minute she was fully merged in the lane, she started in on me again. I was vaguely aware of her speaking, my attention more focused on the way she handled the Bentley. She drove fast and with confidence, her grip light and easy on the wheel. She kept her gaze on the road, but I couldn't take my eyes off her. My California girl. On an open road, she was fully in her element.

I found myself pleasantly aroused by watching Eva handle the powerful SUV. Or maybe it was that she was chastising me, challenging me.

"Are you listening to me?" she demanded.

"Not really, angel. And before you get more riled, it's entirely your fault. You're sitting there looking hot and sexy, and I'm distracted."

Her hand whipped out and smacked my thigh. "Seriously? Stop cracking jokes!"

"I'm not kidding. Eva . . . you want me to share, so you can support me. I get it. I'm working on it."

"Not hard enough apparently."

"I'm not going to share things that aggravate you unnecessarily. There's no point."

"We have to be straight with each other,

Gideon. Not just occasionally, but all the time."

"Really? I don't expect the same from you. For example, feel free to keep all the unflattering comments your father and Cary make about me to yourself."

Her lips pursed. She chewed on that for a bit, then, "Using that logic, wouldn't it be okay for me to not say anything about Brett?"

"No. Kline impacts our relationship. My mother does not."

She snorted.

"I'm right about this," I said evenly.

"Are you telling me that your mom talking crap about me doesn't bother you?"

"I don't like it. That said, it doesn't change how I feel about you or her. And telling you won't change your feelings about her, either. Since the result is the same either way, I choose the path of least disruption."

"You're thinking like a guy."

"I should hope so." I reached over and brushed the hair off her shoulder. "Don't let her cause trouble between us, angel. She's not worth it."

Eva glanced at me. "You're pretending that what your mom says and does has no effect on you, but I know that's not true."

I debated denying it, just to shut down the topic, but my wife saw everything I'd rather hide. "I don't let it affect me."

"But it does. It hurts and you push it into that place where you push everything you don't want to deal with."

"Don't analyze me," I said tightly.

Her hand touched my thigh. "I love you. I want to stop the pain."

"You already have." I gripped her hand. "You've given me everything she took away. Don't let her take any more."

With her eyes on the winding road, Eva lifted our joined hands and kissed my wedding band. "Point taken."

She gave me a quick smile that told me she was done — for now — and drove us home.

12

I dared anyone to come up with a more awe-inspiring sight than Gideon Cross taking a shower.

It amazed me that he could be so matter-of-fact about running his hands over all that taut, tanned skin and those perfectly defined slabs of muscle. Through the misted glass of my bathroom shower, I watched the rivulets of soapy water run down the hard ridges of his abdomen and the length of his strong legs. His body was a work of art, a machine he kept in prime shape. I loved it. Loved looking at it, touching it, tasting it.

Reaching out, he swiped a hand through the condensation, revealing that breathtaking face. One darkly winged brow arched in silent query.

"Just enjoying the show," I explained. The scent of his soap teased senses that had become trained to recognize the fragrance as belonging to my mate. The man who stirred and pleasured my body to delirium.

I licked my lips when he casually stroked the heavy length of his cock. He'd once told me he used to masturbate every time he took a shower, a release he had considered as routine as brushing his teeth. I could see why, knowing how powerful his sexual appetite was. I would never forget the way he'd looked when he had jacked off in the shower for me, so virile and potent and hungry for orgasm.

Since he'd met me, he didn't pleasure himself anymore. Not because he couldn't still satisfy me if he did, and not because I took care of him enough to make the effort redundant. For both of us, being ready for sex with each other was never a problem, because the hunger we felt was deeper than physical.

Gideon teased me by saying he saved himself to satisfy my insatiability, but I saw the self-restraint for what it was — he gave me the right to his pleasure. It was mine and mine alone. He had none without me, which was a tremendous gift. Especially in light of his past, when sexual release had been used as a weapon against him.

"It's an interactive exhibition," he said, his eyes warm with amusement. "Join me."

"You're an animal." My thighs were wet

with his semen beneath my robe, since I was the lucky girl who woke up to his desire.

"Only for you."

"Ooh, right answer."

He smirked. His cock lengthened. "You should reward me."

I moved away from the threshold and stepped closer. "How would you suggest I do that?"

"Any way you like."

That was a gift, too. Gideon rarely relinquished control, and then only to me.

"I don't have enough time to do you justice, ace. I'd hate to cut things short when they're just getting interesting." I set my hand on the glass. "How about we revisit after my workout tonight? You, me, and whatever I want to do to you?"

He shifted and faced me head on, his hand lifting to press against mine through the glass. His gaze slid over my face in a heated caress that was damn near tangible. His face was impassive, a strikingly handsome mask that revealed nothing. But his eyes . . . those stunning blue depths . . . they exposed tenderness and love and vulnerability.

"I'm all yours, angel," he said, his words so quiet I saw them more than heard them.

I pressed a kiss to the cool glass. "Yes," I

agreed. "You are."

New week. Same ultrafocused Gideon. He started working as soon as the Bentley pulled away from the curb, his fingers flying across the keyboard built into a dropdown tray table. I watched him, finding his intense concentration and confidence extremely sexy. I was married to a powerful, driven man, and watching him flex that ambition was a major turn-on.

I was so into watching him that I jumped when my smartphone vibrated in my purse against my hip.

"Jeez," I muttered, digging it out.

Brett's name and photo appeared on the lock screen. Knowing I needed to deal with him at some point if I expected him to stop calling, I answered.

"Hey," I answered cautiously.

"Eva." The timbre of Brett's now-famous voice hit me as forcefully as it always had, but not in the same way. I loved the way he sang, but that love wasn't intimate anymore. It wasn't personal. I admired him the way I did a dozen other singers. "Damn it, I've been trying to reach you for a week!"

"I know. I'm sorry, I've been busy. How are you?"

"I've been better. I need to see you."

My brows rose. "When are you coming to town?"

He laughed harshly, a humorless sound that rubbed me the wrong way. "Incredible. Listen, I don't want to get into it on the phone. Can we get together today? We need to talk."

"You're in New York? I thought you were on tour . . . ?"

Gideon's rapid-fire typing didn't slow and he didn't look at me, but I could feel his energy shift. He was paying attention, and he knew who was on the line.

"I'll tell you what's going on when I see you," Brett said.

I frowned out the window as we idled at a light, my gaze on the flood of pedestrians crossing the street. New York was teeming with life and frenetic energy, gearing up to do world-changing business. "I'm on my way to work. What's going on, Brett?"

"I can meet you for lunch. Or after you get off for the day."

I debated saying no, but the determination in his tone gave me pause. "Okay."

Reaching over, I set my hand on Gideon's thigh. The toned muscle was hard beneath my palm, even though he was at rest. The tailored suits polished his form into civility, but I knew the truth about the vigorously fit body that was only hinted at underneath. "I can see you at lunch, if we stick close to the Crossfire Building."

"All right. What time should I be there?"

"A little before noon would be best. I'll meet you in the lobby."

We hung up and I dropped the phone back into my purse. Gideon's hand captured mine. I glanced at him, but he was reading a lengthy e-mail, his head bent slightly so that the ends of his hair brushed his sculpted jaw.

The warmth of his touch soaked into me. I looked down at the band he wore on his finger, the one that told the world he belonged to me.

Did his business associates pay attention to his hands? They weren't those of a man who pushed paper and tapped on keyboards all day. They were the hands of a fighter, a warrior who practiced mixed martial arts and pounded out his aggression with both boxing bags and sparring partners.

Kicking off my shoes, I curled my legs under me and leaned into Gideon's side, setting my other hand on top of his. I ran my splayed fingers between his knuckles and fingers, forward and back, carefully resting my head against his shoulder so that I didn't mess up his pristine black jacket with my makeup.

I breathed him in, feeling the effect of him — his nearness, his support — permeate my being. The smell of his soap was muted now, the naturally seductive scent of his skin altering the fragrance into something richer and more delicious.

When I was restless, he settled me.

"There's nothing for him," I whispered, needing him to know that. "I'm too filled with you."

His chest expanded abruptly, his sharp inhalation audible. He pushed the tray table up and away, then patted his lap in invitation. "Come here."

I crawled into his lap, sighing happily when he shifted me into a spot that felt made for me. Every peaceful moment we had with each other was treasured. Gideon deserved the respite, and I longed to be that for him.

His lips touched my forehead. "You okay, angel mine?"

"I'm in your arms. Life doesn't get better than this."

I spotted three paparazzi outside the Crossfire when we arrived.

With a hand at the small of my back, Gideon ushered me through the entrance ahead of him, escorting me quickly but unhurriedly into the cool lobby.

"Vultures," I muttered.

"Can't be helped that we're such a photogenic couple."

"You're such a humble man, Gideon Cross."

"You make me look good, Mrs. Cross."

We stepped into the elevator with a few other people and he took the rear corner, hooking me to him with an arm around my waist, his hand pressed flat against my belly, his chest warm and hard against my back.

I savored those few minutes with him, refusing to think about work or Brett until we parted on the twentieth floor.

Megumi was already at her desk when I approached the glass security doors, and the sight of her made me smile. She'd trimmed her hair since I'd seen her Friday night and polished her nails a bright red. It was good to see the small signs that she was reclaiming her spirit.

"Hey, you," she greeted me after buzzing me in, pushing to her feet.

"You look great."

Her smile widened. "Thanks. How'd it go with Gideon's sister?"

"Awesome. She's a lot of fun. It makes me melt seeing Gideon with her."

"He makes me melt, period. You lucky bitch. Anyway, I put a call through to your line earlier. They wanted to leave a message."

I shifted on my feet, thinking of Brett. "Was it a guy?"

"No, a woman."

"Hmm, I'll go check it out, thanks."

I headed back to my desk and got settled in, my gaze coming to rest on the collage of photos of Gideon and me. I still needed to talk to him about Crossroads. There hadn't been a good time over the weekend. We'd had enough on our plates having Ireland over.

He hadn't slept Saturday night. I'd hoped he would but hadn't really expected him to. It was hard for me, thinking of his inner struggle, his worry and fear. He carried shame, too, and an inherent belief that he was broken. Damaged goods.

He didn't see in himself what I saw — a generous soul who wanted so much to belong to something greater than himself. He didn't recognize what a miracle he was. When he didn't know what to do in a given situation, he let instinct and his heart take over. Despite all he'd been through, he had such an amazing capacity to feel and to love.

He'd saved me, in so many ways. I was

going to do whatever needed to be done to save him, too.

I listened to my messages. When Mark came in, I stood, and met him with a grin and bouncing anticipation.

His brows rose. "What's got you so excited?"

"A gal from LanCorp called this morning. They want to meet with us sometime this week to talk a bit more about what they're hoping to achieve with the launch of the PhazeOne system."

His dark eyes took on a familiar sparkle. He'd become a happier man overall since he and Steven had become engaged, but there was a whole different energy to him when he was eager about a new account. "You and me, kid, we're going places."

I hopped a little on my feet. "Yeah. You've got this. Once they meet with you in person, you'll have them eating out of your hand."

Mark laughed. "You're good for my confidence."

I winked at him. "I'm good for you, period."

We spent the morning working on the PhazeOne RFP, putting together comps to better grasp how we might position the new gaming system against its competition. I had a momentary pause when I realized how much buzz surrounded the upcoming release of the next-generation GenTen console — which happened to be a product of Cross Industries, making it PhazeOne's primary rival in the marketplace.

Pointing the situation out to Mark, I asked, "Is it going to be a problem? I mean, could LanCorp possibly see a conflict of interest with me working for you on this?"

He straightened in his chair, leaning back. He'd shucked his coat earlier but remained smartly attired in a white dress shirt, bright yellow tie, and navy slacks. "It shouldn't be an issue, no. If our proposed positioning wins out over the other RFPs they're collecting, the fact that you're engaged to Gideon Cross isn't going to make a damn bit of difference. They're going to make their decision based on our ability to deliver their vision."

I wanted to feel relieved, but I didn't. If we were awarded the PhazeOne campaign, I'd be helping one of Gideon's competitors steal some of his market share. That really bothered me. Gideon worked so hard and had overcome so much to lift the Cross name up from infamy to a level where it inspired awe, respect, and a healthy amount of fear. I never wanted to set him back, in anything.

I'd thought I would have a little more time before I was forced to make a choice. And I couldn't help feeling like the choice to be made was between my independence and my love for my husband.

The dilemma niggled at me all morning, chipping away at the excitement I felt over the RFP. Then the hours crept toward noon and Brett took over my thoughts.

It was time to take responsibility for the mess I'd made. I had opened the door to Brett, and then I'd kept it open because I couldn't get my head on straight. It was my job now to fix the problem before it impacted my marriage any more than it already had.

I headed down to the lobby at five minutes to noon, having asked permission from Mark to leave a little early. Brett was already waiting for me, standing near the entrance with his hands shoved into his jeans pockets. He wore a plain white T-shirt and sandals, with sunglasses propped atop his head.

My stride faltered a little. Not just because he was hot, which was undeniable, but because he looked so out of place in the Crossfire. When he'd met me here before the video launch in Times Square, we had rendezvoused outside. Now, he was in the

319

building, occupying a spot too near to where I'd first run into Gideon.

The differences between the two men were stark and didn't have anything to do with clothing or money.

Brett's mouth curved when he saw me, his body straightening, shifting in that way men moved when their sexual interest was piqued. Other men, but not Gideon. When I'd first met my husband, his body, his voice, gave nothing away. Only his eyes had betrayed his attraction, and only for an instant.

It was later I realized what had happened in that moment.

Gideon had claimed me . . . and given himself to me in return. With a single look. He'd recognized me the moment he saw me. It took me longer to understand what we were to each other. What we were meant to be.

I couldn't help but contrast the possessive, tender way Gideon looked at me against the earthier, lustful way Brett raked me from head to toe.

It seemed so obvious suddenly, that Brett had never really thought of me as *his*. Not the way Gideon did. Brett had wanted me, still did, but even when he'd had me, he hadn't asserted any ownership and he certainly hadn't ever given anything *real* of himself to me.

Gideon. My head tilted back, my gaze searching for and finding one of the many black domes in the ceiling that hid the security cameras. My hand went to my heart, pressing over it. I knew he probably wasn't looking. I knew he'd have to deliberately access the feed in order to see me and that he was far too busy with work to think of it, but still . . .

"Eva."

My hand dropped to my side. I looked at Brett as he approached me with the easy prowl of a man who knew his appeal and was confident of his chances.

The lobby was swarming with people flowing around us in steady streams, as one would expect in a midtown skyscraper. When his arms lifted as if to embrace me, I stepped back and held out my left hand instead, just as I had done when we last met in San Diego. I would never again cause Gideon to feel the pain I'd inflicted when he saw me kissing Brett.

Brett's brows lifted and the heat in his eyes cooled. "Really? Is this where we're at now?"

"I'm married," I reminded him. "Hugging each other isn't appropriate."

"What about the women he's tapped all over the tabloids? That's okay?"

"Come on," I chided. "You know you can't always believe what the press feeds you."

His lips pursed. He shoved his hands back in his pockets. "You can believe what they say about how I feel about you."

My stomach fluttered. "I think *you* believe it."

Which made me a little sad. He didn't know what Gideon and I had, because he'd never had it. I hoped he would someday. Brett wasn't a bad guy. He just wasn't meant to be *my* guy.

Cursing under his breath, Brett turned and gestured toward the exit. "Let's get out of here."

I was torn. I wanted privacy, too, but I also wanted to stay where there were witnesses who could reassure Gideon. In any case, we couldn't exactly have a picnic in the Crossfire lobby.

Reluctantly, I fell into step beside him. "I had some sandwiches delivered a little bit ago. Figured that would give us more time to talk."

Brett nodded grimly and held out his hand for the bag I was carrying.

I took him to Bryant Park, weaving beside

him through the frenetic lunchtime crowds on the sidewalks. Taxis and private cars honked insistently at the streams of pedestrians too time-strapped to obey the signals. Heat shimmered off the asphalt, the sun high enough in the sky to spear down between the towering skyscrapers. An NYPD squad car hit its siren, the piercing robotic chirps and rumbles doing little to expedite the cruiser's movement through the clogged street.

It was Manhattan on an average day and I loved it, but I could tell Brett was frustrated by the intricate dance required to get through the city. The shifting of shoulders and hips to let people pass, the quick inhales to squeeze by too-big bags or too-slow pedestrians, the swift-footedness needed to avoid the abrupt appearance of new bodies filing out of the many doorways that lined the sidewalks. Life as usual in NYC, but I remembered how overwhelming it felt when you weren't used to so many people occupying relatively little space.

Entering the park just behind the library, we found an unoccupied bistro table and chairs in the shade near the carousel and settled in. Brett pulled out the sandwiches, chips, and bottled water I'd ordered, but neither of us started eating. I scouted our surroundings instead, aware that we could be photographed.

I'd considered that when I chose the location, but the alternative was a noisy, crowded restaurant. I was hyperconscious of my body language, trying to ensure that nothing could be misconstrued. The world at large could think we were friends. My husband would know, in every way I could show him, that Brett and I had actually said good-bye.

"You got the wrong impression in San Diego," Brett said abruptly, his eyes shielded behind his shades. "Brittany isn't a serious thing."

"It's none of my business, Brett."

"I miss you. Sometimes, she reminds me of you."

I winced, finding the comment anything but flattering. I lifted one hand and gestured helplessly. "I couldn't go back to you, Brett. Not after Gideon."

"You say that now."

"He makes me feel like he can't breathe without me. I couldn't settle for less." I didn't need to say that Brett had never made me feel like that. He knew.

He stared at his steepled fingertips, then straightened abruptly and dug his wallet out of his back pocket. He pulled a folded photograph out and set it on the table in front of me.

"Look at that," he said tightly, "and tell me we didn't have something real."

I picked up the photo and spread it open, frowning at the image. It was a candid shot of Brett and me, laughing together over something lost to memory. I recognized the interior of Pete's in the background. There was a crowd of blurred faces around us.

"Where did you get this?" I asked. There'd been a time when I would've given anything to have an unposed photo with Brett, believing that such an insubstantial thing would give me some kind of proof that I was more than a piece of ass.

"Sam took that after one of our sets."

I stiffened at the mention of Sam Yimara, abruptly reminded of the sex tape. I looked at Brett, my hands shaking so hard I had to put the photo down. "Do you know about . . . ?"

I couldn't even finish the sentence. Turned out, it wasn't necessary for me to.

Brett's jaw tensed, his forehead and upper lip beaded with sweat from the summer heat. He nodded. "I've seen it."

"Oh my God." I recoiled from the table, my mind filled with all the possibilities of what was captured on video. I had been desperate to win Brett's attention, with a complete lack of self-respect that shamed me now.

"Eva." He reached for me. "It's not what you think. Whatever Cross told you about the video, I promise it isn't bad. A little raw sometimes, but that's the way it was between us."

No . . . Raw was what I had with Gideon. What I'd had with Brett was something much darker and unhealthy.

I clasped my trembling hands together. "How many people have seen it? Have you shown it to — Has the band watched it?"

He didn't have to answer; I saw it on his face.

"Jesus." I felt sick. "What do you want from me, Brett?"

"I want —" Shoving up his sunglasses, he rubbed at his eyes. "Hell. I want you. I want us to be together. I don't think we're over yet."

"We never got started."

"I know that's my fault. I want you to give me a chance to fix it."

I gaped. "I'm married!"

"He's no good, Eva. You don't know him like you think you do."

My legs quivered with the urge to get up and leave. "I know he'd never show footage of us to anyone! He respects me too much."

"The whole point was to document the rise of the band, Eva. We had to sort through it all."

"You could've watched it alone first," I said tightly, horribly aware of the people sitting not too far away. "You could've cut us out before the others saw it."

"We're not the only ones Sam got on video. The other guys had stuff, too."

"Oh God." I watched as he shifted restlessly. Suspicion bloomed. "And there were other girls with you," I guessed, my nausea worsening. "What did it matter when I was just one of many."

"It mattered." He leaned forward. "It was different with you, Eva. *I* was different with you. I was just too young and full of myself to appreciate it at the time. You need to see, Eva. Then you'll understand."

I shook my head violently. "I don't want to see it. Ever. Are you crazy?"

That was a lie. What was in the video? How bad was it?

"Goddamn it." He yanked off his shades, throwing them on the table. "I didn't want to talk about the fucking video."

But there was a defensiveness to his posture that made me doubt him. His shoulders were high and tight, his mouth a hard line.

Whatever Cross told you . . .

He knew Gideon was aware of the tape. He had to know Gideon was fighting to keep it buried. Sam would've told him.

"What do you want?" I asked again. "What was so damned urgent you had to come out to New York?"

I waited for him to answer, my heart pounding. It was hot as hell and humid, but my skin felt chilled and clammy. He couldn't tell me he loved me, not after I'd caught him with Brittany. He couldn't warn me away from Gideon; I was already married. Brett was in Manhattan midtour, something the band had to agree with. And Vidal. Why would they do that? What would they get out of interrupting their schedule?

When Brett just sat there, his jaw working, I stood and turned blindly away, hurrying across the grass toward the nearest gate in the wrought-iron fence.

He called after me, but I kept my head down, achingly aware of the number of people in the park whose heads turned in my direction. I was making a scene, but I couldn't stop. I left my bag behind and didn't care.

Get away. Get somewhere safe. *Get to Gideon.*

"Angel."

The sound of my husband's voice made me stumble. I turned my head. He rose from a chair near the piano by Bryant Park Grill. Cool and elegant, seemingly impervious to the sultry heat.

"Gideon."

The concern in his eyes, the gentle way he enfolded me in a hug, gave me strength. He'd known this meeting with Brett wouldn't go well. That I would be upset and needy. That I would need *him*.

And he was there. I didn't know how, and I didn't care.

My fingers dug into his back, practically clawing at him.

"Shh." His lips brushed against my ear. "I've got you."

Raúl appeared beside us with my bag in hand, his stance conveying a protectiveness that added to the shield Gideon's body gave me. The riotous panic inside me began to ease. I wasn't freefalling anymore. Gideon was my net, always prepared to catch me.

He led me down the steps to where the Bentley waited, with Angus standing ready to open the back door. I slid inside and Gideon joined me, his arm wrapping around me when I curled into him.

We were right back to where we'd started

that morning. But in a matter of hours, everything had changed.

"I've got this," he murmured. "Trust me."

I lifted my nose to his throat. "They want to use the footage, don't they?"

"They won't. No one will." There was a razor-sharp edge to his words.

I believed him. And I loved him more than I ever thought possible.

What an afternoon. I avoided thinking about Brett by working hard on game console comps, including GenTen; my mind was firmly on Gideon when five o'clock rolled around.

It wasn't just PhazeOne that worried me anymore. It was also me, the girl I'd once been. The sex tape could do more damage to the Cross name than anything a rival company could do.

I texted Gideon. I hoped for a quick answer but didn't expect one. Are you in your office?

He replied almost instantly. Yes.

Heading home, I typed back. Want to say bye first.

Come up.

I released the breath I hadn't realized I'd been holding. See you in ten.

Megumi was already gone when I passed

330

reception, so I reached Gideon faster than I'd planned on. His receptionist was still at her station, her long red hair hanging sleekly around her shoulders. She gave me a curt nod and I gave her a smile, unfazed.

Scott wasn't at his desk when I got back there, but Gideon was standing at his, his hands on the desktop as he perused documents spread out in front of him. Arash was seated in one of the chairs, his posture relaxed and easy as he spoke. Neither of them wore a coat, and both of them looked mighty fine.

Arash glanced at me as I came closer, and Gideon's head came up. My husband's eyes were so blue, the hue struck me even across the distance between us. His face remained austerely handsome, so classically Gideon, and yet his gaze softened at the sight of me. My mouth curved when he beckoned me with a crook of his finger.

I entered his office and held out my hand to Arash when he stood. "Hey," I greeted him. "You keeping him out of trouble?"

"When he lets me," the lawyer replied, catching my hand and pulling me in for an air kiss on my cheek.

"Back off," Gideon said dryly, his arm sliding around my waist.

Arash laughed. "This new jealous streak

331

of yours is vastly entertaining."

"Your sense of humor is not," Gideon shot back.

I leaned into my husband, loving the feel of his hard body against mine. There was no give to him, no yielding. Except when he looked at me.

"I've got a meeting in thirty," Arash said, "so I'll head out. Thanks for Friday night, Eva. I'd love to do it again sometime."

"We will," I told him. "For sure."

As he left the office, I turned to Gideon. "Can I hug you?"

"You never have to ask."

My heart felt squeezed by the warm indulgence in his eyes. "The glass is clear."

"Let them see," he murmured, wrapping his arms around me. He exhaled long and slow when I clung to him. "Talk to me, angel."

"I don't want to talk." Didn't want to think about the mess I'd made of my life, which was now impacting the man I loved. "I want to hear your voice. Say anything, I don't care."

"Kline won't hurt you. I promise you that."

My eyes squeezed shut. "Not about him. Tell me about work."

"Eva . . ."

I felt the tension in his body, the strain of concern and worry, so I explained. "I just want to close my eyes for a minute and feel you. Smell you. Hear you. I need to just soak you in for a minute, and then I'll be okay."

His hands rubbed up and down my back, his chin resting on the top of my head. "We're going away. Soon. For at least a week, although I'd prefer two. I was thinking we might go back to Crosswinds. Spend the time naked and lazy —"

"You're never lazy. Especially when you're naked."

"Especially when *you're* naked," he corrected, nuzzling me. "But I've never had you that way for an entire week. You could wear me out."

"I doubt that's possible, fiend. But I'm willing to try my best."

"It won't be our honeymoon, per se. I want a month for that."

"A month!" I pulled back and looked at him, my mood lifting. "The entire economy of New York could collapse if you're out of the game that long."

He cupped the side of my face, his thumb brushing over my brow. "I think my highly capable team can manage a few weeks without me."

I caught his wrist and let a little of my anxiety out. "I couldn't manage it. I need you too much."

"Eva." He lowered his head and pressed his lips to mine, his tongue teasing them open.

Gripping his nape in my hand, I held him still while I deepened the kiss. Fell into it. He pulled me closer, lifting me onto my tiptoes. His head tilted, tightening the seal until every breath was shared, every moan and whimper.

I gasped when we broke for air. "When will you be home?"

"When you want me there."

"That would be when your day is done. You've lost enough time over me today." I smoothed his perfectly placed tie. "You weren't just spying on me this afternoon. You knew my lunch with Brett was going to go south."

"It was a possibility."

"The spying? Or the heading south?"

He shot me a look. "You're not going to give me a hard time about being there for you. You would've done the same had the situation been reversed."

"How did you know what he wanted?" Was the video's existence eating at him, too? What I'd done and who I'd been before?

"I know he's getting pressure from Christopher, who's also putting pressure on the rest of the band."

"Why? To get to you?"

"In part. You're not just some random hot blonde. You're Eva Tramell and you're news."

"Maybe I should dye my hair. Get rid of the 'Golden.' How about red?" I couldn't go brunette, not with Gideon's history of dark-haired women. It would kill me to look in the mirror every day.

His face shuttered, closed up like a steel trap even though nothing else about him gave away any tension. I got a tingle at the back of my neck, a prickling warning that something had shifted.

"Don't like the idea?" I prodded, abruptly reminded of a redhead from his past — Dr. Anne Lucas.

"I like you just the way you are. That said, if you want a change, I won't object. It's your body, your right. But don't do it just because of them."

"Would you still want me?"

The tightness around his mouth eased, the inflexibility on his face fading away nearly as swiftly as it had appeared. "Would you still want me if I had red hair?"

"Hmm." I tapped my chin with my finger,

pretending to contemplate the change. "Maybe we should stick with what we've got."

Gideon kissed my forehead. "That's what I signed up for."

"You also signed up for letting me have my way with you tonight."

"Name the time and place."

"Eight o'clock? Your apartment on the Upper West Side?"

"*Our* apartment." He kissed me softly. "I'll be there."

13

"By the way, congratulations on your engagement."

My gaze shifted from the project engineer's face on my monitor to the photo of Eva blowing kisses. "Thank you."

I would much rather look at my wife. For an instant, I pictured Eva as she'd been the night before, those plush lips wrapped around my cock. I had given her carte blanche with my body and all she'd wanted was to suck me off. Again and again. And again. *Christ.* I had been thinking about the night we'd had all day long.

"I'll keep you posted on the impact of the storm," he said, bringing my attention back to work. "I appreciate you calling personally to check on us. The weather conditions may set us back a week or two, depending, but we'll open on time."

"We have a cushion. Take care of yourself and your crew first."

"Will do. Thanks."

I closed the chat window and checked my schedule, needing to know exactly how much time I had to prepare for my next meeting with the lead R and D team at PosIT.

Scott's voice projected from my phone's speaker. "Christopher Vidal Sr. is on line one. It's his third call today. I've already told him you'll get back to him when you can, but he's insistent. How do you want me to handle?"

Calls from my stepfather never boded well, which meant delaying them ate into the time I had to fix whatever problem he needed to impose on me. "I'll take it."

I hit the speaker button. "Chris, what can I do for you?"

"Gideon. Listen, I'm sorry to disturb you, but you and I need to talk. Would it be possible for us to meet today?"

Prodded by the urgency in his voice, I picked up the receiver and took him off speaker. "My office or yours?"

"No, your penthouse."

I sat back, surprised. "I won't be home until close to nine."

"That's fine."

"Is everyone all right?"

"Yes, everyone's fine. Don't worry about that."

"It's Vidal, then. We'll take care of it."

"God." He laughed harshly. "You're a good man, Gideon. One of the best I know. I should've told you that more often."

My gaze narrowed at the edge in his tone. "I've got a few minutes now. Just lay it out."

"No, not now. I'll see you at nine."

He hung up. I sat for a long minute with the receiver in my hand. There was a knot in my gut, one that was cold and sharp.

I returned the receiver to its cradle and my attention to work, pulling up schematics and reviewing the packet Scott had placed on my desk earlier. Still, my mind raced.

I couldn't control what happened with my family, had never had any power there. I could only clean up the messes Christopher made and try to keep Vidal from going under. I drew the line, however, at using the footage of Eva. Nothing Chris could say would change that.

Time was racing toward the PosIT meeting when the message app popped up on my monitor and Eva's avatar appeared.

I can still taste you. Yummy. ☺

A dry laugh escaped me. The knot I'd been ignoring eased, then disappeared. She was my clean slate. My fresh start.

Soothed, I replied. The pleasure was mine.

"I've got a lead."

My head turned to find Raúl entering my office.

He came to my desk with brisk strides. "I'm still running through the guest list for that event you attended a couple weeks ago. I've also been running twice-daily searches for photos. Got an alert on this one today. I secured a copy and made some zoom views."

I glanced at the photos he slid across my desk. Picking them up, I examined them more closely, one by one. There was a redhead in the background. In each successive picture, she was brought closer to the fore. "Emerald green dress, long red hair. This is the woman Eva saw."

It was also Anne Lucas. Something about the way she was standing, with her face averted, spurred a familiar sickness in my gut.

I looked up at Raúl. "She wasn't on the guest list?"

"Not officially, but she was on the red carpet, so I'm thinking she had to have been someone's plus-one. I don't know who her escort was yet, but I'm on it."

Restless, I stood, shoving my chair back.

"She went after Eva. You need to keep her away from my wife."

"Angus and I are developing new protocols for event security."

Turning, I retrieved my jacket from its hook. "You'll tell me if you need more men."

"I'll let you know." He scooped up the photos and started toward me. "She's at her office today," he said, accurately gauging my intention. "Was still there when I headed up to see you."

"Good. Let's go."

"Excuse me." The petite brunette behind the desk stood in a rush as I walked by. "You can't go in there. Dr. Lucas is with a patient now."

I grabbed the knob and opened the door, walking into Anne's office without breaking stride.

Her head snapped up, her green eyes widening the instant before her red mouth curved in a satisfied smile. The woman on the couch across from her blinked at me in confusion, swallowing whatever she'd been about to say.

"I'm so sorry, Dr. Lucas," the brunette said breathlessly. "I tried to stop him."

Anne slithered to her feet, her eyes on me. "An impossible task, Michelle. Don't worry, you can go."

The receptionist backed out. Anne glanced at her patient. "We'll have to cut today's appointment short. I apologize for this incredibly rude interruption" — she glared at me — "and of course I won't charge you. Please talk to Michelle about rescheduling."

I waited in the open door as the flustered woman gathered her stuff, and then I moved aside as she stepped out.

"I could've called security," Anne said, leaning back against the front of her desk and crossing her arms.

"After going to all the trouble of luring me here? You wouldn't."

"I don't know what you're talking about. Regardless, it's good to see you." She dropped her arms and gripped the edge of her desk in a deliberately provocative pose, exposing her bare thigh as the slit in her blue wrap dress slid open.

"I can't say the same."

Her smile tightened. "Break your toys, then throw them away. Does Eva know her days are numbered?"

"Do you?"

Unease dimmed her bright eyes and shook her smile. "Is that a threat, Gideon?"

"You'd like for it to be." I stepped closer, watched her pupils dilate. She was becoming aroused and that revolted me as much as the smell of her perfume. "Might make your game more interesting."

She straightened and came toward me, her hips swaying, her red-soled black stilettos sinking into the plush carpet.

"You like to play, too, lover," she purred. "Tell me, have you tied up your pretty fiancée? Flogged her into a frenzy? Shoved one of your extensive array of dildos into her ass, so that it fucked her while you pounded her pussy for hours? Does she know you, Gideon, the way I do?"

"Hundreds of women know me the way you do, Anne. Do you think you were special? The only thing memorable about you is your husband and how it eats at him that I've had you."

Her hand swung up to slap me and I didn't stop her, taking the hit unflinchingly.

I wish what I'd said were true, but I had been particularly depraved with her, seeing ghosts of her brother in the curve of her smile, her mannerisms —

I caught her wrist when she made a grab for my cock. "Leave Eva alone. I won't tell you twice."

"She's the chink in your armor, you heartless piece of shit. You've got ice in your veins, but she bleeds."

"Is that a threat, Anne?" I asked, calmly tossing her words back to her.

"Absolutely." She yanked free of my grip. "It's time to pay, and your billions won't cover the debt."

"Raising the stakes with a declaration of war? Are you that stupid? Or don't you care what this will cost you? Your career . . . your marriage . . . everything."

I moved toward the door, my stride leisurely even as fury burned through me. I'd brought this down on Eva. I had to clean it up.

"Just watch me, Gideon," she called after me. "See what happens."

"Have it your way." I paused with my hand on the doorknob. "You've started this, but make no mistake, the final move will be mine."

"Have you had any nightmares since we last saw each other?" Dr. Petersen asked, his demeanor laid back and quietly interested, the requisite tablet in his lap.

"No."

"How often would you say you have them?"

I sat as comfortably as the easygoing doctor but was irritably restless inside. I had too much to deal with to waste an hour of

344

my time. "Lately, once a week. Sometimes a little longer in between."

"What do you mean by *lately*?"

"Since I met Eva."

He jotted something down with his stylus. "You're facing unfamiliar pressures as you work on your relationship with Eva, but the frequency of your nightmares is lessening — at least for now. Do you have any thoughts as to why?"

"I thought you were supposed to be explaining that to me."

Dr. Petersen smiled. "I can't wave a magic wand and give you all the answers, Gideon. I can only help you sort through it."

I was tempted to wait for him to say more, make him do most of the talking. But the thought of Eva and her hopes that therapy was going to make some sort of difference goaded me to speak. I'd promised to try, so I would. To a degree. "Things are smoothing out for us. We're in sync more than we're not."

"Do you feel that you're communicating better?"

"I think we're better at gauging the motives behind each other's actions. We understand each other more."

"Your relationship has moved very quickly. You're not an impulsive man, but many would say marrying a woman you've known such a short time — and one you admit you're still getting to know — is extremely impulsive."

"Is there a question there?"

"An observation." He waited a moment, but when I didn't say anything, he went on. "It can be difficult for spouses of individuals with Eva's history. Her commitment to therapy has helped both of you; however, it's likely she'll continue to change in ways you may not expect. It will be stressful for you."

"I'm no picnic myself," I said dryly.

"You're a survivor of a different sort. Have you ever felt that your nightmares were aggravated by stress?"

The question irritated me. "What does it matter? They happen."

"You don't feel there are changes that can be made to lessen their impact?"

"I just got married. That's a major life change, wouldn't you say, Doctor? I think that's enough for now."

"Why must there be a limit? You're a young man, Gideon. You have a variety of options available to you. Change doesn't have to be something avoided. What's the harm in trying something new? If it doesn't work out, you always have the option to go back to what you were doing before."

I found that wryly amusing. "Sometimes, you can't go back."

"Let's try a simple change now," Dr. Petersen said, setting his tablet aside. "Let's go for a walk."

I found myself standing when he did, not wanting to be seated while he towered above me. We stood face-to-face with the coffee table between us. "Why?"

"Why not?" He gestured toward the door. "My office may not be the best place for us to talk. You're a man used to being in charge. In here, I am. So we'll level the playing field and hit the hallway for a bit. It's a public space, but most of the individuals who work in this building have gone home."

I exited his office before him, watching as he locked both his inner and outer office doors before joining me.

"Ah, well. This is certainly different," he said, his mouth curving wryly. "Knocks me off my stride a bit."

I shrugged and started walking.

"What are your plans for the rest of the evening?" he asked, falling into step beside me.

"An hour with my trainer." And then I said more. "My stepfather is coming over later."

347

"To spend time with you and Eva? Are you close to him?"

"No, to both." I stared straight ahead. "Something's wrong. That's the only reason he ever calls me."

I sensed his gaze on my profile. "Do you wish that were different?"

"No."

"You don't like him?"

"I don't dislike him." I was going to leave it at that, but again I thought of Eva. "We just don't know each other very well."

"You could change that."

I huffed out a laugh. "You're really pushing that angle tonight."

"I told you, I don't have an angle." He stopped, forcing me to stop, too.

Tipping his chin up, he eyed the ceiling, clearly thinking. "When you're considering an acquisition or exploring a new avenue of doing business, you bring in people to advise you, right? Experts in their respective fields?" He looked at me again, smiling. "You could think of me the same way, as an expert consultant."

"On what?"

"Your past." He resumed walking. "I help you with that, you can figure out the rest of your life yourself."

■ ■ ■ ■

"Get your head in the game, Cross."

My gaze narrowed. Across the mat, James Cho hopped on his bare feet, taunting me. He grinned evilly, knowing the unspoken challenge would spur me on. Half a foot shorter than me and lighter by at least thirty pounds, the former MMA champion was lethally quick and had the belt to prove it.

Rolling my shoulders back, I adjusted my stance. My fists came up, closing the opening that had allowed his last punch to connect with my torso.

"Make it worth my while, Cho," I fired back, irritated that he was right. My brain was still back in Dr. Petersen's office. A switch had been thrown tonight and I couldn't get a handle on what it was or what it meant.

James and I circled, feinting and striking out, neither of us scoring a hit. As always, it was just the two of us in the dojo. The driving beat of taiko drums rumbled in the background from speakers cleverly hidden in the floor-to-ceiling bamboo paneling.

"You're still holding back," he said. "Falling in love turn you into a pussy?"

"You wish. Only way you'd beat me."

James laughed, then came at me with a roundhouse kick. I dropped low and swept him, taking him down. He scissored his legs with lightning speed, taking me down with him.

We hopped back up. Squared off again.

"You're wasting my time," he snapped, his fist lashing out.

I ducked to the side. My left fist shot out, grazing his side. His fist hit my ribs straight on.

"No one piss you off today?" He came at me in a rush, giving me no option to do anything but defend myself.

I growled. Rage was simmering in the back of my mind, tucked away until I had the time and attention to deal with it.

"Yeah. I see that fire in your eyes, Cross. Let it out, man. Bring it on."

She's the chink in your armor . . .

I lashed out with a left/right combo, driving James back a step.

"That all you got?" he jeered.

I feigned a kick and then threw out a punch, snapping his head back.

"Fuck yeah," he gasped, flexing his arms, getting pumped. "There you are."

She bleeds . . .

Snarling, I lunged forward.

■ ■ ■

Refreshed from a shower, I had barely finished dressing by pulling a T-shirt over my head when my smartphone started ringing. I picked it up off the bed where I'd left it and answered.

"A couple things," Raúl said after greeting me, the background noise of a crowd and music quickly fading, then disappearing completely. "I've noticed that Benjamin Clancy is still keeping an eye on Mrs. Cross. Not constantly, but consistently."

"Is that so," I said quietly.

"Are you good with that? Or should I talk to him?"

"I'll deal with him." Clancy and I were due for a chat. It had been on my list, but I would move it up.

"Also — and you may know this already — Mrs. Cross had lunch with Ryan Landon and some of his executives today."

I felt that terrible quiet settle over me. Landon. Fuck.

He'd slid in somewhere I hadn't been watching.

"Thank you, Raúl. I'll need a private number for Eva's boss, Mark Garrity."

"I'll text it to you when I have it."

Ending the call, I shoved the phone in my pocket, barely resisting the urge to throw it at the wall instead.

Arash had warned me about Landon and I'd brushed his concerns off. I'd been focused on my life, my wife, and while Landon had a wife of his own, his primary focus had always been me.

The ringing of the penthouse phone jolted me. I went to the receiver on the nightstand and answered with an impatient, "Cross."

"Mr. Cross. It's Edwin at the front desk. Mr. Vidal is here to see you."

Jesus. My grip tightened on the receiver. "Send him up."

"Yes, sir. Will do."

Grabbing my socks and shoes, I carried them out to the living room and pulled them on. As soon as Chris left, I was heading home to Eva. I wanted to open a bottle of wine, find one of the older movies she knew by heart, and just listen to her recite the corny lines of dialogue. No one could make me laugh like she did.

I heard the elevator car arrive and pushed to my feet, running a hand through my damp hair. I was tense and despised the weakness.

"Gideon." Chris paused on the threshold of the foyer, looking grim and worn, which he so rarely did and only then because of my brother. "Is Eva here?"

"She's at her place. I'm heading over there when you leave."

He gave a jerky nod, his jaw working but nothing coming out of his mouth.

"Come in," I said, gesturing at the wing-back chair by the coffee table. "Can I get you something to drink?"

God knew I needed one myself after the day I'd had so far.

He stepped wearily into my living room. "Anything strong would be great."

"Sounds good to me." I went to the kitchen and poured us both a glass of Armagnac. As I was setting the decanter down, my phone vibrated in my pocket. Pulling it out, I saw a message from Eva.

It was a selfie of her bare leg glistening with water and draped over the rim of her bathtub with candles in the background. Join me?

I swiftly revised my plans for the evening. She'd been sending me provocative texts all day. I was more than happy to both satisfy and reward her.

I saved the photo and typed back. Wish I could. Promise to make you wet again when I get there.

Tucking my phone away, I turned and

found Chris joining me at the island. I slid a tumbler over to him and took a sip from mine. "What's going on, Chris?"

He sighed, both of his hands wrapping around the crystal. "We're going to reshoot the 'Golden' video."

"Oh?" That was an unnecessary expense, something Chris wisely avoided as a rule.

"I overheard Kline and Christopher arguing in the offices yesterday," he said gruffly, "and got the story. Kline wants a redo and I agreed."

"Christopher doesn't, I'm sure." I leaned back against the counter, my jaw set. Apparently, Brett Kline had some serious feelings for Eva after all. I wasn't okay with that. Not even close.

"Your brother will get over it."

I doubted that, but it would do no good to say so.

But Chris read what I didn't say and gave a nod. "I know the video has caused stress for you and Eva. I should've been paying more attention."

"I appreciate you being flexible about it."

He stared into his glass and then took a long drink, nearly downing the contents in a single swallow. "I've left your mother."

I took a quick, deep breath, grasping that the reason for his visit had nothing to do with work. "Ireland told me you two had a fight."

"Yeah. I hate that Ireland had to hear it." He looked at me, and I saw the knowledge in his eyes. The horror. "I didn't know, Gideon. I swear to God, I didn't know."

My heart jerked in my chest, then began to pound. My mouth went dry.

"I, uh, went to see Terrence Lucas." Chris's voice grew hoarse. "Barged into his office. He denied it, the lying son of a bitch, but I could see it on his face."

The brandy sloshed in my glass. I set it down carefully, feeling the floor shift under my feet. Eva had confronted Lucas, but Chris . . . ?

"I decked him, knocked him out cold, but God . . . I wanted to take one of those awards on his shelves and bash his head in."

"Stop." The word broke from my throat like slivers of glass.

"And the asshole who did . . . That asshole is dead. I can't get to him. Goddamn it." Chris dropped the tumbler onto the granite with a thud, but it was the sob that tore out of him that nearly shattered me. "Hell, Gideon. It was my job to protect you. And I failed."

"Stop!" I pushed off the counter, my hands

355

clenching. "Don't fucking look at me like that!"

He trembled visibly, but didn't back down. "I had to tell you —"

His wrinkled dress shirt was in my fists, his feet dangling above the floor. "Stop talking. Now!"

Tears slipped down his face. "I love you like my own. Always have."

I shoved him away. Turned my back to him when he stumbled and hit the wall. I left, crossing the living room without seeing it.

"I'm not expecting your forgiveness," he called after me, tears clogging his words. "I don't deserve it. But you need to hear that I would've ripped him apart with my bare hands if I'd known."

I rounded on him, feeling the sickness clawing up from my gut and burning my throat. *What the fuck do you want?*

Chris pulled his shoulders back. He faced me with reddened eyes and wet cheeks, shaking but too stupid to run. "I want you to know that you're not alone."

Alone. Yes. Far away from the pity and guilt and pain staring out at me through his tears. "Get out."

Nodding, he headed toward the foyer. I stood immobile, my chest heaving, my eyes burning. Words backed up in my throat; violence pounded in the painful clench of my fists.

He stopped before he left the room, facing me. "I'm glad you told Eva."

"Don't talk about her." I couldn't bear to even think of her. Not now, when I was so close to losing it.

He left.

The weight of the day crashed onto my shoulders, dropping me to my knees.

I broke.

14

I was dreaming of a private beach and naked Gideon when I was jerked awake by the sound of my phone ringing. Rolling to my side, I thrust my arm out and smacked around on the top of my nightstand, trying to find my smartphone in the dark. My fingers brushed against the familiar shape and I grabbed it, sitting up.

Ireland's face lit up my screen. I frowned and glanced at the space beside me in the bed. Gideon wasn't home. Of course, he could've found me sleeping and gone next door to go to bed . . .

"Hello?" I answered, noting that the time on the cable box said it was after eleven o'clock.

"Eva. It's Chris Vidal. I'm sorry to call so late, but I'm worried about Gideon. Is he all right?"

My stomach dropped. "What do you mean? What's wrong with Gideon?"

There was a pause. "You haven't talked to him tonight?"

I slid out of bed and turned on the lamp. "No. I fell asleep. What's going on?"

He cursed with an intensity that made the hairs rise on my arms. "I met with him earlier about . . . the things you told me. He didn't take it well."

"Oh my God." I spun around blindly. Something to wear. I needed something to put on over the racy teddy I'd planned to seduce Gideon with.

"You have to find him, Eva," he said urgently. "He needs you now."

"I'm going." I tossed the phone on my bed and yanked a wool trench coat out of my closet before racing out of my room. I grabbed the keys to the next-door apartment from my purse and ran down the hall. Fumbling with the deadbolt, I took too long to open the door.

The place was as shadowy and silent as a tomb, the rooms empty.

"Where are you?" I cried into the darkness, feeling the scratch of panicked tears in my throat.

I ended up back in my apartment, my fingers trembling as I opened the app on my smartphone that would track his.

He didn't take it well.

God. Of course, he didn't. He hadn't taken it well when I'd told Chris initially. Gideon had been furious. Aggressive. He'd had a horrible nightmare.

The blinking red dot on the map was right where I was hoping it would be. "The penthouse."

I shoved my feet into flip-flops and hurried back out to my purse.

"What the hell are you wearing?" Cary asked from the kitchen, jolting me.

"Jesus, you just scared the shit out of me!"

He sauntered up to the breakfast bar in just his Grey Isles boxer briefs, his chest and neck glistening with sweat. Since the air-conditioning was working fine and Trey was spending the night, I knew exactly how and why Cary was overheated.

"It's a good thing I did — you can't go out like that," he drawled.

"Watch me." I slung my bag over my shoulder and headed toward the door.

"You're a freak, baby girl," he shouted after me. "A woman after my own heart!"

Gideon's doorman didn't bat an eye when I climbed out of the back of the taxi in front of his building. Of course, the man had seen me in worse shape before. So had the concierge, who smiled and greeted me by

name as if I didn't look like a crazy home-
less person. Albeit one in a Burberry coat.

I walked as fast as I could in flip-flops to
the private penthouse elevator, waited for it
to descend to me, then keyed in the code. It
was a straight shot up, but the ride felt endless. I wished I could pace the confines of
the small, elegantly appointed car. My worried face stared back at me from the spotless mirrors.

Gideon hadn't called. Hadn't sent me a
text after the flirtatious one promising me a
steamy night. Hadn't come to me, even if
only to sleep next door. Gideon didn't like
being away from me.

Except when he was hurting. And
ashamed.

The elevator doors slid open and pounding, screaming heavy metal music poured
in. I cringed and covered my ears, the
volume of the ceiling-mounted speakers so
loud it hurt to hear them.

Pain. Fury. The raging violence of the
music crashed over me. I ached deep in my
chest. I knew. I understood. The song was
an audible manifestation of what Gideon
felt inside himself and couldn't let out.

He was too controlled. Contained. His
emotions so tightly leashed, along with his
memories.

I dug into my purse for my phone and ended up dropping the whole bag, spilling the contents onto the elevator car floor and across the checkerboard foyer. I left it all where it fell except for my smartphone, which I picked up and swiped through to get to the app that controlled the surround sound. I synced it to softer music, lowered the volume, and hit enter.

The penthouse fell silent for an endless moment, and then the gentle chords of "Collide" by Howie Day began to play.

I felt Gideon approaching before I saw him, the air crackling with the violent energy of an impending summer storm. He rounded the corner from the hallway leading to the bedrooms. I lost my breath.

He was shirtless and barefooted, his hair a silky tousled mane that brushed his shoulders. Black sweats clung to the lowest point of his hips, underlining the tight lacing of his abs. He was bruised on his ribs and up by his shoulder, the signs of battle only strengthening the impression of rage and ferocity tightly leashed.

My choice of music clashed with the emotion seething from him. My beautiful, savagely elegant warrior. The love of my life. So tormented that the sight of him brought hot, stinging tears to my eyes.

He jerked to a halt when he saw me, his hands clenching and releasing at his sides, his eyes wild and nostrils flaring.

My phone slid out of my hand and hit the floor. "Gideon."

He sucked in a breath at the sound of my voice. It changed him. I watched the shift come over him, like a door slamming shut. One moment, he was bristling with emotion. The next, he was cool as ice, his surface as smooth as glass.

"What are you doing here?" he asked, his voice dangerously even.

"Finding you." Because he was lost.

"I'm not fit company now."

"I can deal with it."

He was too still, as if he were afraid to move. "You should go. It's not safe for you here."

My pulse leaped. Awareness sizzled across my senses. I felt the heat of him from across the room. His need. The demand. I was suddenly melting in my jacket. "I'm safer with you than anywhere else on earth." I took a deep breath for courage. "Does Chris believe you?"

His head went back. "How do you know?"

"He called. He's worried about you. I'm worried about you."

"I'll be fine," he snapped. Which told me

he wasn't fine now.

I made my way to him, feeling the burn of his gaze as it tracked me. "Of course, you will be. You're married to me."

"You need to go, Eva."

I shook my head. "It almost hurts worse, doesn't it, when they believe you? You wonder why you waited to tell them. Maybe you could've stopped it sooner, if you'd just told the right person?"

"Shut up."

"There's always that little voice inside us that thinks we're to blame for what happened."

His eyes squeezed as tightly closed as his fists. "Don't."

I closed the distance between us. "Don't what?"

"Don't be what I need. Not now."

"Why not?"

Those fiercely blue eyes snapped open, pinning me so thoroughly that I paused midstep. "I'm hanging on by a thread, Eva."

"You don't have to hang on," I told him, holding my hands out to him. "Let go. I'll catch you."

"No." He shook his head. "I can't . . . I can't be gentle."

"You want to touch me."

His jaw worked. "I want to *fuck* you. Hard."

I felt the heat sweep up to my cheeks. It was a testament to how much he wanted me that he could still find me desirable despite my ridiculous clothes. "I'm totally up for that. Always."

My fingers went to the lapels of my coat. I'd partially buttoned up on the cab ride over, not wanting to flash anyone by accident. Now the trench was sweltering, my skin damp with perspiration.

Gideon lunged and caught my wrists, squeezing them too hard. "Don't."

"You don't think I can handle you? After all we've done together? All we've talked about and plan on doing?"

God. His entire body was straining, tense, every muscle thick and hard. And his eyes, so bright against his tanned skin, so agonized. My Dark and Dangerous.

He gripped my elbow and started walking.

"What — ?" I stumbled.

He dragged me toward the elevator. "You have to go."

"No!" I struggled, kicking off my flip-flops and digging my feet in.

"Damn it." He rounded on me and yanked me up, facing me nose to nose. "I can't promise to stop. If I take you too far and you safe word, I might not stop and this — *us* — will all go to hell!"

"Gideon! For chrissakes, don't be afraid to want me too much!"

"I want to punish you," he snarled, gripping my face in both hands. "You did this! You brought this on. Pushing people . . . pushing me. Look what you've done!"

I smelled the liquor on him then, the rich vapor of some expensive spirit. I'd never seen him truly drunk — he valued his control too much to completely dull his senses — but he was drunk now.

The first hint of wariness rippled through me.

"Yes," I said shakily, "this is my fault. I love you too much. Will you punish me for that?"

"God." He closed his eyes. His hot, damp forehead touched mine, nuzzling hard. His sweat coated my skin, imprinting me with the lushly masculine scent that was his alone.

I felt him soften, relaxing infinitesimally. I turned my head and pressed my lips to his feverish cheek.

He stiffened. "No."

Gideon pulled me toward the elevator, yanking me into the foyer and kicking the scattered contents of my purse out of the way.

"Stop it!" I yelled, trying to tug my arm free.

But he wouldn't listen. His finger stabbed at the call button. The car doors opened instantly, the private elevator always waiting to take him down. He threw me in and I stumbled into the rear wall.

Desperate, I yanked at the belt of my coat, my urgency giving me strength. I tore at the buttons, sending them rolling in every direction. The doors were closing when I spun to face him, holding the lapels of my coat wide open so he could see what I was wearing beneath.

His arm shot out, blocking the door from closing. He shoved it open. The teddy I'd worn was bloodred — our color — and had scarcely any material to it at all. Sheer mesh exposed my breasts and sex, while bandage-like cutouts caged my waist.

"Bitch," he hissed, stalking into the confined space, shrinking it too small. "You can't stop pushing."

"I'm *your* bitch," I shot back, feeling the tears well and fall. It was painful to have him so angry with me, even though I understood. He needed an outlet and I'd positioned myself as the target. He'd warned me . . . tried to protect me . . . "I can take you, Gideon Cross. I can take whatever you've got."

He tackled me back into the wall so hard the impact knocked the breath from me. His mouth covered mine, his tongue plunging deep. His hands squeezed my breasts roughly, his knee pressing hard between my legs.

I arched into him, fighting to shrug off my coat. I was too hot, sweat sliding down my back and belly. Gideon wrenched the trench off, tossing it aside, his mouth sealed to mine. A moan of gratitude escaped me, my arms wrapping around his neck, my heart swelling with the relief of holding him. My fingers pushed into his hair, my grip tightening to give me leverage to crawl up him.

Gideon tore his mouth away, then my hands. "Don't touch me."

"Fuck you," I snapped, too hurt to hold the words back. Just to spite him, I broke free of his grip and let my hands roam over his rock-hard shoulders and biceps.

He pushed me back, holding me to the wall with a single hand against the middle of my chest. No matter how I shoved or scratched at his steely arm, I couldn't budge him. I could only watch as he yanked the drawstring free of his sweats.

Desire and apprehension twisted together inside me. "Gideon . . . ?"

His gaze met mine, so dark and haunted. "Can you keep your hands off me?"

"No. I don't want to."

With a nod, he released me, only to spin me around to face the rear of the car. Caged by his body, I had little room to maneuver.

"Don't fight me," he ordered, his lips to my ear.

Then he tied my wrists to the handrail.

I froze, startled that he was actually restraining me. So surprised and disbelieving that I barely struggled. It was only after I watched him knot the thin cord that I realized he was serious.

Gripping my hips, he nuzzled my hair aside and sank his teeth into my shoulder. "I say when."

I gasped, tugging at my hands. "What are you doing?"

He didn't answer me.

He just left.

Twisting around as much as I was able, I caught him walking into the living room just as the doors slid shut.

"Oh my God," I breathed. "You wouldn't."

I couldn't believe he'd send me away like this . . . tied up in the elevator in only lingerie. He was presently screwed up in the head, yes, but I couldn't believe my wildly jealous husband would expose me that way, to whoever might be in the lobby, just to get rid of me.

"*Gideon!* Goddamn it. Don't you dare leave me in here like this! Do you *hear* me?! Get your ass back in here!"

I wrenched at the cord binding my wrists, but it was knotted tight. Seconds passed, then minutes. The car didn't move and after screaming myself hoarse, I realized it wouldn't. It waited for the push of a button, standing by for Gideon's command.

Just like I was.

I was going to kick his fucking ass when I got loose. I'd never been so pissed. *"Gideon!"*

Bending over, I walked backward, then lifted and stretched one leg to reach the button that opened the doors. I pushed it with my big toe. As they slid open, I sucked in a deep breath to scream . . .

. . . then promptly lost it in a startled rush.

Gideon strode through the living room toward the foyer . . . *completely naked.* And drenched from head to toe. His cock was so hard it curved up to his navel. His head was tipped back as he guzzled bottled water, his stride loose and easy, yet entirely predatory.

I straightened as he drew closer, panting from both the riot of my emotions and the depth of my hunger. Asshole or not, I wanted him with a ferocity I couldn't fight. He was complicated and sexy, damaged and perfect.

"Here." He brought a crystal tumbler to my lips that I hadn't noticed because I'd been too busy ogling his magnificent body. The glass was nearly full, the reddish-gold liquid sloshing against my lips as he tipped it.

My mouth opened by instinct and he poured the liquor in, the potent proof burning my tongue and throat. I coughed and he waited, his gaze heavy-lidded. He smelled clean and cool, refreshed from a shower.

"Finish it."

"It's too strong!" I protested.

He simply poured another large swallow past my parted lips.

I kicked at him, cursing when I hurt my foot — and didn't do any damage to him at all. "Stop it!"

He dropped the empty water bottle and cupped my face in his hand. His thumb brushed away the drops of liquor on my chin. "You need to let me settle, and you need to mellow out. We go at it like this, we'll tear each other apart."

A stupid tear slipped out of the corner of my eye.

Gideon groaned and bent toward me, his tongue licking the trail of the droplet off my cheek. "I'm shattered and you're beating at me with your fists. I can't take it, Eva."

"I can't take you shutting me out," I whispered, tugging at the damned cord. The liquor was spreading fire through my veins. I could feel the tendrils of intoxication curling around my senses already.

He put his hand over mine, stilling my restless movements. "Stop that. You'll hurt yourself."

"Cut me loose."

"You touch me and I can't keep it together. I'm hanging by a thread," he said again, sounding desperate. "I can't snap. Not with you."

"With someone else?" My voice became shrill. "You need someone else?"

I couldn't keep it together, either. Gideon was the rock in our relationship, the anchor. I thought I could be the same for him. I wanted to shelter him, be his haven. But Gideon didn't need shelter from the storm; he *was* the storm. And I wasn't strong enough to bear up under the weight of his crashing mood.

"No. Christ." He kissed me. Hard. "You

need me in control. *I* need to be in control when I'm with you."

I felt the panic building. He knew. He knew I wasn't enough. "You were different with the others. You didn't hold back —"

"Fuck!" Gideon spun away, slamming his fist into the control panel. The doors opened to the sound of Sarah McLachlan singing about possession and he threw the tumbler, shattering it against the foyer wall. "Yes, I was different! *You* made me different."

"And you hate me for that." I started crying, my body sagging into the car wall.

"No." He wrapped himself around me, his water-chilled body curving over my back. He rubbed his face against me, his embrace so tight I could barely breathe. "I love you. You're my *wife.* My goddamn life. You're everything."

"I just want to help you," I cried. "I want to be here for you, but you won't let me!"

"God. Eva." His hands began to move, to pet and glide. To stroke. To soothe. "I can't stop you. I need you too much."

I gripped the handrail with both hands, my cheek pressed to the cool mirror. The liquor began to work its magic. A heated languor slid through me, drowning my anger and what fight I had left until they drifted away, leaving me sad and afraid and so desperately, terrifyingly in love.

His hand pushed between my legs, rubbing, searching. With a forceful tug, he opened the snaps that held the front and back of the teddy together. I moaned at the sudden release of pressure. My sex was wet and swollen from the skilled movements of his hands and the image in my mind of the way he'd looked walking toward me.

My head fell back against his shoulder and I saw his reflection. His eyes were closed, his lips parted. The vulnerability etched on his gorgeous face undid me. He was hurting so badly. I couldn't bear it.

"Tell me what I can do," I whispered. "Tell me how to help."

"Shh." His tongue rimmed the shell of my ear. "Let me settle."

The featherlight stroke of his thumb over the mesh covering my nipple was driving me mad. The slide of his fingers between the slick folds of my cleft had me quivering. He knew where to touch me, how much pressure.

I cried out when he pushed two fingers inside me, my feet flexing, lifting me onto my toes. My knees weakened, my legs quivering with the strain. The air in the elevator felt thick and steamy, heavy with the need that pumped off him in waves.

"Ah, Christ." He groaned when my sex tightened around him, his hips rolling against me to grind his erection into my buttocks. "I'm going to bruise this sweet cunt, Eva. I can't stop it."

His arm banded around my waist and lifted me, pulling me back so that my arms were straight and I was bent over. He kneed my legs apart, his fingers sliding wetly from my cleft. I felt his hand graze my hip, and then he was dragging the wide crest of his penis through the seam of my buttocks and notching it between the lips of my sex.

I held my breath, squirming against that plush pressure. I'd wanted him all day, craving the feel of his big cock inside me, needing him to make me come.

"Wait," he groaned, reaching for both my waist and my shoulder, his fingers flexing impatiently. "Let me —"

My sex clenched, tightening around the thick head.

Gideon cursed and thrust, one hard stroke that shoved him deep. I cried out in pleasured pain, arching away from the rigid fullness, feeling the burn of stretching inner muscles and tender tissues.

"Yes," he hissed, yanking me back into him until the lips of my sex hugged the thick root of his penis. His hips circled, his balls lying heavily against my engorged clitoris. "Fucking tight . . ."

I moaned and tried to hold on to the handrail; my body rocked as he began to fuck. The sensation was devastating, being filled so completely, then emptied abruptly. My knees gave out, my core spasming in delight as he reamed me hard and thoroughly. All the emotion he'd pent up inside him was hammered into me, the relentless drives of his cock massaging every sensitive nerve.

I was coming before I knew the orgasm was on me, gasping his name as pleasure racked my body in violent trembles.

My head dropped between my arms, my muscles weak and useless. Gideon held me up with his hands, with his erection. Using my body. Taking it. Grunting primitively every time he hit the end of me.

"So deep," he growled. "So good."

In the periphery, I caught movement, my dazed eyes focusing on our reflection. With a low, pained cry I started coming again, if I'd ever stopped. Gideon was the most searingly erotic thing I'd ever seen — his biceps thick and hard as he supported my weight, his thighs straining with exertion, his ass flexing as he pistoned, his abs rippling with power as he rolled his hips with every stroke.

He'd been built to fuck, but he had mastered the skill, using every inch of his amazing body to enslave a woman to pleasure. It was innate to him, instinctive. Even drunk and near feral with anguish, his rhythm was tight and precise, his focus absolute.

Every thrust took him deep inside me, hitting the sweetest spots again and again, driving the ecstasy into me until I couldn't resist the onslaught. Another climax churned through me like a tidal wave.

"That's it," he groaned. "Milk my dick, angel. God . . . You're making me come."

I felt his cock thickening, lengthening. Tingles raced across my skin; my lungs heaved for air.

Gideon threw back his head and roared like an animal, spurting hotly. Gripping my hips, he pumped me onto his ejaculating cock, coming hard and forever, filling me until semen slicked my sex and inner thighs.

He slowed the thrust of his hips, gasping, bending over to press his cheek to my shoulder.

I started sinking to my knees. "Gideon . . ."

He pulled me up. "I'm not done," he said roughly, still thick and stiff inside me.

Then he started again.

I woke to the feel of his hair brushing over my shoulder and the press of warm, firm lips. Exhausted, I tried to roll away, but an arm around my waist pulled me back.

"Eva," he rasped. His hand cupped my breast, clever fingers rolling my nipple.

It was dark and we were in bed, although I barely remembered him carrying me there. He'd undressed me, washed me with a damp cloth, and rained kisses over my face and wrists. They were bandaged now, slicked with ointment and wrapped with care.

It had turned me on to feel his tender caresses over the chafing, the mix of pleasure and pain. He'd noticed.

With eyes hot with lust, he'd spread my legs and eaten me with an insistent demand that robbed me of the ability to think or move. He'd licked and sucked my cleft endlessly, until I lost count of how many times he made me come around his wicked tongue.

"Gideon . . ." Turning my head, I looked at him over my shoulder. He was propped on one arm, his eyes glittering in the faint light of the moon. "Did you stay with me?"

Maybe it was reckless to hope he'd stayed

with me while I slept, but sharing a bed with him was something I loved. And craved.

He nodded. "I couldn't leave you."

"I'm glad."

He rolled me over and into him, taking my mouth, kissing me softly. The coaxing licks of his tongue stirred me again, made me moan.

"I can't stop touching you," he breathed, gripping my nape to hold me still as he deepened the kiss, his teeth tugging gently on my lower lip. "When I touch you, I don't think about anything else."

Tenderness blended with the love. "Can I touch you, too?"

Closing his eyes, he begged. "Please."

I surged into him, my hands sliding into his hair to hold him as he held me. I brushed my tongue against his, our mouths hot and wet. Our legs tangled, my body arching to press against the hardness of his.

He hummed softly and slowed me down, rolling to pin me to the bed. Pulling back, he broke the seal of our mouths, nibbling, sucking. Tracing the curves of my lips with the tip of his tongue.

I whimpered in protest, wanting deeper, harder. Instead, he licked leisurely, stroking the roof of my mouth, the lining of my cheeks. I tightened my legs, dragging him closer. He rocked his hips, pressing his erection into my thigh.

Gideon kissed me until my lips were hot and puffy and the sun was rising in the sky. He kissed me until he came in a hot rush against my skin. Not once but twice.

The feel of him coming, the sound of his low pained moans of pleasure, knowing I could bring him to orgasm with just my kiss . . . I slicked his thigh with my need and ground against him until I climaxed.

As the new day began, he closed the distance he'd put between us in the elevator. He made love to me without sex. He pledged his devotion by making me the center of his world. There was nothing beyond the edges of our bed. Only us and a love that stripped us bare even as it made us whole.

When I woke again, I found him sleeping beside me, his lips as kiss-swollen as mine. Gideon's face was soft in repose, but the faint frown between his brows told me he wasn't resting as deeply as I would wish. He lay on his side, his body stretched long and lean across the mattress, the sheet tangled around his legs.

It was late, nearly nine, but I didn't have the heart to either wake him or leave him. I hadn't been at my job long enough to miss a day, but I decided to do it anyway.

I'd been putting my needs first when it came to my career, giving it the power to someday put a wedge between us. I knew my desire to be independent wasn't wrong, but at that moment, it didn't feel right, either.

Pulling on a T-shirt and boyshorts, I slipped out of the bedroom and down the hall to Gideon's home office, where his smartphone was bitching that he was ignoring the alarm to wake him up. I turned it off and went to the kitchen.

Mentally checking off the things I needed to do, I called and left a message for Mark about missing work due to a family emergency. Then I called Scott's desk and left a message telling him that Gideon wasn't going to make it in by nine and might not be there at all. I told him to call me and we could talk about it.

I hoped to keep Gideon home all day, although I doubted he would agree to that. We needed time together, alone. Time to heal.

I retrieved my smartphone from the foyer and called Angus. He answered on the first ring.

"Hello, Mrs. Cross. Are you and Mr.

Cross ready to go?"

"No, Angus, right now we're staying put. I'm not sure we'll be leaving the penthouse today. I was wondering, do you know where Gideon gets those bottles of hangover cure?"

"Yes, of course. Do you need one?"

"Gideon might when he wakes up. Just in case, I'd like to have one waiting for him."

There was a pause. "If you don't mind me asking," he asked, his Scottish burr more pronounced, "does this have something to do with Mr. Vidal's visit last night?"

I rubbed at my forehead, feeling the warning signs of an impending headache. "It has everything to do with it."

"Does Chris believe?" he asked quietly.

"Yes."

He sighed. "Ach, that's why, then. The lad wouldna been prepared for that. Denial is what he knows and can handle."

"He took it hard."

"Aye, I'm certain he did. It's good he has you, Eva. You're doing the right thing for him, though it may take him time to appreciate it. I'll get that bottle for you."

"Thank you."

With that accomplished, I turned my attention to cleaning the place up. I washed the empty decanter and tumbler I found on the kitchen island first, then took the broom and dustpan into the foyer to clean up the shattered glass. I talked to Scott when he called while I was picking up all the crap that had fallen out of my purse, and when we hung up, I turned my attention to scrubbing the foyer wall and floor to remove the dried traces of brandy.

Gideon had said he felt shattered the night before. I didn't want him to wake up and find his place that way.

Our place, I corrected myself. Our home. I needed to start thinking of it that way. And so did Gideon. We were going to have a conversation about him trying to kick me out. If I was going to make a better effort at entwining our lives, then he had to as well.

I wished there were someone I could talk to about it all, a friend to listen and give sage advice. Cary or Shawna. Even Steven, who had a way about him that made him so easy to talk to. We had Dr. Petersen, but that wasn't the same thing.

For now, Gideon and I had secrets we could share only with each other, and that kept us isolated and codependent. It wasn't only innocence our abusers had taken away from us; they'd also taken our freedom. Even after the abuse was long over, we were still caged by the false fronts we lived behind. Still caged by lies, but in a different way.

I had just finished polishing all the smudges off the mirror in the elevator when it began descending with me inside. In only a T-shirt and underwear.

"Seriously?" I muttered, yanking off my rubber gloves to try to put order to my hair. After rolling around with Gideon all night, I looked like an epic mess.

The doors slid open and Angus started to step in, his footstep halting midair when he spotted me. I shifted position, trying to hide the cord still tied to the handrail behind me. Gideon had cut me loose with scissors, freeing my wrists but leaving the evidence.

"Uh, hi," I said, squirming with embarrassment. There was no good way to explain how I happened to be in the elevator, scarcely dressed and holding yellow rubber gloves, when Angus had called it down to pick him up. To make things worse, my lips were so red and swollen from kissing Gideon for hours that there was no way to hide what I'd been up to all night.

Angus's pale blue eyes lit with amusement. "Good morning, Mrs. Cross."

"Good morning, Angus," I replied, with as much dignity as I could manage.

He held out a bottle of the hangover

"cure," which I was pretty sure was just a shot of alcohol mixed with liquid vitamins. "Here you go."

"Thank you." The words were heartfelt and carried additional gratitude for his lack of questions.

"Call me if you need anything. I'll be nearby."

"You're the best, Angus." I rode back up to the penthouse. When the doors opened, I heard the penthouse phone ringing.

I made a run for it, sliding into the kitchen on my bare feet to snatch the receiver off its base, hoping the noise hadn't woken Gideon.

"Hello?"

"Eva, it's Arash. Is Cross with you?"

"Yes. He's still sleeping, I think. I'll check." I headed down the hall.

"He's not sick, is he? He's never sick."

"There's a first time for everything." Peeking into the bedroom, I found my husband sprawled magnificently in sleep, his arms wrapped around my pillow with his face buried in it. I tiptoed over to put the hangover bottle on his nightstand, and then I tiptoed back out, pulling the door closed behind me.

"He's still crashed," I whispered.

"Wow. Okay, change of plan. There are

385

some documents you both have to sign before four this afternoon. I'll have them messengered over. Give me a call when you're done with them, and I'll send someone to pick them up."

"*I* have to sign something? What is it?"

"He didn't tell you?" He laughed. "Well, I won't ruin the surprise. You'll see when you get them. Call me if you have any questions."

I growled softly. "Okay. Thanks."

We hung up and I stared down the hall toward the bedroom with narrowed eyes. What was Gideon up to? It drove me crazy that he set things in motion and handled issues without talking to me about them.

My smartphone started ringing in the kitchen. I ran back across the living room and took a look at the screen. The number was an unfamiliar one but clearly based in New York.

"Good grief," I muttered, feeling like I'd already put in a full day of work and it was just past ten thirty in the morning. How the hell did Gideon manage being pulled in so many directions at once? "Hello?"

"Eva, it's Chris again. I hope you don't mind that Ireland gave me your number."

"No, it's fine. I'm sorry I didn't call you

back sooner. I didn't mean to make you worry."

"Is he okay, then?"

I went to one of the bar stools and sat. "No. It was a rough night."

"I called his office. They told me he was out this morning."

"We're home. He's still sleeping."

"It's bad, then," he said.

He knew my man. Gideon was a creature of habit, his life rigidly ordered and compartmentalized. Any deviation from his established patterns was so rare it was cause for concern.

"He'll be all right," I assured him. "I'll make sure of it. He just needs some time."

"Is there anything I can do?"

"If I think of anything, I'll let you know."

"Thank you." He sounded tired and worried. "Thank you for saying something to me and being there for him. I wish I had been when it was happening. I'll have to live with the fact that I wasn't."

"We all have to live with it. It's not your fault, Chris. Doesn't make it easier, I know, but you need to keep it in mind or you'll beat yourself up. That won't help Gideon."

"You're wise beyond your years, Eva. I'm so glad he has you."

"I got lucky with him," I said quietly. "Big-time."

I ended the call and couldn't help but think of my mother. Seeing what Gideon was going through made me appreciate her all the more. She had been there for me; she'd fought for me. She had the guilt, too, which made her overprotective to the point of craziness, but there was a part of me that hadn't gotten quite so damaged as Gideon because of her love.

I called her and she answered on the first ring.

"Eva. You've been deliberately avoiding me. How am I supposed to plan your wedding without your input? There are so many decisions to make and if I make the wrong one, you'll —"

"Hi, Mom," I interrupted. "How are you?"

"Stressed," she said, her naturally breathy voice conveying more than a little accusation. "How could I be anything else? I'm planning one of the most important days of your life all by myself and —"

"I was thinking we could get together on Saturday and hash it all out, if that fits into your schedule."

"Really?" The hopeful pleasure in her voice made me feel guilty.

"Yes, really." I had been thinking of the

second wedding as being more for my mother than anyone else, but that was wrong. The wedding was important to Gideon and me, too, another opportunity for us to affirm our unbreakable bond. Not for the world to see, but for the two of us.

He had to stop pushing me away to protect me, and I had to stop worrying that I would disappear when I became Mrs. Gideon Cross.

"That would be wonderful, Eva! We could have brunch here with the wedding planner. Spend the afternoon going over all our options."

"I want something small, Mom. Intimate." Before she argued, I pressed forward with Gideon's solution. "We can go as crazy as you want with the reception, but I want our wedding to be private."

"Eva, people will be insulted if they're invited to the reception and not the ceremony!"

"I really don't care. I'm not getting married for them. I'm getting married because I'm in love with the man of my dreams and we're going to spend the rest of our lives together. I don't want the focus to ever shift from that."

"Honey . . ." She sighed, as if I were clueless. "We can talk more about this on Saturday."

"Okay. But I'm not changing my mind." I felt a tingle race down my back and turned.

Gideon stood just beyond the threshold to the kitchen, watching me. He'd pulled on the sweatpants from the night before and his hair was still mussed from sleep, his eyes heavy-lidded.

"I've got to go," I told my mom. "I'll see you this weekend. Love you."

"I love you, too, Eva. That's why I only want the best for you."

I killed the call and set my phone down on the island. Sliding off the seat, I faced him. "Good morning."

"You're not at work," he said, his voice raspier, sexier, than usual.

"Neither are you."

"Are you going in late?"

"Nope. And you're not, either." I went to him, wrapping my arms around his waist. He was still warm from the bed. My sleepy, sensual dream come true. "We're going to hole up today, ace. Just you and me hanging out in our pajamas and relaxing."

His arm cinched around my hips, his other hand lifting to brush the hair back from my face. "You're not mad."

"Why would I be?" Lifting onto my tiptoes, I kissed his jaw. "Are you mad at me?"

"No." He cupped my nape, pressing my cheek to his. "I'm glad you're here."

"I'll always be here. Until death do us part."

"You're planning the wedding."

"You heard that, huh? If you've got requests, tell me now or forever hold your peace."

He was quiet for a long time, long enough that I figured he didn't have anything to add.

Turning my head, I caught his lips and gave him a quick, sweet kiss. "Did you see what I left you by the bed?"

"Yes, thank you." A ghost of a smile touched his mouth.

He looked like a man who'd been well fucked, which filled me with feminine pride. "I got you off the hook at work, too, but Arash said he had some papers to send over to us. He wouldn't tell me what they were."

"Guess you'll have to wait and find out."

I brushed my fingertips over his brow. "How are you doing?"

His shoulder lifted in a shrug. "I don't know. Right now, I just feel like shit."

"Let's revisit that bath you missed last night."

"Umm, I'm feeling better already."

Linking our fingers together, I started leading him back toward the bedroom.

"I want to be the man of your dreams, angel," he said, surprising me. "I want that more than anything."

I looked back at him. "You've got that in the bag already."

I stared down at the contract in front of me, my heart racing with a dizzying combination of love and delight. I looked up from the coffee table as Gideon entered the room, his hair still damp from our bath, his long legs encased in black silk pajama bottoms.

"You're buying the Outer Banks house?" I asked, needing his confirmation despite having the proof in front of me.

His sexy mouth curved. "*We're* buying the house. We agreed we would."

"We talked about it." The agreed-upon price was a bit staggering, telling me the owners hadn't been easy to persuade. And he'd asked them to convey the copy of *Naked in Death* with the property, along with the furnishings in the master bedroom. He always thought of everything.

Gideon settled on the couch beside me. "Now, we're doing something about it."

"The Hamptons would be closer. Or Connecticut."

"It's a quick hop down by jet." He tipped my chin up with his finger and pressed his lips to mine. "Don't worry about the logistics," he murmured. "We were happy there on the beach. I can still picture you walking along the shore. I remember kissing you on the deck . . . spreading you across that big white bed. You looked like an angel and that place, for me, was like heaven."

"Gideon." I rested my forehead against his. I loved him so much. "Where do we sign?"

He pulled back and slid the contract over, finding the first yellow *sign here* flag. His gaze roved over the coffee table and he frowned. "Where's my pen?"

I stood. "I've got one in my purse."

Catching my wrist in his hand, he tugged me back down. "No. I need my pen. Where's the envelope this came in?"

I spotted it lying on the floor between the couch and table, where I'd dropped it when I realized what Arash had sent over. Picking it up, I realized it was still weighted and upended it over the table to let the rest of the items inside spill out. A fountain pen clattered onto the glass and a small photo floated out.

"There we go," he said, taking the pen and

slashing his signature on the dotted line. As he went through the rest of the pages, I picked up the picture and felt my chest tighten.

It was the photo of him and his dad on the beach, the one he'd told me about in North Carolina. He was young, maybe four or five, his small face screwed up in concentration as he helped his dad build a sand castle. Geoffrey Cross sat across from his son, his dark hair blowing in the ocean breeze, his face movie-star handsome. He wore only swimming trunks, showing off a body very much like the one Gideon boasted today.

"Wow," I breathed, knowing I was going to make copies of the image and frame one for each of the places we lived in. "I love this."

"Here." He pushed the contract, with the pen lying atop it, over to me.

I set the photo down and picked up the pen, turning it over to see the *GC* engraved on the barrel. "You superstitious or something?"

"It was my father's."

"Oh." I looked at him.

"He signed everything with it. He never went anywhere without it tucked in his pocket." He raked his hair back from his face. "He destroyed our name with that pen."

I set my hand on his thigh. "And you're building it back up with the same pen. I get it."

His fingertips touched my cheek, his gaze soft and shining. "I knew you would."

15

"His-and-hers master suite — a classic."
Blaire Ash smiled as his pen flew across the
large notepad clipped to a board.

His gaze lifted to roam the entirety of
Eva's bedroom in the penthouse, the one
I'd had him design specifically to look
exactly like the room my wife had in her
Upper West Side apartment.

"How big a change are you looking for?"
the designer asked. "Do you want to start
with a blank slate, or are you just looking
for the easiest structural change that will
combine the two rooms?"

I left it to Eva to answer. It was difficult
for me to participate, knowing this change
was one neither of us really wanted. Our
home would soon reflect how fucked up I
was and how badly our marriage was affected because of it. The whole exercise was
like a knife in the gut.

She glanced at me, then asked, "What

would the easy way look like?"

Ash smiled, revealing slightly crooked teeth. He was attractive — or so Ireland assured me — and sported his usual attire of ripped jeans and a T-shirt under a tailored blazer. I couldn't care less about his looks. What mattered was his talent, which I'd admired enough to hire him to decorate both my office and my home. What I didn't like was the way he was looking at my wife.

"We could simply adjust the layout of the master bath and knock out an arched entry through this wall, effectively joining the two rooms via the bathroom."

"That's just what we need," Eva said.

"Right. It's quick and efficient, and the actual construction wouldn't be all that disruptive to your lives. Or" — he went on — "I could show you some alternatives."

"Like what?"

He moved to her side, so close that his shoulder pressed against hers. Ash was nearly as blond as Eva, the image of them striking as he bent his head to hers.

"If we work with the square footage of all three bedrooms and master bathroom," he replied, speaking only to her as if I weren't there, "I could give you a master suite that's balanced on both sides. Both bedrooms would be the same size, with his-and-hers adjoining home offices — or sitting room, if you prefer."

"Oh." She nipped absently at her lower lip for a second. "I can't believe you sketched that up so quickly."

He winked at her. "Fast and thorough is my motto. And getting the job done so well that you think of me when you want to do it again."

I lounged against the wall, my arms crossing as I watched them. Eva seemed oblivious to the designer's double entendre. I was anything but.

The house phone rang and her head came up. She looked at me. "I bet Cary's here."

"Why don't you get that, angel?" I drawled. "Maybe you should bring him up yourself, share your excitement."

"Yes!" She ran her hand over my arm as she hurried from the room, a fleeting touch that reverberated through me.

I straightened, focusing on Ash. "You're flirting with my wife."

He stiffened abruptly, the smile leaving his face. "I'm sorry. I didn't mean anything by it. I just want Miss Tramell to feel comfortable."

"I'll worry about her. You worry about me." I didn't doubt that he questioned the arrangement we'd consulted him to implement. Everyone who saw it would. What red-blooded man in his right mind would have a wife like Eva, yet sleep not just in a different bed but a different room altogether?

The knife dug in a little deeper and twisted.

His dark eyes went flat and hard. "Of course, Mr. Cross."

"Now, let's see what you've sketched so far."

"What do you think?" Eva asked, between bites of pepperoni and basil pizza. She leaned over the island, with one leg kicked up behind her, having chosen to stand on the opposite side from where Cary and I sat.

I debated my reply.

"I mean the idea of a master suite with two mirroring sides is lovely," she went on, wiping at her mouth with a paper napkin, "but if we go the easy route, it'll be faster. Plus we could close up the wall again one day, if we want to use the room for something else."

"Like a nursery," Cary said, shaking crushed red pepper onto his slice.

My appetite died and I dropped the slice I'd been eating onto my paper plate. Lately, eating pizza at home hadn't been working out for me.

"Or a guest room," Eva corrected. "I liked what you talked to Blaire about for your apartment."

Cary shot her a look. "Quick dodge."

"Hey, you may have babies on your mind, but the rest of us have other things to check off our lists first."

She was saying exactly what I wanted her to say, but . . .

Did Eva have the same fears I did? Maybe she'd taken me as a husband because she couldn't help herself, but drew the line at taking me as a father to her children.

I carried my plate to the trash and tossed it in. "I have some calls to make. Stay," I said to Cary. "Spend time with Eva."

He gave me a nod. "Thanks."

Leaving the kitchen, I crossed the living room.

"So," Cary began, before I stepped out of earshot, "hot-designer-dude's got a thing for your man, baby girl."

"He does not!" Eva laughed. "You're crazy."

"No argument there, but that Ash guy barely glanced at you all night and kept his eyes glued on Cross."

I snorted. Ash had gotten the message,

which reaffirmed my belief in his intelligence. Cary was free to read that however he liked.

"Well, if you're right," she said, "I have to admire his taste."

I headed down the hallway and entered my home office, my gaze landing on the collage of Eva's photos on the wall.

She was the one thing I couldn't tuck neatly away in my mind. She was always at the forefront, driving everything I did.

Settling down at my desk, I got to work, hoping to catch up on what I could so that the rest of the week wouldn't be thrown completely off. It took me a bit to get my head in the game, but once I did, I felt relief. It was a reprieve to focus on problems with concrete solutions.

I was making headway when I heard a yell from the living room that sounded like it had come from Eva. I paused, listening. It was quiet a moment, and then I heard it again, followed by Cary's raised voice. I went to the door and opened it.

"You could talk to me, Cary!" my wife said angrily. "You could tell me what's going on."

"You know what the fuck is going on," he retorted, the edge in his tone drawing me out of my office.

"I didn't know you were cutting again!"

I moved down the hall. Eva and Cary squared off in the living room, the two friends glaring at each other across the span of several feet.

"It's none of your business," he said, his shoulders high and chin canted defensively. He glanced at me. "Not yours, either."

"I don't disagree," I replied, although that wasn't quite true. How Cary self-destructed wasn't my concern; how it affected Eva was.

"Bullshit. That's total fucking bullshit." Eva's gaze shot to me as she turned to bring me into their conversation. Then she looked back at Cary. "I thought you were talking to Dr. Travis."

"When do I have time for that?" he scoffed, raking his hair back off his forehead. "Between my work and Tat's, plus trying to keep Trey, I don't have time to sleep!"

Eva shook her head. "That's a cop-out."

"Don't lecture me, baby girl," he warned. "I don't need your shit right now."

"Oh my God." She tipped her head back and looked at the ceiling. "Why the fuck do the men in my life insist on shutting me out when they need me most?"

"Can't speak for Cross, but you're not around for me anymore. I'm getting by the best I can."

Her head snapped down. "That's not fair! You have to tell me when you need me. I'm not a damn mind reader!"

Turning on my heel, I left them to it. I had problems of my own to work out. When Eva was ready, she'd come to me and I would listen, being careful not to offer too much of my opinion.

I knew she didn't want to hear that I thought she would be better off without Cary.

The early-morning light slanted across the bed and caught the ends of Eva's hair as she slept. The soft blond strands glowed like burnished gold, as if they were lit from within. Her hand curled gently on the pillow beside her beautiful face, the other tucked safely between her breasts. The white sheet was draped over her from hip to thigh, her tanned legs exposed by the tangle we'd made before falling asleep.

I wasn't a man given to whimsy, but at that moment my wife looked like the angel I believed she was. I focused the camera on the sight she made, wanting to preserve that image of her for all time.

The shutter snapped and she stirred, her lips parting. I took another shot, grateful I'd bought a camera that just might do justice to her.

Her eyelids fluttered open. "What are you doing, ace?" she asked, in a voice as smoky as her irises.

I set the camera on the dresser and joined her in the bed. "Admiring you."

Her lips curved. "How are you feeling today?"

"Better."

"Better is good." Rolling, she reached for her breath mints. She turned back to me smelling of cinnamon. Her gaze slid over my face. "You're ready to tackle the world today, aren't you?"

"I'd much rather stay home with you."

Her eyes narrowed. "You're just saying that. You're itching to get back to global domination."

Bending down, I kissed the tip of her nose. "You know me so well."

It still amazed me how well she could read me. I was feeling restless, a bit shaky. Distracting myself with work — seeing concrete progress made on any of the projects I was personally overseeing — would ease that. Still, I pointed out, "I could work the morning at home, and then spend the afternoon with you."

She shook her head. "If you want to talk, I'll stay home. Otherwise, I've got a job to get back to."

"If you worked with me, you could cyber-commute, too."

"You'd rather push me on that, huh? That's the tack you wanna take?"

I rolled onto my back and slung my forearm over my eyes. She hadn't pushed me the day before and I knew she wouldn't push me today. Or tomorrow. Like Dr. Petersen, she'd wait patiently for me to open up. But knowing she was waiting was pressure enough.

"There's nothing to say," I muttered. "It happened. Now Chris knows. Talking about it after the fact won't change anything."

I felt her turn toward me. "It's not talking about the events themselves that matters, it's how you feel about them."

"I don't feel anything. It . . . surprised me. I don't like surprises. Now, I'm over it."

"Bullshit." She slid out of bed faster than I could catch her. "If you're just going to lie, keep your mouth shut."

Sitting up, I watched her round the foot of the bed, the tight set of her shoulders doing nothing to detract from how stunning she was. My need for her was a constant thrumming in my blood, so easily provoked by her fiery Latin temper into a restlessly impatient craving.

I'd heard some say my wife was as breathtaking as her mother, but I disagreed. Monica Stanton was a cool beauty, one who gave off the air of being slightly out of reach. Eva was all heat and sensuality — you could reach her, but her passion would scorch you.

I jumped out of bed and waylaid her before she reached the bathroom, gripping her by the upper arms. "I can't fight with you right now," I told her honestly, staring down into the roiling depths of her turbulent gaze. "If we're out of sync, I won't make it through the day."

"Then don't tell me you're over it when you're struggling to keep it together!"

I growled, frustrated. "I don't know what to do with this. I don't see how Chris knowing changes anything."

Her chin tilted up. "He's worried about you. Are you going to call him?"

My head turned away. When I thought of seeing my stepfather again, my stomach churned. "I'll talk to him at some point. We do manage a business together."

"You'd rather avoid him. Tell me why."

I pushed back from her. "We're not suddenly going to be the best of friends, Eva. We rarely saw each other before, and I see no reason for that to change."

"Are you angry with him?"

"Jesus. Why the fuck is it my job to make him feel better?" I headed for the shower.

She followed. "Nothing is going to make him feel better, and I don't think he expects that of you. He just wants to know that you're back on your stride."

I reached into the stall and turned the taps on.

Her hand touched my back. "Gideon . . . you can't just shove your feelings into a box. Not unless you want an explosion like the other night. Or another nightmare."

It was the mention of my recurrent nightmares that had me rounding on her. "We managed the last two nights just fine!"

Eva didn't back down in the face of my fury the way others did, which only aggravated me further. And seeing the myriad reflections of her naked body in the mirrors didn't help.

"You didn't sleep on Tuesday night," she challenged. "And last night you were so exhausted, I doubt you even dreamed at all."

She didn't know I'd slept part of the night in the other bedroom, and I didn't see any reason to mention it. "What do you want me to say?"

"This isn't about me! It helps to talk things over, Gideon. Laying it all out helps us gain perspective."

"Perspective? I've got that just fine. There was no mistaking the pity on Chris's face last night. Or yours! I don't need anyone feeling sorry for me, damn it. I don't need their fucking guilt."

Her brows shot up. "I can't speak for Chris, but that wasn't pity you saw on me, Gideon. Sympathy, maybe, because I know what you're feeling. And pain, certainly, because my heart is connected to yours. When you're hurting, I'm hurting, too. You'll have to learn to deal with that, because I love you and I'm not going to stop."

Her words ripped into me. Reaching out, I gripped the edge of the shower's floating glass.

Relenting, she came to me, wrapped herself around me. My head bowed as I soaked her in. The smell of her, the feel. My free arm slid around her hips, my hand cupping the full curve of her ass. I wasn't the same man I'd been when we met. I was stronger in some ways and weaker in others. It was the weakness I struggled with. I used to feel nothing. And now —

"He doesn't see you as weak," she murmured, reading me the way she always could. Her cheek lay over my heart. "No one could. After what you've been through . . . to be the man you are today. *That's* strength, baby. And I'm impressed."

My fingers flexed into her supple flesh. "You're biased," I muttered. "You're in love with me."

"Of course I am. How could I be anything else? You're amazing and perfect —"

I grunted.

"Perfect for *me,*" she corrected. "And since you belong to me, that's a good thing."

I tugged her back and into the shower, leading her under the pounding jets of warm water. "I feel like this changed things," I admitted, "but I don't know how."

"We figure it out together." Her hands ran over my shoulders and down my arms. "Just don't push me away. You have to stop trying to protect me, especially from yourself!"

"I can't hurt you, angel. Can't take any risks."

"Whatever. I can take you down, ace, if you get out of hand."

If that were true, it might have been a comfort.

I switched gears, hoping to avoid a fight that would send ripples through the rest of my day. "I've been thinking about the penthouse renovations."

"You're changing the subject."

"We exhausted the subject. It's not

closed," I qualified, "just tabled until there are additional variables to address."

She eyed me. "Why does it turn me on when you go all alpha mogul on me like that?"

"Don't tell me there are times when I don't turn you on."

"God, I wish. I'd be a more productive human being."

I brushed the wet hair back from her forehead. "Have you thought about what you want?"

"Whatever ends with your cock inside me."

"Good to know. I was talking about the penthouse."

She shrugged, her eyes lit with mischievous amusement. "Same goes either way."

It was the sort of local eatery that tourists never spared a glance. Small and lacking in aesthetics, it boasted a vinyl marquee that did nothing to brand it as unique or welcoming. It specialized in soup, with sandwich options for those with heartier appetites. A cooler by the door offered a limited selection of beverages, while an ancient register was only capable of taking cash.

No, travelers would never come to this

place run by immigrants who'd decided to take a bite out of the Big Apple. They'd head to the spots made famous by movies or television shows, or those that dotted the garish spectacle of Times Square. The locals, however, knew the gem in their neighborhood and lined up outside the door.

I slid through that line to reach the back, where a tiny room held a handful of chipped enamel-topped tables. A lone man sat at one of them, reading the day's paper while steam curled out of his cup of soup.

Pulling out the chair opposite him, I sat.

Benjamin Clancy didn't look up when he spoke. "What can I do for you, Mr. Cross?"

"I believe I owe you thanks."

He folded the paper leisurely and then set it aside, his gaze meeting mine. The man was solidly built, thick with muscle. His hair was dark blond, cut short in a military style. "Do you? Well, then, I accept. Although I didn't do it for you."

"I didn't think you did." I studied him. "You're still keeping watch."

Clancy nodded. "She's been through enough. I'm going to see she doesn't go through any more."

"You don't trust me to do that?"

"I don't know you enough to trust you. In

my opinion, neither does she. So I'll keep an eye on things for a while."

"I love her. I think I've proven how far I'll go to protect her."

His gaze hardened. "Some men need to be put down like rabid dogs. Some men need to be the ones to do it. I didn't peg you as one of those guys either way. That makes you rogue in my book."

"I take care of what's mine."

"Oh, you took care of it all right." His smile didn't quite reach his eyes. "And I took care of the rest. As long as Eva is happy with you, we'll leave it at that. You decide someday she's not what you want, you cut her off clean and with respect. If you hurt her in any way at all, then you've got a problem, whether I'm still breathing or in the grave. You got me?"

"You don't have to threaten me to be good to her, but I heard you." Eva was a strong woman. Strong enough to survive her past and to pledge her future to me. But she was vulnerable, too, in ways most people didn't see. That was why I would do anything to shield her, and it seemed Benjamin Clancy felt the same.

I leaned forward. "Eva doesn't like being spied on. If you become a problem for her, we'll sit down like this again."

"You planning on making it a problem?"

"No. If she catches you at it, it won't be because I tipped her off. Just keep in mind that she's spent her life looking over her shoulder and being suffocated by her mother. She's breathing easy for the first time. I won't let you take that away from her."

Clancy narrowed his eyes. "I guess we understand each other."

I pushed back from the table and stood, extending my hand. "I'd say we do."

As my day ended and I cleared off my desk, I felt solid and settled.

There in my office, at the helm of Cross Industries, I had a handle on every detail. I doubted nothing, least of all myself.

The ground had leveled beneath my feet. I'd smoothed the feathers ruffled by my Wednesday cancellations, while staying on track with my Thursday. Despite missing a full day, I was no longer behind.

Scott walked in. "I've confirmed your agenda for tomorrow. Mrs. Vidal will meet you and Miss Tramell at The Modern at noon."

Shit. I'd forgotten about lunch with my mother.

I glanced at him. "Thank you, Scott. Have

413

a good night."

"You, too, Mr. Cross. See you tomorrow."

Rolling my shoulders back, I walked over to the window and looked out at the city. Things had been easier before Eva. Simpler. During the day, while consumed with work, I'd taken a moment to miss that simplicity.

Now, with the evening upon me and time to think, the prospect of major alterations to the home I'd come to see as a refuge bothered me more than I would admit to my wife. On top of the other personal pressures we faced, I felt almost crushed by the scale of the adjustments I was making.

Waking up to Eva as she'd been that morning was worth it all, but that didn't mean I wasn't struggling with the aftermath of her entry into my life.

"Mr. Cross."

I turned at the sound of Scott's voice and found him standing in the doorway to my office. "You're still here."

He smiled. "I was on my way out to the elevators when Cheryl caught me at reception. There's a Deanna Johnson in the lobby asking for you. I wanted to confirm that I should tell her you're no longer available today."

I was tempted to turn her away. I had little patience for reporters and even less for former lovers. "They can send her up."

"Do you need me to stay?"

"No, you can go. Thank you."

I watched him leave, then watched Deanna arrive. She strode toward my office on long legs and high heels, her thin gray skirt skimming the tops of her knees. Long dark hair swayed around her shoulders, framing the zipper that gave her otherwise traditional blouse an edge.

She tossed me a megawatt smile and held out her hand. "Gideon. Thanks for seeing me on such short notice."

I shook her hand briefly and briskly. "I expect you wouldn't go to the trouble of coming here directly unless it was important."

The statement was both fact and a warning. We had come to an understanding, but it wouldn't last if she thought she could exploit our connection beyond what I'd already conceded.

"Worth it for the view," she said, her eyes on me for just a second too long before shifting sideways to the window.

"I'm sorry, but I've got an appointment, so we'll have to make this quick."

"I'm in a hurry, too." Tossing her hair over her shoulder, she moved to the nearest chair and sat, crossing her legs in a way that showed more of her toned thigh than I wanted to see. She started digging into her large bag.

I pulled my smartphone out of my pocket, checked the time, and called Angus. "We'll be ready in ten," I told him when he answered.

"I'll bring the car around."

Ending the call, I glanced at Deanna, impatient for her to get to the point.

"How's Eva?" she asked.

"She'll be here in a few moments. You can ask her yourself."

"Oh." She looked up at me, one eye hidden behind the fall of her hair. "I should probably be gone before she gets here. I think our . . . history makes her uncomfortable."

"She knows how I was," I said evenly, "and she knows I'm not that way now."

Deanna nodded. "Of course she does, and of course you're not, but no woman likes when her man's past gets rubbed in her face."

"Then you'll have to make sure you don't do that."

Another warning.

She withdrew a thin folder from her bag. Standing, she walked toward me. "I wouldn't. I accepted your apology and appreciate it."

"Good."

"It's Corinne Giroux you might want to worry about."

What patience I'd had disappeared. "Corinne is her husband's concern, not mine."

Deanna held the folder out to me. I took it and opened it, finding a press release inside.

As I read, my grip tightened until I crumpled the edges.

"She's sold a tell-all book about your relationship," she said redundantly. "The release officially hits the wire Monday morning at nine."

16

"Other couples meet, hit things off, their friends nitpick a little but are mostly supportive, and they coast for a while in that couple stage just enjoying each other." I sighed and glanced at Gideon, who sat beside me on the couch. "We, on the other hand, can't seem to catch a break."

"What kind of breaks are you referring to?" Dr. Petersen asked, eyeing us with fond interest.

That fondness gave me hope. As soon as Gideon and I had arrived, I'd noticed the change in the dynamic between him and Dr. Petersen. There was something looser between them, a new ease. Less wariness.

"The only people who really want us to be together are my mother — who thinks us loving each other is a bonus to his billions — and his stepfather and sister."

"I don't think that's a fair assessment of your mother," Dr. Petersen said, sitting back

418

and holding my gaze. "She wants you to be happy."

"Yeah, well, a lot of being happy for my mom is being financially secure, which I just don't understand. It's not like she's ever struggled for money, so why is she so afraid of not having any? Anywayyyy . . ." I shrugged. "I'm just irritated with everyone right now. Gideon and I get along great when it's just the two of us. I mean we fight sometimes, but we always get through it. And I feel like we're always stronger once we do."

"What do you fight about?"

I glanced at Gideon again. He sat beside me totally at ease, looking gorgeous and successful in his beautifully tailored suit. It was on my to-do list to go with him the next time he updated his wardrobe. I wanted to watch them measure that stunning body of his, see them select the materials and style.

I found him sexy as sin in jeans and a T-shirt, and mind-blowing in a tuxedo. But I'd always have a special fondness for the three-piece suits he favored. They reminded me of how he'd been when I first met him, so beautiful and seemingly unattainable, a man I'd wanted so desperately that the need overrode even my sense of self-preservation.

I looked back at Dr. Petersen. "We still

argue about the things he doesn't tell me. And we argue when he tries to shut me out."

He turned his gaze to Gideon. "Do you feel the need to maintain a certain distance from Eva?"

My husband's mouth curved wryly. "There is no distance between us, Doctor. She wants me to dump everything on her that's an irritant to me and I won't do that. Ever. It's bad enough if one of us has to bother with it."

I narrowed my eyes at him. "I think that's crap. Part of a relationship is sharing the load with someone else. Maybe sometimes I can't do anything about the problem, but I can be a sounding board. I think you don't tell me things just because you'd rather shove them into a corner where you can ignore them."

"People process information in different ways, Eva."

I wasn't buying Gideon's dismissive reply. "You're not processing, you're ignoring. And I'm never going to be okay with you pushing me away when you're hurting."

"How does he push you away?" Dr. Petersen asked.

I looked at him. "Gideon . . . separates himself. He goes somewhere else where he can be alone. He won't let me help him."

420

" 'Goes somewhere else' how? Do you emotionally withdraw, Gideon? Or physically?"

"Both," I said. "He shuts down emotionally and goes away physically."

Gideon reached over and took my hand in his. "I can't shut down with you. That's the problem."

"That's not a problem!"

I shook my head. "He doesn't need space," I said to Dr. Petersen, "he needs me, but he cuts me off because he's afraid he'll hurt me if he doesn't."

"How would you hurt her, Gideon?"

"It's . . ." He exhaled harshly. "Eva has triggers. I keep them in mind, all the time. I'm careful. But sometimes, when I'm not thinking clearly, it's possible I could cross the line."

Dr. Petersen studied us. "What lines are you worried about crossing?"

Gideon's grip tightened on my hand, the only outward sign he gave of any uneasiness. "There are times when I need her too much. I can be rough . . . demanding. Sometimes, I don't have the control I need."

"You're talking about your sexual relationship?" He returned Gideon's nod. "We've touched on that briefly before. You said you have sex multiple times a day, every day. Is that still the case?"

I felt my face heat.

Gideon's thumb stroked over the back of my hand. "Yes."

Dr. Petersen set his tablet aside. "You're right to be concerned. Gideon, you may be using sex to keep Eva at an emotional distance. When you're making love, she's not talking, you're not answering. There's a point when you're not even thinking, your body is in charge and your brain is just along for the endorphin ride. Conversely, sexual abuse survivors like Eva often use sex as a way to establish an emotional connection. Can you see the problem there? You may be trying to achieve distance through sex, while Eva is trying to get closer."

"I've already told you there's no distance." Gideon leaned forward, pulling my hand into his lap. "Not with Eva."

"So tell me, when you're struggling emotionally and you initiate sex with Eva, what is it you're looking for?"

I twisted a little to look at Gideon, totally invested in his answer. I'd never questioned *why* he needed to be inside me, only *how*. For me, it was as simple as him needing and me giving.

His gaze met mine. The shield over his

eyes, that mask of his, slipped away. I saw the longing there, the love.

"The connection," he answered. "There's this moment. She opens and I . . . I open, and we're there. Together. I need that."

"You need it rough?"

Gideon looked at him. "Sometimes. There are times when she holds back. But I can get her there. She wants me to get her there, needs it like I do. I have to push. Carefully. With control. When I don't have the control, I need to back off."

"How do you push?" Dr. Petersen asked quietly.

"I have my ways."

Dr. Petersen turned his attention to me. "Has Gideon ever gone too far?"

I shook my head.

"Do you ever worry that he might?"

"No."

His gaze was soft and capped with a frown. "You should, Eva. You both should."

I was stirring vegetables and cubed chicken into a curry mix on the stove when I heard the front door opening. Curious, I waited to see who came into view, hoping Cary had come home alone.

"Smells good," he said, walking up to the breakfast bar to watch me. He looked cool and casual in an oversized white V-neck T-shirt and khaki shorts. Sunglasses hung off his collar and wide brown leather cuffs hugged each forearm, hiding the threadlike cuts I'd spotted the night before.

"Got enough for me?" he asked.

"Just you?"

He smiled his cocky smile, but I saw the tightness around his mouth. "Yep."

"Then I've got enough, *if* you pour the wine."

"You got yourself a deal."

Joining me in the kitchen, he looked over my shoulder and into the pot. "White or red?"

"It's chicken."

"White it is, then. Where's Cross?"

I watched him head to the wine fridge. "With his trainer, working out. How was your day?"

He shrugged. "Same shit as always."

"Cary." I lowered the heat and turned to him. "Just a few weeks ago, you were so happy to be here in New York and getting jobs. Now . . . you're so unhappy."

Pulling a bottle out, he shrugged again. "That's what I get for fucking around."

"I'm sorry I haven't been here for you."

He glanced at me as he dug out the bottle opener. "But . . . ?"

I shook my head. "No buts. I'm sorry. I will say that you've had company most nights I'm home, so I figured that's why we weren't talking as much, but that doesn't excuse me from not reaching out when I know you're going through a difficult time."

Cary sighed, his head bowing. "It wasn't fair to dump everything on you last night. I know Cross has got his own shit to wade through and you're dealing with that."

"That doesn't mean I'm not here for you." I put my hand on his shoulder. "Anytime you need me, just let me know and I'll be there."

Turning abruptly, he caught me up in a powerful hug, squeezing the air out of me. Sympathy did the rest of the work, squeezing my heart.

I hugged him in return, one hand stroking the back of his head. His dark brown hair was as soft as silk, his shoulders as hard as granite. I guessed they'd have to be to hold up the weight of the stress he was carrying. Guilt made me hold him even tighter.

"God," he muttered. "I've fucked this all up to hell and back."

"What's going on?"

He set me down, then turned back to the bottle to open it. "I don't know if it's hormones or what, but Tat is a raging fucking bitch right now. Nothing is good enough. Nothing makes her happy, especially being pregnant. What shot has the poor kid got with me as a father and a self-centered diva who hates him as his mother?"

"Maybe it's a girl," I said, handing over the wineglasses I'd pulled out of the cupboard.

"Jesus. Don't say that. I'm panicked enough as it is." He poured two hefty glasses, slid one over to me, and drank deep from his own. "And I feel like an asshole talking about the mother of my baby that way, but it's the truth. God help us, it's the damned truth."

"I'm sure it's just the hormones. It'll all settle in, and then she'll get that glow and be happy." I took a sip, hoping like hell everything I was saying would come true. "Have you told Trey yet?"

Cary shook his head. "He's the one sane thing I've got going on right now. I lose him, I'll lose my mind."

"He's stayed with you so far."

"And I have to work for it, Eva. Every day. I've never worked so hard. And I'm not talking about fucking."

"I didn't think you were." I pulled two clean bowls out of the dishwasher, along with spoons. "What I think is that you're an

426

amazing guy and anyone would be lucky to have you. I'm pretty sure Trey feels the same way."

"Don't. Please." His gaze met mine. "I'm trying to be real here. I don't need you to blow smoke at me."

"I'm not. Maybe what I said wasn't deep, but it's true." I paused in front of the rice cooker. "Gideon doesn't tell me what's going on with him a lot of the time. He says he's trying to protect me, but what he's really doing is protecting himself."

And it took saying the words aloud to really make them sink in for me.

"He's afraid that the more he tells me, the more reason he gives me to walk away. But it's just the opposite, Cary. The more he doesn't say, the more I don't feel like he trusts me, and that's hurting us. You and Trey have been together as long as Gideon and I have." I reached out and touched his arm. "You have to tell him. If he finds out about the baby some other way — and he will — he might not forgive you."

Cary sagged against the island, suddenly looking so much older and so tired. "I feel like if I just had more time to get a handle on things, I could deal with Trey."

"Waiting isn't helping," I said gently, scooping rice into the bowls. "You're backsliding."

"What else have I got?" His voice came hard with anger. "I don't fuck around anymore. A monk gets off more than I do."

I winced, knowing Cary was a man who exemplified what Dr. Petersen had talked about. When Cary had sex, he could turn his brain off and let his body make him feel good, if only for a little while. He didn't have to think or feel beyond the sensory. It was a coping mechanism he'd had to perfect back when he was the one being fucked, long before he was old enough to even want to.

"You've got me," I countered.

"Baby girl, I love you, but you're not always what I need to get by."

"Cutting yourself and banging everyone who'll let you isn't getting you by, either. They certainly don't help you feel good about yourself."

"Something has to."

I poured curry over the rice and passed the bowl over along with a spoon. "Taking care of yourself will do it. Trusting the people you love will help, too. Being honest with yourself and with them. Sounds simple, but we both know it's not. Still, it's the only way, Cary."

He flashed me a quick, sad smile and took

the food I handed him. "I'm scared."

"There," I said softly, returning his smile. "That was honest. Would it help if I'm with you when you talk to Trey?"

"Yeah. I'll feel like a pussy for not doing it alone, but yeah, it'd help."

"Then I'll be there."

Cary caught me in a hug from behind, his cheek resting against my shoulder. "You really are always there for me. I love you for that."

Reaching back, I ran my fingers through his hair. "I love you, too."

The comforter lifted away from my skin, waking me, and then the mattress shifted under the weight of the man sliding into my bed.

"Gideon."

Eyes closed, I turned to him. Breathing deep, I inhaled the scent of his skin. My hands found the cool strength of his body, slid over him, pulled him close to warm him.

He took my mouth in a deep, urgent kiss. The shock of his hunger woke me the rest of the way; the greed in his touch sent my heart racing. He slid over me, then down, his mouth searing my nipples, then my belly, then my sex.

I gasped and arched. He tongued my clit

with demanding focus, driving me higher, his hands pinning my hips as I writhed under the lash of his tongue.

I came hard, crying out. He wiped his lips on my inner thigh and rose, a seductive looming shadow in the dark of night. He mounted me, thrust hard inside me.

Over my moan, I heard him growl my name as if the pleasure of taking me were too great to bear. I gripped his waist; he gripped the sheets. His hips surged and rolled, stroking that magnificent penis deep and tirelessly inside me.

When I woke again the sun was up, and the place beside me in the bed was cold and empty.

17

I was fixing a cup of coffee for Eva the next morning when my smartphone started ringing. Leaving the half-and-half on the counter, I crossed to the bar stool where I'd hung my coat and pulled my phone out of the pocket.

Steeling myself, I answered, "Good morning, Mother."

"Gideon. I'm sorry to cancel on such short notice" — she took a shaky breath — "but I won't be able to make lunch this afternoon."

I returned to my coffee, knowing I'd need it for the long day ahead. "That's fine."

"I'm sure you're relieved," she said bitterly.

I took a drink, wishing it were something stronger though it was barely past eight. "Don't. If I didn't want to have lunch with you, *I* would've canceled."

She was quiet a minute, then asked, "Have

431

you seen Chris lately?"

I took another sip, my gaze on the hallway as I waited for Eva. "I saw him Tuesday."

"That long ago?" There was a note of fear in her voice. It gave me no pleasure to hear it.

Eva rushed into the living room in bare feet, her body encased in a pale beige sheath dress that managed to be professional while still hugging all her curves. I'd picked it out for her knowing the color would showcase the color of her skin and the paleness of her hair.

Pleasure at the sight of her slid through my veins like the liquor I'd wished were in my coffee. She could do that to me, intoxicate and captivate me.

"I have to go," I said. "I'll call you later."

"You never do."

I set my mug down to pick up Eva's. "I wouldn't say it if I didn't mean it."

Ending the call, I shoved the phone in my pocket and handed the coffee to my wife. "You look stunning," I murmured, bending to press a kiss to her cheek.

"For a man who claims not to know a damn thing about women, you sure know how to dress one," she said, eyeing me over the lip of her mug as she took a sip.

A low moan of pleasure escaped her as

432

she swallowed, a sound very similar to the one she made when I slid my cock inside her. Coffee, I'd learned, was one of Eva's addictions.

"I've made mistakes, but I'm learning." I leaned back against the counter and pulled her between my spread legs. Had she noticed one less Vera Wang dress in the closet? I'd removed it from her wardrobe after realizing just how much of her luscious tits it exposed.

She held the mug up. "Thank you for this."

"My pleasure." I brushed my fingertips across her cheek. "I have to talk to you about something."

"Oh? What's up, ace?"

"Do you still have a Google alert on me?"

She looked into her mug. "Is this when I should plead the Fifth?"

"That won't be necessary." I waited until she looked up at me again. "Corinne has sold a book about our time together."

"What?" Her eyes darkened from pale gray to slate.

I cupped her nape and stroked over her racing pulse with my thumb. "From what I read in the press release, she kept a diary during that time. She's also sharing personal photos."

"Why? Why would she sell that stuff for people to paw through?"

The hand holding her mug trembled, so I took it from her and set it back on the counter. "I don't think she knows why."

"Can you stop it?"

"No. However, if she lies outright and I can prove it, I can go after her for that."

"But only after it's released." Her hands came to rest on my chest. "She knows you'll have to read it. You'll have to see all the photos and read about how much she loves you. You'll read about things you did that you don't even remember now."

"And it won't matter." I pressed my lips to her forehead. "I never loved her, not the way I do you. Looking back on that time isn't going to make me suddenly wish I were with her and not you."

"She didn't push you," she whispered. "Not like I do."

I spoke against her skin, wishing I could press the words into her mind in a way that she would never doubt them. "She also didn't make me burn. Didn't make me hunger, and hope, and dream like you do. There's no comparison, angel, and no going back. I would never want to."

Her beautiful eyes closed. She leaned into

me. "The hits just keep on coming, don't they?"

I looked over her head and out the window beyond, at the world that waited for us once we stepped outside. "Let 'em come."

She exhaled roughly. "Yeah, let 'em come."

I entered Tableau One and spotted Arnoldo immediately. Dressed in his pristinely white chef's jacket paired with black slacks, he stood by a small table for two in the back, talking to the woman I'd come to see.

Her head turned toward me as I approached, her long dark hair sliding across her shoulder. Her blue eyes lit brightly for a moment when she spotted me, and then that light was quickly banked. Her smile when she greeted me was cool and more than a little smug.

"Corinne." I greeted her with a nod before shaking hands with Arnoldo. The restaurant he ran and I backed was crowded with lunch guests, the buzz of numerous conversations loud enough to drown out the instrumental Italian-themed music piping through recessed speakers.

Arnoldo excused himself to see to the kitchen, lifting Corinne's hand to his lips in farewell. Before he walked away, he shot me a look that I understood to mean we'd talk later.

I took the seat across from Corinne. "I appreciate your taking the time to see me."

"Your invitation was a pleasant surprise."

"I don't believe it was unexpected." I leaned back, absorbing the soft lilt of Corinne's speech. While Eva's throaty voice stirred a deep craving, Corinne's had always soothed me.

Her smile widened as she brushed at an invisible speck on the plunging neckline of her red dress. "No, I suppose not."

Irritated by the game she was playing, I spoke curtly. "What are you doing? You value your privacy as much as I do mine."

Corinne's lips flattened into a firm line. "I thought the exact same thing when I first saw that video of you and Eva arguing in the park. You say I don't know you, but I do, and having your private life splashed all over the tabloids isn't something you would ever allow under normal circumstances."

"What's normal?" I shot back, unable to deny that I was a different man with Eva. I'd never indulged women who tested me expecting some grand gesture. If they pursued me aggressively enough, I let them catch me for a night. With Eva, I'd always been the one chasing.

"That's exactly my point — you don't remember. Because you're wrapped up in a passionate affair and you can't see beyond it."

"There is nothing beyond it, Corinne. I will be with her until I die."

She sighed. "You think so now, but stormy relationships don't last, Gideon. They burn themselves out. You like order and calm, and you won't have that with her. Ever. Somewhere inside you, you know that."

Her words struck home. She had unwittingly echoed my own thoughts on the subject.

A server came by our table. Corinne ordered a salad; I ordered a drink — a double.

"So you've sold a tell-all to do . . . what?" I asked, when the server walked away. "Get back at me? Hurt Eva?"

"No. I want you to remember."

"This isn't the way."

"What is the way?"

I held her gaze. "It's over, Corinne. Exposing your memories of us isn't going to change that."

"Maybe not," she conceded, sounding so sad it sent a pang of regret through me. "But you said you never loved me. At the very least, I'll prove that wrong. I gave you

437

comfort. Contentment. You were happy with me. I don't see that same sort of tranquillity when you're with her. You can't tell me you feel it."

"Everything you're saying tells me you don't care if I end up with you. But if you're leaving Giroux, maybe you care about the money. How much did they pay you to prostitute your 'love' for me?"

Her chin lifted. "That's not why I'm writing the book."

"You just want to be sure I don't end up with Eva."

"I just want you to be happy, Gideon. And since you've met her, I've seen you be anything but."

How would Eva take the book when she read it? No better, I imagined, than I was taking "Golden."

Corinne's gaze dropped to my left hand, which rested on the tabletop. "You gave Eva your mother's engagement ring."

"It hasn't been hers for a long time."

She took a sip of the wine she'd had on the table when I joined her. "Did you have it when you and I were together?"

"Yes."

She flinched.

"You can tell yourself that Eva and I are incompatible," I said tightly, "that we're either fighting or fucking with nothing of substance in between. But the truth is that she's the other half of me and what you're doing is going to hurt her, which will hurt me. I'll buy you out of the publishing contract if you'll withdraw the book."

She stared at me for a long minute. "I . . . I can't, Gideon."

"Tell me why."

"You're asking me to let you go. This is a way for me to do that."

I leaned forward. "I'm asking you, Corinne, if you feel anything for me at all, to please drop this."

"Gideon . . ."

"If you don't, you're going to turn what were good memories for me into something I hate."

Her turquoise eyes shone with tears. "I'm sorry."

I pushed back from the table and stood. "You will be."

Turning away, I walked out of the restaurant to the waiting Bentley. Angus opened the door, his gaze shifting to look beyond me into Tableau One's massive front window.

"Damn it." I slid into the back. "God fucking damn it!"

People who felt I'd wronged them in some

way were crawling out of the shadows like spiders, lured by the presence of Eva in my life.

She was my biggest vulnerability, one I wasn't hiding well. And that was becoming a problem I had to get a handle on. Christopher, Anne, Landon, Corinne . . . they were only the beginning. There were others who had grievances against me. Still more who held grudges toward my father.

I'd long dared them all to come at me, enjoying the challenge. Now, the bastards were coming at me through my wife. All at once. And I was being stretched thin because of it. If I didn't have my guard up completely, my focus absolute, I would leave Eva open and unprotected.

Whatever I had to do, I had to prevent that.

"I still want to see you tonight," Eva said, her seductive voice drifting through the phone receiver like smoke.

"That's not in question," I told her, leaning back in my desk chair. Outside the windows, the sun hung lower in the sky. The workday was over. Somewhere in the madness of the week, August had given way to September. "You deal with Cary, I'll sit down with Arnoldo, and you and I will start the weekend when we're done."

"God, this week just flew by. I need to work out. I skipped too many days."

"Spar with me tomorrow."

She laughed. "Yeah, right."

"I'm not joking." I thought of Eva in her sports bra and body-hugging pants, and my dick stirred with interest.

"I can't fight you!" she protested.

"Of course you can."

"You know too much. You're too good."

"Let's put those self-defense skills of yours to the test, angel." The idea I'd thrown out on a whim suddenly seemed like the best one I'd had all day. "I want to know you can take care of yourself in the unlikely case that you have to."

She never would, but it would give me peace of mind to know that she could get away from a threat.

"I've got wedding stuff tomorrow, but I'll think about it," she said. "Hang on."

I heard the car door open and Eva greet her doorman. She said hi to her concierge, and then I heard the ding of an arriving elevator in her lobby.

"You know" — she sighed — "I'm putting on a brave face for Cary, but I'm worried about what's going to happen with Trey. If he walks out, I think Cary just might totally

441

self-destruct."

"He's asking a lot," I warned her, hearing another ding from the elevator. "Cary's basically telling this guy that he's got a pregnant sidepiece that he intends to hang on to. No, scratch that. He's saying that Trey is going to be the sidepiece. I can't see that going over well with anyone."

"I know."

"I'll have my phone on me all night. Call me if you need me."

"I always need you. I'm home, so I have to go. See you later. I love you."

Would those words always hit me hard enough to steal my breath?

We hung up just as a familiar figure rounded the corner leading to my office. I stood as Mark Garrity reached my open doorway, and I met him halfway with my hand extended.

"Mark, thank you for making time for me."

He smiled and shook my hand in a strong grip. "I'm the one feeling thankful, Mr. Cross. There are a large number of people in this city — in the world, actually — who'd kill to be where I am right now."

"Call me Gideon, please." I gestured toward the seating area. "How's Steven?"

"He's doing great, thank you. I'm beginning to think he missed a calling as a wedding planner."

I smiled. "Eva's about to dig into that this weekend."

Unbuttoning his suit jacket, Mark tugged up the legs of his slacks and sat on the sofa. His gray suit contrasted well with his dark skin and striped tie, pulling together the appearance of an urban professional on the rise.

"If she has half as much fun with it as Steven," he said, "she'll have the time of her life."

"Let's hope she doesn't have too much fun," I drawled, remaining on my feet. "I'd like to get past the planning and into the actual wedding."

Mark laughed.

"Can I get you something to drink?" I asked.

"I'm good, thanks."

"Okay. I'll make this quick." I took a seat. "I asked you to meet me after work, because it wouldn't be appropriate for me to offer you a position with Cross Industries while you're on Waters Field and Leaman's time."

His brows shot up.

I let that sink in for a second or two. "Cross Industries has a number of diverse international holdings, with a concentration

443

on real estate, entertainment, and premium brands — or assets we believe we can elevate to that status."

"Like Kingsman Vodka."

"Precisely. For the most part, advertising and marketing campaigns are managed on the ground level, but brand overhauls or adjustments to messaging are approved here. Due to the diversity I mentioned, we're always reviewing new strategies for rebranding or strengthening an established brand. We could use you."

"Wow." Mark rubbed his palms over his knees. "I'm not sure what I was expecting, but this has caught me off guard."

"I'll pay you twice what you're making, to start."

"That's a hell of an offer."

"I'm not a man who likes the word *no.*"

His grin flashed. "I doubt you hear it very often. I guess this means Eva is leaving Waters Field and Leaman?"

"She hasn't made that decision yet."

"No?" His brows shot up again. "If I leave, she'll lose her job."

"And gain another one here, of course." I kept my replies as brief and unrevealing as possible. I wanted his cooperation, not questions he might not like the answers to.

"Is she waiting for me to agree before she

takes any steps?"

"Your decision will be a catalyst."

Mark ran a hand over his tie. "I'm both flattered and excited, but —"

"I understand it's not a move you were planning on making," I interjected smoothly. "You're happy where you're at, and feel a measure of job security. So I'm prepared to guarantee you the position — and reasonable bonuses and annual raises — for the next three years, barring any misconduct on your part."

Leaning forward, I set my fingers on the folder that Scott had left atop the table. I pushed it toward Mark. "All the information is laid out in detail in this. Take it home with you, discuss it with Steven, and let me know your decision on Monday."

"Monday?"

I stood. "I expect you'll want to give Waters Field and Leaman ample notice and I don't have a problem with that, but I'll need to have your commitment as soon as possible."

He picked up the folder and rose to his feet. "What if I have questions?"

"Call me. My card is in the folder." I glanced at the watch on my wrist. "I'm sorry. I have another appointment."

"Oh, yes, of course." Mark accepted my

extended hand. "I'm sorry. This happened so fast I feel like I haven't quite processed it all yet. I understand you've offered me a fantastic opportunity, though, and I appreciate that."

"You're good at what you do," I told him honestly. "I wouldn't make the offer if you weren't worth it. Think about it, then say yes."

He laughed. "I'll give it some serious thought and you'll hear from me on Monday."

As he left, my head turned toward the building that housed LanCorp's headquarters. Landon wouldn't find me with my back turned again.

"She started crying the minute you walked out."

I looked at Arnoldo over the rim of my tumbler, which held two fingers of scotch. I swallowed, then asked, "Do you want me to feel guilty about that?"

"No. I wouldn't feel sorry for her, either. But I thought you should know that Corinne isn't completely heartless."

"I never thought she was. I just thought she'd given that heart to her husband."

Arnoldo lifted one shoulder in a shrug. Dressed in well-worn jeans and a tucked-in white dress shirt that was open at the collar and rolled up at the cuffs, he was drawing a lot of female attention.

The bar was packed, but our section of the VIP balcony was guarded well, keeping the rest of the patrons at bay. Arnoldo sat on the crescent-shaped sofa where Cary had sat the first night I'd met with Eva outside the Crossfire. The place would always hold strong memories because of her. It was that night when I realized she was changing everything.

"You look tired," Arnoldo said.

"It's been one of those weeks." I caught his look. "No, it's not Eva."

"Do you want to talk about it?"

"Nothing to say, really. I should've been smarter. I let the world see how much she means to me."

"Passionate kisses on the street, even more passionate fights in the park." He smiled ruefully. "What is it they say? Wearing your heart on your sleeve?"

"I opened the door, now everyone wants to walk through it. She's the most direct way to fuck with my head, and everyone knows it."

"Including Brett Kline?"

"He's not an issue any longer."

Arnoldo studied me and must have seen

whatever he needed to. He nodded. "I'm glad, my friend."

"So am I." I took another drink. "What's new with you?"

He waved off the question with a careless sweep of his hand, his gaze sliding around us to take in the women nearby who were swaying to the music of Lana Del Rey. "The restaurant is doing well, as you know."

"Yes, I'm very pleased. Exceeded profit projections in every way."

"We just filmed some promotional teasers for the new season earlier this week. Once the Food Network starts airing them and the new episodes, we should see a nice boost in business."

"I can always say I knew you when."

He laughed and clinked his glass to mine when I held it up in a toast.

We were back on track, which settled some of the unrest I'd been feeling. I didn't lean on Arnoldo the way Eva leaned on her friends or Cary leaned on her, but Arnoldo was important to me all the same. I didn't have many people in my life who were close to me. Finding the rhythm he and I had lost was at least one major victory in a week that had seemed like a losing battle.

18

"Oh my God," I moaned around a bite of chocolate toffee cupcake, "this is divine."

Kristin, the wedding planner, beamed. "It's one of my favorites, too. Hold on, though. The butter vanilla is even better."

"Vanilla over chocolate?" My gaze slid over the yummies on the coffee table. "No way."

"I would usually agree," Kristin said, making a note, "but this bakery made me a convert. The lemon is also very good."

The early-afternoon light poured in through the massive windows that made up one side of my mother's private sitting room, illuminating her pale gold curls and porcelain skin. She'd redecorated recently, opting for soft gray-blue walls that lent a new energy to the space — and complemented her well.

It was one of her talents, showcasing herself in the best light. It was also one of her major flaws, in my opinion. She cared so damn much about appearances.

I didn't understand how my mom could not get bored with decorating to the latest trends, even if it did seem to take over a year to cycle through every room and hallway in Stanton's six-thousand-plus-square-foot penthouse.

My one meeting with Blaire Ash had been enough to tell me that the decorating gene had skipped my generation. I'd been interested in his ideas but couldn't get worked up over the details.

While I popped another mini cupcake into my mouth with my fingers, my mother daintily speared one of the coin-sized cakes with a fork.

"What are your floral arrangement preferences?" Kristin asked, uncrossing and recrossing long, coffee-hued legs. Her Jimmy Choo heels were elegant but still sexy; her Diane von Furstenberg wrap dress was vintage and classic. She wore her shoulder-length dark hair in tight curls that framed and flattered her narrow face, and pale pink gloss highlighted full, wide lips.

She looked fierce and fabulous, and I'd liked her the moment we met.

"Red," I said, wiping frosting from the corner of my mouth. "Anything red."

450

"Red?" My mother gave an emphatic shake of her head. "How garish, Eva. It's your first wedding. Go with white, cream, and gold."

I stared at her. "How many weddings do you expect me to have?"

"That's not what I meant. You're a first-time bride."

"I'm not talking about wearing a red dress," I argued. "I'm just saying the primary accent color should be red."

"I don't see how that will work, honey. And I've put together enough weddings to know."

I remembered my mother going through the wedding planning process before, each successive nuptial more elaborate and memorable than the last. Never overdone and always tasteful. Beautiful weddings for a youthful, beautiful bride. I hoped I aged with half as much grace, because Gideon was only going to get hotter as time went on. He was just that kind of man.

"Let me show you what red can look like, Monica," Kristin said, pulling a leather portfolio out of her bag. "Red can be amazing, especially with evening weddings. The important thing is that the ceremony and reception represent both the bride and groom. To have a truly memorable day, it's important that we visually convey their style, history, and hopes for the future."

My mother accepted the extended portfolio and glanced at the collage of photos on the page. "Eva . . . you can't be serious."

I shot a look of appreciation at Kristin for having my back, especially when she'd come on board expecting my mother to be footing the bill. Of course, the fact that I was marrying Gideon Cross probably helped sway her to my side. Using him as a future reference would certainly help her draw new clientele.

"I'm sure there's a compromise, Mom." At least I hoped so. I hadn't dropped the biggest bomb on her yet.

"Do we have an idea of the budget?" Kristin asked.

And there it was . . .

I saw my mom's mouth open in slow motion and my heart lurched into a semipanicked beat. "Fifty thousand for the ceremony itself," I blurted out. "Minus the cost of the dress."

Both women turned wide eyes toward me.

My mom gave an incredulous laugh, her hand lifting to touch the Cartier trinity necklace that hung between her breasts. "My God, Eva. What a time to make jokes!"

"Dad's paying for the wedding, Mom," I

told her, my voice strengthening now that the moment I'd dreaded had passed.

She blinked at me, her blue eyes revealing — just for an instant — a sweet softening. Then her jaw tightened. "Your dress alone will cost more than that. The flowers, the venue . . ."

"We're getting married on the beach," I said, the idea just coming to me. "North Carolina. The Outer Banks. At the house Gideon and I just bought. We'll only need enough flowers for the members of the wedding party."

"You don't understand." My mom glanced at Kristin for support. "There's no way that would work. You'd have no control."

Meaning *she* wouldn't.

"Unpredictable weather," she went on, "sand everywhere . . . Plus, asking everyone to travel that far out of the city will make it likely some won't be able to attend. And where would everyone stay?"

"Who's everyone? I told you, the ceremony is going to be small, for friends and family only. Gideon's taking care of travel. I'm sure he'd be happy to take care of lodging arrangements, too."

"I can help with that," Kristin said.

"Don't encourage her!" my mother snapped.

453

"Don't be rude!" I shot back. "I think you're forgetting that it's *my* wedding. Not a publicity op."

My mom took a deep, steadying breath. "Eva, I think it's very sweet that you want to accommodate your father this way, but he doesn't understand what a burden he's placing on you by asking this. Even if I matched him dollar for dollar, it wouldn't be enough —"

"It's plenty." My hands linked tightly together in my lap, pressing the rings on my fingers uncomfortably against the bone. "And it's not a burden."

"You're going to offend people. You have to understand that a man in Gideon's position needs to take every opportunity to solidify his network. He's going to want —"

"— to elope," I bit out, frustrated by the too-familiar clash of our viewpoints. "If he had his way, we'd run off somewhere and get married on a remote beach with a couple of witnesses and a great view."

"He may say that —"

"No, Mother. Trust me. That's *exactly* what he would do."

"Um, if I may." Kristin leaned forward. "We can make this work, Monica. Many celebrity weddings are private affairs. A limited budget will keep us focused on the details. And, if Gideon and Eva are open to it, we can arrange to have select photographs sold to the celebrity lifestyle magazines, with the profits going to charity."

"Oh, I like that!" I said, even as I wondered how that could work with the forty-eight-hour exclusive deal Gideon had offered Deanna Johnson.

My mom looked distraught. "I've dreamed of your wedding since the day you were born," she said quietly. "I always wanted you to have something fit for a princess."

"Mom." I reached over and took her hand in mine. "You can go wild with the reception, okay? Do whatever you want. Skip the red, invite the world, whatever. As for the wedding, isn't it enough that I found my prince?"

Her hand tightened on mine and she looked at me with tears in her blue eyes. "I guess it'll have to be."

I'd just slid into the back of the Benz when my smartphone started ringing. Pulling it out of my purse, I looked at the screen and saw it was Trey. My stomach twisted a little.

I couldn't get the shattered look on his face last night out of my mind. I'd stayed tucked away in the kitchen while Cary sat with Trey in the living room and told him about Tatiana and the baby. I had put a pot roast in the oven and sat at the breakfast bar with my tablet, reading a book while staying in Cary's line of sight. Even in profile, I could see how hard Trey had taken the news.

Still, he'd stayed for dinner and then overnight, so I hoped things would work out in the end. At least he hadn't just walked out.

"Hi, Trey," I answered. "How are you?"

"Hey, Eva." He sighed heavily. "I have no idea how I am. How are you doing?"

"Well, I'm just leaving my mother's place after spending hours talking about the wedding. It didn't go as badly as it could have, but it could've been smoother. But that's pretty usual when dealing with my mom."

"Ah . . . well, you've got a lot on your plate. I'm sorry to bother you."

"Trey. It's fine. I'm glad you called. If you want to talk, I'm here."

"Could we get together, maybe? Whenever it's convenient for you?"

"How's now?"

"Really? I'm at a street fair on the west side. My sister dragged me out and I was miserable company. She ditched me a few minutes ago and now I'm wondering what the hell I'm doing here."

"I can meet you."

"I'm between Eighty-second and Eighty-third, close to Amsterdam. It's packed here, just FYI."

"Okay, hang tight. I'll see you in a few."

"Thanks, Eva."

We hung up and I caught Raúl's gaze in the rearview mirror. "Amsterdam and Eighty-second. Close as you can get."

He nodded.

"Thanks." I looked out the window as we turned a corner, taking in the city on a sunny Saturday afternoon.

The pace of Manhattan was slower on the weekends, the clothes more casual, and the street vendors more plentiful. Women in sandals and light summer dresses window-shopped leisurely, while men in shorts and T-shirts traveled in groups, taking in the women and discussing whatever it was men discussed. Dogs of all sizes pranced on the ends of leashes, while children in strollers kicked up their heels or napped. An elderly couple shuffled along hand in hand, still lost in the wonder of each other after years of familiarity.

I was speed-dialing Gideon before I realized I'd thought of it.

"Angel," he answered. "Are you on your way home?"

"Not quite. I'm done at my mom's, but I'm going to meet Trey."

"How long will that take?"

"I'm not sure. Not more than an hour, I think. God, I hope he doesn't tell me he's done with Cary."

"How did it go with your mother?"

"I told her we were getting married on the beach by the Outer Banks house." I paused. "I'm sorry. I should've asked you first."

"I think that's an excellent idea." His raspy voice took on the special timbre that told me he was moved.

"She asked me how we're planning on lodging everyone. I kinda dropped that on you and the wedding planner."

"That's fine. We'll work something out."

Love for him spread through me in a warm rush. "Thank you."

"So the big hurdle's behind you," he said, understanding as he so often did.

"Well, I don't know about that. She got all teary about it. You know, she had big dreams that aren't coming true. I hope she lets them go and gets on board."

"What about her family? We haven't talked about making arrangements for them to come."

I shrugged, then remembered he couldn't

see me. "They're not invited. The only things I know about them are what I found with a Google search. They disowned my mom when she got pregnant with me, so they've never been a part of my life."

"All right, then," he said smoothly. "I've got a surprise for you when you get home."

"Oh?" My mood instantly brightened. "Will you give me a hint?"

"Of course not. You'll have to hurry home if you're curious."

I pouted. "Tease."

"Teases don't deliver. I do."

My toes curled at the rough velvet of his voice. "I'll be home as soon as I can."

"I'll be waiting," he purred.

The traffic near the fair was impossible. Raúl left the Benz in the garage beneath my apartment building, then walked me over to the street fair.

When we were half a block away, I started smelling the food and my mouth watered. Music drifted in the air and when we reached Amsterdam Avenue, I saw that it came from a woman singing on a small stage for a packed audience.

Vendors lined either side of the overflowing street, their wares and heads shielded from the sun by white tent tops. From scarves and hats, to jewelry and art, to fresh produce and multinational eats, there was nothing one could want that couldn't be found.

It took me a few minutes to spot Trey in the crowd. I found him sitting on steps not too far from the corner we'd agreed upon. He was dressed in loose jeans and an olive-hued T-shirt, with sunglasses perched on the crooked bridge of his once-broken nose. His blond hair was as unruly as ever, his attractive mouth tightened into a firm line.

He stood when he saw me, holding out his hand for me to shake. I pulled him into a hug instead, holding him until I felt him relax and hug me back. Life flowed by around us — New Yorkers were comfortable with all sorts of public displays. Raúl moved a discreet distance away.

"I'm a fucking mess," Trey muttered against my shoulder.

"You're normal." I pulled back and gestured toward the steps where I'd found him. "Anyone would be reeling right now."

He sat down on the middle step. I perched next to him.

"I don't think I can do this, Eva. I don't think I should. I want someone in my life full-time, someone who's there to support me while I get through school, then try to build my practice. Cary's going to be supporting that model instead and fitting me in when he can. How am I not going to resent that?"

"That's a valid question," I said, stretching out my legs in front of me. "You know Cary won't be sure the baby is his until a paternity test is done."

Trey shook his head. "I don't think it'll matter. He seems invested."

"I think it'll matter. Maybe he won't just walk away, maybe he'll play uncle or something. I don't know. For now, we have to go with the assumption that he's the dad, but maybe he's not. It's a possibility."

"So you're telling me to hang in there for another six months?"

"No. If you want me to give you answers, I don't have any. All I can tell you for sure is that Cary loves you, more than I've ever seen him love anyone. If he loses you, it's going to break him. I'm not trying to guilt you into staying with him. I just think you should know that if you leave, you're not the only one who'll be hurting."

"How is that helpful?"

"Maybe it's not." I set my hand on his knee. "Maybe I'm just small enough to find that comforting. If Gideon and I didn't work out, I'd want to know he was as miserable as I was."

Trey's mouth curved in a sad smile. "Yeah, I see your point. Would you stay with him if you found out he'd knocked someone else up? Someone he was sleeping with while dating you?"

"I thought about that. It's hard for me to imagine not being with Gideon. If we weren't exclusive at the time and the woman was in his past, if he was with me and not her, maybe I could handle it."

I watched a woman hang yet another bag of purchases onto the overburdened handle of her kid's stroller. "But if he was mostly with her and seeing me on the side . . . I think I'd walk."

It was tough being honest when the truth was the opposite of what Cary would want me to say, but I felt like it was the right thing to do.

"Thanks, Eva."

"For what it's worth, I wouldn't think less of you if you toughed it out with Cary. It's not weak to stand by the person you love when they're trying to fix a big mistake, and it's not weak to decide to put yourself first. Whatever decision you make, I'll still think you're a helluva guy."

Leaning into me, he rested his head on my shoulder. "Thanks, Eva."

I linked my fingers with his. "You're welcome."

"I'll go get the car and pull it around," Raúl said, as we entered the lobby of my apartment building.

"Okay. I'm just going to check the mail." I waved at the concierge as we passed the desk. I turned into the mailroom, while Raúl headed to the elevator.

Sliding my key into the lock, I pulled the brass door open and bent low to peer inside. There were a few postcard advertisements and nothing else, which saved me a trip upstairs. I slid them out, tossed them in the nearby trash can, then shut and locked the mailbox.

I headed back into the lobby just in time to catch a woman exiting the building. Her spiky red hair caught my attention and held it. I stared hard, waiting for her to turn onto the street, hoping I'd catch a glimpse of her profile.

My breath caught. The hair was familiar from a Google image search. The face I remembered from the shelter fund-raiser Gideon and I had attended a few weeks back.

Then she was gone.

I ran after her, but when I reached the

sidewalk she was already sliding into the back of a black town car.

"Hey!" I shouted.

The car sped off, leaving me staring after it.

"Everything all right?"

I turned to face Louie, the weekend door-man. "Do you know who that was?"

He shook his head. "She doesn't live here."

Going back inside, I asked the concierge the same question.

"A redhead?" she asked, looking per-plexed. "We haven't had any visitors who came in without a tenant today, so I haven't really paid attention."

"Hmm. Okay, thank you."

"Your car's here, Eva," Louie said from the doorway.

I thanked the concierge and headed out to Raúl. I spent the ride between my place and Gideon's thinking about Anne Lucas. By the time I stepped out of the private elevator into the foyer of the penthouse, my spinning thoughts had me distracted.

Gideon was waiting for me. Dressed in worn jeans and a Columbia T-shirt, he looked so young and handsome. Then he flashed me a smile and I almost forgot the world altogether.

"Angel," he purred, crossing the black-and-white checkerboard flooring on bare feet. He had that look in his eye I knew well. "Come here."

I walked right into his open arms, cuddling up tightly to his hard body. I breathed him in. "You're going to think I'm crazy," I mumbled against his chest, "but I could swear I just saw Anne Lucas in the lobby of my building."

He stiffened. I knew the shrink wasn't his favorite person.

"When?" he asked tightly.

"Twenty minutes ago, maybe. Right before I came over here."

Releasing me, he reached into his back pocket and pulled out his smartphone. His other hand caught mine and pulled me into the living room.

"Mrs. Cross just saw Anne Lucas in her apartment building," he said to whoever answered.

"I *think* I did," I corrected, frowning at his hard tone.

But he wasn't listening to me. "Find out," he ordered, before hanging up.

"Gideon. What's going on?"

He led us to the couch and sat. I settled next to him, putting my purse down on the coffee table.

"I saw Anne the other day," he explained, holding on to my hand. "Raúl confirmed that the woman who spoke to you at the fund-raiser was her. She admitted it, and I warned her to stay away from you, but she won't. She wants to hurt me and she knows she can do that if she hurts you."

"Okay." I processed that.

"You need to tell Raúl the moment you see her anywhere. Even if you just *think* it's her."

"Hold on a minute, ace. You went to see her the other day and didn't tell me?"

"I'm telling you now."

"Why didn't you tell me then?"

He exhaled roughly. "It was the day Chris came over."

"Oh."

"Yeah."

I gnawed on my lower lip a minute. "How would she hurt me?"

"I don't know. It's enough for me that she wants to."

"Like would she break my leg? My nose?"

"I doubt she'd resort to violence," he said dryly. "It would be more fun for her to play mind games. Showing up where you are. Letting you catch glimpses of her."

Which was more insidious. "So that you'll go to her. That's what she really wants," I

466

muttered. "She wants to see you."

"I won't be obliging her. I said what I needed to."

Looking down at our joined hands, I played with his wedding band. "Anne, Corinne, Deanna . . . It's a bit crazy, Gideon. I mean, I don't think this is normal for most men. How many more women are going to lose their minds over you?"

He shot me a look that was patently not amused. "I don't know what's gotten into Corinne. None of what she's done since she returned to New York is like her. I don't know if it's the medication she was on, the miscarriage, her divorce . . ."

"She's getting divorced?"

"Don't take that tone, Eva. It doesn't make a damn bit of difference to me if she's married or single. *I'm* married. That's never going to change, and I'm not a man who cheats. I have more respect for you — and me — than to be that kind of husband."

I leaned forward, offering my mouth, and he took it in a soft, sweet kiss. He had said exactly what I needed to hear.

Gideon pulled back, nuzzling his nose against mine. "As for the other two . . . You have to understand that Deanna was collateral damage. Fuck. My entire life has been a war zone and some people have gotten caught in the line of fire."

I cupped his jaw, trying to stroke the tension away with soothing brushes of my thumb. I knew just what he meant.

He swallowed hard. "If I hadn't used Deanna to send a message to Anne that the door was closed between us, she would've been just a one-night stand. Over and done with."

"But she's okay now?"

"I think so." His fingertips brushed my cheek, the touch reflecting the one I'd given him. "Since I'm sharing, I'll say that I don't think she'd turn me down if I tried to hook up — which I won't — but I don't think she falls in the woman-scorned category any longer."

"Yeah, I knew she'd hit the sheets with you again if she could. Not that I blame her. Do you have to be so damn good in bed? Isn't it enough that you're hot, and have an amazing body and a huge cock?"

He shook his head, clearly exasperated. "It's not *huge.*"

"Whatever. You're hung. And you know how to use it. And women don't get awesome sex very often, so when we do, we can go a little nuts over it. I guess that answers my question about Anne, since she had you repeatedly."

"She never had me." Gideon sat back, slouching. Scowling. "At some point you're going to get sick of hearing what an asshole I am."

I curled into his side, resting my head on his shoulder. "You're not the first insanely hot guy on the planet to use women. And you won't be the last."

"It was different with Anne," he grumbled. "It wasn't just about her husband."

I stilled, then forced myself to relax so that I didn't make him any more nervous than he already was.

He sucked in a quick, deep breath. "She reminds me of Hugh sometimes," he said in a rush. "The way she moves, some of the things she says . . . There's a familial resemblance. And more. I can't explain it."

"Then don't."

"Sometimes the line between them blurred in my mind. It was like I was punishing Hugh through Anne. I did things to her I've never done with anyone else. Things that made me feel sick when I thought about them later."

"Gideon." I slid my arm around his waist.

He hadn't told me this. He'd said before that it was Dr. Terrence Lucas he was punishing, and I was sure that was part of it. But now I knew it wasn't all of it.

Gideon sat back. "It was twisted between Anne and me. I twisted her. If I could go back and do things differently —"

"We'll deal with it. I'm glad you told me."

"Had to. Listen, angel, you need to tell Raúl the moment you see her anywhere. Even if you're not sure. And don't go anywhere alone. I'll figure out how to deal with her. In the meantime, I need to know that you're safe."

"Okay." I wasn't sure how that plan would work over the long haul. We lived in the same city with the woman and her husband, and Lucas himself had approached me before. They were a problem and we needed a solution.

But we weren't going to come up with it today. Saturday. One of the two days of the week I most looked forward to because I got to spend so much private time with my husband.

"So," I began, sliding my hand up beneath Gideon's shirt to touch his warm skin. "Where's my surprise?"

"Well . . ." The sexy rasp in his voice deepened. "Let's wait a bit before that. How about we start with some wine?"

Tilting my head back, I looked up at him. "Are you trying to seduce me, ace?"

He kissed my nose. "Always."

"Umm . . . Go right ahead."

I knew something was up when Gideon didn't join me in the shower. The only time he missed an opportunity to put his hands on me while drenched and dripping was in the mornings, after he'd already had his way with me.

When I came back out to the living room dressed in shorts and tank top sans bra, he was waiting for me with a glass of red wine. We settled on the couch with *3 Days to Kill,* which only proved to me that my husband knew me well. It was just the sort of movie I enjoyed — a bit funny, a lot over-the-top. And it had Kevin Costner, who was always a win for me.

Still, as much fun as I had just being lazy with Gideon, the anticipation started to make me twitchy as the hours passed. And Gideon, the devious man, knew it. He built on it. He kept my wineglass full and his hands on me — tangled in my hair, brushing over my shoulder, running along my thigh.

By nine o'clock, I was crawling all over him. I slid into his lap and pressed my lips to his throat, my tongue darting out to stroke over his pulse. I felt it leap, then accelerate, but he made no move in response.

He sat as if absorbed in the rerun we'd channel-surfed to after the movie ended.

"Gideon?" I whispered in my fuck-me voice, my hand sliding between his legs to find him as hard and ready as always.

"Hmm?"

I caught the lobe of his ear in my teeth, tugging gently. "Would you mind if I fucked myself on your big cock while you're watching TV?"

His hand rubbed absently down my back. "I might not be able to see around you," he replied, sounding distracted. "Maybe you better get on your knees and suck it instead."

Pulling back, I gaped at him. His eyes laughed at me.

I shoved at his shoulder. "You're terrible!"

"My poor angel," he crooned. "Are you horny?"

"What do you think?" I gestured at my chest. My nipples were hard and tight, straining against the thin cotton in a silent demand for his attention.

Cupping my shoulders, he pulled me closer and caught the tip of my breast in his teeth, his tongue stroking softly. I moaned.

He released me, his eyes now so dark they were like sapphires. "Are you wet?"

I was getting there, fast. Whenever Gideon looked at me like that, my body softened for him, grew moist and eager. "Why don't you find out?" I teased.

"Show me."

The authoritative bite in his command made me hotter. I slid off him carefully, feeling inexplicably shy. He pushed the coffee table back with one foot, giving me more room to stand in front of him. His gaze slid over me, his face expressionless. The lack of encouragement made me even more anxious, which I guessed was his intention.

He was pushing in that way he had.

Rolling my shoulders back, I caught his gaze with my own and ran my tongue along my bottom lip. His eyes became heavy-lidded. I slid my thumbs beneath the elastic waistband of my athletic shorts and pushed them down, wriggling my hips a little to make it look more like a striptease and less like I was feeling awkward.

"No panties," he murmured, his gaze on my sex. "You're a bad girl, angel."

I pouted. "I'm trying to be good."

"Open yourself for me," he murmured. "Let me see you."

"Gideon . . ."

He waited patiently and I knew that patience would hold. Whether it took me five minutes or five hours, he would wait for me. And that was why I trusted him. Because it was never a question of whether I would submit, but *when* I was ready to, and that was a decision he most often left to me.

I widened my stance and tried to slow the quickness of my breathing. Reaching down with both hands, I touched the lips of my sex and spread them, exposing my clit to the man it ached for.

Gideon straightened slowly. "You have such a pretty cunt, Eva."

As he leaned closer, I held my breath. His hands lifted from his thighs, reaching for mine to hold me steady. "Don't move," he ordered.

Then he licked me in a leisurely glide.

"Oh God," I moaned, my legs shaking.

"Sit down," he said hoarsely, sliding to his knees on the floor as I obeyed.

The glass was cool against my bare buttocks, a sharp contrast to the heat of my skin. My arms stretched back, gripping the far edge of the table for balance as he pressed my thighs wide with his palms, splaying me open.

His breath was hot against my damp flesh, his focus fully on my sex. "You could be wetter."

I watched, panting, as he lowered his head

and wrapped his lips around my clit. The heat was searing, the lash of his tongue devastating. I cried out, wanting to writhe but held fast by his grip. My head fell back, my ears ringing with the rush of blood and the sound of Gideon's groan. His tongue fluttered over the tight bundle of nerves, driving me relentlessly toward orgasm. My stomach tightened as the pleasure built, the soft silk of his hair brushing along my sensitive inner thighs.

A low moan escaped me. "I'm going to come," I gasped. "Gideon . . . God . . . I'm going to come."

He drove his tongue inside me. My elbows weakened, dropping me lower. His tongue fucked into the clutching opening of my sex, stroking through the sensitive tissues, teasing me with a promise of the penetration I truly craved.

"Fuck me," I begged.

Gideon pulled back, licking his lips. "Not here."

I made a sound of protest as he stood, so close to orgasm I could taste it. He held his hand out to me, helped me straighten and then stand. When I wobbled, he caught me up, tossing me over his shoulder.

"Gideon!"

But then his hand was between my legs,

massaging my wet, swollen sex, and I didn't care how he carried me, as long as he got me someplace where he'd take me.

We reached the hallway and turned, then stopped too quickly to have reached his bedroom. I heard the doorknob turn and then the light flicked on.

We were in the bedroom that was mine. He set me down on my feet, facing him.

"Why here?" I asked. Maybe some men would head to the nearest bed, but Gideon had more control than that. If he wanted me in the second bedroom, he had a reason for it.

"Turn around," he said quietly.

Something about his voice . . . the way he looked at me . . .

I looked over my shoulder.

And saw the swing.

It wasn't what I expected.

I'd looked up sex swings on the Internet when Gideon had first mentioned one. What I'd found were rickety things you hung from door frames, not-so-rickety things that hung from four-legged frames, and ones that hung from an eyebolt in the ceiling. All of them consisted of some combination of chains and/or straps that acted as slings for various body parts. Pictures of women actually harnessed in the damn things looked uncomfortable.

Honestly, I couldn't see how anyone could get past the awkwardness and fear of collapse, let alone manage an orgasm.

I should've known Gideon would have something else in mind.

Turning, I faced the swing head-on. Gideon had cleared out the bedroom at some point. The bed and furnishings were gone. The only object in the room was the swing itself, suspended from a sturdy cage-like structure. A wide, solid metal platform anchored steel sides and roof, which supported the weight of a padded metal chair and chains. Red leather cuffs for wrists and ankles hung in the appropriate places.

His arms wrapped around me from behind, one hand sliding up beneath my shirt to cup my breast, while the other slid between my legs to push two fingers inside me.

Nuzzling my hair out of the way, he kissed my throat. "How do you feel, looking at that?"

I thought about it. "Intrigued. A little apprehensive."

His lips curved against my skin. "Let's see how you feel once you're in it."

A shiver of expectation and apprehension

moved through me. I could see from the position of the cuffs that I would be helpless, unable to move or pull away. Unable to exert any control whatsoever over what might happen to me.

"I want to do this right, Eva. Not like that night in the elevator. I want you to feel it when I'm in control and we're in it together."

My head fell back against him. Somehow, it was harder giving the consent he wanted. There was less . . . responsibility when he just took charge.

But that was a cop-out.

"What's your safe word, angel?" he murmured, his teeth scoring gently across my throat. His hands were magic, his fingers gliding shallowly inside me.

"Crossfire."

"You say the word and everything stops. Say it again."

"Crossfire."

His dexterous fingers tugged at my nipple, milking it expertly. "There's nothing to be afraid of. You just have to sit back and take my cock. I'm going to make you come without you having to do a thing."

I took a deep breath. "I feel like that's always how it is between us."

"Try it this way," he coaxed, his hands

moving to pull my shirt off. "If you don't like it, we'll hit the bed instead."

For a moment, I wanted to delay, take more time to let it all settle in. I'd promised the swing, but he wasn't holding that over me . . .

"Crossfire," he breathed, hugging me from behind.

I didn't know if he was reminding me of my safe word or telling me he loved me so much there were no words for how he felt. Either way, the effect on me was the same. I felt safe.

I also felt his excitement. His breathing had quickened the moment I'd spotted the swing. His erection was like steel against my buttocks and his skin was hot against mine. His desire spurred my own, made me want to do whatever it took to give him as much pleasure as he could stand.

If he needed something, I wanted to be the woman who gave it to him. He gave so much to me. Everything.

"Okay," I said softly. "Okay."

He kissed my shoulder, then stepped beside me, taking my hand in his.

I followed him to the swing, studying it intently. The narrow seat hung at waist level for Gideon, which meant he had to turn me to face him, then lift me up into the chair.

His mouth touched mine as my bare ass touched the cool leather, his tongue teasing the seam of my lips. I shivered. Whether that was from the chill, his kiss, or anxiety, I didn't know.

Gideon pulled away, his gaze heavy-lidded and hot. He eased me into position, holding the chains steady as I leaned into the seat back, which was angled away from him, making me want to stretch my legs out for balance.

"You settled?" he asked, watching me intently.

I knew the question was about more than my physical comfort. I nodded.

He stepped back, his gaze never leaving my face. "I'm going to secure your ankles. You tell me if anything doesn't feel right."

"All right." My voice was breathy, my pulse racing.

His hand slid down my leg, the stroke warm and provocative. I couldn't look away as he wrapped the crimson leather around my ankle and cinched the metal buckle. The cuff was fit securely but not too tightly.

Gideon moved quickly and confidently. A moment later, my other leg was suspended as well.

He looked at me. "Okay so far?"

"You've done this before." I pouted. His

actions seemed too practiced to be those of a beginner.

He didn't answer. Instead he began to strip as slowly and methodically as he'd restrained me.

Mesmerized, I greedily drank in every inch of skin he revealed. My husband had such an amazing body. He was so hard and tight, so virile. It was impossible not to become aroused seeing him naked.

His tongue slid along the bottom curve of his mouth in a leisurely, erotic caress. "Still good, angel?"

Gideon knew exactly what the sight of him did to me, and it turned me on even more that he was arrogant enough to use that weakness against me. God knew I did the same to him when I could.

"You are so fucking hot," I told him, licking my own lips.

He smiled and came toward me, his thick, long cock curving upward to his navel. "I think you'll really enjoy this."

I didn't have to ask why he said so, because it was evident as he reached me and took my hands in his. My vantage of him from the swing seat was completely unhindered. From the thighs upward, he was totally exposed between the spread of my legs.

He bent and kissed me again. Softly. Sweetly. I moaned at the unexpected tenderness and the lushness of his flavor.

Releasing one of my hands, he reached between us, gripping his cock and angling it downward to stroke between the lips of my sex. The wide head slid through the slickness of my desire, then nudged against my exposed clit. Pleasure rippled through me and I discovered just how vulnerable I was. I couldn't arch my hips. I couldn't tighten my inner muscles to chase the sensation.

A low whimper escaped me. I needed more, but could only wait for him to give it to me.

"You trust me," he whispered against my mouth.

It wasn't a question, but I answered anyway. "Yes."

Gideon nodded. "Grab the chains."

There were wrist restraints above my head. I wondered why he didn't use them, but I trusted him to know best. If he didn't think I was ready, it was because he knew me so well. In some ways, he knew me better than I knew myself.

The love I felt for him unfurled in my chest until it filled me, pushing aside the vestiges of fear that hovered in the dark corners of my mind. I'd never felt so close to him, never known it was possible to believe in someone so completely.

I did as Gideon ordered and gripped the chains. He stepped close again, his abs glistening with the first mist of perspiration. I could see his pulse throbbing in his neck, his arms, his penis. His heart was racing like mine. The head of his cock was as wet with excitement as my sex. The hunger between us was a living thing in the room, sliding sinuously around us, narrowing the world to just the two of us.

"Don't let go," he ordered, waiting until I nodded my agreement before he proceeded.

He gripped a chain where it met with the seat. His other hand guided his cock to my cleft. The thick crown pressed teasingly against me, taunting me with the promise of pleasure. I was panting as I waited for him to take the step forward that would slide him into me, my core aching with the need to be filled.

Instead, he gripped the seat of the chair in both hands and pulled me onto his cock.

The sound that ripped from my throat was inhuman, the savagely erotic feeling of being so deeply penetrated driving me wild. He sank deep in that one easy glide, my body unable to offer any resistance.

Gideon snarled, a tremor running through

his powerful body. "Fuck," he hissed. "Your cunt is so good."

I started to reach for him, but he pushed the swing back, gliding me off his rock-hard erection. The feeling of being emptied made me moan in distress.

"Please," I begged softly.

"I told you not to let go," he said, with a wicked gleam in his eyes.

"I won't," I promised, gripping the chains so hard it hurt.

His arms flexed as he pulled me back, sliding me onto his cock. My toes curled. The feeling of weightlessness, of total surrender, was indescribable.

"Talk to me," he bit out. "Tell me you like this."

"Damn it," I gasped, feeling sweat slide down my nape. "Don't stop."

One moment I was held stationary, the next I was swinging fluidly, my sex sliding on and off Gideon's rigid cock with breathtaking speed. His body worked like a well-oiled machine, his arms, chest, abs, and thighs straining with the exertion of masterfully handling the swing. The sight of his powerful movements, the intensity of his focus on pleasuring us both, the feel of him pumping so deep and fast into me . . .

I orgasmed with a scream, unable to

contain the rush that surged through me. He fucked me through it, growling roughly, his face flushed and etched with lust. I'd never come so hard, so fast. I couldn't see or breathe for an endless moment, my body wracked by a pleasure more ferocious than any I'd ever felt before.

The swing slowed, then stopped. Gideon took an extra step toward me that kept him buried inside me. He smelled decadent, primal. Pure sin and sex.

His hands cupped my face. His fingers brushed tendrils of hair off my damp cheeks. My sex spasmed around him, all too aware of how hard and thick he still was.

"You didn't come," I accused, feeling far too vulnerable after the insanity of my orgasm.

Gideon took my mouth in a harsh, demanding kiss. "I'm going to restrain your wrists. Then I'm going to come in you."

My nipples tightened into painful points. "Oh God."

"You trust me," he said again, his gaze searching my face.

I touched him while I still could, my hands sliding over his sweat-slick chest, feeling the desperate beat of his heart. "More than anything."

19

"Good morning, Ace."

I looked over my shoulder at the sound of Eva's voice, smiling as I watched her circle the island on her way to the coffeemaker. Her hair was a wild tangle, her legs sexy beneath the hem of the T-shirt she wore.

Returning my attention to the stove and the French toast I was browning in the pan, I asked, "How are you feeling?"

"Umm . . ."

I looked at her again and found her blushing.

"I'm sore," she said, inserting a coffee pod into the machine. "Deep inside."

I grinned. The swing had positioned her perfectly, allowing for optimal penetration. I'd never been as deep in her before. I had been thinking about it all morning and decided that I would be speaking to Ash about his plans for the renovations. One of the bedrooms would need to have two closets — one for clothes, the other for the swing.

"Jeez," she muttered, "Look at that cocky smirk. Men are pigs."

"And here I am, slaving over a hot stove for you."

"Yeah, yeah." She swatted my ass as she passed me with a steaming cup of coffee in hand.

I caught her by the waist before she got too far, giving her a quick hard kiss on the cheek. "You were amazing last night."

I'd felt something click into place between us so strongly that the change had been as tangible as the rings I wore on my fingers, and I cherished it as dearly.

She flashed me a dazzling smile, then opened the fridge to pull out the carton of half-and-half. While she took care of that, I plated the finished French toast.

"I've been wanting to talk to you about something," she said, joining me at the island and wriggling onto a bar stool.

My brows lifted. "Okay."

"I'd like to become involved with the Crossroads Foundation — financially and administratively."

"That could encompass a lot of things, angel. Tell me what you have in mind."

Shrugging, she picked up her fork. "I've

487

been thinking about the settlement money I got from Nathan's dad. It's just sitting in the bank, and after what Megumi has been through . . . I've realized that I need to put that money to work and I don't want to wait. I'd like to help fund the programs offered by Crossroads and help brainstorm ways to expand them."

I smiled inwardly, pleased to see her moving in the right direction. "All right. We'll work something out."

"Yeah?" She brightened like the sun, the shining light in my world.

"Of course. I'd like to commit more time to it, too."

"We can work together!" She bounced up and down. "I'm excited about this, Gideon."

I let the smile show. "I can tell."

"It just feels like a natural progression for us. An extension of *us*, really." She cut into her food and forked a bite to her mouth. She hummed her appreciation. "Yummy," she mumbled.

"I'm glad you like it."

"You're hot *and* you can cook. I'm a lucky girl."

I decided not to tell her I'd just downloaded the recipe that morning. Instead, I considered what she'd said.

Had I made a tactical error by moving too

quickly with Mark? It was possible that if I'd left it alone just a little longer, Eva might have come around to working at Cross Industries on her own.

But did I have the luxury of giving her more time with Landon closing in? Even now, I didn't think so.

Seeking to mitigate any possible fallout, I debated the merits of broaching the topic of Mark's move to Cross Industries now versus later. Eva had opened the door by talking about us working together. If I didn't walk through it, I ran the risk of her finding out another way.

I had taken that chance on Saturday, knowing Eva and Mark were friends who talked outside work. He could've called her at any time, but I'd banked on him thinking it over first, discussing it with his partner, and coming to peace with leaving Waters Field & Leaman.

"I have to talk to you about something, too, angel."

"I'm all ears."

Shooting for nonchalance, I grabbed the maple syrup and poured some onto my plate. "I offered Mark Garrity a job."

There was a moment of stunned silence, and then, "You did what?"

The tone of her voice confirmed that I'd

been right to be up front sooner rather than later. I looked at her. She was staring at me.

"I've asked Mark to work for Cross Industries," I repeated.

Her face paled. "When?"

"Friday."

"Friday," she parroted. "It's Sunday. You're just bringing this up now?"

Since the question was rhetorical, I didn't reply, choosing to wait for a clearer assessment of the situation before possibly making things worse.

"Why, Gideon?"

I took the same tack I'd used with Mark — I told the parts of the truth most likely to be accepted. "He's a solid employee. He'll bring a lot to the team."

"Bullshit." The color came back into her face in an angry rush. "Don't patronize me. You're putting me out of a job and you didn't think that was something you should discuss with me first?"

I switched tactics. "LanCorp asked for Mark directly, didn't they?"

She was silent a minute. "That's what this is about? The PhazeOne system? Are you fucking serious?"

I'd wondered what product Ryan Landon would use as an excuse to approach Eva. I was surprised he'd gone with a product so vital to his bottom line, then chastised myself for not expecting it. "You didn't answer my question, Eva."

"What the hell does it matter?" she snapped. "Yeah, they asked for Mark. So what? You don't want your competitors using him? Are you trying to say this was a business decision?"

"No, this was personal." I set my utensils down. "Eric Landon, Ryan Landon's father, invested heavily with my dad and lost everything. Ryan Landon has been gunning for me ever since."

A frown marred the space between her brows. "So you didn't want us working on any campaigns for him? Is that what you're saying?"

"I'm saying that Ryan Landon asked for Mark as a way to get to you."

"What? Why?" Irritation mixed with anger on her face. "He's married, for chrissakes. He brought his wife to lunch with us the other day. You've got no reason to be jealous."

"He wouldn't be interested in you that way," I agreed. "It's more of a triumph to have you working for him. He wants the satisfaction of knowing he can give an order and you'll have to jump to get it done."

"That's ridiculous."

"You don't know the whole of it, Eva. How many years he's spent trying to under-cut me in every way possible. Every business decision he makes is driven by the need to rewrite the connection between the Landon and Cross names. Every success he's had has been accompanied by a mention of his father's failure to see my dad as a fraud and what that cost the Landons."

"Of course I don't know," she said coldly. "Because you didn't see fit to tell me."

"I'm telling you now."

"When it doesn't matter anymore!" She slid off the bar stool and stalked out of the kitchen.

I went after her, as I always did. "Eva."

I caught her by the elbow, but she yanked free, spinning to face me.

"Don't touch me!"

"Don't walk away from me," I growled. "If we're going to fight, let's get it over with."

"That's what you were counting on, right? You figured you'd do whatever you wanted, then sweet-talk or fuck your way through it later. But you can't fix this, Gideon. You can't say a few words or screw me brainless and get away with it this time."

"Fix what? I saw someone maneuvering

to take advantage of you and I took care of it."

"Is that how you see it?" Her hands went to her hips. "I don't see it that way at all. Landon is taking the risk. What if Mark and I do a crappy job? He's got a lot riding on PhazeOne."

"Exactly. He has in-house advertising, marketing, and promotion, just like I do. Why take something he's sunk a fortune into — even by my standards — and set himself up for leaks or a massive fail?"

She threw her hands up with a snort.

"Right," I bit out. "You can't answer that because there is no good answer. It's an unnecessary gamble. The only people handling the launch of the next-generation GenTen are people whose souls I own."

"What are you saying?"

"That Landon's waited a long time for his pound of Cross flesh. Maybe he doesn't care that you married into the name. I don't know what he has in mind. At the very least, he's forcing us into a place where we're unable to share information with each other."

Her brow arched. "How is that any different from how our relationship usually works?"

"Don't." I clenched my hands at my sides, frustrated by her stubbornness. "Don't make this about us when it's about him. I'll be damned if Landon drags you through hell because of me."

"I'm not saying you're wrong! If you'd told me about this, I would've made the right decision on my own. Instead, you forced me out of a job I love!"

"Back up. What decision would that have been?"

"I don't know." She gave me a cold, hard smile that chilled my blood. "And now we'll never find out."

She turned her back to me again.

"Stop."

"No," she tossed over her shoulder. "I'm getting dressed. Then I'm leaving."

"Like hell." I followed her into the bedroom.

"I can't be around you right now, Gideon. I don't even want to look at you."

My mind raced, searching for something to say that would calm her down. "Mark hasn't taken the job."

She shook her head and yanked open a drawer to pull out a pair of shorts. "He will. I'm sure you made him an offer he can't refuse."

"I'll withdraw it." God. I was backpedaling and it rankled, but she was so angry I couldn't reach her. She was as distant as I'd ever seen her. Remote and untouchable. After the wildly erotic night we'd had, when we had been as close as ever, her attitude was unbearable.

"Don't bother, Gideon. The damage is done. But you'll get a solid employee who'll bring a lot to your team." She tugged the shorts on and went into the closet.

I was right behind her, blocking the doorway while she shoved her feet into flip-flops. "Listen to me, damn it. They're coming after you. Everyone. They want to get at me through you. I'm doing the best I can, Eva. I'm trying to protect us the only way I know how."

She paused, facing me. "That's a problem. Because this way doesn't work for me. It will *never* work for me."

"Goddamn it, I'm *trying*!"

"All you had to do was talk to me, Gideon. I was halfway there on my own. Working with you on Crossroads was just the first step. I was going to make the decision to work with you, and you took that away from me. You took it away from both of us. And we'll never get it back."

The icy finality in her tone made me crazed. I could deal when discussions went sideways. I could spin and switch strategy on the fly. What I couldn't handle was when my grip on Eva slipped. When we'd said our vows, I had made the irrevocable decision to let everything go — my ambition, my pride, my heart — to hang on to her. If I couldn't do that, I had nothing.

"Don't throw that at me now, angel," I warned. "Every time I've brought up working together you shut me down."

"So you just bulldoze right through me?"

"I was willing to give you time! I had a plan. I was going to seduce you with the possibilities, let you decide that the best way to develop your potential was alongside me."

"You should've stuck with the plan. Get out of my way."

I held my ground. "How could I stick with any plan the last few weeks? While you're feeling righteous, think about what I've dealt with. Brett, the damned tape of you with him, Chris, my brother, therapy, Ireland, my mother, Anne, Corinne, fucking Landon —"

Eva crossed her arms. "Gotta handle it all yourself, don't you? Am I really your wife, Gideon? I'm not even your friend. I bet Angus and Raúl know more about your life than I do. Arash, too. I'm just the pretty cunt you fuck."

"Shut up."

"You need to get out of my way before

496

this gets any uglier."

"I can't let you leave. You know I can't. Not like this."

Her jaw tightened. "You're asking me to give you something I don't have right now. I'm hollowed out, Gideon."

"Angel . . ." I reached for her, my chest so tight I found it hard to breathe. The devastation on her face was killing me. I'd destroy anyone who put that look on her face, but this time, I had done it. "What does it matter if you would've made the same decision anyway?"

"You need to stop talking," she said hoarsely. "Because every word coming out of your mouth makes me think we're so far apart on this that we've got no business being married."

If she'd stabbed me in the chest, it couldn't have hurt worse. The air in the closet became hot and stale, drying my throat and making my eyes burn. The floor seemed to tilt beneath my feet, the foundation of my life shifting as Eva slipped further and further away.

"Tell me what to do," I whispered.

Her eyes glistened. "Let me go for now. Give me some space to think. A few days —"

"No. *No!*" Panic swelled until I was forced

to grip the door frame to stay upright.

"Maybe a few weeks. I need to find a new job, after all."

"I can't," I gasped, panting for air. A black ring encroached on my vision, until Eva was the lone pinpoint of light. "For God's sake, something else, Eva!"

"I have to figure out what to do now." She rubbed at her forehead with rough fingers. "And I can't think when you're looking at me like that. I can't think . . ."

She moved to pass me and I grabbed her by the arms, kissing her, groaning when I felt her soften for an instant. I tasted her, tasted her tears. Or maybe they were mine.

Her hands went to my hair, fisting it, pulling it hard. She turned her head, breaking the seal of my mouth.

"Crossfire," she sobbed, the word cracking like a gunshot.

I released her abruptly, stumbling back, even as my mind screamed at me to hang on.

I let her go, and she left me.

The sea breeze blows through my hair and I close my eyes, absorbing the feel as it buffets me. The rhythmic push and pull of the waves against the beach and the raucous cries of seagulls anchor me in the moment, in this place.

It's home in a way I haven't known for a long time, although I've spent less than a handful of days here. It is a place I've shared only with Eva, so all of my memories of here are as drenched with her as the sand is with rays of the sun. Like the sand, I've been crushed down into fine, tiny bits by the forces around me. And like the sun, Eva has brought joy and warmth to my existence.

She joins me on the deck, standing behind me at the railing. I feel her hand on my shoulder, then the press of her cheek against my bare back.

"Angel," I murmur, and place my hand over hers.

This is what we needed, to come back to this place. It's our retreat when the world closes in on us, trying to separate us. We heal each other here.

Relief washes through me. She's back. We're together. She understands now why I did what I did. She was so angry, so hurt. For a moment, I had felt crippling fear that I'd destroyed the most precious part of my life.

"Gideon," she breathes, in that husky siren's voice. One arm slides around my waist to hold me from behind.

I tilt my head back and let the power of her

love pour through me. Her fingers glide over my hip, and then she's holding my cock in her hand. Stroking it from root to tip. I harden and thicken, ready for her. I live to serve her, to please her. How could she have doubted it?

A moan rumbles up from the very depths of my soul, the desire I always feel for her climbing through me. Pre-cum leaks from the swollen head of my dick, my balls growing heavy and full.

Her hand on my shoulder glides down my back, pressing lightly, urging me to bend forward.

I obey because I want her to see how she owns me. I want her to understand that I would do anything, give anything, to make her safe and happy.

Her hand traces my spine, kneading lightly. I grip the wooden handrail that circles the deck and spread my legs at her urging.

Now, both of her hands are between my thighs, her breath hot and panting against my back. She's pumping my cock with a firm, practiced grip. Harder than I'm used to from her. Demanding. Her other hand is massaging my sac, driving the urgency into me.

Her grip slickens as the pre-cum streams steadily from the slit at the tip of my dick. The salty air washes over me, cooling the sweat misting my skin.

"Eva . . ." I gasp her name, so hard for her, so desperately in love.

Her fingers, now creamy and always cleverly agile, slide back and tease the dark rosette of my anus. It feels good, even though I don't want it to. The stroking of my penis is making it hard to breathe, to think, to fight . . .

"That's it," she coaxes.

I try to arch away, but she's got me trapped with my dick in her hand.

"Don't," I tell her, squirming.

"You like it," she purrs, working my cock, her touch something I crave and can't resist. "Show me how much you want me."

She pushes two slick fingers inside my ass. I cry out, writhing away, but she's rubbing and thrusting into me, hitting the spot that makes me want to come more than anything. The pleasure grows despite the tears burning my eyes.

My head falls forward. My chin touches my heaving chest. It's coming. *I'm* coming. I can't stop it. Not with her . . .

The fingers inside me thicken, lengthen. The thrusting becomes frenzied, the slap of flesh against flesh drowning out the sounds of the ocean. I hear a rough, lusty growl but it's not mine. A cock is in me, fucking me. It hurts and yet the pain is tinged with a sick, unwanted pleasure.

"Keep stroking it," he pants. "You're almost there."

Agony explodes in my chest. Eva isn't here. She's gone. She's left me.

Vomit rises into my throat. I throw him off violently, hearing him crash through the sliding door behind us, the glass shattering. Hugh laughs hysterically and I round on him, finding him sprawled amid the glistening slivers, his hair as red as his blood, his eyes lit with that vile lustful avarice.

"You think she'd want you?" he taunts, clambering to his feet. "You told her everything. Who'd want you after that?"

"Fuck you!" I lunge and tackle him back down. My fist pounds into his face again and again.

The shards of glass pierce me, cut into me, but the pain is nothing next to what I feel inside.

Eva is gone. I'd known she would leave, that I couldn't keep her. I'd known it, but I had hoped. I couldn't fight the hope.

Hugh won't stop laughing. I feel his nose shatter. His cheekbone, his jaw. His laughter turns to gurgles, but it's still laughter.

My arm pulls back to hit him again —

Anne is lying beneath me, her face battered nearly beyond recognition. Horrified at what I've done, I jerk away, scrambling to my feet.

The glass digs deep into the soles of my feet.

Anne laughs as bubbling blood pours from her nose and mouth, spreading through the home that was once a sanctuary. Staining everything, the taint washing away the sun until only a blood moon remains . . .

I woke up with a scream in my throat. Sweat drenched my hair and skin. Darkness suffocated me.

Scrubbing at my eyes, I rolled onto my hands and knees, sobbing. I crawled toward the only light I could see, the weak silver glow that was my only guide.

The bedroom. God. I collapsed on the floor, racked by tears. I'd fallen asleep in the closet, unable to move after Eva left me, afraid to take one literal step in any direction toward a life without her in it.

The face of the clock glowed brightly in the darkened room.

It was one A.M.

A new day. And Eva was still gone.

"You're here early."

Scott's cheery voice lured my gaze from the photo of Eva on my desk.

"Good morning," I greeted him, feeling as if I were still in a nightmare.

I'd come to work shortly after three A.M., unable to sleep anymore and unable to go

503

to Eva. I wanted to, would have — nothing could keep me away from her — but when I tracked her phone I found her at Stanton's penthouse, a place I couldn't reach. The anguish of that, knowing she was deliberately keeping herself from me, ate at me from the inside out like acid.

I couldn't stay home and go through the morning routine of preparing for work without Eva. It had been easier to revert to the schedule I'd often kept before her, coming into work while the moon was high, finding peace in the place where I exercised complete control.

But today there was no peace. Only the torment of knowing that she was in the same building I was by now, so damn close and yet farther away than she'd ever been.

"Mark Garrity was waiting by reception when I came in," Scott continued. "He said you'd discussed having him come in today . . . ?"

My gut knotted. "I'll see him."

I pushed back from my desk and stood. I'd thought of nothing but Eva and the offer I had made to Mark, trying to reason out how I could have done anything differently. I knew Eva too well. Telling her about Ryan Landon wouldn't have made her leave Waters Field & Leaman any more than telling her about Anne would cause her to be more cautious.

Eva would face them head-on instead, growling like a lioness to defend me and failing to see the danger to herself. It was her way and I loved her for it, but I would also protect her when the situation called for it.

"Mark." I extended my hand as he entered, knowing immediately that he was going to say yes. Energy radiated off him and his dark eyes were lit with anticipation.

We agreed that he would begin in October, giving Waters Field & Leaman nearly a month's notice. He wanted to bring Eva along with him and I encouraged him to make the offer, even as I doubted that she would accept it. He countered some of my terms and I negotiated by instinct, keeping him in check without my heart being in it.

In the end, he left happy and pleased with his changed situation. I was left with the deepening fear that Eva would not forgive me.

Monday blurred into Tuesday. There were only three times a day when I felt any life at all — at nine when I knew Eva arrived for work, at lunch, and again at five when she finished for the day. I waited with endless hope for her to reach out to me. To call or communicate in any way. Another horrible fight would be better than the aching silence.

She didn't. I could only watch her on the security monitors, devouring the sight of her coming and going like a man dying of hunger, scared to approach her and risk widening the chasm between us.

I stayed in the office overnight, afraid to go home. Afraid of what I would do if I entered any of the residences I shared with her. Even my office was a torment, the couch where I had fucked her an inescapable reminder of what I'd had only days before. I showered in my office's washroom and changed into one of the many suits I kept at work.

I'd never thought it strange to live for work before. Now, I was overwhelmed by emotion I couldn't express, comprehending just how much of my life Eva had come to fill.

She stayed at Stanton's again. It didn't escape my notice that she preferred to spend time with her mother than to risk having to deal with me.

I texted her constantly. Pleas for her to call me. *I just need to hear your voice.* Notes about nothing. *Cooler today, isn't it?* Comments about work. *Never realized Scott always wears blue.* And most of all, *I love you.* For some reason, it was easier to type those three words than to say them. I typed them a lot. Over and over again. I didn't want her to forget that. Whatever my faults and fuck-ups, everything I did or thought or felt was love for her.

Sometimes I got mad, hating what she was doing to me. To us. *Goddamn you! Call me. Stop doing this to me!*

"You look like shit," Arash said, eyeing me as I reviewed the contracts he'd placed on my desk. "You getting sick again?"

"I'm fine."

"My man, you are anything but fine."

I glared at him, shutting him up.

It was nearly six and I was on my way to Dr. Petersen's office when Eva finally reached out to me.

I love you, too.

The words wavered as my eyes stung. I typed back with shaking fingers, nearly dizzy with relief. I miss you so much. Can't we talk, please? I need to see you.

She didn't reply before I reached Dr. Petersen's, which blackened my mood to the point of violence. She was punishing me in the worst possible way. I was as jittery as

507

a junkie, desperate for a hit of her to function. To think.

"Gideon." Dr. Petersen greeted me at the door to his office with a smile that quickly faded when he saw me. Concern drew his brows down. "You don't look well."

"I'm not," I snapped.

He calmly gestured for me to take a seat. I remained standing, roiling inside, debating leaving and searching for my wife. I couldn't stand around and wait anymore. It was too much to ask of me.

"Maybe we should walk again," he said. "I could stand to stretch my legs."

"Call Eva," I ordered. "Tell her to come here. She'll listen to you."

He blinked at me. "You're having trouble with Eva."

Shrugging out of my suit jacket, I threw it on the couch. "She's being irrational! She won't see me . . . won't talk to me. How the fuck are we supposed to work things out if we're not even talking?"

"That's a reasonable question."

"Damn right! I'm a reasonable man. She, however, is out of her damn mind. She can't keep doing this. You have to get her here. You have to make her talk to me."

"All right. But first I need to understand what's happened." He sat in his chair. "I'm not going to be much use to you if I don't know what's going on."

I pointed a finger at him. "Don't play your head games with me, Doc. Not today."

"I think I'm being as reasonable as you are," he said smoothly. "I want you to work things out with Eva, too. I think you know that."

Exhaling in a rush, I sank onto the edge of the sofa, then dropped my head into my hands. It was throbbing viciously, pounding front and back.

"You're fighting with Eva," he said.

"Yes."

"When's the last time you spoke with her?"

I swallowed hard. "Sunday."

"What happened on Sunday?"

I told him. It came out in a rush that had him scribbling frantically on his tablet. The words spewed out in an angry purge, leaving me feeling wiped out and exhausted.

He continued to write for a few moments after I finished, and then his gaze lifted to my face. I saw compassion and it tightened my throat.

"You cost Eva her job," he pointed out, "a job she's told us both that she enjoys very much. You can see why she'd be upset with you, can't you?"

"Yeah, I get it. But I had valid reasons. Reasons she understands. That's what I don't get. She understands and she's still cutting me off."

"I'm not sure *I* understand why you didn't discuss this with Eva beforehand. Can you explain that to me?"

I rubbed at the back of my neck, where the tension felt like steel cables. "She would've stewed over it," I muttered. "It would've taken her time to come around. In the meantime, I'm trying to manage a ton of other shit. We're getting hit from all sides."

"I saw the news about Corinne Giroux's book about you."

"Oh, yeah." My mouth curved grimly. "She probably got the idea from Six-Ninth's 'Golden' video. Landon got to Eva through a hole in my guard. I couldn't risk giving him another opening while I was distracted with everything else Eva and I are dealing with right now."

Dr. Petersen nodded. "You're facing a lot of pressure. Don't you trust Eva to help you reach the decisions you're making? You have to know that her conflicts with her mother often stem from not being consulted before actions are taken."

"I know that." I tried to articulate my

chaotic thoughts. "But I need to take care of her. After what she's lived through . . ."

My eyes squeezed shut. Knowing what she'd suffered was almost too much for me to think about sometimes. "I have to be strong for her. Make the tough calls."

"Gideon, you're one of the strongest men I know," he said quietly.

I opened my eyes and looked at him. "You haven't seen me the way she has."

Crying like a child. Brutalized by memories. Masturbating while unconscious. Violent in my sleep. Weak, so weak. Helpless.

"Do you think she doubts you because you've let her see you vulnerable? That doesn't sound like Eva to me."

My eyes stung. "You don't know everything. You just . . . You don't know."

"But Eva does. And she married you anyway. She loves you — very much — anyway." He offered a kind smile that somehow slashed like a blade, cutting me open. "You asked me once if relationships were about compromise. Do you remember that?"

I jerked a nod.

"That compromise means you don't always have to be the strong one, Gideon. You can do the heavy lifting on occasion, and you can let Eva do it sometimes. Marriage isn't about whether you're strong enough as an individual. It's about how strong you are together and the luxury of taking turns carrying the load."

"I . . ." My head bowed again. Eva had said the same thing. "I'm trying. I swear to God, I'm trying."

"I know you are."

"She has to take me back. She has to come back. I need her. She's killing me right now. She's ripping me apart." I stared at my hands, at the rings she'd given me that made me hers. "What do I do? Tell me what to do."

"Eva is going to want to know that you're willing to change. She'll want to see you taking steps to demonstrate that. You won't face these big decisions too often, so she may adopt a wait-and-see attitude. That will be hard for you, I think. Very hard."

I nodded slowly, but I couldn't wait anymore. If Eva needed proof that I'd do anything to keep her, I would give it to her.

My hands clenched into fists. My gaze stayed on the carpet between my feet. "I was —" I cleared my throat. "The therapist. The one I had when I was a child."

"Yes?"

"He . . . he molested me. For nearly a year. He . . . raped me."

20

I miss you so much. Can't we talk, please? I need to see you.

"Still staring at that text?" Cary asked, rolling onto his back on the bed beside me and pressing his temple to mine.

"I can't sleep." It was torture to stay away from Gideon. I spent every minute — waking and sleeping — feeling like someone had hacked out my heart and left a gaping hole in my chest.

I looked up at the canopy above my mom's guest bed. Like her sitting room, the bedroom she'd put me in was newly redecorated. With its palette of cream and moss green, the room was soothing and tastefully elegant. The guest bedroom Cary occupied was done in a more masculine style with grays and navy, with walnut furnishings on the opposite end of the spectrum from the white gilded pieces in my room.

"When are you going to talk to him,

baby girl?"

"Soon. I just . . ." I lowered the phone to my chest and pressed it against my heart. "I think we both need a little time."

It was so hard to think when Gideon and I were fighting. I hated it.

And it was worse because he was the one who'd fucked up, and like everything he did, he had done so spectacularly. I couldn't imagine how I could forgive him and live with myself. On the other hand, I couldn't imagine how I could go forward without him and live, period. I felt dead inside. The only thing keeping me going was the belief that somehow we'd work things out and be together. How could we not? How could I give so much of myself to someone and then let that person go?

I thought about the advice I'd given to Trey and how we were both facing the same decision — did we choose love or did we choose ourselves? I was so pissed off at Gideon for being the one who forced my hand. I'd recognized that certain situations were pushing me into that spot, but I had never thought my husband would.

And why the hell did the two choices have to be mutually exclusive? It wasn't fair.

"You're running him through the wringer," Cary pointed out, unnecessarily.

"*He's* done it, not me." Gideon had taken something precious from me, but worse, he had taken something precious away from *us* — my free will and the trust I'd given him to respect it. After that last night we'd had . . . as much as I had trusted him and opened myself to him . . . And he'd already talked to Mark. The feeling of betrayal was heartrending. "Thanks for sticking with me."

He shrugged. "I like Stanton. It's no hardship hanging at his place a few days. We *are* eventually going home, right?"

"I can't hide forever."

"So you've always said," he muttered. "Personally, I like hiding. Just taking a fucking break and forgetting about all the crap."

"But the crap's always out there waiting for you." And knowing that, I always preferred to face it head-on. Get it out of the way and behind me.

"Let it wait," he said, reaching up to ruffle my hair.

Turning my head, I pressed a kiss to his cheek. I'd cried gallons on him the last three days and curled up against him at night. At times, it felt like his arms were the only things holding me together.

God. I hurt all over. I was a fucking mess,

a zombie in the vibrantly lively city of New York.

Where was Gideon now? Was the pain of our separation starting to ease? Or was he still as devastated by it as I was?

"Mark asked me to move to Cross Industries with him," I said, just to force my mind onto something else.

"Well, you saw that coming."

"I guess, but it was still surreal when he brought it up." I sighed. "He's so excited, Cary. He's getting a hefty raise, and that will change a lot of things for him and Steven. They'll be able to afford a really fancy wedding plus a long honeymoon, and they're looking for a condominium now. It's hard to hold on to my resentment when this is such a good thing for him."

"Are you going to work for Gideon?"

"I don't know. I wasn't kidding when I told him I was halfway toward making that decision on my own. But now . . . I kinda want to apply elsewhere just to spite him."

Cary lifted his fists and shadowboxed. "Show him he's not the boss of you."

"Yeah." I threw a few punches, too, just to give myself a little lift. "But that's stupid. I'd never know if I got hired for me or for his name, whether that turned out to be a good or a bad thing. Anyway, I've got a month before Mark moves on. I've got time to think about it."

"Maybe Waters Field and Leaman will keep you. Have you considered that?"

"It's a possibility. I'm not sure how I would respond. It would save me a job search, but I wouldn't have Mark, and he's the reason I love my job. Would I still want to be there without him?"

"You'd still have Megumi and Will."

"There's that," I agreed.

We lay there in companionable silence for a while.

Then he said, "So it looks like you and me are just floating around in the hell-if-I-know boat."

"Trey *is* going to call," I assured him, even though I still had no idea what Trey would say when he did.

"Sure. He's a nice guy. He won't leave me hanging." Cary sounded so weary. "It's *what* he's going to say, not *when,* that's the kicker."

"I know. Love should be easier than this," I complained.

"If this were a romantic comedy, it'd be called *Love Actually Sucks.*"

"Maybe we should've stuck with *Sex and the City.*"

"Tried that. Ended up *Knocked Up.* I

should've gone for being a *40-Year-Old Virgin,* but I had way too much of a head start."

"We can write a manual on How to Lose a Guy in 10 Weeks."

Cary looked at me. "Fucking perfect."

Wednesday morning hit me like a hangover.

Getting ready for work at my mom's place helped me to not miss Gideon so much, but it sure as hell didn't separate me from my mother, who was driving me nuts talking about the wedding nonstop. Even Stanton, with his endless capacity for indulging my mom's neurosis, gave me sympathetic looks when he was around.

I couldn't think about the wedding now. I couldn't think beyond each and every hour of the day. That was how I was getting by — one hour at a time.

When I stepped out of the lobby onto the street, I found Angus waiting for me with the Bentley rather than Raúl with the Benz. I managed a smile, genuinely pleased to see him, but I was wary, too.

"Good morning, Angus." I jerked my chin toward the car and whispered, "Is he in there?"

He shook his head, then touched the brim of his vintage chauffeur's hat. "Good morning, Mrs. Cross."

I squeezed his shoulder briefly before sliding past the door he opened and into the backseat. In short order we were easing into the snarl of morning traffic and heading toward midtown.

Leaning forward, I asked, "How is he?"

"Worse than you, I expect." He glanced at me briefly before returning his attention to traffic. "He's suffering, lass. Last night was the hardest."

"God." I sank back into the seat, at a loss for what to do.

I didn't want Gideon to hurt. He'd been hurt too much already.

Pulling out my smartphone, I texted him. I love you.

His reply was almost immediate. Calling. Pls answer.

A moment later the phone vibrated in my hand and his picture appeared on my screen. It was like a quick stab to the heart to see his face after spending the last few days avoiding any image of him. I was equally afraid to hear his voice. I didn't know if I could be strong. And I didn't have the answers he needed from me.

My voice mail kicked in and the phone quieted. It started vibrating again right away.

I answered, lifting the phone to my ear without speaking.

There was silence on the line for a long, breathless moment. "Eva?"

My eyes watered at the sound of Gideon's voice, the rasp in it so deep, as if his throat were rough. What was worse was the hope I heard in the way he said my name, the desperate longing.

"It's okay if you don't talk," he said gruffly. "I just . . ." He gave a shaky exhale. "I'm sorry, Eva. I want you to know I'm sorry and that I'll do whatever you need me to. I just want to fix this."

"Gideon . . ." I heard him suck in a sharp inhalation when I said his name. "I believe that you're sorry we're not together now. But I also believe that you would do something like this again. I'm trying to figure out if I can live with that."

Silence hung on the line between us.

"What does that mean?" he asked finally. "What would be the alternative?"

I sighed, suddenly feeling so tired. "I don't have any answers. That's why I've stayed away. I want to give you everything, Gideon. I never want to say no to you, it's so hard for me. But right now, I'm afraid that if I make this compromise, if I stay with you knowing how you are and that you're not going to change, I'm just going to resent you and, eventually, fall out of love with you."

"Eva . . . Christ. Don't say that!" His breath snagged. "I told Dr. Petersen. About Hugh."

"What?" My head snapped up. "When?"

"Last night. I told him everything. About Hugh. Anne. He's going to help me, Eva. He said some things . . ." He paused. "They made sense to me. About me and the way I am with you."

"Oh, Gideon." I could imagine how difficult that must have been for him. I'd lived through that confession myself. "I'm very proud of you. I know it wasn't easy."

"You have to stick with me. You promised. I told you I was going to fuck this up. I'll fuck up again. I don't know what the hell I'm doing, but God . . . *I love you.* I love you so fucking much. I can't do this without you. I can't live without you. You're breaking me, Eva. I can't . . ." He made a low, pained noise. "I need you."

"Ah God, Gideon." Tears poured down my face and splattered onto my chest, sliding down beneath the neckline of my dress. "I don't know what to do, either."

"Can't we figure it out together? Aren't we better — *stronger* — together?"

I wiped at my face, knowing my makeup

was ruined and not caring. "I want us to be. I want that more than anything. I just don't know if we can get there. There hasn't been a single time when you've let me figure things out with you. Not once."

"If I did . . . if I do — and I *will* — you'll come back to me?"

"I haven't left you, Gideon. I don't know how." I looked out the window, spotted a young couple kissing each other good-bye in front of a revolving door before the man ran off. "But yes, if we could really be a team, nothing could keep me away."

"Heard you guys landed the PhazeOne campaign."

I turned my attention from the coffee I was sweetening to raise my brows at Will. "I haven't heard that."

He grinned, his eyes sparkling behind his glasses. He was such a happy guy, anchored solidly in a relationship that worked. I was so envious of that serenity. I had felt it only a few times since I'd been with Gideon, and every time it was . . . bliss. How amazing would it be if we could get there and *stay* there?

"That's the buzz I've been hearing," he said.

"Man." I gave an exaggerated sigh. "I am

always the last to know."

I'd been putting on an Oscar-worthy performance all week. Between Mark's excitement, the imminent adjustment in my work situation, starting my period, and dealing with the mess in my private life, I was focusing every ounce of energy I had left on acting calm. As a result, I'd avoided the office gossip cliques to limit my contact with people. There was only so much happiness/joy/contentment I could fake.

"Mark's going to kill me for telling you." Will looked completely unapologetic. "I wanted to be the first to congratulate you."

"Okay. Thank you. Maybe."

"I'm dying to get my hands on that system, you know. The tech blogs are wild with rumors about PhazeOne's features." He leaned against the counter next to me and gave me a hopeful look.

I wagged my finger at him. "You won't be hearing any leaks from me."

"Damn it. A guy's gotta hope." He shrugged. "They're probably going to lock you in solitary somewhere until the release just to keep a lid on it."

"Makes you wonder why LanCorp would take it to an outside agency, doesn't it?"

He frowned. "Yeah. I guess. Hadn't thought about it."

Neither had I. But Gideon had.

I looked back down at my mug, stirring absently. "There's a new GenTen coming out soon."

"I heard. That's a no-brainer, though. Everyone's going to buy it."

Flexing my fingers, I studied my wedding ring and thought about the vows I'd made when I accepted it.

"You got plans for lunch?" he asked.

I picked up my mug and faced him. "Yes, I'm going out with Mark and his partner."

"Oh, right." He moved toward the coffeemaker when I got out of the way. "Maybe we could grab drinks after work sometime this week. Drag our significant others with us. If Gideon's up for it. I know he's a busy guy."

I opened my mouth. Closed it again. Will had given me the perfect opening to excuse Gideon. I could take it, but I wanted to share the social parts of my life with my husband. I wanted him with me. If I started excluding him from my life, wasn't that the beginning of the end?

"Sounds like fun," I lied, imagining a tension-fraught evening. "I'll talk to him about it. See what we can work out."

Will nodded. "Cool. Lemme know."

"I've got a problem."

"Oh?" I looked across the table at Mark. The Cuban restaurant Steven had chosen was both large and popular. Sunlight streamed in through a massive skylight, while colorful murals decorated the space with parrots and palm fronds. Festive music made me feel like I'd gone on vacation to somewhere exotic, while the rich smell of spices made my tummy perk up for the first time in days.

I rubbed my hands together. "Let's fix it."

Steven nodded. "Eva's right. Lay it on us."

Mark pushed the menu aside and set his elbows on the table. "So Mr. Waters told me this morning to start working on the LanCorp brief."

"Yay!" I applauded.

"Not so fast. In light of that, I had to give him my notice. I'd been hoping to wait until Friday, but they need someone who can stick with the client all the way through, not just the first month."

"You've got a point," I conceded, my smile fading. "What a bummer, though."

"It sucked, but . . ." He shrugged. "It is what it is. Then he called in the other partners. They told me that the LanCorp brass was insistent that I head the campaign when they first approached the agency, enough so that the partners are worried they'll lose the account if I'm not managing it."

Steven grinned and slapped him on the shoulder. "That's what we like to hear!"

Mark gave a sheepish smile. "Yeah, it was a boost, for sure. So anyway, they offered me a promotion and a raise if I'll stay."

"Whoa." I sat back. "That's a *serious* boost."

"They can't offer what Cross did. Not even half, but let's be honest, he's overpaying me."

"Says you," Steven scoffed. "You're worth every penny."

I nodded, even though I had only a vague idea of what Gideon had put on the table. "I agree with that."

"But I feel like I owe Waters Field and Leaman some loyalty." Mark rubbed at his jaw. "They've been good to me and they want to keep me, even knowing I can be poached by someone else."

"You've given them good work for years," Steven countered. "They got a lot out of you. You don't owe them any favors."

"I know that. And I was fine with leaving

an empty office behind, because they could fill that quick enough. But I'm having a hard time with possibly costing them the Lan-Corp campaign when I go."

"But that decision isn't yours to make," I pointed out. "If LanCorp doesn't retain the agency, that's up to them."

"I've tried spinning it that way, too. But it's still not something I want to see happen."

The server came by to take our order. I looked at Steven. "Can you do the honors?"

"Sure." He looked at Mark, who gave a quick nod to signal the same request. Steven ordered for all of us.

I waited until we were alone again to speak, unsure of how to say what needed to be said. In the end, I went with blunt. "I can't work on the PhazeOne campaign."

Mark and Steven stared at me.

"Look, the Landons and the Crosses go way back," I explained, "and there's bad blood between them. Gideon's got some concerns, and I see his point. It's strong enough for me to be cautious."

Mark frowned. "Landon knows who you are. He doesn't have a problem with it."

"I know. But the PhazeOne system is a pretty big deal. There's risk involved with having access to it, and I don't need to contribute to that in any way." It was hard admitting that Gideon was right, because I knew I was right, too. Which left us at an impasse I didn't know how to get around.

Steven leaned closer and studied me. "You're serious."

"Afraid so. Not that your decision is in any way affected by me, Mark, but I thought I should put that out there."

"I'm not sure I understand," Mark said.

"She's telling you that if you stay with your job, you'll be losing both the money and your assistant," Steven clarified. "Or you can move to Cross Industries as you've already agreed to do, get the money, and keep Eva."

"Well . . ." God. This was harder than I'd thought it would be. I had heard it but now I was living it: Any woman who loses or gives up a job she loves because of a man will resent it . . . What had ever made me think I would be somehow exempt? "I can't say yet that I'll be making the move with you."

Mark fell back against the burgundy vinyl booth. "This just keeps getting worse."

"I'm not saying definitively that I won't." I tried to shrug it off as no big deal. "I'm just not sure that Gideon and I should be working together. I mean I'm not sure he should be my boss . . . or whatever. You know what I mean."

"I hate to say it," Steven said, "but she's got a point."

"This is not helping my problem," Mark muttered.

"I'm sorry." I couldn't tell them how sorry I really was. I didn't even feel like I could offer advice. How could I be nonbiased about Mark's options?

"On the bright side," I offered instead, "you're definitely a hot commodity."

Steven elbowed Mark with a grin. "I knew that already."

"So" — Cary slung his arm around me when I curled into his side — "here we are again."

Another night at my mom's. She'd finally gotten suspicious, considering it was our fourth night in a row at her place. I confessed to arguing with Gideon, but not why. I didn't think she would understand. I'm sure she would think it was perfectly normal for a man in Gideon's position to handle all the pesky little details. And as for me possibly losing my job? Why would I want to work when I had no financial reason to?

She didn't understand. Some daughters wanted to grow up to be just like their mothers; I wanted the opposite. And my need to be the anti-Monica was the main reason I struggled so much with what Gideon had done. Any advice from her would only make things worse. I almost resented her as much as I did him.

"We'll go home tomorrow," I said.

After all, I'd be seeing Gideon at Dr. Petersen's office at the very least. I was desperately curious about how that would go. I couldn't help but hope that Gideon had turned a major corner with therapy. If so, maybe there were other corners we could turn. Together.

I crossed my fingers.

And really, I had to give Gideon credit for doing his best to give me the space I'd asked for. He could've caught me in an elevator or the lobby of the Crossfire. He could have told Raúl to drive me to him instead of wherever I directed. Gideon *was* trying.

"Have you heard from Trey?" I asked.

It was kind of miraculous how often Cary and I ended up in the same place at the same time. Or maybe it was a shared curse.

"He sent me a text saying he was thinking about me but wasn't ready to talk yet."

"Well, that's something."

His hand ran up and down my back. "Is it?"

"Yes," I said. "I'm in the same place with Gideon. I think about him all the time, but I don't have anything to say to him right now."

"So what's next? Where do you go from here? When do you decide you've got something more to say?"

I thought about that a minute, absently watching Harrison Ford hunt for answers in *The Fugitive,* which we had on mute. "When something changes, I guess."

"When *he* changes, you mean. What if he doesn't?"

I didn't have that answer yet, and when I tried to think about it, I went a little crazy.

So I asked Cary a question instead. "I know you want to put the baby first and that's the right thing to do. But Tatiana's not happy. And you're not, either. Trey's definitely not. This isn't working out for any of you. Have you thought about being with Trey and the two of you helping Tatiana with the baby?"

He snorted. "She's not gonna go for that. If she's miserable, everyone else has to be, too."

"I don't think that should be her choice to make. She's as responsible for getting pregnant as you are. You don't have to do some sort of penance, Cary." I put my hand

531

over the arm he had lying in his lap, my thumb brushing carefully over the fresh scars on his inner forearm. "Be happy with Trey. Make him happy. And if Tatiana can't be happy with having two hot guys looking after her, then she's . . . not doing something right."

Cary laughed softly and pressed his lips to the crown of my head. "Solve your own problem that easily."

"I wish I could." I wished for that more than anything. But I knew it wouldn't be easy.

And I feared it might be impossible.

The vibration of my smartphone woke me.

When I realized what the buzzing was, I began searching blindly for my phone, my hands sliding around the bed until I found it. By then, I'd missed the call.

Squinting at the glaringly bright screen, I saw it was just past three A.M. and Gideon had called. My heart skipped as worry chased away sleep. Once again I'd gone to bed cradling my phone, unable to stop reading the many texts he had sent me.

I called him back.

"Angel," he answered on the first ring, his voice hoarse.

"Is everything okay?"

"Yes. No." He blew out his breath. "I had a nightmare."

"Oh." I blinked up at the canopy that I couldn't see in the dark. My mother was a fan of blackout drapes, saying they were necessary in a city that was never truly dark. "I'm sorry."

It was a lame reply, but what else could I say? It would be pointless to ask if he wanted to talk about it. He never did.

"I'm having them a lot lately," he said wearily. "Every time I fall asleep."

My heart hurt a little more. It seemed impossible that it could take so much pain, but there was always more. I'd learned that long ago.

"You're stressed, Gideon. I'm not sleeping well, either." And then, because it had to be said, "I miss you."

"Eva . . ."

"Sorry." I scrubbed at my eyes. "Maybe I shouldn't say that."

Maybe it was a mixed signal that would only make things worse for him. I felt guilty for staying away, even though I knew I had good reason to.

"No, I need to hear it. I'm scared, Eva. I've never felt fear like this. I'm afraid you won't come back . . . that you won't give me another chance."

"Gideon —"

"I dreamed about my father at first. We were walking on the beach and he was holding my hand. I've been dreaming about the beach a lot lately."

I swallowed hard, my chest aching. "Maybe that means something."

"Maybe. I was little in the dream. I had to look up a long way to see my dad's face. He was smiling, but then I always remember him smiling. Even though I heard him fighting with my mom a lot toward the end, I can't remember any other expression on his face but a smile."

"I'm sure you made him happy. And proud. He probably always smiled when he looked at you."

He was quiet for a minute, and I thought maybe that was it. Then he went on. "I saw you up ahead on the beach, walking away from us."

I rolled onto my side, listening intently.

"Your hair was blowing in the breeze and the sun lit it up. I thought it was beautiful. I pointed you out to my dad. I wanted you to turn your head so we could see your face. I knew you were gorgeous. I wanted him to see you."

Tears welled in my eyes and slid down to wet my pillow.

"I tried to run after you. I was pulling at his hand and he was holding me back, laughing about chasing pretty girls at my age."

I could picture the scene so clearly in my mind. I could almost feel the brisk breeze whipping through my hair and hear the seagulls calling. I could see the young Gideon in the picture he'd given me and the handsome, charismatic Geoffrey Cross.

I wanted a future like that. With Gideon walking down the beach with our son who looked just like him, my husband laughing because our troubles were behind us and a bright, happy future lay ahead of us.

But he'd called it a nightmare, so I knew that future I envisioned wasn't one he saw.

"I was tugging so hard on his hand," he continued, "digging my bare feet into the sand for traction. But he was so much stronger than me. You were walking farther and farther away. He laughed again. Only this time, it wasn't his laugh. It was Hugh's. And when I looked up again, it wasn't my father anymore."

"Oh, Gideon." I sobbed his name, unable to hold back the sympathy and grief. And the relief that he was talking to me at last.

"He told me you didn't want me, that you were going away because you knew every-

535

thing and it made you sick. That you couldn't get away fast enough."

"That's not true!" I sat up in bed. "You know that's not true. I love you. It's because I love you so much that I'm thinking so hard about this. *Us.*"

"I'm trying to give you space. But I feel like it would be so easy for us to drift apart. A day goes by, then another. You'll find a new routine without me in it . . . Christ, Eva, I don't want you to get over me."

I spoke in a rush, my thoughts tumbling out of my mouth. "There's a way to get through this, Gideon, I know there is. But when I'm with you I lose myself in you. I just want to be with you and to be happy, so I let things ride and put them off. We make love and I think we'll be okay, because we have that and it's perfect."

"It *is* perfect. It's everything."

"When you're inside me, looking at me, I feel like we can conquer anything. But we've really got to work on this! We can't be afraid to deal with our baggage because we don't want to lose each other."

He growled softly. "I just want us to spend time together not dealing with all this other shit!"

"I know." I rubbed at the pain in my chest. "But we have to earn it, I think. We can't manufacture it by running away for a week-end or a week."

"How do we earn it?"

I swiped at the tears drying on my cheeks. "Tonight was good. You calling me, telling me about your dream. It's a good step, Gideon."

"We'll keep making steps, then. We have to keep moving together or we're going to end up moving apart. Don't let that happen! I'm fighting here, with everything I've got. Fight for me, too."

My eyes stung with fresh tears. I sat for a while, crying, knowing he could hear me and that it was hurting him.

Finally, I swallowed the pain down and made a snap decision. "I'm going to that all-night café on Broadway and Eighty-fifth for coffee and a croissant."

He was silent for a long minute. "What? *Now?*"

"Right now." I tossed back the covers on the bed and slid to the floor.

Then he got it. "Okay."

Killing the call, I dropped the phone on the bed and fumbled for the light. I ran to my duffel bag, digging out the butter yellow maxi dress I'd shoved in there because it was easy to pack and comfortable to wear.

Now that I was decided on seeing Gideon, I was anxious to get to him, but I had my vanity, too. I took the time to brush out my hair and put a little makeup on. I didn't want him to see me after four days and wonder why he was so gone over me.

My phone buzzed a notification of a text and I hurried over to it, seeing a note from Raúl: I'm out front with the car.

A little zing went through me. Gideon was anxious to see me, too. Still, he never missed a trick.

I shoved my phone into my purse, my feet into sandals, and hurried out to the elevator.

Gideon was waiting on the street when Raúl pulled up to the curb. Many of the storefronts on Broadway were shuttered and dark, although the street itself remained well lit. My husband stood within the light cast by the café's awning, his hands shoved into the pockets of his dark jeans and a Yankees ball cap tugged low over his brow.

He could've been any young man out late at night. Clearly attractive by the way his hard body filled his clothes and the confidence in the way he carried himself. I would've given him a second and third look. He wasn't as intimidating outside the three-piece suits he wore so well, but he was still dark and dangerous enough to hold me back from the lighthearted flirting most devastatingly handsome men inspired.

In jeans or Fioravanti, Gideon Cross was not a man to be taken lightly.

He was at the car almost before Raúl pulled to a complete stop, yanking the door open and then freezing in place, staring at me with such scorching hunger and possessiveness that I found it hard to breathe.

I swallowed past the lump in my throat, my equally ravenous gaze sliding all over him. He was unbelievably more beautiful, the expertly sculpted planes of his face honed further by his torment. How had I lived the past few days without seeing that face?

He held his hand out to me and I reached for it, my own trembling in anticipation of his touch. The brush of his skin against mine sent tingles of awareness racing through me, my bruised heart surging with life at being in contact with him again.

He helped me out, then pushed the door closed, rapping twice on the roof to send Raúl away. As the Benz left us, we stood barely a foot apart, the air crackling with tension between us. A taxi raced by, honking its horn as another car turned onto Broadway without looking. The harsh sound jolted Gideon and me both.

He took a step toward me, his eyes dark and hot beneath the brim of his hat. "I'm going to kiss you," he said roughly.

Then he cupped my jaw and tilted his head, fitting his mouth over mine. His lips, so soft and firm and dry, pressed mine open. His tongue slid deep and rubbed, withdrew, slid deep again. He groaned as if he were in the greatest pain. Or pleasure. For me, it was both. The hot stroke of his tongue into my mouth was like a sweet, slow fucking. Smoothly rhythmic, skilled, with just the perfect tease of leashed passion.

I moaned as euphoria sparkled through me like champagne, the ground shifting beneath my feet so that I clung to him for balance, my hands wrapping around his wrists.

I whimpered in protest when he pulled away, my lips feeling achy and swollen, my sex wet with desire.

"You'll make me come," he murmured, unable to resist brushing his lips over mine one last time. "I'm right there."

"I don't care."

His mouth curved and chased the shadows away. "The next time I come will be inside you."

I sucked in a shaky breath at the thought. I wanted that, and yet I knew it would be too soon now. That we'd fall too easily back into the unhealthy pattern we had established. "Gideon . . ."

His smile turned rueful. "Guess we'll settle for coffee and a croissant for now."

I loved him so much in that moment. Impulsively, I pulled off his hat and gave him a great big smacking kiss on the mouth.

"God," he breathed, his gaze so tender it made me feel like crying again. "I've missed you so damn much."

I slid the hat back on his head and grabbed his hand, leading him around the little metal fences cordoning off an outside seating area from the pedestrian traffic. We entered the café and settled at a table by the window, Gideon on one side and me on the other. But we didn't stop holding hands, our fingers stroking and rubbing, each of us touching the other's wedding bands.

We ordered when the server walked over with the menus, then turned our attention back to each other.

"I'm not even hungry," I told him.

"Not for food, anyway," he rejoined.

I shot him a mock glare that made him smile. Then I told him about the retention offer Waters Field & Leaman had made Mark.

It seemed wrong to talk about something

541

so practical, so mundane, whe[...]
was giddy with love and relief,[...]
to keep talking. Reconnecti[...]
enough; I wanted a full and tota[...]
tion. I wanted to move into the[...]
penthouse with him, start our li[...]
To do that, we had to keep com[...]
about the things we'd spent our [...]
avoiding.

Gideon nodded grimly when[...]
"I'm not surprised. An accou[...]
should be handled by one of th[...]
Mark's good, but he's a junio[...]
LanCorp would've had to push[...]
And you. The request is unusua[...]
give the partners cause for conc[...]

I thought about Kingsman V[...]
did the same thing."

"I did, yes."

"I don't know what he's goin[...]
looked at our joined hands. "Bu[...]
I couldn't work on the PhazeOn[...]
even if he stayed to manage it."

Gideon's grip tightened on mi[...]

"You have good reasons for[...]
things you do," I said quietly,[...]
don't like them."

He took a slow, deep breath[...]
come with him to Cross Indu[...]
moves?"

"I'm not sure yet. I'm feeling pretty resentful right now. Unless that changes, it wouldn't be a healthy working relationship for either of us."

He nodded. "Fair enough."

The server came back with our order. Gideon and I released each other by necessity to give her room to put the plates on our settings. When she walked away, a heavy silence descended between us. There was so much to say, but so much that had to be figured out first.

He cleared his throat. "Tonight — after Dr. Petersen — could I take you out to dinner?"

"Yes." I accepted eagerly, grateful to move past the awkwardness into action. "I'd like that."

I could see similar relief soften the hard line of his shoulders and wanted to do my share to build it. "Will asked if we'd be up for grabbing a drink with him and Natalie this week."

A hint of a smile touched Gideon's mouth. "I think that'd be great."

Small steps. We would start with those and see where they took us.

I pushed back from the table and stood. Gideon pushed to his feet quickly, eyeing me warily. I rounded the table and took the seat next to him, waiting until he sat again so that I could lean into him.

His arm came around me and he settled me into the crook of his neck. A soft sound escaped him when I snuggled in.

"I'm still mad at you," I told him.

"I know."

"And I'm still in love with you."

"Thank God." His cheek rested against the top of my head. "We'll figure out the rest. We'll get back on track."

We sat together and watched the city rouse from sleep. The sky lightened. The pace of life quickened.

It was a new day, bringing with it a new chance to try again.